MW01118242

Sandaman's Riposte

Tom Trabulsi

iUniverse, Inc.
Bloomington

Sandaman's Riposte

iUniverse books may be ordered through booksellers or by contacting:

iUniverse
1663 Liberty Drive
Bloomington, IN 47403
www.iuniverse.com
1-800-Authors (1-800-288-4677)

Because of the dynamic nature of the Internet, any Web addresses or links contained in this book may have changed since publication and may no longer be valid. The views expressed in this work are solely those of the author and do not necessarily reflect the views of the publisher, and the publisher hereby disclaims any responsibility for them.

ISBN: 978-1-4502-7317-6 (pbk)
ISBN: 978-1-4502-7318-3 (cloth)
ISBN: 978-1-4502-7319-0 (ebk)

Library of Congress Control Number: 2010917270

Printed in the United States of America

iUniverse rev. date: 12/28/2010

Map image used on cover used with permission of the
Publisher - American Map Corporation

For

Jason Ellis Young

May 16, 1970—February 13, 2002

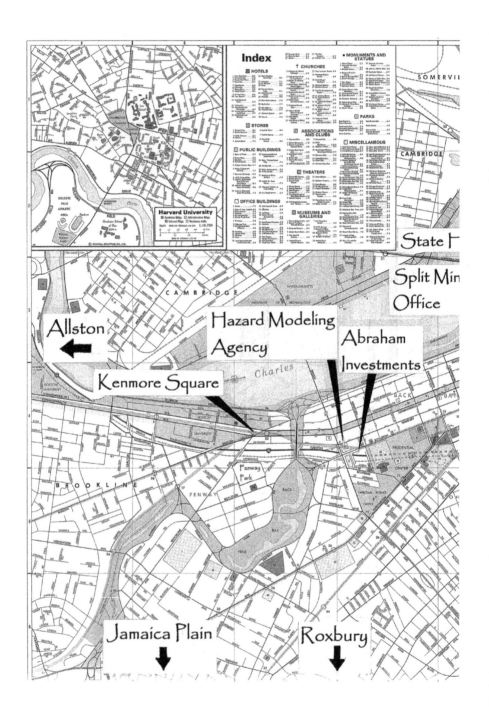

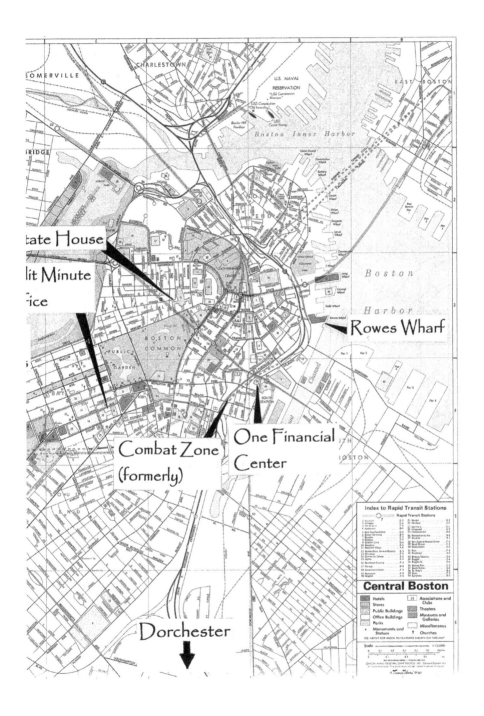

State House

Split Minute
Office

Rowes Wharf

BOSTON
COMMON

PUBLIC
GARDEN

Combat Zone
(formerly)

One Financial
Center

Dorchester

Index to Rapid Transit Stations

Central Boston

Hotels
Stores
Public Buildings
Office Buildings
Parks
Monuments and
Statues
Associations and
Clubs
Theaters
Museums and
Galleries
Miscellaneous
Churches

Scale 1:12,000

Make friends with pain, and you will never be alone.

—Ken Chlouber,
Colorado miner and creator of the Leadville Trail 100

Acknowledgments

The author would like to thank:

The Massachusetts Department of Parole and Probation
The Environmental Protection Agency
The National Library of Medicine
The Agency for Toxic Substances and Disease Registry
The Unified Air Toxics website
The National Kidney and Urologic Diseases Clearinghouse
The Anti-Defamation League
The Texas and Florida Departments of Corrections websites

The following texts proved invaluable:

Dr. Joe Graedon and Teresa Graedon. *People's Guide to Deadly Drug Interactions.* New York: St. Martin's Press, 1995.
Jill Krementz. *How It Feels to Fight for Your Life.* Boston: Joy Street Books, 1989.
Wendy Lader Ph.D. and Karen Conterio, with Jennifer Kingson Bloom. *Bodily Harm.* New York: Hyperion, 1998.
Kerry A. McGinn and Pamela J. Haylock. *Women's Cancers.* Alameda: Hunter House, 1993.
Marilee Strong. *Bright Red Scream.* Introduction by Armando Favazza. New York: Viking, 1998.
Liz Tilberis with Aimee Lee Ball. *No Time to Die.* Boston: Little, Brown and Company, 1998.

The following Catholic prayers were also excerpted:

Raccoltas #597, 600
Enchiridion of Indulgences #46
The Itinerarium
Gradual Psalms (Psalmi Graduales)
2 Corinthians 5:1
Romans 8:38–39

Special thanks to criminal defense attorney Anthony Traini, whose expert guidance made the legal transitions seamless.

A debt of gratitude is owed to Adam Dunn and Jason Young, editors at large.

Additional thanks to Leila Trabulsi, who illustrated the bike wheel and granted permission for its republication.

Although they wish to remain anonymous, several doctors provided technical advice which proved instrumental.

The map image on the front inside pages of this book was used with permission of the publisher—American Map Corporation.

The epigraph in the beginning of the novel was taken from page 57 of *Born to Run*, by Christopher McDougall, New York: Alfred A. Knopf, 2009.

The definition of "riposte" was reprinted by permission from Merriam-Webster's Collegiate® Dictionary, Eleventh Edition©2010 by Merriam-Webster, Incorporated (www.merriam-webster.com).

Riposte: a fencer's quick return thrust following a parry
a retaliatory verbal sally
a retaliatory maneuver or measure

Chapter One

Boston, mid-1990s
Wednesday, July 20

HE HIT COMMONWEALTH AVENUE in a full downpour and already running twenty minutes late. This was no morning mist. He had heard in passing the day before about an approaching Nor'easter, but it was only late July. The rain was practically blowing horizontally, soaking him through despite the rear fender and zipped-up slicks.

Accounting for the rain-smeared brakes, he geared down early, fighting the headwind as he blew into Kenmore Square and hopped two lanes toward the curb. Locking up outside a row of five-story brownstones, he passed pizza shops, record joints—the college part of town. Fenway Park was a block up Brookline on the left, which meant traffic would be fucked up as early as three o'clock.

Inside 522 Commonwealth Avenue, the cleats of his Specializeds clacked like tap shoes across the wood-floor lobby. A pretty brunette office worker smiled uncomfortably as they waited for the elevator, shifting left as the growing puddle at his feet ominously pooled her way.

Come on, he thought, cursing the clock. *Come on, come on …*

Up on five, he cut right and passed a handful of small businesses run by people who were semi-successful and maybe had a secretary or two. Their names and titles were carefully printed across each opaque glass door like

1

product descriptions. At Pierce Investigations, Esq., he knocked once and entered a single office where a middle-aged man was surrounded by file stacks and fast-food rubbish.

"Unbelievable," he said, a gold tooth beaming among the smoke-stained yellow that comprised his smile. He clapped his hands appreciatively. "You're a fucking miracle, kid, honest to God." He nodded towards the window. "You wouldn't catch me walking across the street, much less pedaling all day in this shit, lemme tell ya."

Zeke grunted, peeling off a soaked Red Sox ball cap to reveal a plain face with a twice-broken nose, the pretty boy now grown salty. Double-checking the thin single-ply blue Izumi rain gear, he slung the water from his face, replaced the cap, and said, "What's going on, Don?"

"Nothing." Donald Pierce sipped his coffee. "Want some? Christ, I'm your first hit and you're already soaked like a rat."

"Can't. Goddamn it!" He silenced his beeper without even looking at the number. "I'm on the fly today."

"Rain?"

"Yeah." He wiped a swelling drop off his nose. "Fuckin' sunny-day pussies leave me all the money."

Donald Pierce laughed, causing a column of cigarette ash to collapse across a plaid tie and brown shirt as he grabbed nonchalantly at his crotch. Leaning forward, he tossed a sealed manila envelope on top of a stack of old betting slips. "It's a petition for contempt against a husband for failure to make child support payments. If you could get it there right as they open, before the rest of today's shitstorm floods their already feeble process, I'd be most obliged."

"No problem."

Donald Pierce laid a ten-dollar bill on top of it. "So that it doesn't get lost in the shuffle."

"Never does, Don. Here." He handed Pierce the stainless-steel contractor case where he kept his blank, current, and finished slips. Donald Pierce scrawled an account number next to his signature and detached the pink copy off the back like a veteran.

"There you go, Zeke."

"Cool." Zeke filed the remaining two copies in a left-side slot.

"What's that say on the back?"

"Of what?"

"Your case." Donald Pierce nodded. "And not the giant whore part. The other, littler writing. I've always meant to read it."

Zeke Sandaman held up the case as Donald Pierce squinted and recited,

"It used to be,
In a man like me …
Whore."

Donald Pierce shook his head and said, "What the hell . . .?"

"Who knows." Zeke frowned at the waste of time. "Goddamn it, can I use your phone? Stuey's lightin' up my beeper for like the eighth fucking time."

"Sure. Just don't drip on my desk."

Zeke dialed the eight-hundred number and it was answered immediately.

"Split Minute."

"Stuey. It's Z, what's up?"

"Zach-a-riah!" a high-pitched singsong voice replied. "You're being naughty to me today."

"Jesus, Stu, I just got here. I'm out the door."

"Naughty boys, Zachariah. Need to be disciplined, spanked."

"Stu—"

"Across those lovely, well-muscled ass cheeks and firm thighs, where their—"

"Stu!" Zeke sighed. "Come on, man."

"Come on indeed, Zekey-boy. Come on and in and all around those sweet little edges—"

"Stuart!"

"Fine! Pickup at Abraham, going to Link, 155 Summer. And then, let's see …"

Hearing his boss flip through the giant dispatcher sheets, Zeke knew the game was one of resources and personnel kept in constant motion. Ideally, like an air-traffic controller imposing synchronization, the dispatcher juggled up to two dozen bikes, vans, and cars that made no profit in haphazard deployment. As he moved from point to point, organizing pickups and drops, it was like placing cubes of cheese in front of hungry mice who ate only what they earned in volume. Having worked with some of the worst dispatchers in the trade, where one was led in disjointed circuits filled with backtracks and drops in no particular order, Zeke knew Stuart was as greedy as he was, and sometimes thought his routes works of pure genius.

"Are you still there, Zeke?"

"Yep."

"Two Guy Design in the same building. Going to Paul Art Brothers, 135 Milk. And, oh, the lovely Jessica Hazard Modeling Agency on a round tripper to Ferrelly Publishing, 122 North."

Zeke Sandaman scribbled out each ticket and snapped his case shut.

"Got it."

"You sure do, Zekey-boy. And don't dawdle with those lovely honeys at the Hazardous place. Stuey will be awaiting yesterday's tickets, dear, so drop in on your way through Copley."

"Yeah, yeah."

"Do you know what I love about your last name, Zeke-a-licious? It's like Gland-a-man, but with a Z!"

"Stuart!"

"Four call-ins already, sweet pea. I'm gonna be riding you all day, filling those tight pockets with cash, cash, cash!"

"Goddamn it, Stu, good-bye."

"Answer your beeps!"

Zeke Sandaman hung up, shoved Pierce's envelope into a quadruple-ply garbage bag just in case, and then jammed both it and the contractor case into his courier sack.

"All right, Don, I'm outta here."

"Good luck, kid. Stay dry."

It was an old joke but Zeke smiled nonetheless.

"Yeah," he said and pocketed the ten-dollar bill. "We'll see about that."

Donald Pierce watched the door close and listened to the clacking shoes, thankful he was not, nor ever had been, in a spot so bad that he had to fill them.

———————————

Straddling his bike, Zeke faced the headwind and downpour like a sea captain on the Grand Banks. He cursed every ten seconds and finally put on his sunglasses just so he could see. Inbound on Commonwealth Avenue, he bent a right onto Massachusetts Avenue and then a quick left the wrong way down Newbury Street. He locked up mid-block against a thigh-high wrought-iron fence in between a place that sold fur hats for a thousand dollars and an Italian shoe boutique one of his old girlfriends had managed. Most of the stores were still closed. He two-hopped the six stairs, blew snot out of his left nostril, and hit an intercom buzzer, which caused a tired voice to sigh, "Hazard Inc."

"Split Minute." Zeke cleared the other nostril onto the doorstep. "Gotta pick up, Cherise."

"That you, Zeke? God, it's early."

"It sure is."

"I feel so bad for you guys. This weather is just so fucked up."

"Tell me about it."

"You really should get more money if the weather's bad. I mean, that's not totally unreasonable, is it?"

"Not at all. Listen, Cherise, think maybe you could buzz me in before I fucking drown out here?"

He heard her laugh before the lock disengaged with an ear-rattling complaint. His beeper sang out and three flights later he found Cherise Maxwell in a small lobby studded with framed cover pages of top industry magazines hung like trophies. Cherise did not look well. Her usually beautiful brown eyes were spider-webbed and glassy, her black hair yanked into an uncombed ponytail. Zeke had bumped into her a few times on Lansdowne Street and knew she liked dancing and sniffing blow and running herself down enough so that she now rode the front desk instead of facing a camera.

"Tell me it's not a tube." Zeke reached into his bag for the slipcase. "God, Cherise, you look totally fucked up."

Sipping hot coffee, Cherise Maxwell smiled guiltily and said, "Kiefer Sutherland was in town last night."

"At Axis?"

"Oh my God, Zeke, he didn't even have anyone with him. He just walked in and sat down at the bar."

"Wow." Zeke wiped his face and slung the water towards the rug. "Did you get me his autograph?"

"Fuck you."

"I heard his dick is small."

"You an expert on celebrity dick sizes, Zeke?" Cherise smiled despite her hangover. "The rain sure hasn't dampened your bitterness."

Zeke flipped open the contractor case and noted the time, 7:10 AM. "It's the only way I can show affection."

"Well, at least that explains your desperation. I mean, what is it exactly that you see in her?"

"Honestly?" Zeke half-grinned and held out the case. "I've just been waiting for you to say yes so we can elope to Vegas."

"Vegas ..." She smiled, but the blush was already there, left over from last night and the whiff of vodka Zeke caught face first as he leaned in. She etched what looked like a signature in the wrong place but Zeke said nothing. "Where is it?" he asked.

"Please don't be angry." She meekly pointed towards a pair of three-foot cardboard tubes in the far corner. "Zeke—"

"What the fuck?" He stalked over and grabbed the tubes. "On a day like this? Are you people out of your fucking minds?"

"Zeke, easy, Linda's just around—"

"Screw Linda." Zeke shook his head and took a deep breath in surrender. "Call Stu. Tell him what they are and that I'm hitting you for two oversizes, two overweights, and maybe even two expresses if I have to dump them first."

Reaching for the phone, Cherise bit the smile from her lips. Despite her thumping headache, she caught an image of Zeke cursing his head off in the middle of that downpour and abruptly started to laugh.

"What's so funny, Cherise?"

"I'm not laughing at you."

"Yeah, right."

But the way his face was scrunched with rage, coupled with the fact that laughing now would only piss him off even further, helplessly doubled her over.

"Cherise!" He knelt down and began bookending the tubes into garbage bags.

"I'm sorry." She blew her nose and wiped carefully under each red eye. "It's just ... you're funny. What's in that bag that's so godawful precious, anyway?"

"I don't hear any dialing."

Sighing, she worked the digits and carried the handheld over to where Zeke was crouched. Kneeling as well, she began poking through his courier bag. "Hi, Stu … Yeah, he's right here … No, I wouldn't say that. He seems to be very irritated this morning. Tools, pump, long black rubber thing—"

Zeke paused and looked over his shoulder. "That's an inner tube, Mrs. Sutherland."

Cherise frowned and gave him the finger. "No, Stu, I'm just going through his bag. He's really pissed about our tubes. Wait a sec. Zeke, what's this?"

Zeke looked back. "Chain tool."

"What's it do?"

"Lets you screw out the rivets. Replace the chain-link if you blow something."

"I don't know, Stu," Cherise said, returning it into the sack before grimacing at her grease-smeared hand. "He's telling me all about some tool that lets you blow something."

Cherise laughed, and Zeke could only imagine what the perverted little voice was saying. "Now, Stu. Be a good boy. I don't think Zeke's a meat eater … All right. Hold on, I'll ask him. Zeke? Stuart wants to know if you like fish or sausage?"

"Tell him I'm going home."

"Sausage, Stu … Who? Me? Not really. Zeke, how tall are you?"

"Five ten."

"Yeah. I like my guys to be around six feet though, Stu. And besides, his nose is all smushed in the middle … That's true. Hey Zeke, you do have pretty green eyes … I'm not sure, Stu, hang on. Zeke, what are you?"

"The employee of the month."

"Seriously."

Zeke shoved the makeshift sarcophagus into his courier bag on an angle. He put his contractor case in next, followed by Donald Pierce's envelope, which would lie flat against his back. Fastening the straps, he said, "I'm half Norwegian, half Colombian."

"Oh, that's gotta be it, Stu. He's half Colombian. Every Spanish guy I've ever dated has a temper like his."

"I'm not Spanish."

"You're right, Stu. You could never tell otherwise … Yeah, you should see him. All wet and frumpled in his little blue jumpsuit. He looks like a really deranged smurf … No, Stu, he sure isn't, he's wearing a ball cap. Hey, Zeke, why don't you ever wear a helmet?"

"Because of conversations like this. Listen, Cherise, it's been fun chatting with you two ladies. Tell Stu I'll call him from Abraham."

"He says he'll call you from Abraham. Hang on, Stu. Bye, sweetie!" she called out and Zeke tossed her a wave. Downstairs, in the tiny hall, he slung the satchel over his left shoulder, adjusted his jacket, and double-checked the tubes that hovered near his left ear. Putting on the sunglasses, he took a peek outside and then instantly regretted it. Like the rain fifteen feet away, the first of the day's two rush hours was only now just flooding through the streets.

———————————

His next stop was only one street over, so Zeke Sandaman again buzzed the wrong way down Newbury, hung a right on Fairfield, and then headed the wrong way up Boylston Street. The trip took all of thirty seconds. He clacked through a busy lobby where a security guard had nothing better to do than shoot him dirty looks. At the fourth floor, Zeke found a manila envelope propped against the locked front door of Two Guy Design. The attached note read,

MR. MESSENGER, PLEASE DON'T GET ME WET.

There was a bagel on a paper plate next to the envelope bearing another note that said,

EAT ME.

Zeke unslung his bag, stuck the envelope in with the one from Pierce Investigations, and scribbled out a ticket, the pink part of which he slipped beneath the glass doors. Chewing off half a bagel, he tasted how stale it was and spat it out immediately. He ground the other half under his shoe before turning for the elevator which arrived almost full even though it was not yet 7:30 AM. On the sixth floor, he walked off into a lobby with maroon walls, thick black carpet, and several landscape paintings. Six-inch silver letters attached to the left wall read,

Abraham Investments

Below it, three black leather couches formed a horseshoe around a glass table fanned with financial magazines.

"Good morning, Zeke," an enthusiastic voice called out.

Letting a grin slip past his mood, Zeke grunted. "Hi, Elaine."

Already strapped into her headset like a battlefield radioman awaiting the first salvo, Elaine was surrounded by switchboards, phones, and pictures of likewise obese children framed in two neat rows. Zeke had heard all their names and ages—the roll call of mothers everywhere—but today he was in a rush. "Whaddaya got, Elaine?"

"Oh, Zeke," she replied, and her round face pursed into a frown. "You poor thing. Do you want some coffee? I just made it."

"No thanks." He stopped about five feet away, unslung his bag, and carefully, in a gesture he did not afford everyone, shook off the excess water before approaching her desk.

"Please? Here, I've only taken one sip."

She stuck out her coffee cup like a demand. Zeke decided she was a nice lady, always a little garishly dressed but with big brown eyes that held no pretense. If Abraham Investments was like a class-oriented hierarchy where people with no power could easily feel stepped upon, she never seemed to sense it. Dealing with couriers, running her phones, and making connections for more than three hundred calls an hour made her virtually indispensable. Zeke took the cup. "Thanks."

It was too sweet and milky but felt warm, so he finished it in three huge gulps. Her gaze up at him was so pleasant and simple he blinked and said thanks again.

"Stuey called." She put down the empty cup. "Gosh, I just love him. He is such a nice man. Isn't he, Zeke?"

"Depends."

"Oh, you." She smiled and batted a hand. "He is too. And charming on top of it."

Zeke grinned as if she should know the half of it. "Where am I going, Elaine? Link?"

"Yes."

He jotted down the address, the water dripping from his cap onto the slip until he swung the case a hundred and eighty degrees for her to sign. "Do you want more coffee?" she asked.

He shook his head and tore off her receipt. "I'm tweaked enough, but thanks. What'd Stu want?"

"For you to call him before you left. But you knew that already, didn't you, Zeke?"

"My beeper hasn't stopped yet."

"Geez. I am not envious. This is my favorite part of the day, though. I get about an hour of this before the real hell breaks loose."

Zeke tapped his foot anxiously. "I don't know how you do it."

"It's sick, isn't it?" She smiled brightly. "I'll tell you, between you and me, there are days where all of this just makes me nuts. And then there are days where I just fall in love with the rush."

"Tell me about it."

She smiled again and said, "Here. I know you're in a hurry."

Zeke took the envelope, double-checked the address, and reached for his bag.

"Did you eat breakfast, Zeke? I've got some bagels and cream cheese."

"Naw, no more bagels. But would you mind calling Stu while I wrap and stuff this thing?"

She hit one button and three seconds later cheerily said, "Hi again, Stuart ... No, not yet. Funny, though, I was just telling Zeke about this golden hour ... Yes, he's already here. And all wet too. Isn't this weather just awful?"

Zeke stored the envelope with the others and called over his shoulder, "Tell him I want a raise."

"Zeke says he wants a raise ... Gosh, Stu, I can't say that!" And Elaine chuckled despite her blush. "Oh, Stuart, you're too much ... No, I've never dated any Colombians. Brad was from my hometown and I never dated anyone else before we got married ... Oh yes, they're all fine. In fact, my youngest starts nursery school this year ... It is super. I'm a very lucky woman ... Now, Stuart, be nice ... You're such a naughty little thing!"

Zeke tucked the garbage bag into his courier bag, which he checked for signs of moisture. The material was the same used in firemen's jackets, tripled over with a Gore-Tex lining. The tubes sticking up out of the left corner were the only possible breach. He buckled the straps and made sure the garbage bag covering the tubes was puffed into a half-ass seal before standing up.

"Yes, in fact he's getting ready to leave right now, Stu. Okay, I will ... Bye-bye, honey." Clicking off, she lifted the tiny microphone forehead-high. "Zeke, tell me, how are you ever going to be warm enough in that little blue thing?"

"Elaine—"

"You must be half frozen already."

"It's the middle of July, Elaine."

"Still, it's fifty degrees outside. Your mother must worry something awful."

"Huh."

"She must be used to it."

"Did Stu want anything?"

"Yes. He said to make sure you stop in before heading downtown."

"Cocksucker!"

"Zeke!"

"I'm sorry. It's just ... aw, never mind. He knows I know to stop in. And this goddamn beeper—"

"Zeke—"

"I'm sorry. I know you hate that. But he's already driving me nuts this morning."

"Be careful on those wet roads, Zeke."

"I will. Absolutely. And thanks for the coffee." He headed for the elevator. Once inside, he thought about his route and drops after he saw Stuart. The door slid closed and there he stood, in the middle of the empty car, staring at his own reflection with a dour look like someone caught peeping in on his own life.

Split Minute's office was located on St. James Avenue, so Zeke got up to speed before shooting off the curb. Dropping in on the left rear bumper of a delivery van, he checked right, geared down, and then took the white line in between the second and third lanes down Boylston. The pavilion of the public library whizzed past on the right. He hunched forward, the rain smacking his face and near-useless glasses. Even though he kept pace downhill, he was punished in the mists fanning off the car tires ahead. Near the corner of Exeter, the street leveled off as he plowed through an eight-inch puddle. Outside of a cheap coffee shop on the left, Zeke knew that this part of the Back Bay was nothing but office buildings and ground-level stores catering to those who could pay ten dollars for a sandwich or thirty dollars for a haircut.

Blowing through the Dartmouth Street intersection into Copley Square, he saw that the corners were mass clusters of trench coats and umbrellas streaming out of the T-stations below. He had only one block left and nothing but green lights, so he clicked into the highest gear, checked right, and shot through a four-foot gap as the car horn behind wailed in anger. On Berkeley Street, he bent a tight leaning right and waited for the back tire to slip out. St. James Avenue was barely thirty feet ahead against traffic, so he pedaled as fast as he could before the light went green.

Split Minute Messenger Service was on the eighth floor of a fourteen-floor building that spanned an entire block. The lobby had sixteen elevators in a U-shaped bank and a concierge desk set in the middle. The ground floor also had two corridors extending either way with eateries, drycleaners, and stationery stores. Zeke strode into the first available eight-through-fourteen elevator when he heard his beeper begin to pulse. He could not believe it. He wanted to curse but instead said, "Could you hit eight, please?"

A miserable-looking lady punched the button as if she was sick of putting herself out for the world. Zeke thought about asking what the fuck could be so bad but then decided he might cheer her up with a confrontation and instead lifted his sunglasses as if to dare her. *Bitch*, he thought, *and what the fuck is wrong with me?*

A computerized voice announced his floor, and he walked out before the doors swooshed closed. He stood still and stared at the far wall while the water slowly dripped off his cuffs, nose, and hat brim.

Tap ... tap ... tap...

Zeke knew what his mother used to say, that like his older brother and father before him, it was just something he would have to work through. Yet the irony was, growing up and dodging his father's horrific mood swings,

Zeke had wondered how anyone else could live like that. *It's too early in the day for this*, he thought.

Split Minute's office was at the end of the hall, which meant it was nearly half a block away. His right hand blindly reached over his right shoulder and into his bag, pulling out the contractor case. Flipping it open as he walked, he organized yesterday's receipts into a neat stack, closed the case, and eventually pushed through a door with the company name stenciled above a slanted bicycle and featureless rider bent forward for speed. The office itself was actually a four-room suite, the first of which contained nothing other than an empty water cooler and a small mountain of bike parts backed into a corner. The lights were never on. Besides rent, liability insurance, office supplies, and taxes, the only other overhead cost was the phone bill, which, some months, topped the twenty-five hundred dollar rent.

"Hi, Zeke."

Zeke Sandaman waved to Richard Parks, Stuart's partner, who handled nearly all the billing, outside business, and payroll. On top of living together, he and Stuart had adjoining offices, a situation Zeke knew had its hazards. For an older man in his early forties Richard Parks carried only a slight paunch on his otherwise fit six-foot-two-inch frame. His face was plain except for a neatly trimmed mustache and expressionless brown eyes.

"Zekey!" Stuart's voice sang out. "Wherefore art thou?"

The damp morning and overcast sky shadowed the room in gray. Striding in, Zeke unslung his bag, tossed a salute, and took a seat across from his boss.

"Goddamn," he said, taking off the ball cap. He ran a hand through his soaked hair, which was cut short and wetly spiked. "It's fucking raining out there, man."

Stuart Rigby twitched his lips, the oversized mustache jerking like a stuffed sock. Except for the conservative slacks and oxford button-downs each of his employers preferred, any similarities ended there. At five feet two inches, Stuart Rigby was almost a foot shorter than Richard Parks and obstreperous to the point of offense. Poorly wired, Zeke had always thought, the electricity like a barely contained static field snapping off Stuart's small, pudgy body. Now in his late thirties, Stuart's wavy black hair was speckled with gray but neatly trimmed.

Currently, Zeke watched him sip coffee from a gigantic mug, spy him through the steam, and arch a single finger-thick eyebrow as if to say, *And ...?*

"Here's yesterday." Zeke placed the tickets on the desk and saw the black button eyes twinkle momentarily, the hand motion a quick and greedy snap as Stuart fanned the receipts into a geisha's prop over which he peeked. "Oh Zachariah?" Batting his eyes lasciviously, he said, "Take a guess at what I'm thinking now?"

"Stu ..."

"Fantastic! He won't even try!" Stuart shuffled the fan back into a neat stack and placed a hand upon it. Then, as if in a shaman's jig, his body seized as his eyes rolled back into their whites.

"Stu, Jesus Christ—"

"Ahhhhhhh!"

"You look like a coked-up squirrel."

Zeke smiled when he heard Richard Parks begin laughing through the two-way intercom next to the telephone.

"You!" Stuart screamed at the box. "Stop eavesdropping on me!"

"Actually," Richard Parks deadpanned, "he left out preppy."

"A preppy coked-up squirrel! Is that what you're calling me!"

"Exactly."

"Oh my God." Stuart looked at Zeke as if this might be the end of the road for Richard Parks. "Casting the first stone, eh, Richie? Before I forget, your waistband called. Seems your steady diet of donuts and fried crap has just got it a promotion to a fatso forty-six! Congratulations, Jabba!"

"You obsequious little *turd*."

Stuart Rigby bounced up and down in his chair, repeatedly screaming, "Fatty!"

"I can't believe you're saying that." Richard Parks sounded hurt. "You are such a little prick. Zeke, help me out."

"He's got you there, Stu." Zeke flipped open his contractor case, looked up, and said, "You are a total fucking mess."

"Fuck you both."

The phone rang and Stuart said, "Like that donut in your hand, fatty, business calls. Bye-bye now."

"Stuart—"

It came from doing it a million times a day, Zeke decided, watching the self-styled gunslinger kill the intercom, hit the flashing line-two button, and palm the phone—elapsed time a second and a half. Stuart shot him a quick wink. "Split Minute … Oh hi, Doris … " Stuart picked up a pen and cleared Zeke's receipts off the top sheet. Stapled into groups of ten, the three-foot dispatcher sheets were dissected into thirty-five rows by six columns capable of handling approximately half an hour's worth of calls. In his own shorthand, the package's vital signs were noted in columns headed by Company Name, Caller Name, Destination, Contact's Name, Time, and Contractor … "Yes, as a matter of fact, I'll send over one of my best little boys … " Stuart nodded at Zeke, so he pulled out his slipcase and put a fresh ticket on top of the ones already holding. "Harris Publishing, 150 Milk … Got it, darling … Oh, yes … You know Zeke … Doris! Oh my, I think he's blushing. Zeke, you should hear the things she's saying … You're a dirty bird, Doris … He's on the way, sweetie. Bye-bye now!"

Chuckling as he hung up, Stuart looked at Zeke. "You're still here? Let's go, money, money, money!"

"Who else you got out there?" Zeke asked, leaning over and storing the case in his bag.

"What possible concern is that of yours?"

"Stuart."

Stuart Rigby pouted, his giant frowning mustache making Zeke think of a cruller stapled to a kid's face. "Danny's downtown, Remo's still in Allston, Fudgie's working the South End, Mother's fucking off somewhere, and Cammi's in Cambridge."

"Pretty meager, Stu."

"You don't have to tell me. Fucking Spike woke up, saw the rain, and called in saying he had to go to court."

"But he did, didn't he?"

"Yes, Zeke. Yesterday. I mean, how stupid do these miscreant employees of mine consider me to be? That in between six o'clock last night and six this morning he miraculously remembered another court date? Please … Spike, Larry, Mumbles, X-Man—all no-shows."

"Fuck 'em." Zeke put the soaked ball cap back on his head and stood up.

Stuart grinned. "You can't say you weren't warned."

"Tell me about it."

"Listen ... " Stuart held out his hands as if he had no choice. "You and Cammi are the only way I make it through today."

"That's no problem. But Stu, please don't spend the day stepping on my fucking beeper. You know that shit drives me nuts."

"But I love—"

"I know. But not today. I'll fucking walk." Zeke cocked an eyebrow. "You know I will."

"All right! All right! I won't fondle your buttons! Now can we please make some money?"

Zeke slipped into the strap, shrugged the load to center, and said, "How'd she look this morning?"

"Who?"

"The first lady. Who the fuck do you think?"

"Haven't seen her yet." Stuart Rigby was already busy checking off Zeke's receipts against yesterday's register. "Don't tell me you got her all fucked up last night."

"You've got that reversed again."

Zeke turned for the door as Stuart called out, "What's your first stop?"

"155 Summer."

"Call me!"

"Bye, Stu."

"We're gonna make you rich today, Zekey!"

As he passed, Zeke Sandaman waved good-bye to Richard Parks, who rolled his eyes in the universal gesture of those unfortunate enough to have heard it all before.

Cammi Sinclair was making excellent time despite the rain blowing sideways across the Harvard Bridge. Her right cheek was beaten red from this assault as a cab wandered in too close, almost force-feeding her the curb. While downtown was in a feeding frenzy, she had two measly cross-zones returning from Cambridge and felt as if she were working for free. *Fucking Stuart*, she cursed, but this gave her no relief.

Trying to escape the yellow menace on her left, she geared down and rose forward on the pedals, the water skidding off her face in streams. Rhythmically working the handlebars side to side, she thought about tonight, and Zeke, when the same cab swung back in.

"Hey, douche bag! Fucking wake up!"

Quickly peering inside, she saw the cabbie mouth something that caused a woman in the backseat with giant gold earrings to clutch her purse. Facing front, Cammi winced at the upcoming sewer grates flooding over, and at the same instant she decided to give up position, the cab inched her towards the curb again.

"Motherfucker!"

With thirty feet to go and a building fury, she reached back into her bag and yanked out the U-bar lock. The cabbie must have seen the backed-up lakebed approaching, because he was pinning her directly towards its center until the lock ripped a downward arc across his side mirror with a horrendous crack a second before she heaved with all her might, missing the flood and curb. Grinning from the sidewalk, flush with adrenaline, she saw the smashed mirror hanging like a broken limb.

"Bite me!" she yelled.

At the congested corner, she found a seam and hit the Beacon Street intersection at full speed. With the cab jammed up at the stoplight, she eased up and reached back, tucking away the lock one-handed.

Marlborough Street was the next left and virtually empty. Letting go of the handlebars, Cammi raised up to massage her low back as she passed immaculate two- and three-story brownstones. Entirely residential, it was where the professional class could have a quiet slice of status without a horrific commute from the suburbs. She came to a stop at 255, next to a foreign car and a tree outrageously in bloom. She locked up, then slipped a hand beneath the black poncho slick with rain. Tugging at a seam on her left shoulder, she noted the discomfort for future adjustment. While far from a seamstress, she nonetheless took great pride in her designs, no matter how ornate or mundane the purpose.

Yanking out her slipcase, she double-checked the address before walking up five steps to a doorway with the name Justin Arding III above a button she then depressed. Pushing off her hood, she was wringing out a soaked red bandana as the door swung open to reveal an attractive late-twentyish blond in a bathrobe and perfect white-toothed smile.

"Hey there," he said, and she saw a certain interest appear in his eyes.

"When they said they were sending it by courier, I had no idea it would be carried by a woman of such beauty."

"Oh my God." Cammi caught herself laughing as she re-knotted the bandana around her head before shrugging back into her hood. She pulled a manila envelope from a black plastic bag in her courier sack and handed him the slipcase. Proffering a pen, she said, "I'm sorry about that."

"Don't be." He leaned against the doorjamb with a suggestive smile. "Did you know this was sent from my law firm?"

"Wow."

He leaned forward as if sharing a secret. "I'm the youngest junior partner they have."

"That's nice."

"You don't seem to believe me."

Impatient, Cammi watched him sign the case. "You must be very proud."

"Of course I am." He gave her a lascivious smile before handing back the case and pen. "If only I were joking, right?"

"Well, you must be. Seriously, you're one of the cheesiest things I've ever seen."

Dismay spread across his gaping face. "You fucking *bitch*."

"Wipe your chin." Cammi dabbed at her own for example. "Your boyfriend left a bit of a mess."

"I'm calling your company!"

"Ha-ha!" She skipped down the steps as he lurched forward in pursuit until the rain stopped him cold.

Ignoring a tirade of insults, she unlocked her bike and set herself in motion. "Call my service! We'll do lunch!" she yelled back.

"Bitch!"

Gearing down, catching her stride, she swooped in on an empty pay phone at the corner of Fairfield and Marlborough and punched in the eight-hundred number.

"Split Minute!"

"Stu, it's Cam. I'm on Marlborough with a single fucking downtown."

"Cammi! Thank God! I'm positively swamped! How was Cambridge, dear?"

"Unprofitable."

"Please, sweetums, bear with Uncle Stu. Who else would I send? Fudgie? Mother Hubbard?" Stuart sighed as if that were impossible. "It would take them two fucking hours. Literally, Cammi, I've been staring at those calls for over an hour and had nowhere else to go. Jeepers! Wait one second."

On hold, Cammi Sinclair had a moment to picture either Fudgie or Mother Hubbard pedaling to Cambridge through this maelstrom and knew two hours might not be long enough. Stuart clicked back in. "You know I can't be mad at you," she said.

"Yeah, baby, make it hurt!"

"Stuart!"

"Yes, right. Well, you had to take a hit for the team and so now comes the reward. Pickup at Schuster Film, 325 Berkeley, with an express to Desmond, 415 Washington … Another express at Parsons Art, 225 Clarendon, going to Wisement, a private residence at 45 Milk Street, number four … And let's see, Hazard has a triple heading down to Fillmont Processing, 320 Washington Street, and while we're there let's stop at Abraham Investments, where the lovely Elaine has a deuce going to Link, 155 Summer."

"I take it all back." Hurriedly scribbling out slips for the two expresses, a triple, and the deuce, she blew a drop of rain from the tip of her nose and said, "I think I'm in love with you all over again."

"As it should be, Miss Sinclair. Call me after your second pickup in case anymore downtowns come in."

"Where's Zeke?"

"Currently? In the South End fixing a flat tire amid a string of obscenities."

"Nothing like switching out inner tubes on a crowded sidewalk during a downpour, right?"

"I know." Stuart tittered wickedly. "How he hates the petty tortures." Cammi Sinclair laughed along with Stuart. "Oh my," he said, then coughed. "Please, dear, keep up your pace—which is, by the way, simply fantastic. The two of you are my only legs to stand on."

"Thanks, Stu."

Cradling the receiver, she stared up the street and saw the rain like a pixelized curtain offering no way out.

———————————————————

Graphic Art was on the same floor as Split Minute, and over the years Zeke had heard every story about all the participants in Stuart Rigby's rise to fame. Started fifteen years before, Graphic Art had risen from one man's bedroom to an eighteen-room suite and print plant downtown. The owner, one of Stuart's oldest friends, was also his best customer, and Zeke considered him a gifted, if not incredibly maladjusted, genius. By chance, Zeke also figured he had at least twenty album covers in his own collection, all with the tiny Lane DeSanto signature tagging the bottom right corner. A twisted hobby gone mad is how Zeke remembered DeSanto describing the origination of his multimillion-dollar operation. Beginning with hardcore promotion posters stapled across Allston, then moving on to print advertising contracts on Madison Avenue, Graphic Art had always stood on the extreme fringe of the acceptable, thereby classifying itself as a corporate institution run by dissidents.

The office décor, like its owner, seemed to relish the role of provocateur. The walls were painted black with curling pink flames that licked the ceiling. Gothic candelabras shone on sneering gargoyles poised on pedestals like artifacts awaiting their master's return.

Beyond it all, he saw Doris Lytol perched behind a huge black desk on a platform that was more like an altar erected at the back of the room. She couldn't have looked more bored, Zeke decided, as he watched her nod hello while nonchalantly filing her maroon-glossed nails. An industrial-metal hybrid was blasting in surround-sound as an old John Woo film played on three different televisions, and in that instant, Zeke figured he pretty much loved this place.

"Hey, Doris."

She looked down at him and put a finger behind her repeatedly pierced ear.

"I said, hey Doris!"

She clicked her gum, dialing down the stereo. "What's up, Zeke? Staying dry?"

Zeke Sandaman reached over his shoulder for the slipcase as Doris Lytol grinned. Zeke knew she relished her role as gatekeeper inside the daily nightclub of Graphic Art. The steel door to her left was locked and two cameras in either corner behind her went directly to DeSanto's desk. Zeke remembered she once told him that the walk-ins were the worst part of her day, but that sometimes a reasonably famous person or good idea might cross her desk.

"And that's what the cameras are for," she had said. "I hit this button and Lane looks at the screen, and if he thinks it's worthy he tells me so through my headset."

"Fantastic," he had answered, and Doris had raised one perfectly plucked eyebrow, sucker as she was for sarcasm.

Zeke walked up the four steps to her desk, penned the time on the slip, and said, "You don't look so good this morning."

"Yeah? How so?"

"You're a little paler than usual."

"I'm a vampire, Zeke." Her blue eyes, beneath the straight black hair and white powdered face, glowed as if provoked. "Victims, Zeke. I'm always looking for someone new to suck on."

"Wow." Zeke finished writing and held out the contractor case. "People tell me I'm the exact opposite."

"Yeah, right." She took the proffered case and signed it. "Too bad you're so unattractive."

"Tell me about it."

"The spiky hair is cute but, like the tattoos, so predictable. And your nose, why's it so mushed in the middle? It looks like someone bashed you with a steel rod."

"My boyfriend can be a real dick sometimes."

"I bet." She handed Zeke a manila envelope. "How old are you, anyway?"

He knelt down and sandwiched it into the garbage bag with the others. "Twenty-four."

"And how long have you been doing this?"

"Too long."

"How long?"

"Off and on? Seven years."

"Well," her blood-red lips parted into a smile, "all that cycling sure has given you a great ass. Does your boyfriend ever tell you that?"

"Only after he's finished."

"Gross, Zeke."

He checked his pager. "I can't believe he's already beeping."

"Sacrify was at Man Ray last night. Thought for sure I'd see you and those other hoodlums."

"We had a previous engagement." He held out his hand for the phone.
Doris rolled her eyes. "One can only imagine."

He snapped the bag closed and took the phone as Stuart Rigby said, "Split Minute."

"Stu."

"Zekey! Oh my. The phones are positively ringing off the hook!"

"What's up?"

"Pickup at Cross, One Financial, going to Ferrelly, 145 Oliver … Hanover, at Three Rowes Wharf, coming back to Distinct Instinct, 240 Commonwealth, which will go nicely with your Hazard round trip. And I think that's all for now."

"Cool," Zeke said as he scribbled out the tickets.

"I'm giving Danny most of the downtowns. He's an old man, you know."

"Don't forget Pierce. I've got to be at the courthouse no later than 8:50."

"Zeke—"

"8:50, Stu. And please, load me up with shit heading back. I'm not making any money staying in the same goddamn zone. Can't you kick Danny the Cross?"

"But you're heading right there! Don't micromanage me, Zachariah!"

"Yeah, you're right. I'll call from One Financial. What time you got?"

"7:58."

"Bye, Stu."

"Zekey—"

Zeke handed her the phone as Doris Lytol sipped coffee from a Miss Piggy mug. "You know," she said, "when you walked in just now, with the music blasting, and reached over your shoulder for that metal case thingy, I meant to tell you that you looked like Mad Max."

"What?"

"His gun. He used to reach over … just … never mind. You're not even listening."

"What?"

She gave him the finger. "Fuck. You. Did you hear that okay?"

Zeke grinned and turned for the stairs. "Bye, Doris."

"I hope you get run over by a taxi!"

"You said that last time."

"Yeah, but this time I mean it. Fuck you, Zeke!"

Zeke pushed through the glass front doors, not quite sure why his mood was so suddenly improved.

The clock in the lobby tolled for the eighth time as Zeke hustled towards the doors. *Five on me*, he thought, *got to be at the courthouse by nine*. Outside, he decided it must have been like the *Poseidon Adventure* for the soaked commuters caught in between warm cab rides and the mad dash for their cubicle-filled spaces. Zipping up, Zeke pushed through the carousel front door and immediately broke for his bike. The keys, which were on a two-foot chain snapped onto the base of the bag's strap, were out of Zeke's pocket and in his hand twenty feet before he got to the No Parking sign. He stored the Kryptonite U-bar lock in a front-side pocket of his bag and swung the bike the opposite direction. Ignoring the horn blast and extended middle finger of a passing cabdriver, he launched himself from the curb like a preset missile oblivious to consequence.

He made the right turn back onto Boylston and powered uphill past the Public Garden and Boston Common, which shimmered like gigantic empty lawns drinking in the downpour. Boylston turned into Essex Street where ten years before the once-formidable Combat Zone had flourished. Surviving the most recent purge were a handful of strip clubs and porno shops which Zeke passed before burning a tight left onto Chauncy. Catching Summer Street at the very end of Downtown Crossing, he eventually glided up onto the wide brick pavilion outside One Financial Center. The rain, which was nearly blowing sideways, swirled around the sixty-floor skyscraper as if confused. He pushed through one of six carousel front doors and practically walked right into a security guard, who hastily asked, "That your bike?"

"What bike?"

"Right there." The guard jabbed his walkie-talkie towards a custom slung-back roadster leaning against the far atrium window.

"I wish," Zeke said.

He walked past into a canyon-sized ground-floor lobby with two restaurants and a small armada of tables facing the street. A water fountain pulsed upward next to an escalator scrawling participants to and from the second-floor conference center. Hearing his name called out, Zeke tossed a wave at a dozen couriers sipping coffee around their usual tables near the door. Deadbeat Central, Zeke dryly noted, was nearly standing room only even at this early hour. How they could not be out there sucking up all that money, Zeke could never figure out. Some still lived at home, some worked for crappy companies, and others were just in it for a taste of the lifestyle. Striding through another set of glass doors into a separate elevator lobby, he nodded at a fat balding concierge, who had been behind this same desk for as long as Zeke could remember.

"Hey, Mort."

"Zeke. How's it going?"

"Cross's on forty, right?"

"Yes, sir."

"Be cool, Mort." He headed towards the appropriate elevator bank and twenty seconds later shot upward like an astronaut in a box. He walked out and down the hall and took a right into the mailroom of Cross Digital Communications, where he picked up the outgoing Ferrelly.

Downstairs, at one of six pay phones stuck into a stone wall, he dialed the eight-hundred number.

"Split Minute."

"Stuey."

"Zeke! Oh, hooray!"

"I'm at One Financial heading for Rowes Wharf."

"You've got the Cross on you already?"

"Yep."

"You're the best, Zeke, a real thigh-and-butt man."

"Stu—"

"Pickup at Simon, 550 High, coming back to Barney, 260 Commonwealth."

Zeke scribbled hastily. "Got it."

"Call me from Rowes."

"The 8:50, Stu, I've got to start working that way."

"Don't tell me how to do my job!"

"Talk to you soon."

Hanging up, Zeke felt a tap on his shoulder as someone said, "Yo, Z, what up?"

Turning, Zeke felt the recognition ignite his smile as he said, "Fuckin A, Faustis, how goes it?"

"Same old trauma." Faustis swung a batch of soaked dreadlocks off his face, then clasped Zeke's hand. He seemed to scrutinize Zeke. "See you got some new slicks."

"Yeah. You remember my old getup."

"Sure do. Them digs were dug. How much?"

"Eighty-five. With discount."

"No shit. Izumi no less. Where at? Bill's?"

Zeke shook his head. "Community. Fuck, you live up Tremont. You need to score a pair while they're still trying to clear them out."

"I will. You cool with the phone?"

"All yours. And watch out for Supercop. I walked in and he was hawking your gearbox something awful."

"Yeah." Faustis rolled his eyes. "In this weather, fuck that curb shit."

"I hear you."

"Wait, Z, what you doin' later on?"

"Tonight?"

"Yeah."

"Nothing. I was out tweaking until 3:30 last night."

Faustis grinned. "Right on. But we're playin' tonight. At Chase's. Come by, man."

"Maybe. That's that place in Jamaica Plain, right?"

"Yeah. And Z," Faustis placed a hand on Zeke's chest, "we got a whole new set, yo. You won't be disappointed. And what about C, yo, you still with her?"

Zeke shrugged. "You know how that goes. Love and hate. I was actually with her last night."

"Bring her. Tell her I said it's been a decade, man, what the fuck?"

"I will."

"Here." Faustis reached into his army green fatigues and handed Zeke two free passes. "We're opening for the Red Land Band. And they just opened for Kravitz. Ripe-ass reggae, Z, serious."

"Sweet." Zeke reached back for his wallet, which, like his keys, and because of his daily movements, had to be chained to his body. "What time you go on?"

"Nine o'clock."

"Sweet."

"Damn, suit, that's my phone!" Faustis jumped in front of a middle-aged man who immediately frowned. "I'll check you, Z."

Heading for the door, Zeke zipped up his jacket, double-checked that his bag was closed, and stepped back outside like someone who had yet to learn his lesson.

Like giant steps extending off Atlantic Avenue and Commercial Street, there were twelve wharves ringing Boston's financial district and North End. A lifetime before, and for two centuries before that, much of New England's commercial shipping had landed on these downtown docks. Yet business growth and soaring land values, even through the recession-filled 1970s and '80s, eventually pushed the boats across the harbor into Charlestown and East Boston.

Built from brick and stone four stories high, Rowes Wharf was now home to a number of high-end law firms. From One Financial Center, it was a short trip three blocks down Atlantic Avenue. Zeke peeled off from the bumper-to-bumper traffic and almost killed a woman naively jaywalking with an umbrella held directly across her line of sight. Hopping the curb, he clicked his right foot free, legged over the bar, and coasted sidesaddle until stopping beneath a stone archway dividing the building in two. Locking up, he scanned for security. They were a hassle here, he knew, but each building, especially downtown, had its own rules and degrees of enforcement. In particular, the guardians of Rowes Wharf were notorious for locking up bikes parked anywhere but in the bike rack conveniently located two blocks away. Tucking his rig behind a giant stone planter, Zeke eyeballed the storm and decided even the most inspired pseudo-lawman might think twice about venturing forth.

Adjusting his bag, he blinked through a gust and saw, just beyond the archway, the Inner Harbor and far shore where Logan Airport twinkled like Christmas come early. Inside, he clacked across the marble floor to the elevator and watched the omnipresent cameras watching him.

Hanover, Pembroke, and Wright was located on three, and when the elevator doors opened, Zeke walked into a chaotic vortex where secretaries and associates alike were kneeling down to work an assembly line of paper while yapping into cell phones they could not dial fast enough. After standing there for a good thirty seconds, he saw half a dozen people look his way, only to ignore him, and so he finally called out, "Split Minute! Whose got the Instinct?"

"Did anyone call for a courier?" one guy yelled, slacking his tie to unbutton the collar. His head, Zeke noted, was egg shaped and prematurely balding. Pushing his glasses back up, the man paused with a frown. "Wait a minute. Aren't you supposed to be going to the courthouse?"

"Nope."

"But we … Mary, didn't I tell you to call for the courthouse?"

Mary, Zeke soon saw, looked to be a woman who was rapidly losing her sense of humor. She let both arms slap her sides. "Christ, Bob, I did. It was—"

"Hold on." Zeke dug for his beeper. "Did you just call in?"

"Two minutes ago," Mary said and Zeke nodded.

"That's him right now. I hope you're going to Suffolk, because I've got to be there in twenty minutes."

"Perfect," Bob said, then hopped over two lines of people and paper to get to Mary, who handed him the envelopes like a baton in a relay race. Making his way to Zeke, he tried to smile through the stress. "Here you go. Jesus, you're soaked. Heard it's a mess out there. I've been stuck in this goddamn office since yesterday morning."

"That really sucks." Zeke quickly filled out the extra ticket and had Bob sign both. "It's like Vietnam in here, man."

Bob grunted. "Just wait. In about an hour we're gonna need eight of you guys just to get all of this out of here."

"What's going on?"

"Class action. You've got the preliminary. I don't know what the fuck this Distinct's for."

"Cover and graphics," Mary called out.

The guy nodded. "Yeah. Whatever."

"Hope it's not a roundtrip," Zeke said, tearing off the receipts. "I'll never make it back by then."

"Well, that ain't my department."

His cell phone rang and Bob turned away, so Zeke grabbed the next elevator down and called from the lobby.

"Split Minute."

"Stuey."

"Zeke! Did you get the deuce at Hanover?"

"Yes, sir."

"Oh, marvelous. Zeke, you are spectacular!"

"Listen, Stu, I've got twenty minutes left. I'm picking up the High Street, dumping the Oliver and two Milks, and then banging for the courthouse."

He heard Stuart Rigby anxiously clicking his tongue, no doubt scanning the dispatcher sheets. "Okay. You're right. Time's running out."

"Stockpile and I'll call you from Suffolk."

"Wait, Zeke! Did you spit out a bagel on the door of Two Guy Design?"

"Yep."

"Zeke!"

"It was staler than hell, Stu, what the fuck? I'm not some homeless guy they can pawn off day-old crap on."

"But—"

"And Hanover said they're gonna need a convoy in about an hour."

"Don't you worry about that. Uncle Stuey's got it covered, Zeke-a-licious."

"I'll call you."

"Don't piss off any more of my clients!"

"Sure thing." Hanging up, Zeke Sandaman checked his bag while jogging for the door.

It was 8:26 when he pedaled beneath the I-93 underpass, which, because of weather and construction, was little more than a three-lane parking lot. 550 High Street was directly opposite Rowes Wharf, and Zeke was in and out of the building barely two minutes later. Continuing one block up, he took a right on Oliver and locked up outside a five-floor walkup. Ferrelly Incorporated was on four, and Zeke pushed through the door as if the building were on fire. He yanked out the two tubes from the Jessica Hazard Modeling Agency, fished out the Cross Digital Communications envelope, and practically threw them and his contractor case at a pretty young receptionist who stopped smiling the second the barrage hit her desk.

"What's up?" Zeke asked rhetorically. "The tubes are a roundtrip from

Jessica Hazard and the envelope's from Cross at One Financial. Could you please sign here?"

"Um, sure," she said, and Zeke watched her check the packages before picking up the pen. "Um, this might be a problem."

"What's that?"

"The roundtrip. They're addressed to Ms. Danright and she won't be in the office for another fifteen minutes at least. I have no idea what's going back."

"Jesus … Is there anything you can do? I've got to be at the courthouse by 8:50 or I'm totally fucked."

"Hang on."

Zeke listened as she dialed and explained the situation. He felt the individual seconds slipping off the face of the clock until she finally hung up and said, "Okay, we're in luck. Her assistant says the tubes stay here and this goes back."

Reaching behind her, she procured yet another tube, and Zeke was in too big a hurry to curse. He wrapped it in the garbage bag, thanked her for her help, and took the stairs back down three at a time. Outside, the morning rush hour was approaching its apex, which meant absolute dead-stop madness. Laid out nearly three hundred years before, the streets of downtown Boston read like indecipherable hieroglyphics. There were consecutive one-ways, tiny lanes tucked off alleyways, practically no parking anywhere, and one-lane roads that might have accommodated the horse and buggy but could in no way handle the sheer crushing demands of twentieth-century traffic. A single wrong turn could cost a motorist half an hour of frustrating U-turns and horn-honking rage. Zeke blasted through all of it and had the two Milk Streets delivered by 8:45. He caught State Street off Broad and motored uphill through the driving rain. Banging a left onto Cambridge, he felt the back end slip out and cursed himself again for not having his mountain bike up and running. These thin European tires were no match for this weather, a fact reiterated by the grueling, tractionless climb up a rain-slicked Beacon Hill.

On Somerset, he locked onto a black steel handrail, then got on line for the metal detectors. Usually, if Oscar Jimenez was working, Zeke would merely toss his bag onto the conveyor belt, expecting only a cursory inspection. However, no Oscar meant he had to remove his belt, keys, wallet, beeper, and sunglasses while still tripping the detector with the metal fasteners in his shoes.

Since the morning session was nearing commencement, the hallways were a description of anxious lawyers and stone-faced clients awaiting their fates. Zeke passed them all and made it to a door on the second-floor marked INTAKE as a hall clock listed the time at 8:56 AM. He would have smiled, but his beeper abruptly chirped, so he unloaded his parcels in front of a half-asleep clerk at the pinnacle of his ambition. Downstairs, he snagged a phone before an old lady with a cane could take possession, and fifteen seconds later heard Stuart Rigby ecstatically proclaim, "Eight fifty-nine, Zeke-a-licious. You are such a god!"

"I got three on me. A Newbury and two Comm. Aves."

"I know. Quickly then. Pickup at Marshall, 200 Congress, going to Proffered Properties, 980 Boylston … Uplink Software, 320 Franklin, going to Richmond, 220 Berkeley, and—let's see what else—Bellflower, 80 Pearl Street, heading to Bowser, 565 Tremont … and—"

"Damn it, lady, I'll be off the phone in one second!"

"Zeke, I may be a fairy but I'm certainly no lady."

"Not you. This old hag behind me's whacking me with her cane because I stole her phone." Stuart laughed, but Zeke said, "It's not funny. I think she just told me to go fuck myself."

"Ha-ha!"

"Damn it, hurry up. She's beating the hell out of my calves!"

Stuart Rigby purred perversely and said, "Do you like to get beat, Zeke?"

"Stu!"

"Okay, okay! I've got a Circumspect, 232 Broad, coming back here for a car ride to Waltham."

"It better not be oversized."

"Zeke—"

"Forget it, Stu. Not in this weather. You've already fucked me with three tubes and it's barely nine o'clock."

"I'll call and double-check, okay? Gosh, you can be so moody sometimes."

"What else?"

"What else? You'll have seven on you, oh greedy Zeke-a-licious! Call me from your first stop. Which will be ..."

"Congress Street."

"Excellent."

"Hey, what's the weather?"

"Fucked until two PM. Richie's checking WBZ every fifteen minutes."

"Then please, Stu, no Kenmore Squares after four o'clock. They're probably gonna try and get that fucking game in."

"Don't you worry about that. I'm gonna wing you through downtown, get you back here, and then turn you around again for the Rowes Wharf fuckfest. They just called and ten thirty's our new time to fret over."

"Whatever."

"See you soon, Zekey."

"Yeah, man."

Zeke hung up as the woman behind him said, "Bastid," and gave him one last whack for the road.

It was just gonna be that kind of day, Zeke decided, throwing the old woman the fakest smile he could muster.

———————————

At 11:36 AM, Zeke walked out of the federal courthouse and into the downpour, which did not show the slightest sign of abatement. One fortunate side effect of this was that almost every outside pay phone was unoccupied, so Zeke pulled up on the corner of Milk and Congress and dialed the eight-hundred number while still seated, balancing on the bike.

"Split Minute."

"Stuey."

"Zachariah!" Stuart Rigby singsonged. "Oh brave knight in the foulest of tempests! Wherefore art thou?"

"Corner of Milk and Congress. Got two on me heading for Southie."

"Ah ..."

Zeke heard Stuart flipping through the dispatcher sheets. "Nope. Call me from Southie, Zeke. I'll load you up and ram it home!"

"Gross, Stu."

"Call me."

Hanging up, Zeke jumped the curb and took a right. He banged another right on Atlantic before swinging through a tight left onto Summer. He passed One Financial Center, South Station, and the giant South Post Office Annex before rumbling across the steel-grid road of the Summer Street Bridge. This part of South Boston was dominated by warehouse spaces filled with upstart companies cashing in on the cheap rent, artists' studios, and lofts where it seemed half the bands in Boston rehearsed. Zeke pulled up outside 345 and locked into a finely crafted wrought-iron gate that looked horribly out of place. Inside, the walls were unadorned cinder blocks, and the building directory was simply spray-painted on the wall next to an elevator that did not work. He took the stairs two at a time until he reached the top and stumbled through a door like a SWAT team off balance. Tripping to the floor, he heard someone say, "Oh my God. Are you all right?"

It was a second before she came into focus, standing up as Zeke rolled over to his knees and said, "Jesus, I'm sorry."

The secretary left her desk and repeated, "Are you okay?"

Fixing his bag through the blush, Zeke tried to smile. "Except for feeling like an ass."

"Here," she said and extended her hand.

Glad he still had on his sunglasses, he glanced up at the shoulder-length brown hair and huge blue eyes like a dumbstruck teen. At five foot three inches, she was small and curvy, the hair framing a pretty face that seemed taken aback by this abrupt encounter. Her long-sleeved dress hung like a thin curtain over the shifting shadows swelling beneath.

"Uh, thanks," Zeke said, accepting her assistance to get to his feet.

"Guess I tripped," he said, swearing he could feel the pulse pounding through his face. "God, I feel like such a loser. Must've scared the hell out of you too."

"Kind of." She smiled shyly and brushed at his jacket. "Oh, wow. You're totally soaked."

"Yes, I am."

They stood in silence as the gray outside spilled in through the windows. *I don't have time for this*, was all he could think, and it sounded like a warning belatedly posted. He wanted to say something, anything intelligent, but the awful silence only left him dripping onto the carpet.

"Can I get you some coffee?" he heard her say.

"Yes," he said. "Please."

"Do you like cream or sugar?"

"Nope." Watching her head for an alcove, Zeke's eyes feasted on her secrets. "I mean, no thanks."

From the framed mechanical workups tacked onto the bare concrete walls, Zeke guessed it was some kind of architectural design firm. He was still looking at them when he heard her blurt out, "Damn it," and return empty handed seconds later.

"I'm really sorry," she said. "I thought we had some brewed. Can you wait a minute?"

"Um …" It was impossible and he knew it. "Thanks, but I really—fuck me." Palming off his beeper, he said sheepishly, "Reflex. Sorry about that."

Her lips curved into a smile that dragged Zeke with it as he idly wondered how her lipgloss tasted. It was an unnerving sensation, knowing next to nothing and yet swimming so comfortably across that blue-eyed gaze. He watched her watching him until he finally realized what she was waiting for.

"Oh yeah."

He swung his bag to the front and pulled out an envelope and slipcase. She was a good two inches shorter, and as she signed for the package, he looked down the center trench of her parted hair, caught a delicious whiff of shampoo, and decided she had all of his senses on overdrive.

"Is that all you need?" she asked. Zeke thought she might be reading his mind, so he quickly said, "That'll do," and tucked away the case. Re-slinging his bag, he saw a middle-aged man poke his head around the corner.

"If you're going to lunch, Lizzie, can you pick me up the usual?" the man asked.

"Yes, Frank." She waited until he disappeared to roll her eyes.

"I hear you," Zeke said and she smiled at the conspiracy. Grabbing her coat and umbrella, she said, "Walk me out?"

"Hell, yeah."

As he held the door like the gentleman he could not ever remember being, Zeke cracked an ironic grin towards the lone respite in what was otherwise turning out to be just another horrendous day.

"Where are you?"

"Stu—"

"Please tell me you're still in Southie."

"I am." Zeke cleared his throat and spit a phlegm wad twenty feet.

"Gross, Zeke. Must you do that right in my fucking ear?"

Zeke grinned beneath the drenched ball cap pulled low. "Just trying to spread my good cheer."

"Listen carefully. I've got two unbelievably important expresses. Zeke, this is no joke. People are trying to make flights because Logan might close. You're empty, right?"

"Totally."

"Pickup at Hanover, for a change, Three Rowes Wharf, going to Mason-Myer, One State Street. This is hand-to-hand delivery, Zeke—no receptionists, no exceptions. And the first one's got to be there in twenty-three minutes."

"Expresses get half an hour."

"*Zeke!*"

"What else?"

"For you, there is no what else!" Stuart shrieked. "Why do you think I emptied you out?"

"Stu, what the fuck?"

"Two expresses, at cost plus 50 percent. I'm making you rich!"

"And then …?"

"Clear them and believe me, the shitshow continues. I'm staring at two full sheets and you and Cammi are the only ones keeping me alive. Post-lunch hour's gonna be a nightmare."

"Lunch hour. Imagine that. An hour for lunch."

"Yes, well, that's why people go to college, Zeke. Are you with me?"

"To the end, bro."

"Call me from Rowes on the return."

"What time you got?"

"Zeke, really, there's no time for—"

"Listen, could you try and get me back to Rosemont?"

"Three forty-five Summer? But you just came from there!"

"Please? I'll ride till six o'clock if you do."

"Is this about a woman?"

"Nope."

"You're lying. Besides, I'm saving you for me, sir thigh-a-lot."

"Stu!"

"Zeke! I've got zero bodies on the most fucked-up weather day this summer and you're expecting me to play Love Connection? Clock's ticking. You've now got twenty-one minutes."

The phone went dead in his ear, so Zeke slammed it into its cradle. Forgetting to check left, he launched into the foot-and-a-half wake thrown off a barreling tractor-trailer. He was at the bridge and back on Atlantic Avenue twenty-five seconds later. At Rowes Wharf and locked up two minutes after that. Upstairs, the combat conditions preceding the filing of the class-action lawsuit were nowhere to be found.

"Hey, Mary," he said to the stuffy receptionist, who did not seem to appreciate the familiarity. "Picking up a—"

"Oh, thank God."

Zeke turned and saw the same lawyer from this morning come bolting out of the double-glass doors.

"It's a super express," he said, slightly winded. "Going to—"

"Jacoby. One State."

Zeke plucked the envelope out of his hand and gave him the slipcase.

"It's gotta be—"

"Hand-delivered." Zeke took back the case. "Get a soda. I'll be back in seventeen minutes."

The lawyer looked at Zeke, unsure of whether to take offense or thank him. Downstairs, back on Atlantic and pedaling fiercely, he swung left through a freshly turned red light and of all things got blasted by the air horn off an oncoming street sweeper. Accounting for the hill and heavy traffic, he clicked up into second and a minute later pulled onto the pavilion of One State Street. The lobby clock read 12:12 PM as he jumped into an 18–32 floor elevator exactly as the doors slid closed.

The lobby of Mason, Myer, and Tennant had two black leather couches, three tropical plants, and a receptionist making small talk with an impressively dressed man, who took one look at Zeke and said, "Holy shit. I just got off the phone with them." The man smiled and clapped appreciatively as Zeke yanked out the envelope.

"Mr. Myer, I presume?" Zeke said.

"You're not even breathing hard." Vino Myer shook his head, took the envelope, and scribbled out a signature on the proffered case. "Hang on a sec. Beth, get me Phippsy over at Hanover."

The receptionist handed him the phone as Zeke catalogued the envelope returning to Rowes Wharf.

"Yeah, he's right here," Vino Myer said, then turned towards Zeke. "How long did it take you to get here?"

"About four minutes."

"Including the elevator?"

Zeke nodded and stored the envelope. "Incredible," Myer said. "Yeah, Robby, double or nothing."

Vino Myer handed back the phone and told Zeke, "You just cost me fifty bucks." He dug into his pocket and pulled out a roll of bills, peeling back a twenty. "That's for you. No offense, but I hope you blow a tire on the way back."

"We'll see about that." Zeke grabbed his case, said good-bye, and, because of the downhill run back to Atlantic Avenue, handed Robert Phipps the other envelope three minutes and fifty seconds after that.

"Shouldn't have even hung up the phone," he said and smiled broadly. "You just made me a hundred bucks, Mr. Courier Man."

"Sweet." Zeke pointed at the receipt. "Could you sign right there? And initial the time?"

"Sure." Robert Phipps obliged. "You really aren't even breathing hard."

Zeke checked his beeper. "I do this all day long, mister."

"I wonder what your pulse rate is."

"Barely fifty at rest."

Robert Phipps eyed his own slight paunch and shook his head. "That's incredible." He handed Zeke the contractor case and said, "There's something in there for you. You've been here four times today and busted ass through a god-awful monsoon."

"Appreciate it. Have a good one." Zeke tossed him a salute and headed for the elevator where, after he flipped open the contractor case and found two dollars, he would have laughed if anything less was to be expected.

"Split Minute."

"Stuey."

"Zeke! You luscious proboscis! How they hanging?"

"High and tight, bro. Whaddaya got?"

"Are you still at Rowes?"

"And empty as fuck."

"Delicious. Let's see … back to Simon, 550 High, going to a private residence, 263 Comm. Ave … Pickup at Harris, 150 Milk, going to Graphic Art—you know where—pickup at Paul Art Bros., 135 Milk, going to Two Guy Design, 755 Boylston."

Zeke frowned, the rain dripping off his ball cap onto the opened case. "That's it?"

"Ha-ha!" Stuart laughed excitedly. "Every other messenger in the city's hiding in coffee shops and praying for five o'clock, and you, you're just begging for more abuse!"

"Seriously, whaddaya got?"

"A four-inch worm, Zekey, nosing around for a dark moist hole to crawl into."

"Ugh. Can't help you."

"But I can, Zeke-a-licious. Do you happen to know a Mr. Vino Myer?"

"Who?"

"Of Mason-Myer, moron-a-thon. You were just there, loverboy."

"Yeah, Vino Myer. So what?"

"What's he look like?"

"Look like?"

"His voice was *so* sexy on the phone."

"Stu, goddamn, don't drag me—"

"What's he look like!"

Zeke sighed as if standing in a downpour wasn't bad enough. "Six foot, black hair, slicked back all greasy. White teeth and a ten-thousand dollar suit."

"Ahhhhhh …"

"Seemed like he might be a lot fun outside the office, Stu."

"Stop it, Zeke. I'm getting a woody."

"Oh my God! I'm so outta here."

"Wait, Zeke! His office just called. Said you did a fabulous job and wanted to know our rates and times, fair prince of the roadways. Think you might've just landed us another big one."

"Great." Zeke stored his case. "You can put that on my tombstone."

"Fat bonus for you if it's true. But don't tell the others."

"Never do."

"Excellent. And Cammi too. She just got us a whole dentist complex in Kenmore Square an hour ago."

"Hey, when you talk to her tell her I ran into Faustis and got free passes for Chase's tonight."

"No fraternizing with the help, Zeke."

"But I am the help!"

"Still, I won't be an accomplice to your petty seductions."

"Stu!"

"Call me. Bye-bye now."

The phone clicked dead in his ear, and Zeke smashed the receiver down repeatedly. Pushing off from the phone booth, he geared up, checked left, and pointed his bike back out into the tempest.

It was after 2:00 PM when he began to feel the effects of his late night and even longer day. At the Espresso Cart on the corner of Newbury and Dartmouth, a concerned attendant watched as Zeke drained three cups in a row.

"Zeke! What up!"

Zeke swiveled just as Big Billy went cruising by on a tiny BMX. *Good ol' Billy,* Zeke thought, *making absolutely no money at all on that piece of shit.* There had been a time, in between riding for Stuart Rigby, when Billy Campbell had founded his own company with a handful of friends. They rode hard for him, Zeke remembered, clearing a better percentage and even buying into a group employee health insurance plan. Things had been good, which of course meant they could only get worse. Dealing coke as well, Billy began paying his employees half-and-half and then one-quarter to three until finally no one wanted cash at all. Zeke could smile now, recalling the last month of that ill-fated adventure as the pasty-thin, tweaked-out corpses wrecked the only good thing most had ever had, as some went to rehab, some went home, and others, like Zeke, temporarily became property of the state. *Yeah,* Zeke thought, *the good old days.* He shook his head and peeled the cellophane off his first Marlboro of the day as the Espresso Cart attendant leaned out his window and said, "Hey, um, could you not hang out and smoke under the awning?"

Zeke inhaled deeply on the cigarette, shot the attendant an unpleasant look, and said, "Make you a deal. Let me use your phone to page my friend and then I'll be gone."

"But my boss—"

"Buddy, I got nineteen more cigarettes in this pack."

The attendant withdrew, then quickly reappeared with a handheld portable as a middle-aged woman on line for coffee frowned at Zeke's extortion. He ran the numbers by heart, hit the pound sign, and then hung up. Waiting and smoking, he watched the parade of human dollar signs pinball in and out of Newbury Street's high-end stores despite the rain. The store phone rang and Zeke answered.

"Hey, do you guys deliver?" some guy asked.

"Coffee? Are you fucking kidding me?"

Hanging up, Zeke took another deep inhale and managed to catch a buzz. When business was slow, as summers usually were, cigarettes were easily abused. And the die-hards, at least to Zeke, never failed to amuse, legging out a twenty-block run with a smoke dangling from their lips while wondering why they had no wind. The phone rang again.

"Hello?" Zeke said.

"What the fuck number is that?"

"Hey, Cam." Zeke grinned. "I'm at that espresso trap on Newbury."

She laughed. "Making new friends?"

"Absolutely. Fuck, it ain't my fault. Blame the city. Blame the crack dealers. No incoming calls on pay phones was one of the dumbest moves ever."

"Hell, yeah."

"Where are you?"

She grunted, the disgust like an odor oozing through the phone. "Fucking Cambridge, Z, for the second time today. Do you believe this? Stuart is such a prick."

"Yeah." Zeke ground out the smoke. "If you don't have five going and five returning, Cambridge is a total loser."

"Tell me about it. On top of that, I got hung up at some professor's office at Harvard for like forty minutes and Stu wouldn't even let me hit them for any waiting time."

"Drummond, right? In the business school?"

"Yep."

"There must be something going on with Stuey and that guy," Zeke said. "Same thing happened to me last week."

"Think Stuey's two-timing Richie with that hippy fucking loser?"

"Who knows? You know Stu. Him and his little crushes."

"Gross."

"Now, Cammi, be nice."

"Oh yeah?" She laughed. "And this coming from a guy who stepped in front of an old lady on line for a pay phone?"

"Hey—"

"Don't even bother. Stuart told me the whole thing. Classy, Zeke."

Zeke grinned. "It's a young person's world—ain't that what they say?"

"No, Zeke, they definitely do not say that, especially not when the poor thing's trying to get around on a goddamn cane."

"Yeah, well, I'm just trying to save room in heaven."

"I wouldn't worry about that, sweetie. Satan's probably confirming your reservation as we speak."

"Listen. I ran into Faustis at One Financial. He gave me two passes for his show tonight. At Chase's. You in?"

"Ugh. After last night? What time did we get home, anyway?"

"Who knows? I couldn't have read a clock if it was six inches in front of my face."

Cammi Sinclair laughed. "Who's playing?"

"They're opening for Red Land Band."

"No way. That's so cool. Faustis is moving up in the world."

"Maybe. Hope those guys hit it soon."

"You never know."

"Are you in or not? He told me to specifically ask that you come. Said he hasn't seen you in thirty years."

"Yeah," she sighed. "Where and when?"

"Meet you at the Rat, say five-thirty or six? We'll cruise over to Chase's at like eight thirty. I don't think he goes on till nine. Fuck, there goes my beeper."

"Unbelievable," Cammi said. "Mine just popped as you said that."

"He scares me sometimes."

"Light me up if anything changes."

"Bye, Cam."

He was clicking off the phone, facing the slow-moving traffic spasming forward in between stop signs, when an image appeared from behind a tinted passenger-side window descending like a screen upon his past. Caught off guard, wondering if recognition was already mutually established, he felt his pulse explode before cursing this morbid coincidence as their eyes met and Zeke wondered what was next since he had nowhere else to duck.

"Yeah, motherfucker," the voice called out.

Zeke said nothing, frozen by what he thought might be aimed from the backseat shadows.

"Ain't your brother someone's bitch yet?"

"Fuck you, Lindy." Zeke saw a row of parked cars and a stream of pedestrians in between himself and the tricked-out sedan creeping steadily past. *They wouldn't dare*, he thought, before remembering who he was dealing with and that, more than the innocent passersby, caused him to say, "It wasn't ever like you thought."

"Yeah? Well, we haven't forgotten a fucking thing, little man."

Zeke dissected the face. The decade since had not been kind to Lindy, as he was already losing his curly blond hair, the blue eyes cynical chips in a patch of lines gathered around his sneer. "I bet that puke fuck's sucking cock like a real pro. You can tell him I said practice makes perfect."

"You would know," Zeke scoffed. "You never dared before, and now you're talkin' shit behind his back. Ain't you still a gutless fuck."

"We've been watching the calendar, little man." Lindy smirked again. "And we'll be waiting. After all this fucking time and still the parole board's gonna drop him right into our laps."

"Careful what you wish for." Now it was Zeke who wore the smirk. "Big bro's coming home."

"But C.B. and Ju-Ju won't be." Lindy spat out the window. "Remember them? Tell your fucking brother we're gonna be having us a reunion, man. Bank on that."

"Fuck you!"

"He sent them home in boxes, kid."

A cascade of car horns finally propelled the sedan forward as Lindy formed a gun with his hand and blew smoke from the index-finger barrel. Watching the car shriek around the corner, Zeke winced at both the stench of burnt rubber and what he'd thought he'd left behind. Amid new questions, he stared sickly up the street.

Sweeping across western Massachusetts and then into the suburbs, the thick black storm clouds had run out of reinforcements by four o'clock. Zeke was on his way back downtown as the last of them trailed overhead like a rumor blowing out to sea. It was still July, which meant the sun, when it finally clocked in, jacked the temperature thirty degrees within half an hour. *East Coast humidity*, Zeke thought. *Fuck me.*

Despite the hours since his malevolent encounter with Lindy on Newbury Street, Zeke's mind still echoed with the threats of violence. He considered it amazing that even after all this time, almost twelve years, the dead end of days past never seemed to die. Never. A one-way street with no escape …

Tucked inside this reverie, he almost got clipped by a taxi and so cursed his own stupidity. He knew better than to think about this now, especially with rush hour bearing down, so he blanked his mind completely.

Late afternoons were a lot like mornings and post-lunch hour. Zeke had twelve on him and his beeper had chirped twice in two minutes, but he nonetheless pulled to the curb on Boylston and quickly shed his raingear. Folding the blue jacket and pants into tiny squares, he jammed them and his soaked ball cap into the courier bag before saddling back up. He was wearing black army fatigues cut off at mid-calf and a Fugazi T-shirt, which, despite the rear fender, was instantly splattered in roadslime.

His drenched pants and shirt flapped in the now stagnant breeze as he hit the intersection of Boylston and Tremont at twenty-five mph. He tapped the brakes because the roads were still funneling massive quantities of water into the sewers. *Can't believe I'm sweating now*, he silently complained. *It's always something.*

At the corner of Summer and Atlantic, he unclicked his right shoe, legged over the bar, and slalomed in between pedestrians crowding the pavilion outside One Financial Center. Peeking at the atrium windows, he waved to a fresh assortment of messengers still gathered around their tables drinking coffee like a council of amateurs. Inside, he grabbed an elevator and rocketed back up to the fortieth floor and tossed the package at a Cross Digital mailroom employee.

Back downstairs at a pay phone minutes later, he heard Stuart Rigby exclaim, "Split Minute!"

"It's Zeke."

"Zeke! Back in a flash!"

While on hold, Zeke frowned at the increasing traffic on Atlantic Avenue, the late afternoon already in demise.

"Zeke!"

"Still here, buddy."

"The phones are going fucking crazy!"

"Good. I'm at One Financial with eleven on me."

"Eleven! Good Lord. Pickup at Social Services, 15 Chauncy, going to the State House, third floor, and—"

"Name."

"I asked. They didn't have one."

"Stu, goddamn it, I'm not running around the fucking State House at five o'clock so those idiots can bounce me from office to office."

"Zeke!"

"No way."

"I'll get the name! Just pick up the fucking package!"

"Okay."

"Stanley and Morgan, 50 State, going to United Bank, 100 Federal … and let's see, the Irish Trust, 25 Broad, going to the Historical Society, 50 School Street."

"What else?"

"What else? Zeke, that'll be fourteen! Fuck, hold on a second."

On hold again, Zeke finished filling out the newest slips before he heard Stuart Rigby sigh and say, "That was Remo. He just got a flat on Exeter with six on him and no goddamn inner tube!"

"Jesus, what a moron. I can't get there, Stu."

"Fuck!"

"You know I'd try."

"Fuck!" Stuart said rhetorically. "Danny's on Comm., Stretch's in the Back Bay. Guess I'm just gonna have to swing him through."

"All right, I'm outta here."

"Wait, Zeke! You're gonna be my vacuum downtown. I'll start paying you back at five. Get ready to load up with Back Bays on the way home, like we always do."

"Shit." But he wasn't headed home. "I guess that's cool."

"Please, Zeke, I've got no choice. Cammi's way the hell out in the South End sweeping up all the leftovers and Fudgie's fucking off around Newbury somewhere ignoring his beeper."

"He's a non-factor anyway."

"Say it twice, my friend."

"I'll call from Chauncy."

Must be busier than hell, Zeke thought, noting the missing perversion that usually ended each call. Outside, Zeke clicked into his pedals, checked left, and zigzagged through three lanes of stopped red-light traffic. The clock on Federal Street flashed the temperature at 89 degrees, the time 4:15 PM. Rush hour was hanging above them all like the recently departed clouds, and no one knew that better than Zeke. End of the day meant people dodged their phones and fled the office while the courier chased only ghosts. Some buildings even blocked access after 5:00 PM, forcing Zeke to stand around a security desk while those upstairs argued over who would take the long trip down. All of it, he knew, was usually a money loser, making riding late a return courtesy for Stuart Rigby, who always kept his earners fed. It was Operation Dump Bag, so Zeke spent the next thirty minutes unloading half his parcels while picking up three Back Bays.

The State House was located adjacent to the municipal and superior courthouses at the top of Beacon Hill, so Zeke clicked into first and powered up Beacon Street. The state troopers were just beginning to bar access when Zeke slipped through the closing door.

"Nah, nah, nah," one of them said, and when he smiled Zeke thought he saw a thousand teeth. "We're closed."

"Come on, guy, please?" Zeke said, acting as if he was at wit's end, noting the nametag. "Come on, Trooper Collins. It's for the Secretary of State, ultra-important."

"Which ones aren't?" his partner said, and Zeke thought they could have been brothers. Over six feet tall and stacked with muscle until their shirts gripped them like skin, they had haircuts like marines and the sense of humor to match.

"Come back tomorrow," Collins said.

No way, Zeke almost replied. Not going backwards now. For liability purposes, Stuart Rigby's Rule Number 158 stated that all undeliverable government packages be immediately returned and not overnighted. Zeke saw a clock, which read 4:58 P.M., and said, "It ain't even five o'clock. What the fuck?"

"Listen," Collins said. "I told you we're closed up. What part of that do you need clarified?"

"Damn it." Zeke stood there and watched as they went about their closing procedures. "Can I at least take a leak?"

"No."

"Yeah, Willie, let him." Collins pointed down a foyer. "Make it quick. Third door on the right."

"Cool."

Zeke clacked across the shined stone floor, past oil paintings of stately men in powdered wigs two hundred years dead. The empty great hall was a marked contrast to the usual bureaucratic shuffle and tour bus miasma. Glancing over, Zeke made sure the troopers were occupied before throwing a shoulder into the first-floor door marked STAIRWELL. Stealthily ascending, he popped out on the third-floor landing and caught his breath when he found himself directly above the two policemen who were busy below. He eased the door closed and inched along the wall like a shadow until he reached a hallway with a plaque that said HEALTH AND HUMAN SERVICES. Room 304 was halfway down and locked, so Zeke noted the time on the receipt, broke policy, and slipped the unsigned-for parcel beneath the door. He was inching his way back when he heard, "Van, he ain't in here."

"What? Fuck me."

"State's on four."

"That little prick."

"I'm going up."

Zeke grinned and watched below as Collins took out a walkie-talkie while the second cop ran upstairs. Once he was past, Zeke slipped back into the stairwell. At the bottom, he hid beneath the riser as Collins came crashing through next, saying, "That's right, 126 on the fourth floor. Post the south entrance just in case."

I gotta get the fuck outta here, Zeke thought, his pulse like a pinned RPM gauge. *Guess they won't think this is too funny.*

He crept back out into the foyer, made it halfway through the cavernous great hall, and was nearing the metal detectors when he heard from the fourth-floor railing, "Stop right there, motherfucker! You wanna play games?"

Running for the door, Zeke spun the locks, bolted into the sun, and heard, "They're coming for you, dickhead!"

But he was already gone, ass-sliding the banister past forty concrete steps as the huge oak door swung open to reveal alligator-face in full sprint. Misjudging the landing, Zeke crashed and raked himself across the concrete sidewalk before fleeing towards his bike. Frantically, he worked the lock as two other state policemen turned the corner to join alligator-face in hot pursuit. Zeke got a running start and, with only one escape route, found the left pedal and blasted down the opposite side of Beacon Hill. From experience, he knew one-way streets were often law enforcement's worst nightmare, so when he saw Charles Street rapidly approaching on the left, he thought he was in the clear. Yet Beacon Hill was the highest point downtown, which meant he was going to hit the traffic-clogged intersection at thirty miles per hour until he saw the unmarked car suddenly jet out from Spruce Street with its front dash light spinning madly. Swerving at the last possible second, he felt his right pedal clip the bumper and waited to pinwheel through the air until he saw his hands still on the bars, righted himself as best he could, and found he had a second and a half to make a move. Either split two lanes and hope the light went green or try clearing the left curb at speed without slamming into the wrought-iron fence ringing the Boston Common. Swinging left, he pulled up with a prayer and made the sidewalk with thirty feet remaining to create yet another miracle before smashing through the pedestrian-crowded corner.

"Look out! Look out! Look out!" he screamed at the abruptly swiveled heads and panicked faces. "Comin' through!"

He took a right shoulder full of groceries as someone screamed, and, leaning almost to forty-five degrees, bent the left onto Charles Street without skidding into traffic or clipping anyone else. Chancing a look over his shoulder, he saw the unmarked car pinned at the corner of the one-way as four lanes slowly choked past. He would have screamed triumphantly, but he was far from clear, and the adrenaline dropped him into high gear. Boylston was coming up fast and he needed to get out of sight. At the corner, he took a left and then a quick right onto Tremont, turning down an alley behind one of the only triple-X video stores still open for business in the Combat Zone. Braking to a stop next to a leaky drainpipe, he pried his hands off the bar to take a deep breath and immediately felt the sweat explode from his pores.

Jesus Christ, he thought, and held out his hands to check for the shakes. *That was a close one.*

Leaning his bike against the alley wall, Zeke crouched and flexed his burnt quadriceps. Flipping open the bag, he pulled out the blue rain pants and black ball cap, hoping they would be camouflage enough until he somehow fled downtown.

Eight on me, he thought. *Time to go.*

Walking out to Tremont, he checked the street. Five o'clock, people and traffic everywhere. He was on the western fringe of Chinatown, a ten square block section bordering the financial district. Coasting down Tremont, he swung left onto Grange and passed rows of stores splattered in Chinese characters. Heading north through the side streets, he worked his way back to 150 Federal. In the lobby, every elevator disgorged a small population of commuters clutching the morning's umbrellas, raincoats, briefcases, newspapers, and books for the T-ride home. He shared an elevator with another courier who obviously had no fenders on his rig, because he looked like he had taken a daylong bath in road slime.

Six minutes later, downstairs in the huge green-stoned lobby, Zeke punched in the eight-hundred number as a clock read 5:27 PM.

"Split Minute."

"Stuey."

"Zeke! I was just on the way out. Pickup at Nordstrom—"

"Can't do it, Stu."

"What? What do you mean?"

"I'm smoking hot."

"Oh no. What's it this time? Did you mow down a baby carriage in a crosswalk?"

"I got five downtowns. Three Back Bays. I'm dumping it all, like now, and signing off."

"Jeepers. Okay." Stuart clicked his teeth. "How bad is it?"

"It's nothing. No clients."

"You're really fucking me here. I had you all dialed in with five more heading out, but I guess we'll save them for the morning."

"I'll call you for the inbounds."

"Ten-four, Zekey, and please stay away from Cammi. She needs her rest."

"Who doesn't?"

"Okay then. Bye-bye now."

Zeke hung up, checked his slips to order his drops, and as he headed for his bike, idly wondered exactly when he was supposed to have his next cigarette.

The last package was delivered at 6:15 PM on the corner of Massachusetts and Commonwealth avenues. Perfect for Zeke, since the Rat's Nest was barely two blocks up inside Kenmore Square. He had forgotten about the game when he told Cammi where to meet him, and every street within six blocks was jammed with carousing suburbanites in Red Sox ball caps. Some game nights, with nothing else to do, Zeke would sit on the steps of 536 Commonwealth and watch five thousand people stream out of the Kenmore T-station like a colony of ants in mass migration.

Without room to maneuver, he gave up and shouldered his bike through the crowd. The three-foot-high fence outside the bar was already filled with courier bikes stacked five and six feet up like urban modern art. He saw Cammi's bike near the top of the first stack and hoisted his ride up level with hers before sliding the lock around both their middle bars. Like Zeke, she rode a men's frame built up from scrap parts with a customized paint job. Hers was also slathered in stickers, one of which said, IF SATAN'S IN HELL WITH ALL THAT'S BAD, BURY ME UPSIDE DOWN SO HEAVEN CAN KISS MY ASS.

Zeke swung open the door and saw the place was packed. Made famous by Aerosmith in the 1970s, the Rat's Nest Bar had seen its glory days lately fade into a nostalgic twilight frequented by bikers, punks, miscreants, and dozens of local bands hoping to become the next hateful thing. A huge man in a black T-shirt and denim vest flashed a broken-tooth smile when Zeke entered.

"And so it is complete!" he yelled before gathering the twig-like Zeke up into a crushing hug.

Zeke smiled despite the day just finished. "Jesus, Carl—"

"All wet and sweaty!" Carl bellowed, almost lifting Zeke clear above his head. "You smelly roadrash motherfucker!"

Zeke would have laughed, but he could not breathe and so he slapped Carl's bald head until he was once again on the ground. Stretching his back, Zeke said, "Thanks. I needed that."

"Wanna go again?" Carl flexed a foot thick bicep. "Almost felt every bone in your back crack!"

Zeke craned his neck around the bar. "Where they at?"

"You kiddin' me?" Carl nodded at the crowd disdainfully. "Game night, Z. They're all up top coolin' it."

"Nice."

The concert room was in the basement, the main bar was on the first floor, and upstairs was a U-shaped ring with tables overlooking the chaos below. Taking the stairs two at a time, he saw four tables pushed together in the far corner next to where their gear and bags were piled into a mammoth rain-soaked precipice. Once spotted, they called out his name as Zeke found Cammi and squeezed in next to her while slapping the offered hands raised his way. *At least she's smiling*, Zeke thought. He looked over at her and said, "Never thought I'd taste this," then drained her mug completely.

"What an asshole," Cammi said, grinning nonetheless. In baggy T-shirt and shorts, arms and back speckled in tire spray, and with grease smeared across one cheek, she had a sun-wrinkled brown-eyed gaze, two rock-like legs, and the cut arms and torso of someone who pulled over three hundred miles a week. He ran his hand through the brown ponytail, poked playfully at her right breast, and said, "Where's my glass?"

She laughed. "God, whatta perv. How about taking a walk down to the fucking bar, deadbeat?"

"How much fun was your day?"

"A ton." She gave him a guilty smirk. "I was a bad girl today."

"Oh yeah?" Zeke drank thirstily before swiping away the foam. "Misdemeanor bad or felony bad?"

"This moron cabbie was trying to trade paint like NASCAR on the goddamn Harvard Bridge." She took back the beer and gulped. "Let's just say he won't be using his right-side mirror anytime soon."

Zeke laughed and twirled her ponytail. "That's my baby."

"Yo, Zeke!"

Zeke leaned in and waved down towards the other end of the table, raising Cammi's glass in salute.

"Gang's all here," he told her and she smiled warmly, tapping ash from the cigarette onto the floor.

"You're the talk of the town, babe."

"Oh yeah?" He leaned closer as a Motorhead track abruptly tore through the bar. "Great."

"Seriously," Cammi said and ground out the smoke. "Cash saw the whole thing."

"What're you talking about?"

As if on cue, Zeke heard a banshee's scream as Cash Monroe returned from the first-floor bathroom. Approaching the table, he slapped and clasped Zeke's offered hand in both of his. "Fuckin' A, Speed, you are one gnarly motherfucker."

"He sure is," Cammi added, waving at Zeke's armpits.

"Saw the whole deal, brother," Cash said, "comin' the opposite way down Beacon. *Fuck me.*"

Zeke nodded and lit a cigarette. "Oh yeah?"

"You should be tire grease, bro. You know that, right? Hey!" Cash screamed at the others. "Raise a glass for this motherfucker right here!"

They toasted Zeke again as he meekly said, "Yeah, thanks."

"Honestly, if I hadn't seen it …" Cash's eyes glinted appreciatively as he swigged the glass empty. "Just one more miracle, huh?"

"Jesus on wheels, bro."

Cammi punched him again. "Not too humble, are you?"

"Fuck, Cam, Z here don't need no humble pie." Cash Monroe grabbed their pitcher for a refill. "The sidewalk shot was one thing, but when you hit that corner, knuckling your knee on the fucking ground, and didn't touch no one, boy, I just about dropped a nut. All that pork just bunched up at the light and watched you go, too. Did you hear me yelling?"

"Nope."

"Fuckin' A. That was some hairball shit, man, thanks."

Cash guzzled the beer, winked at Zeke, and then retold the story to the other end of the table for the fourth time. After he was gone, Cammi turned to Zeke and said, "Is he full of shit?"

"Total luck." Zeke winced. "I could've killed any one of those people."

"What the fuck did you do? To have six state cops at the corner?"

"First of all, there wasn't six. Cash's already lying. And second," Zeke exhaled through his nose, "you know Stu. All governments go back."

"Courthouse or State House?"

"State House." He grinned. "Fuckers were locking up at like five to five."

"And ...?"

"Told them I was going up to State, which's the fourth floor. They told me to get fucked so I asked to take a leak and that was that."

"And meanwhile ..."

"H and H was on three."

Cammi smiled at the ruse. "That's fucked, Zeke. Tell him, Val."

"*Si, vato, misea su futuro.*" Valdez, who welded discarded bicycles into custom chopper-inspired creations, raised a bottle of beer and grinned. "To nine lives, *cabron.*"

"Thanks, Val."

"I'm gonna use that one too," he said. "Wrong floors and shit. Cold, yo, cold."

"Didn't have a chance, did they?" Cammi stole a pitcher from further down the table. "Here's to it."

"Shouldn't be giving away my secrets," Zeke said, and everyone laughed at that.

Abruptly, he felt the alcohol sponging into his parched muscles. Losing himself inside the thumping music and half-dozen conversations swirling about, he felt the day's events slowly unclaw and retreat into the growing haze. Stretching his legs beneath the table, he leaned back and just observed, listening as Cammi and Valdez traded good-natured insults like playing cards.

Cammi Sinclair. Zeke figured he had known her longer than almost anyone else, both of them on the pedals at sixteen and meeting one day in a horrendous collision that sent both across the asphalt like cheese eaten by a grater. Without question, it had been his fault entirely, and he smiled when he remembered looking up and getting punched in the face twice before swinging back and realizing his attacker had breasts and a scrawny frame that somehow powered a bruising overhand right. He blinked because, like so much else, it all seemed like the day before when in fact it had been seven years since. The first three of it together and the next four pretending it was over. Yet at its end, when long past the point of wondering exactly what it was that made two people love and fight one another almost simultaneously, he just figured she was about the only reason left to listen for anymore.

Traveling along the circumference of the table, his gaze swept across Eddie Z and Rosemont, who rode long-distance for a company out of Cambridge, which basically meant they spent the whole day plowing back and forth across the Charles River. To the left of them were Philly and Double D, a bass player and guitarist, respectively, in a hardcore band based in Allston; James Sylvio, a graphic artist specializing in pornographic web design; Todd the Rod, a college dropout; and next to him Franklin, a protégé of Faustis with the dreadlocks to match; Chink Yang, who wore a full mohawk while still trading in his Mandarin for English; and Isidrio Valdez, the only person at the table who had been riding longer than Zeke. Next to Valdez was Michelle, who had the misfortune of riding for a chain of copy stores, which meant she had health insurance but had to wear a helmet and blue jumpsuit with the company name plastered across her back; and Baby New Year, who was seventeen years old but looked not a day over thirteen; and to his left, the immaculate Cash Monroe, who always thought his wardrobe and sly wink were all the ladies needed, unlike Desmond H, who was a runaway from upstate New York who never spoke much; until finally there was Cammi Sinclair, a street kid since age sixteen, when her father abruptly died drunk at the wheel before her mother left for New York and her older sister kicked her out. All told, in a business with a yearly 70 percent turnover, and with the exception of Baby New Year, Zeke saw the table was pretty much a veterans-only affair.

"Hey," she said. When Zeke felt those familiar brown eyes heat up the side of his face, he turned and saw her cheeks flushed like stop signs beneath the grime. "Are you reading my mind?"

"Maybe." Zeke took a long swallow of cold beer. "It'd be shitty, though. He gave me freebies and everything."

She seemed to contemplate his statement while easing her left bra strap back into position. Observing her, he knew there were times when the two of them could spend an entire night together without wasting a single word. But tied, untied, the same pieces always seemed locked stubbornly at odds. It was, he realized, what made one an absolute perfect disaster for the other. He caught her questioning his expression, so he grinned and said, "Tonight, Cam." He ashed his cigarette into a can. "We need to decide that right now."

"I'm pretty fucked up already."

"Good. Then I won't have to club you too hard later on."

"What a sweet-talker." Cammi rolled her eyes. "Such a romantic."

"I've got all the moves." Zeke spotted a waitress who looked either stoned or half asleep. "Excuse me! Could we get another round of pitchers and two shots of Jack?"

The waitress nodded before shuffling towards the stairs. The in-house stereo switched to Alice in Chains, and the opening riff ran like a chainsaw across the spine. At the same instant Zeke thought about how he should go home, clean his bike, eat a real meal, and go to bed early, the next round arrived like a death sentence handed down upon his evening. He and Cammi clinked glasses, shot the whiskey, and pretended it tasted good. At the end of the table, where the pitchers were being quickly dispatched, Cash Monroe laughed so hard he started hiccupping as Isidrio Valdez leaned relentlessly towards his victim's ear, finishing the joke.

Zeke cracked a grin, drained his glass, and said, "Yeah, Cam, we gotta go. I don't wanna dick Faustis."

"Whatever." Cammi kneaded at a tightening left calf. "I'm down for whatever."

"Val. You done fucking with Cash's brain?"

"Oh man," Cash Monroe said, wiping away the tears. "Too bad you missed it, Z. That was some of the most fucked-up shit ever."

"Where you going tonight?"

"Guess."

"Fuckin' male slut," Cammi scoffed. "Eurotrash wannabe whore."

Cash Monroe's blue eyes twinkled at the insult. Even through the weather, and despite the rigors of the job, Monroe had a reputation to protect—the rest of these greased pigs be damned—which is why he carried a can of mousse and his gear was always coordinated. It might cost more, but what was the point of wearing shitty T-shirts and shorts hacked from ruined jeans? As far as he was concerned, he would leave these mutants to cover themselves in tattoos, wear the same stink-ripe crap for days on end, and basically claim the aesthetic high ground while unknowingly becoming their own cliché. So he winked at the always vitriolic Cammi Sinclair, blew a stream of smoke directly into her face, and said, "You know I'd ask you out tonight, Slammi, but then that would make me gay."

Zeke gagged in mid-sip as the entire table hooted and Cammi scowled. "Fuck you, boy toy." She turned to Zeke. "I don't know what you're laughing at. Guess that makes you a homo too."

"Yeah, well, we gay guys got to stick together. Right, Cash?"

"Fuckin' A, brother. Fuckin' A."

"Polesmokers," Cammi spat. "The both of you."

"Franklin!" Zeke called out. "Homo Monroe's going to Club Z tonight for his usual Euro-infested disaster. Wanna head to Chase's with me and C? Catch Faustis and Red Land?"

Franklin perched one thick eyebrow inquisitively, batting back a natty handful of dreadlocks. He had huge eyes that, along with the two perfect rows of white teeth, seemed to glow within the obsidian face like uncollected gems.

"Can't, Speed. Got class tonight."

"Oh, c'mon. Fuck, I ain't asking you for a loan."

"It's the truth, yo. And fuckin' mid-terms are next week."

"So what?"

"So I'm payin' for this shit, man, fuck. I ain't pushin' all these pedals just to miss a class that's costing me three grand."

"Three grand?" Zeke grinned.

"It's Tufts, yo."

"Tufts? I didn't even know you could read."

Franklin smiled and slowly extended his middle finger.

"Don't listen, Franklin," Cammi said. "You don't want to end up like these other retards."

"Goddamn right he doesn't." Cash Monroe lifted his glass and pulled a joint from a cigarette pack. "Here's to higher education."

"*Simpatico, cabron.*" Isidrio Valdez nodded his head. "*Fumandanos.*"

"*Fumandanos!*" Cash screamed delightedly. "If that means light that motherfucker up, then I'm reading you loud and clear, bean bag!"

Zeke made sure to scan the near-vacant second-floor, spotting a couple of occupied two-tops overlooking Kenmore Square. Lighting up was stupid, he knew, but Zeke had been a Rat's Nest regular since sixteen and eventually an employee of Jamison Ramos, the owner. Originally from Santa Barbara, Zeke knew Ramos had opened the place nearly thirty years before with two other partners now long gone. As legends will, over time, those early years had passed into a strange lore filled with prostrated rock groupies, pharmaceutical-wielding biker gangs, and intermittent law enforcement agencies bucking for a headline. And while serving as errand boy under Ramos's flag, Zeke quickly found the keys to a whole new world practically dropped into his lap. Running packages to the best hotels for VIPs and rock acts, arranging dinner reservations at five-star restaurants for Ramos and his whole tweaked-out entourage, and later, in charge of the bank on concert night, all of it combined to leave Zeke strung out in a never-ending circle of abuse by the ripe old age of nineteen. Thinking back on it, he sometimes smiled, and other times considered it a lost chapter stolen from someone else's life. And Ramos, the last Zeke had heard, was running the place in absentia while living the good life in South Beach. *New faces, new places, and here I still am*, Zeke thought, *growing like a fungus with zero as my hero.*

Cammi gave him a nudge with her elbow. "Hey, space cadet, you're up."

Zeke refocused and took the joint. "If we don't leave soon, I ain't never gonna make it outta here."

Cammi grinned. "Then pass that thing and let's move."

So he did, dropping a twenty-dollar bill on the table and slapping all those hands one last time. Cammi handed him his gear, checked her watch, and on the way out she said, "We're gonna be way early."

"Good." Zeke waved good-bye to Carl, the doorman. "Cause I'm fucking starving."

Outside, the red face of the setting sun bounced off a thousand windows as Kenmore Square patiently awaited the post-game crush.

With the concert over by 11:00 PM, the two shadows that broke north onto the Jamaicaway Riverway owned the road completely. Appearing briefly out of the night at fifty-foot intervals beneath pale streetlights before being swallowed again by the dark, the two hunched figures pedaled madly towards home. Harvard Avenue might have been more direct, but at this late hour, Zeke knew the Riverway would be much faster. Besides, compared to the concrete-and-steel towers he weaved amongst all day, the slow-moving river and tree canopies were a welcome change. He let Cammi push ahead before slipping into her wake and drafting on her hard work. She kept a mean pace—always had—and minutes later she picked up her hands for a breather as Park Drive approached. They exchanged leads and soon rumbled across the B-line train tracks, swinging left onto Commonwealth Avenue. As they crested the hill, the West Campus of Boston University flooded the surrounding streets with drunk revelers lined ten deep at neighborhood bars. They passed the Paradise Rock Club. Since it was Euro night, Zeke idly wondered if Cash Monroe might be in attendance. But after scanning every No Parking sign, bus stop pole, streetlight, and fence, his rig was nowhere to be seen. A quarter mile later, Brighton Avenue peeled off Commonwealth to the right. Behind, he heard Cammi hoot at two well-dressed men and fifty feet later they turned down Linden, cutting across to Cambridge Street.

Lower Allston was similar to Allston in that both the working class and students from all over the city sought out the cheap rent and some semblance of community. Immigrants, artists, and those on the fringe all piled into the narrow streets and triple-decker houses like refugees from the pricey downtown abyss. Since his release five years ago, Zeke had lived in Lower Allston, coincidentally just eight blocks from his old PO's apartment. *Cocksucker*, he habitually thought while pedaling over the six lanes of the Massachusetts Turnpike. Gambling on the green light ahead, he led Cammi downhill at thirty miles per hour and bent a dangerous-leaning left turn onto North Harvard. With enough speed remaining, they coasted the last six blocks before pulling up outside 125 Easton Street.

"Hurry up. Before I collapse," Cammi said.

Zeke grinned into the dark and huffed upstairs to the third floor. Once inside, they propped the bikes against the foyer wall, dumped their gear, and headed for the kitchen.

"Come here," she said, and when he turned, their lips met until she broke the kiss with a tired sigh, placing her head against his chest.

"It's been a long one," he said, massaging gently at her shoulders, "and I'm getting old."

"You will find no pity here." She looked up at him through bloodshot eyes, the intoxicated smile echoing his exhaustion. "I stink, don't I?"

"Not any more than me."

"I'm gonna shower first. Can you cook up the rest of that shit? I don't want to be up all night."

"Yeah."

He fished into his sock for the remaining half-gram as she headed for the bathroom. Pulling open a drawer, he reached beneath and detached a burnt spoon and six-inch glass pipe. The remaining cocaine got dumped onto the spoon along with a pinch of baking soda and four drops of water. He delicately worked the lighter until the mixture eddied and crackled. Using the pick end of a fingernail clipper, he carefully skimmed a thin white chip off the top and placed the clipper on the counter to dry. The back porch was accessed by the kitchen, so Zeke threw open the door to air out the stink of unwashed dishes in an unclean house. His roommate, Booger, was a notorious binge drinker, so Zeke often owned the two-bedroom apartment at night.

Cracking a beer, he ambled into the television room and lit three candles. Powering up the stereo, he put Morphine on low, and soon a tenor saxophone moaned through the otherwise stilled room.

He hit the shower next and ten minutes later they were both in their underwear on the couch, the humidity oppressive despite the midnight hour. When he smiled it was because any secrets were now long gone. In seven years, she had moved from an attractive but thin, safety-pin-pierced punker into an elixir he sometimes drank to addiction. It was a side few others saw, when she wasn't throwing drinks in people's faces or preying on the ignorance of strangers.

Putting a tiny piece of the now-hard rock into the Brillo-stuffed end of the glass tube, he fired up while greedily sucking down the acrid smoke. Holding his breath, he refilled the tube and handed it to Cammi. When he finally exhaled, he decided there was yet to be another feeling quite like this in the world.

"One more," he said and refilled the tube as she gently stroked inside his boxers. She hit the pipe next as he kneaded one breast while sucking on the other, her soft groan cut off by his lips as she exhaled into his mouth. Pushing her back, he made quick work of her Mickey Mouse panties, dragging his tongue from nipple to nipple before finding her belly button. Settling in,

Zeke awaited the bone-crushing thigh squeeze that some nights threatened to pop his skull like a hollow candy as Cammi sank back further, closing her eyes while gently pulling at his hair. Relentlessly, he set to work until she was quivering and arching back and he, to prevent escape, hung on, driving with his legs until her head was jammed sideways against the armrest. Gasping once, he felt her resolve abruptly collapse beneath the butter of his tongue, and soon after she cracked the foolish grin of sweet release.

"Not so fast," she said when he made a move for the pipe. Sitting up, she latched onto his lips and felt that part of him jabbing into her gut as she playfully stripped the boxers before sinking to her knees. Sensing himself disappear into the rhythm, Zeke spent the next fifteen minutes wondering why it ever had to stop. Once his eyes finally opened, she was still down there, alternately licking and pumping until there was nothing left to give.

"My God," he said, seeing her grinning, expectant face. "I can barely feel my legs."

Standing up, Cammi pulled his head against her stomach and after a silent minute said, "We're too good at that."

"No kidding."

"God, Zeke." She brushed affectionately through the spikes of his hair, staring out the blackened window as she felt his breath skim across the flat plain of her belly. "What the fuck is wrong with us?"

He did not have to ask. Knew exactly where this conversation got them every single time. And as smooth as this night had gone, and while others in the future might be just as perfect, there inevitably came the day when they fought over absolutely nothing and swore it was the end. Still, hanging onto her now, he saw how deceptive this bliss could sometimes be. He turned his head to kiss her belly button and said, "Let's get high some more."

She changed the CD while he refilled the pipe, and fifteen minutes later they were both pacing through the apartment and chain-smoking cigarettes. It was after 1:00 AM and the clock was now their enemy. *Five more hours until I call Stuart for the inbounds*, he thought, and instantly regretted it. In the good old days, he would leave work at the Rat's Nest after four o'clock, rage at the nightly after-hours party, and be on the pedals by 6:30 AM. *I'm only twenty-four*, he almost said, but nonetheless cringed at the damage those all-nighters could presently wreak.

They sat on the couch and Cammi lay down, using his lap for a pillow.

"Josie called me yesterday," she eventually said.

"Yeah?" Zeke frowned. "I'm sure it must've been a real treat."

"Fucking cunt."

"She sure is. I don't know how you ended up with a sister like that."

"She said Mommy Dearest was coming to town."

"So what?"

"So she wanted to know if she could stay at my place."

"Oh my God. You're joking, right?"

"Nope."

Zeke shook his head and said, "What's the occasion?"

"For her? Who knows? Probably just one more session of why I am the ungrateful disappointment."

"How long's it been?"

"Like, four years?"

"With no word or nothing ... Fuck her."

"And the other."

"You said it." Zeke gently massaged her back, the muscles knotted into cinched cords painful to the touch. He had been doing this job too long not to know what could happen if he did not stretch his entire body twice a day. Especially since he had no health insurance and injuries, while a nuisance, could bankrupt him within a week. But since she would not listen and derisively called him "yoga boy," she ended every night sprawled across the floor like a wounded specimen unaccustomed to anything else. Zeke ran a stiffened knuckle along her spine and felt the muscles positively vibrating as he said, "So what'd you tell Josie?"

"The same thing I always do. Don't fucking call me ever again."

"And what part of that does she not understand?"

"Who knows? Who cares?"

"And still she calls."

"Mostly to rub in how great her life is."

"Oh yeah. Answering phones and hanging out with a bunch of frauds. Yeah, she's on top of the world all right."

"I don't think she means it like—"

"Cammi, please, she kicked you out of your own house. And now dear mom, the absentee, wants to pull some bullshit reunion scene?"

"Zeke—"

"No. I'm sorry, babe. I'm not buying it."

"Yeah, and you?" She flipped over to look up at him, her gaze tightening into a squint. "You don't hear me telling you to tell your brother to fu—"

"It's totally different. That shit with my mom happened when I was thirteen. And by then, believe me, Josh was already well on his way to Walpole."

"And your father—"

"My old man was a hard-on. Plain and simple."

"But he took care of you."

"You're right. That was never an issue."

"So you told him to fuck off even though—"

"Even though what?" Zeke shrugged. "That mom was in the hospital for months on end and he might've made the trip eight goddamn times?"

"Zeke, you told me he ran his own gig."

"Listen, please." He held up both hands in surrender. "I don't want to talk about this anymore."

"You know, you can be a real bully sometimes."

"Whatever."

"Sucks when the bright light's on you, doesn't it?"

"No. It sucks when I know we're about to start throwing shit at each other and neither one of us can stop it."

She smiled then, looking up at him like a friendly cat.

"Okay," she said. "I'll let tonight be an exception."

"Thank you." But like a magnet, his mind was drawn backwards onto Newbury Street where Lindy lurked again. "I ran into some old friends today."

"Oh yeah?"

He told her about the encounter and could feel her tensing up. His childhood days with the Burgess Street Mob, which his brother had ruthlessly commanded, predated his and Cammi's relationship. "Scumbag punks with guns" is how she usually summed this period up—which wasn't exactly too far from the truth. Having not seen his brother in years, and cognizant of Josh's looming parole, Zeke had started to feel excited before Lindy slithered into view.

We've been watching the calendar, little man.

"Ugh," Cammi said.

"I mean he's not even out yet and these clowns …" Zeke shook his head. "There's just no escaping any of it, man, not ever fucking ever."

"When's he getting out?"

"November." Zeke stared ahead. "Unbelievable."

"Maybe it won't come to that," she said. "Maybe it's just a bunch of macho bullshit."

"What?" He looked down at her upturned face in his lap and did not want to laugh. "Baby, if Josh even gets wind that these guys—his former bros no less—are talking this kind of shit behind his back, he'll hit that corner and waste them all. Josh … you know Josh, man …"

She certainly did. Had even visited him behind bars with Zeke, but she still could not, even now, cut him any slack. "If that's the only reaction he can muster after a fucking decade in prison, maybe they shouldn't even let him out."

Zeke flinched. "Are you out of your mind?"

"Yes." She smiled up at him. "But you already knew that too."

"I certainly did."

"You can't stress about this now, honey. It's still three months away."

"We'll see."

She sighed and closed her eyes.

He wanted to stand and move away but lit another cigarette instead. "The fucking disc is over—"

"No, don't."

"Cam—"

"Just lie here with me, will you? Please? I'll be a good girl."

And he laughed despite himself. "I won't hold my breath."

She opened her mouth to bare her teeth and said, "When you're pissing off a woman who's an inch away from your penis, you really should speak more carefully."

"Hey now. No dick threats."

"What dick?"

"Or insults."

"I'm only kidding. I love your cock."

"Well, thank you."

"You're welcome."

"Hey, cut that out."

"Please? Just one more?"

"Cam, we've got to be up in four and a half hours."

"Are you listening to yourself?"

"God, that feels so good."

"Still sleepy?"

"Apparently not."

He lifted her up so that he could lie down next to her.

"Zeke?"

"What."

"Do you ever think it sucks?"

Zeke smiled. "Not with the moves you got."

"I meant how we're the only thing each other has, moron."

"Jesus, Cam. No more, okay?"

"Okay."

He kissed her, mainly out of fear of what landmine they might stumble over next, and they ended up in a tangle on the floor, sleeping through the night until the ringing phone eventually cracked the deadened calm. *God*, he thought wearily, *I've got fifty miles and twelve more hours to go.*

Chapter Two

"GOOD MORNING, ZACHARIAH! AND how are we feeling today?"

"Man …" Zeke turned his head away from the mellifluous voice and coughed for a solid minute. "What time is it, Stuart?"

"Early. Like six AM kind of early."

"No kidding." Zeke propped himself onto an elbow, careful not to disturb Cammi whose face was nuzzled against his left forearm. Squinting, he tossed off the sleep-dampened sheet that covered them on the floor. "Jesus, it's unbearable already."

Stuart chuckled. "Eighty-one degrees, Zekey-boy, and heading for triple digits by noon."

"God, I almost wish it was raining."

"It's a new day, Zeke. Rise up and greet it!"

"I already got my middle finger pointed out the window."

"Excellent! Are you ready for the inbounds?"

"Hell no. Gimme fifteen minutes."

"I called Cammi's place and got no answer. Please tell me she's right there beside you."

"Affirmative."

"Well, get her sweet little ass up, *mon frère*, cause there's money to be made!"

"Lemme call you back."

"Zeke—"

Clicking off, he lay back down and stared at the ceiling as if it were a mirage-filled pillow.

"Is it that time already?" she asked, and her face was like a little kid's, praying for a snowday.

"He's ringing, Cam. We gotta get moving."

"No." She petulantly flipped the other way and yanked the sheet over her head.

Rising, Zeke coughed again while heading for the kitchen. He fired up the coffeemaker, ate two bananas, and bent slowly towards the floor. Crossing his arms behind his calves, he slowly pulled until his nose brushed against both kneecaps. Holding the stretch, he gradually felt each hamstring loosen until they released like two locks pried open. Then he grabbed the left ankle behind his back and poured the coffee into a Ragu jar that doubled as a glass. After two minutes, he switched legs, inhaling and exhaling every thirty seconds. It was a form of Hatha Yoga, learned entirely by mistake from a former cellmate schooled in various Eastern arts. *Two minutes or don't bother,* Zeke had been instructed, apparently because it took that long for a muscle to realize it was not being asked to perform a function.

"Cammi!" he shouted from the kitchen. "Wake the fuck up!"

He swigged the hot coffee, which added to the humidity, and soon he was sweating despite doing nothing. He heard her get into the shower, and ten minutes later she was frying up half a dozen eggs, ham, cheese, and diced potatoes. Spread out on the floor, he happened to look up at her stoveside pose, jabbing at the skillet as one hand rode a hip poking out like a denim-covered invitation. The tan legs were his momentary feast until she turned, caught his glance, and squinted down as if disgusted by a bug.

"And?"

"What?" He grinned sheepishly. "I can't help it."

"Yeah, right," she deadpanned. "Last night I practically had to jack you off just to fuck me."

"Oh my God, lady, whatever." As her insult settled in, he knew from experience that once Cammi was contacted by her estranged mother and sister, the reverberations could last for days. And here he was, stretched across the floor like road kill just waiting for the wheel. *I should let it slide*, he thought but said instead, "Don't even think about pulling this shit."

"What shit?" She turned away and scraped the skillet onto a plate. "Just don't look at me like that."

"Like what?"

"Like I'm some kind of fucking dick-toy."

"Cam—"

"I know it's not what you meant," she said, landing the plate and tortilla wraps on the kitchen table. "But shit like that pisses me off."

"Shit like what?" He rose slowly out of the stretch and stood up. "Like you're a hottie and I can't help myself?"

"Never mind."

"Seven years and now I can't look at you like a pervert?"

"Exactly."

"This is completely ridiculous."

"Stop talking. Here." She poured out two glasses of milk as the phone rang and Zeke headed for the den. "We're not through here," he said.

When he returned, he handed her a slip of paper that caused her to slam her glass onto the table. "Gimme the phone."

"Cam—"

"Now, please."

He sighed and pushed it across the table. Wrapping up two burritos of the egg mix, he cringed as she shouted, "Stuart, what the fuck is this? … No, I am not amused. I ride too hard to be treated like this … Like what? Like two fucking Cambridge inbounds, that's what. It's gonna take me a half hour in the opposite direction just to pick that shit up … No way. I spent all day yesterday over there losing money. You've got to do better … I said no … Do you want me to take the day off?"

Inhaling his breakfast, Zeke smiled, eavesdropping on Stuart Rigby's verbal demolition.

"Stuart, I'm going to hang up if you call me that again … No, don't pull your hair out. Deep down, you know I'm right … C'mon, sweetie … Okay … Yeah, I'll tell him. I'll see you with yesterday's paper when I roll through Copley."

She clicked off the phone and dug into her meal.

"Well?" Zeke asked.

"Here," she said and pushed her slip across the table. "Where's yours?"

"What?" Zeke dropped his fork, stunned. "Are you fucking kidding me?"

"Call him."

"Fuck him." Zeke stood, balled up his slip of inbounds, and tossed it into her egg. "And fuck you too."

"Zeke—"

"Christ, what a baby." He stormed into the hallway as she called out, "You forgot your list!"

He grabbed his bag, threw the bike onto his shoulder and, as he slammed the door, thought it a perfect start to just another day in the life with Cammi Sinclair.

The first pickup was beyond even Porter Square, at 2300 Massachusetts Avenue, and as far north as a downtown courier could be expected to travel. *I'm practically going into Arlington*, he grumbled, pushing through the pedals and calling her a bitch with every revolution. *Bitch, bitch, bitch.* Twenty minutes later he swooped in along the curb outside a squat brick building ringed by protesters who, despite the early hour, enthusiastically screamed through bullhorns. PLANNED PARENTHOOD, read a building sign in tiny letters, so Zeke locked up across the street. He remembered how the slip had said the address only, which was how these places were now forced to do business. There was another women's clinic on Beacon Street that had been shot up last year with horrific casualties, and while Zeke made no point of other people's politics or principles, he knew he liked bullies even less.

They could have been other people's family and friends, fifty of them neatly dressed and obediently following each other in a tight circle on the sidewalk. Two Cambridge policemen stood an arm's-width apart on the steps leading up, hands clasped behind their backs, the sunglassed eyes staring out like polished stones. Zeke had been here before, and at other places just like it. Among them, the Gay Liberation Task Force, the Black Muslim Society of Boston, and El Mano Vacancia, a Hispanic organization specializing in the documentation of police brutality. Zeke also knew why Stuart Rigby balanced out his upscale financial clientele, and why he ran one of the few courier companies that did not unethically forget entire neighborhoods or socially spurned organizations. It was a story Zeke had heard only once, years ago, after stumbling by chance across Richard Parks in a Back Bay bar. Already inebriated, it was a tale Parks took no pleasure in recounting.

It was also why, if one looked at Stuart Rigby close enough, one might be able to see the slight indent of plastic surgery around an eye that barely functioned. Three months in the hospital, his senior collegiate year just finished, and followed into the Back Bay Fens one naive night after leaving a notorious hardcore gay club on Boylston. It was the thought of those four shadows stepping from the reeds to stomp a harmless kid into a three week coma fifteen years before Zeke Sandaman was even eight years old, that always made those steps towards the cluttered sidewalk so easy. His Specializeds clacked across the asphalt as he approached the curb, eyes unavoidably drawn to the hideous posters of half-formed humans yanked prematurely from their mothers' wombs. Zeke watched the priests with their old books egging on the flock while being men of supposed faith and trust representing a God Zeke believed had not lived or witnessed a single twentieth-century day.

He said excuse me once, and when the line would not yield, he simply pushed through into their circle and then out the other side as people finally parted. Batting away the pamphlets and various propaganda, he shot them the hungover gaze of a sinner covered in tattoos and attitude until he made it to the steps where one policeman politely asked his business.

"Picking up," Zeke said.

"Need some ID, man."

Zeke fished into his back pocket, yanking out the chained-up wallet from which he produced his City of Boston Bicycle Messenger photo identification, a mandatory license issued at police headquarters. The policeman gave it a glance, said something into his radio, and soon a third cop inside unlocked the door.

"Go ahead," the first cop said, handing back the card.

"Lotta muscle here today," Zeke said, and the policeman looked at him as if it was none of his business. Inside, another cop with a goatee asked to look into his bag and Zeke grudgingly obliged.

"Lotta muscle here today," he repeated.

The cop grunted, searching the bag as he said, "Nationals are on the way in. Supposed to be a big protest. Sign here."

"Three of you guys?" Zeke took the clipboard. "Feeling ballsy?"

"Guess you didn't see the two vans a block back." The policeman nodded. "Go ahead. Show the card on the right."

Zeke closed his bag, turned the corner, and faced a pleasant young receptionist behind what he guessed was three-inch bulletproof glass. He pushed the SPEAK button on a wall-mounted intercom and said, "Split Minute." He pressed his card against the window as the receptionist leaned in and, for a brief flash, it reminded him of Cammi visiting him in county, but this place had no phones.

"One minute, please." When she returned, a large manila envelope marked X-RAY slipped beneath a locked door on the right. He carefully placed it inside his bag, keeping it as flat as possible because, unlike the ocean of commerce he daily chauffeured, medical calls meant someone was usually sick enough to require outside consultations. After he got these calls, he might morbidly wonder who had carried the disease-filled news back and forth from his own mother's bedside. Women and Children's Hospital. Fuck, he was sometimes there twice a day. And while Planned Parenthood might not have been the oncology ward at Boston General, he knew all of it only as the same; people stranded at differing points of various desperation.

After the policeman unlocked the door, he shouldered into his bag and felt like a sacrifice being handed to the mob. Stepping outside, Zeke put his sunglasses on and scanned the chaos from over the other two policemen on post. He made his way down the steps and elbowed through each side of the encircled protesters, channeling their ensuing obscenities like dialed-in fuel.

He clicked into his pedals, and their chants for life quickly faded as he geared the chain down to the last cog at top speed. Outside Harvard Square, he took the white line splitting two lanes and braced himself for the tourists and others unprepared for the upcoming forks. Always a huge summer draw, the cobblestone sidewalks were already filling up with shutterbugs despite the time, which a passing bank clock read as 7:15 AM. Outside 950 Massachusetts Avenue, he locked up and six minutes later was back curbside at a pay phone.

"Split Minute."

"Stuey."

"Zeke! We haven't spoken in almost an hour. Where *are* you?"

"Just picked up at 950. Got two on me, one for downtown and one for fucking Beth Israel."

"Now, Zeke, don't be mad at Uncle Stu."

"Okay."

"Please? I didn't want—"

"You sold me out." Zeke hawked up mucus. "You're spineless, man, letting that bitch railroad me."

"Bitch?" Stuart sounded amused. "This the same lady friend you had your dick stuck into last night, otherwise known as your girlfriend?"

"She's no such thing."

"Right. And why haven't you been answering your beeps? I had two more—"

"Turned it off. This whole run's already fucked."

"Zeke-a-licious! Do I have to hear this shit from everyone this morning? I'm the freakin' dispatcher, owner, King of all Fates!"

"Whatever. You could've given this crap to Fudgie or any one of those other maggots who bailed on you yesterday. I hate to say it, but Cammi was right."

"I'm setting you up, okay? Get that thing to Beth Israel and I'll hit you with so many expresses and cross zones you'll be puking by lunch."

"Now you're talking."

"Fine."

"One other thing," Zeke said.

"What now?"

"I'll be a good soldier from here on out, but you've got to get me down to 345 Summer at some point."

"Rosemont?"

"Yes."

"Zeke, I can't have you molesting my clients!"

"I thought we were a full-service operation?"

"Oh, that's real cute."

"Is it a deal, or do I have to act like a bitch for the rest of the day?"

"It's a deal! I can't take any more of your menstruations!"

"Cool."

"Call from B.I."

"Yep." Hanging up, Zeke checked left and, with no further stops, geared down to full power. At the Harvard Bridge, he crossed back into Boston as the sweat dripped steadily from his brow. He bent a hard right onto Beacon

Street and drove through the pedals until his thighs rippled inside the rhythm. A brutal morning run had long been the best elixir, and he felt last night's abuse squeezing slowly from his pores. At a red light inside Kenmore Square, he finally geared up and pried his fingers off the bar. Like most monster intersections in Boston, the traffic lights were timed. After the first of the three oncoming lanes went red, Zeke bolted out into no-man's-land as petulant car horns sounded even though he was already well clear and now powering up Brookline Avenue. A mile later, he pulled into the main entrance of Beth Israel Hospital. On a bench where Zeke locked into, an old white man with a seamed face like a rotten pumpkin tapped a cane, smiled pleasantly, and said, "Thought I was hot."

"Tell me about it." Zeke gave him a wink as he mopped at the sweat seeping down his face. "Say a prayer for me at noon."

"I surely will."

"Cool."

The automatic doors swooshed open and the sudden air-conditioning was more tease than relief. Pulling out the X-ray, he immediately consulted a directory because, from experience, he knew nothing could halt a run dead in its tracks like a mislabeled package sent to a giant metropolitan hospital. *It's a miracle,* he thought, finding Dr. Isaacs on the fifth floor in the same building as people crowded into the elevator and avoided contact with the wet and stinky rider.

Back in the lobby minutes later, he snagged a pay phone.

"Split Minute."

"Stuart."

"Who-ray!" Stuart yelled. "Richie, it's luscious Zeke on the phone!"

"Hello, Zeke."

"What up, Rich?" Zeke tapped his foot anxiously. "Guess I'm on the speakerphone."

"Yes, sir. And guess who else is here?"

"Bob Hope."

Stuart Rigby chuckled and said, "Close. Say hi, mystery guest."

"Fuck you, Zeke."

"Ah, man."

"How was Cambridge, you miserable prick?"

"Stuart, I don't want to talk to her. Pick up the fucking phone before I hang up."

"Zeke—"

He slammed the receiver down hard enough to swivel every head in the lobby. He realized that this morning, in his haste, he had forgotten both bottles, so he found a water fountain and drank until his stomach hurt. Inside the gift shop, he purchased a disposable camera and then, back at the payphone, redialed the number.

"Don't hang up!" Stuart pleaded. "She's gone."

"What's up? I got one downtown on me."

Stuart Rigby sighed as he flipped through the dispatcher sheets. "Boy," he sadly said, "I guess I really messed the two of you up this morning."

Zeke clicked his ballpoint pen half a dozen times. "Whaddaya got?"

"I didn't mean to do that."

"Well, damn, Stu, use your head. I mean, you knew the bitch was sitting right there eating breakfast."

"I just hate it when the two of you fight. It's like Godzilla versus Rodan."

"Fuck her. She is such a basket case."

"You don't mean that."

"I mean that exactly. Now whaddaya got, goddamn it?"

"Okay! Pickup at Back Bay Real Estate, 550 Comm, going to Price, 221 Berkeley. Jessica Hazard, going to Ferrelly, 145 Oliver. And Abraham, 755 Boylston, going to Dedham, which you will drop off here for a car ride with your tickets after I see your shiny face."

"I'll call you from Back Bay."

"Answer your beeps!"

Zeke hung up and stored his case. Once outside, the heat hit him like a blow upside the head. But there was something else on his mind as he approached the same bench where the old man had his face aimed at the sun like a nutrient-starved plant.

"Excuse me," Zeke said and the old man opened his eyes. Holding up the camera, Zeke said, "Do you mind? I kind of collect … well, pictures."

"Oh no, I don't mind." The old man grinned and Zeke decided it was like special effects, the way the skin furrowed deeply into troughs. After snapping the picture, Zeke said, "Thanks. I really appreciate it."

"It's God's work, you know."

"Yeah?" Zeke nodded politely, re-affixing his sunglasses.

The old man smiled again. "All of this," he passed a hand through the air slowly, "you too, you'll see it one day."

"I guess I probably will." Not wanting to be rude, Zeke walked four feet to his bike.

"And do be careful," the old man said, flashing his dentures. "You fellas take such terrible risks."

"Risks are for daredevils." Zeke slipped the U-bar lock into his bag and said, "I just like working outside all day."

"Well, God bless you."

"I hope so." Zeke clicked in and waved. "Take care now."

"I certainly will."

God bless me, Zeke thought nastily, hanging a right back onto Brookline Avenue. *Trying to be nice and the fucking guy hexes me.*

Back Bay Real Estate was located five buildings down from the Rat's Nest in an already busy Kenmore Square. Zeke clung to the far right lane and ignored the horns of the merging traffic sweeping down Beacon Street. He swooped in and hopped the curb, locking up on a fence that led to an office five steps below sidewalk level. Minutes later, he rolled up on a payphone and dialed the eight-hundred number.

"Split Minute."

"Stuey."

"Zeke! I'm on with X-man. Got nothing for ya."

"I'll call from Hazard."

"Okay then. Bye-bye now."

Checking left, Zeke jumped back into the hurtling steel flow just a step away from the curb. He saw thick haze shrouding the city ahead and guessed it was close to ninety degrees already. *Gonna be a nightmare today*, he thought and realized that in this kind of heat, just like the rain, the first hour was always the worst. But since his T-shirt was soaked and his shorts just as damp, he told himself to suck it up and swung left the wrong way down Newbury Street. Outside 254, he locked up, jumped the stairs, and hit the buzzer as a tired voice said, "Hazard Inc."

"Hey, Cherise. Picking up."

"That you, Zeke?"

"Yeah." He already had his stainless steel slipcase out. "Zap me in."

Three flights later, he reached the lobby where two models and a photographer were huddled over layouts. By the sour look on her again hung-over face, he guessed that his lascivious gaze might have lingered a moment too long.

"Hungry, Zeke?" she nastily said.

"Damn, Cherise." Lifting the sunglasses, he watched the models and the photographer disappear into another room. "I don't know how you get any work done around here."

"If I were a lesbian," she said and steadied the coffee mug in both hands, "that might be a problem."

"You look about as good as I feel."

"Thanks, buddy."

Zeke watched Cherise Maxwell breathing slowly, clutching the mug as if it were a life preserver in the tide of sickness etched across her usually flawless face.

"Ugh," she said. "Don't say another word."

"You got the Ferrelly?"

"There." She nodded at an envelope on her cluttered desk.

"Where were you last night?" he asked.

"Like it matters, right?"

"Lansdowne?"

She shook her head slowly, sipping at the mug. "Started at Man-Ray. Stayed in Cambridge fucking myself up completely."

"Thatta girl."

Cherise watched him scrawling out the ticket, her gaze descending from the now transparent white T-shirt to the hacked-off mid-thigh jean shorts, to linger on the tan stalks of sculpted leg.

"Those shoes," she said and grinned slowly. "They always remind me of Peter Pan."

He grunted, rechecking the ticket. She smiled and watched the sweat bead at his blond hairline, run beneath the black sunglasses perched on his forehead like a second pair of eyes, to finally slip across his wide cheekbones and chin cleft where it dripped like a leaky faucet.

"You know," she said, "if I picture myself out there, pedaling in the heat and stink, I almost feel sick to my stomach."

"Yeah?" He noted the time in the corner of the slip. "Well, I just thought of you out there too, and pretty much pictured the same thing."

She laughed. "Seriously? You don't think I could do it if I had to?"

"Without a problem," he said, and handed her the case and pen. "Except, no one in their right mind ever should."

She signed it and detached her copy. "And what about you, Mr. Goody-Two-Shoes. Where'd you end up last night?"

Zeke smiled. "You know Faustis? Black dude, rides for Triple X?"

"Nope."

"His band opened for Red Land at Chase's."

"The pitbull go with you?"

"Now, now. Be nice."

Zeke stored the envelope and case as Cherise Maxwell said, "God, what a bitch. She was already in here this morning, huffing and puffing like the big bad wolf."

"Sounds like her all right."

"What the hell do you see in her, anyway?" Cherise dabbed a tissue at her running nose. "All sweaty, and those outfits, and God, what a mouth."

"Tell me about it."

"You're such a nice guy. Which's why I can't figure it out."

"Can you get me Stu?"

"Here." She handed him the phone and punched one button.

"Split Minute."

"Stuey."

"Zachariah! And how are we? All moist and stinky yet?"

"You know it."

"Excellent. As you know, that's how I like my man flesh!"

"Stu—"

"Moist and puckered and lusciously tonguing—"

"Stuart!"

"Yes, right, sorry about that." Stuart chuckled mischievously. "Must be the coffee. Where are you?"

"Hazard."

"I heard Cherise had a long night last night."

"She sure did." Zeke glanced at Cherise and smiled. "I've had bowel movements that looked better."

Cherise Maxwell extended a middle finger as Stuart said, "Gross, Zeke."

"Whaddaya got?"

"Um …" Stuart flipped through the dispatcher sheets, "remarkably, nothing yet."

"What? Who's in today?"

"Zeke—"

"How many you got?"

"Nineteen." Stuart cleared his throat. "But not to worry. It's Thursday. Should be busy."

"Not with nineteen on. You need to fire some of these morons in the summertime."

"Right, Zeke. I'll just fire everybody except you and Cammi. Would that finally make the two of you miserable bitches happy?"

Zeke grinned. "Probably not."

"No kidding. Just be prepared. Could be a little slow today with the beautiful weather—"

"And with all the deadbeats too scared to ride in the rain."

"Does Daddy ever forget about his luscious little Z?"

"I'll call from Abraham."

"Excellent. Have your tickets ready after that."

"Don't forget about Summer Street."

"Ten-four, Zeke-a-licious. Bye-bye now."

He handed Cherise the phone and said, "Get some sleep tonight. You look like Keith Richards' stepmom after a three-day bender."

"Fuck you, Zeke."

Grinning, he headed for the stairs.

"Hey," she said. "You need to get down to Axis tomorrow night. Freebar and .45 Caliber are gonna be in town."

"Sweet."

"Bye, Zeke."

He waved and two-stepped it back downstairs. Outside, he zipped around the block and pulled up at 755 Boylston thirty seconds later. Abraham Investments was on the sixth floor, and once Zeke entered the tasteful lobby, he knew there would be no small talk with Elaine this morning. It was 8:30 AM and she was already a blur of fingers and phones with nary a wasted second. Her cherubic face beamed as he strode towards her desk where the rows of obese children in framed poses smiled towards their mother.

Raising an index finger at him, she said into her headset, "Abraham Investments, one moment, please." She punched a string of numbers and then said again, "Abraham Investments ... Yes, extension 342 ... Thank you. You too."

She put her hand over the microphone and said, "Morning, Zeke. Gosh, I can't believe it's this busy."

Zeke eyed her switchboard and saw a blinking mess. "Won't keep you then. Picking up for a car ride to Dedham."

"There." She pointed at a sixteen-inch square box. "Sorry, hon. I told them to pack it into the smallest one possible."

"No problem. But I'm gonna have to hit you with an oversize and probably an overweight too."

"Not my problem."

"Absolutely. Sign here and I'm gone."

She hurriedly scrawled her signature and peeled off the pink receipt. "Abraham Investments ... No, I'm sorry, he's not. Would you like his secretary? Yes, you too." She looked up at Zeke and mouthed a silent farewell before saying, "Abraham Investments ... Yes, I sure will. One moment, please."

Zeke grabbed the box, which was heavier than expected. Usually, a parcel this size triggered a burst of obscenities, but seeing as how the normal seven-dollar rate became fourteen with the overweight and oversize, he tucked it under his arm and found a phone in the lobby.

"Split Minute."

"It's Zeke. Got three on me, one a box I'm dropping off right now."

"See you then, Zeke, bye-bye now."

He pushed back out into the heat without even attempting to stuff the box into his bag. He knew most messengers rigged a rack over their back tires for just such an eventuality, but Zeke was thankful that he had only five working parts on his entire bike, the minimization of maintenance ensuring one less headache. Pushing away from the curb, he balanced the box on the bar between his thighs and headed down Boylston. At this time yesterday, he remembered the corners being full of raincoats and umbrellas. Today, it was summer dresses and short-sleeve oxfords as the heat, while welcomed, punished them all beneath its fist. He had one hand on the bike, one on the box, and finally swung a right the wrong way down Clarendon. After another quick right, he was locked up and heading for the elevators. On the eighth floor, he walked the long corridor until pushing into the unlit office. He passed Richard Parks, who smiled and waved from his desk, then heard Stuart Rigby call out, "I smell lusciousness!"

Zeke entered and feigned throwing the box at Stuart's head. He placed it on the desk as Stuart was on the phone in front of an overweight man in soaked camouflage pants and shirt.

"Hey, Mother," Zeke said, pulling up an additional chair and watching his hand disappear into Mother's huge, moist paw. "How goes it?"

"Wet, yo, what up, Speed?"

"Nothing, man. You know."

"Fuck, yo. After this summer, a dollar a degree and we could be retired."

"Absolutely."

Stuart hung up the phone, twitched his mustache, and said, "Okay, Mother Hubbard, you ready to make some dough?"

"Ain't I always?"

No one laughed, because along with the thirteen to fifteen runs he barely made a day, Zeke knew Mother made his real money in the little packets slipped like secrets into others' palms—and occasionally Zeke's as well—the job merely a front for an exceptionally dogged parole officer and concerned girlfriend. With considerable effort, Mother stood up, grabbed a stack of fresh slips, and said to Stuart Rigby, "Beep me."

"You got it."

"Cool. Be cool, Speed."

"Yeah, man."

Stuart Rigby listened for the front door to close, then crinkled his nose. "Worthless. Did you see this?" He held up the tickets. "The busiest day of the summer so far and that fat turd hands me twelve?"

Zeke shrugged as if it was someone else's problem and dropped yesterday's slips onto the desk.

"How many is that?" Stuart asked, eyes pulsing greedily as he let a thumb flip down through the stack.

"Fifty-three."

"Fifty what! Richie!" Stuart screamed. "Pack up your shit! Zeke's gonna be my new lover!"

"Bitch," Richard Parks instantly deadpanned through the intercom, "is that all it takes?"

"Nope." Stuart Rigby spun himself around in his chair, gleefully yelling, "Your ass is too big, thighs too flabby, you're going bald—"

"Stuart!"

"Fatty, fatty!" Stuart screamed with delight.

"At least I'm not a sick little man with a ridiculously large mustache."

"Fatty, fatty!"

"So sad," Richard Parks sighed through the little box. "Zeke, you want to handle this?"

"Stuart," Zeke reloaded his case with blank tickets and said, "stop acting like a fucking retard."

"Thank you, Zeke." Richard Parks clicked off the intercom as Stuart smiled coyly and said, "You almost broke your own record, didn't you?"

"Not really." Zeke placed the unfinished ticket on top of the Abraham box. He initialed the corner to get credit for the pickup and left the rest blank for the driver's pen. "Sixty-one, isn't it?"

"Fifty-three's real close, especially in that weather. No one's ever broke sixty but you."

"Does that mean I'm getting a raise?"

Stuart Rigby squinted at Zeke for a moment. "You don't take compliments well, do you?"

"Nope." Zeke broke eye contact, the other's gaze like a strange hand inside his own back pocket.

"How about insults?"

"You gonna answer the phone or what?"

"Damn it!" Stuart snatched it up. "Split Minute ... Remo, for the love of God, where are you? Link's been calling on that package every five fucking minutes ... Easy, killer, don't make me slip one in you ... Are you wearing those tight black pants that I love?" Stuart winked at Zeke. "Well, that's gonna cost you ... Nope, got nothing here. Call me from Link whenever you decide you would like to make some money. Okay then, deadbeat, bye-bye now."

Hanging up, Stuart consulted a list of beeper numbers and hit speed dial. A minute later the phone rang. "Kofi, where the hell are you? ... Traffic's bad?

Well, no shit. Luscious Zeke was kind enough to drop off your Dedham run and you were supposed to be here twenty minutes ago." Stuart Rigby swung his loafers up onto the desk, his index finger a businesslike jab at every word. "What's that? … No, I have no pity for losers. You've been in this country for three years and still you don't get it. Around the corner means nothing to me. Hurry up."

As Stuart banged his feet down to cradle the receiver, Zeke said, "So what's the deal? Am I gonna work or sit around this office all day like a douche bag?"

"Nope, there can be only one sitting douche bag and that douche bag, *c'est moi*. What do you have on you again?"

"One Back Bay and two downtowns."

Stuart leafed through the oversized call sheets. "Damn it. Hang on one sec and let's see what comes in. I've got too many wheels downtown already."

"Great."

"So you and Cammi got all blown out last night." Stuart leaned back and sipped his coffee. "When I did this job, I couldn't ever get loaded like that."

"I still can't believe you went to college and ended up a pedal pusher."

"Yes, well, it was only for three years." Stuart playfully batted his eyes and added, "Then daddy bought me my own company."

Zeke wiped at his face, the air-conditioning a settling chill. "Well, what were his options? Wait for you to get squashed like a bug after spending a hundred grand on your education? The whole thing probably made him ill."

Zeke saw the gaze abruptly leaden over.

"There certainly was a lot to it," Stuart said.

"That came out all wrong, Stuey. I didn't mean—"

"I know what you meant." Stuart smiled, but there was no amusement. "It's sick, but it is your greatest asset."

"What is?"

"What you just said."

"Stu—"

"I'm serious. Do you know how rare that is?"

"You can't compliment a moron."

"Of course you're a moron. But the difference is, you entirely know it."

"Great. That's great. We're real good at complimenting each other."

"It's sad, really. I mean, aren't you impressed by anything?"

"Jesus, Stu, I don't know—"

"Yes. You do. Answer the question."

"God, I hate this."

"Now, please," Stuart said, "before your head explodes from that clenched jaw."

"Who knows? I guess, well, I guess it's safer not to be."

"And how does *that* feel?"

"What's that?"

"To be one lonely, morose, miserable fuck?"

"You forgot ugly, hateful, and twisted."

Stuart grinned again and said, "Thatta girl."

"Fuck yeah."

"Kofi Asraham!" Stuart abruptly screamed as Zeke turned to see a thin man with a worried look scramble into the room.

"I so sorry, Mr. Rigfree," Asraham said. "I say, straffic on Sorrow Drive so ugly."

"That's Storrow Drive, Kofi."

"Yes. I sorry. Store-row Drive." Kofi Asraham smiled. His Senegalese accent fought every "t" he pronounced. "Yes, Storrow Drive."

"Excellent work, Kofi. And please, accept my most humble apology. I can be such an incredible asshole on the phone. Right, Zeke?"

"Asshole's actually a compliment." He looked at Asraham. "What up, K?"

"Hello, Mr. Speed." Kofi Asraham slapped, clasped, and knocked Zeke's outstretched hand as Stuart Rigby shook his head.

"He barely speaks English and yet he knows how to run a palm like a lifelong gangbanger."

"Hell, yeah, he does." Zeke grinned as he leaned back and winged his arms behind his head. "Tell me a story, K. How's life?"

"Accuse me, Zeke?"

"That's 'excuse me,' Kofi dear." Stuart Rigby placed his coffee cup on the desk. "Do you have yesterday's tickets?"

"Yes, yes." Asraham handed them over. Zeke watched Stuart skim through the slim stack, quickly checking them off against yesterday's register. Zeke knew the van and car guys were lucky to break a dozen runs per day, but with percentage, gas, and thirty cents a mile, averaged as much as the bikes.

Stuart Rigby motioned as if everything was in order and said, "Excellent, Mr. Asraham. There's your Dedham. Address is on it. It's going to an elderly woman's apartment, so she said she might not hear the buzzer. If you have any problems, please call me, okay?"

"I will, yes." Kofi Asraham picked up the box and told Stuart, "I will call from there."

"Certainly do."

"Okay, Mr. Rigfree."

"Be cool, K," Zeke said and Kofi smiled, saying, "I am, Zeke, yes."

Once he heard the front door click closed, Stuart said, "Nice guy, but totally clueless."

"Yeah, right. I'd like to see you in his shoes."

Stuart began organizing slips as he said, "And that means …?"

Zeke shrugged. "The guy's got a fucking family, man. Imagine going to school to be an engineer, then moving over here to get door after door slammed in your face?"

"Oh, say it ain't *so*." Stuart Rigby placed a hand over his heart and said dramatically, "The travails of a poor immigrant have Mr. Stoneheart weeping."

"Fuck you."

"If only you'd let me, sweetmeat, I'd show you things you'd not soon—"

"Answer the phone, pervert."

"Damn it!" Stuart grinned and grabbed the receiver. "Split Minute … Oh, hi, Doris, how's things at Graphic Art? … Really … But you're just down the hall … No, our air-conditioning's working just fine … Right. And where are we going?" Stuart looked up, so Zeke took out his slipcase. "Ryan Publications, 50 Milk Street. Got it. I'll send my best little boy … Who do you think? He's got a sunny disposition and an ass that just won't quit … Yes! Yes!" Stuart squealed delightedly. "He's sitting right here, all wet and smelly. I'll send him right over … Ha-ha! Okay, bye-bye, honey."

"That's makes three downtowns and one Back Bay," Zeke said, closing his case. "You want me to stick or split?"

Stuart gnawed a lip as he studied the dispatcher sheets. "No, Zeke, let's split. Pick up the GA and call from your Back Bay before heading downtown."

"Yes, sir."

Peeling himself off the chair, Zeke shrugged into his bag. "Don't forget—"

"About Rosemont. Yes, Zeke, I heard you the first eighty fucking times."

"Righteous." Zeke grinned, lowered his sunglasses, and said, "Beep me if anything hits."

"Oh, I surely will. Now back out into the heat with you."

A minute later, down the hall, Zeke pushed through a door and saw Doris Lytol glance away from the wall-mounted televisions where, in between the animated horror movie silently playing and the cranked stereo blasting on five channels, the chaos was near complete. At the exact moment she lowered the music, he screamed out into the now dead-quiet calm, "Hey, Doris!"

As he approached the raised altar of her desk, he said, "Jesus, do you ever do any work around here?"

"Good morning, Zeke." She pinched her nose and said, "Stuart wasn't kidding. Your odor really does precede you."

"Fuck, wait till noon." He reached over his shoulder for the slipcase. "Fifty Milk, right?"

She nodded drolly, holding out the envelope as he stepped up to her desk. She was wearing a tight black T-shirt, black skirt, and an expression just as colorful.

"Fucking heat," she said, using her hand for a fan. "I can't wait for winter."

"I can." Zeke slipped the envelope in with the rest and said, "Believe me, it's always something."

"Nice platitude, Zeke. You are a deep one."

"Blow me."

She cracked a smile so rare Zeke thought her face might break. He turned for the door as she said, "You should be so lucky."

"You've got that backwards again."

"It's always nice to see you!" she yelled, but he was already out the door. Watching him wait for the elevator, Doris Lytol found herself oddly sniffing at the aroma's trail, thoughts triggered by the smell of boy and other things concealed roughly in the dark.

He pulled into Winthrop Square at half past eleven as the sun neared its apex. The square itself was nothing more than a thirty-foot patch of grass created by the convergence of Devonshire and Kingston streets in the Financial District's south end. Laid out centuries before, downtown had a handful of tiny parks, playgrounds, and common areas made nearly extinct by the concrete squeeze from all sides. Zeke Sandaman saw there were about fifteen other messengers already spread out beneath the few trees, so he veered left, hopped the sidewalk, and found shade in the shadow of 25 Devonshire Street. Completely empty and sick of calling Stuart every five minutes, he had swallowed two hot dogs off a cart before deciding to find a cool spot and maybe a cigarette or two.

Like his bike, he was leaning against the red brick wall, the sun just out of reach. He lit a smoke, slid to the ground, and watched the buildings begin emptying for lunch. *It's summer*, he decided. *It's just gonna be that kind of day.* He knew Stuart Rigby catalogued the courier trade as a type of parasite dependent exclusively upon the whims of business. When it looked like the fax machine was going to kill the entire industry, Stuart refocused Split Minute towards law firms, advertising, and modeling agencies, professions that required signed documents, large copy rolled into tubes, and pictures of beautiful people that were simply unfaxable. Fall and winter were always busy, spring was tax season, and summertime meant vacations for the corporate culture and a flood of college kids into the trade on two-thousand-dollar mountain bikes. Zeke knew most of them just liked being outside, hanging with their friends and cruising through the city in the sun. He did not blame them, but he also knew what cost a taste of the life could mean. The Boston College basketball star trying to stay in shape and paralyzed after getting clipped by a garbage truck on Harvard Avenue two years back; the Emerson scholarship playwright raped in an alley off Tremont in the South End last August; and, worst of all, the Australian kid from Tufts who began riding for Split Minute in June and got killed six weeks later after smashing his head through a Yellow Cab's windshield. It was, Zeke knew, just something no one could take for granted. The same something the more experienced never talked about because injury and death, if acknowledged as one's worst fear, eroded confidence, stalking each corner as if provoked. It was not an easy guess, but it happened maybe three or four times a week, where reaction to a certain situation within the span of a single second could determine one's entire life.

And for those easily rattled or quick to panic, the gravest consequences could be found curbside in a splash of EMS lights and sirens.

He finished the cigarette and flicked it into the gutter, watching a handful of messengers toss a Frisbee. Zeke guessed he had made only twenty runs, but he had a thing about counting slips before the day was done. He smiled pleasantly at a gaggle of women headed to lunch, watched an obese white man in a soaked suit huff and puff through the heat, and basically cursed because he was sitting on his ass making no money.

Yanking the bag over, he dug for his tool pouch, the eye-level glance at his slime-covered chain more than he could bear. After days like yesterday, where every particle and pebble sprayed up from the wet street, a nightly cleaning was almost a necessity. If it had been winter, with its slush and salt, there would have been no choice.

He broke out a set of Allen wrenches and a pair of pliers. Having trouble gearing from fourth into fifth, he knew the derailleur cable must be loose. Outside of his two brake cables, this was the only other working part on the entire bike. Built up from an old Knottingham racing frame that must have been thirty years old, it had ten-speed handlebars installed upside down and sawed off in mid-loop. The gear lever was plugged into the right-side handlebar like a thumb. From there, he had scored a deal on a handcrafted five-speed Regina racing derailleur and chain, a four-hundred-dollar purchase cut in half because he sometimes did odd jobs for an old Italian named Riffiscutti who ran a shop in the North End. And while the majority of stores ran a 10- to 15-percent messenger discount, Zeke had been wrenching long enough to know that without a few necessary connections and a bike tech for a best friend, the over-inflated retail prices and exorbitant repair costs could easily devour an already slim net profit. Besides Riffiscutti downtown, Bicycle Bob's was just around the corner from Zeke's apartment, and an old buddy named Dirty Dave did practically all the wrenching Zeke had no patience to complete.

He thumbed down the gear lever as far as it would go, lifted up the back end, and wound the pedals until the chain dropped into fourth instead of fifth. Kneeling down, he again almost gagged at the sight of his high-end Italian drivetrain encrusted in yesterday's abuse. With the appropriate-sized Allen wrench, he loosened the nut holding the derailleur cable and yanked with the pliers until the chain finally dropped into the fifth-gear cog. He then re-tightened the nut and tested the repair, finding no problem. Despite having next to nothing for accessories, Zeke knew it was a heavy bike compared to the featherweight titaniums that were now the rage. And while the true stoic couriers rode fixed-gear bikes that had no brakes, Zeke was addicted to speed. He ran a maxed out fifty-six-tooth front chain-ring at the pedals to an eleven-tooth cog in the rear fifth gear. With those kinds of numbers, and in lieu of its humble appearance, he still passed by like an afterthought on one of the fastest bikes in the city. Outside of Linus Pine, a monstrous black triathlete who ran an unheard of custom-forged sixty-two up front, mid-forties were the norm.

Lighting another cigarette, he heard a clock on Franklin Street chime twelve times as the noon lunch rush commenced. They came in numbers and usually clustered by age or class. Groups of older executives, secretaries, or kids in their twenties dressed in suits for the work life yet to come. White, black, Hispanic, fat, thin, beautiful, ugly—Zeke sat ringside as they stepped all around him. He glanced at the messengers across the street and guessed there must have been fifteen thousand dollars in bikes strewn lavishly about the lawn. It was something he could never figure out, how anyone in their right mind would ride something that expensive and just lock it up on the street. A good thief could have a bike in four seconds, a lesson Zeke quickly learned the hard way. U-bar locks, Kryptonites, huge industrial chains—anything could be broken. Zeke remembered a promotion he once heard about on Tremont Street, where a brand-new lock was being debuted. Supposedly impenetrable to even the most sophisticated tools, a professional stepped forward with a tiny vial containing liquid nitrogen, poured it on the locking mechanism, and ten seconds later simply smashed it to pieces with a ten-ounce hammer. The possibilities were endless. Slipjacks, prybars, leveraged industrial-grade cutters—Zeke knew that anything, anywhere, at any time could be stolen. The whole key was speed—getting in and out of buildings before the operators got their chance. Besides, there were only a handful of thieves who might even know what a Regina derailleur was, so his bike, while it might look like a simple five-speed piece of shit built up from spare parts, certainly was no twenty-five-hundred-dollar Cannondale with front-fork suspension and hydraulic brakes just begging to be stolen.

Dragging on the cigarette, he grimaced when his thoughts ran back to Cammi Sinclair and this morning's fiasco. He decided that he hated it, absolutely hated it, when she set her sights unprovoked. What had he done? Step into the crossfire as the Sinclair family history reemerged like a giant toxic spill? He shook his head, exhaling like a dragon, sick of the mood swings. *What two people could do to each other*, he thought, and inhaled one last time.

Flicking away the butt, he stood, shrugged into his bag, clicked in, and set off in search of a phone. He felt the other couriers scoping his departure and knew how cold this business could be. When he had first started at sixteen, Zeke had been in awe that people could actually get paid to ride a bike all day. As young as he was, the money was merely a bonus on top of pulling outrageous tricks on the BMX bikes he used to favor. Rocketing wheelies down the stairs outside the Government Center T-station, flinging tabletops off concrete walls at the public library, and even front flips off the piers of Charlestown, Zeke figured he spent as much time delivering packages as he did dodging the police, who, as far as he knew, only hated skateboarders more. Having been called "New Meat" and "Freshy" by the other couriers he at first tried to befriend, Zeke remembered yearning for a fraternity that only turned out to be a loose conglomeration of nearly impenetrable cliques and syndicates run like fiefdoms. It would be a year before he realized there was no alliance, no unity, nothing like loyalty anywhere in sight when most of the people out here were just like him.

He rolled up on an empty phone on Franklin Street, still clicked in, and dialed up the number.

"Split Minute."

"Please, tell me you've got something."

"Zeke! How is it out there? Hot?"

Zeke watched the lunch crowd sweating around him and said, "The office heads are grabbing their grub and heading right back up into the AC."

"No titties in the park for Zeke this noon? How sad."

"Whaddaya got?"

"Our old friend Castalone, 122 Friend, has a deuce. One for 250 Hanover and the other for 50 State. Also, and here you'll love me again, pickup at Rosemont, 345 Summer, going to Image Concepts, 115 Berkeley."

"Nice."

"Call me from Friend and I'll try to load you up with more Back Bays."

"Thanks, Stu."

"Oh my goodness, someone said thank you!"

"Stu—"

But the line was already dead. Checking left, he hopped the curb and headed the wrong way down Franklin. At Congress Street, he swung left and nearly broadsided a mail truck whose driver held out a middle finger in thanks. *Time to drop the hammer,* Zeke thought, gearing down and tearing through the lunchtime crosswalks until the unreality almost transformed it into a video game, the pedestrians merely a brief terror-stricken pose as he passed by within inches. His luck held with the green lights, and a mile later he bent a right onto Causeway Street. Lifting his hands off the bar, he cruised downhill at twenty miles per hour and rubbed an aching low back. Near North Station and the Boston Garden, he hung a right onto Friend Street and pulled up outside ONE ON ONE TICKETS. Leaning his unlocked bike against the storefront window, he walked inside and tossed a salute at Jimmy Castalone, who returned the gesture, his left ear pinning the phone against his shoulder while he rapidly counted down a stack of twenties.

"Yeah, right, Booch, what the fuck? I'm already carryin' a quarter season and now you want me to spot another on your marker? Are you serious, or just trying to put me out of fucking business?"

Zeke wiped the sweat from his nose and watched as Fat Sam, seated next to the door, munched the leafy end of a giant cigar. His bulbous eyes were like egg yolks slowly scanning the tiny store and TV screen on which last night's Red Sox game quietly replayed. Besides the two chairs and counter, One on One was little more than a three-walled celebration of local sports heroes, whose autographed posters hung like icons through the smoke. Framed pictures sat propped on the counter showing Castalone with members of the Red Sox and Celtics. And for a small, thin man with a fake tan and big black eyes, he clearly stood out in every shot with that patented wide white smile.

"Booch, listen to me." Castalone placed rubber bands around three stacks of twenties. "Don't play the heavy with me. Do I look like a fucking credit card or what?"

Zeke tried to act like he was busy with his slips but grinned nonetheless. Including his stint inside the Rat's Nest ticket office, he figured he had been dealing with Jimmy Castalone in one capacity or another for almost six years. Which also meant he knew that, besides Ticketmaster, One on One moved more tickets than any other un-enfranchised business in the city. Currently,

Zeke watched Jimmy Castalone shaking his head as if he wanted nothing more than silence.

"Boochie, for a run like that I gotta check upstairs … No, you know the ropes. An extension like that and it gets bumped up the chain … Fine, then I'm sure he won't care. Call me tomorrow."

Jimmy cradled the receiver and said, "Fat fuck. Jesus Christ, like I'm supposed to give a shit about his problems?" He took a deep breath, ran a hand through the greased-back black hair, and lit a cigarette. "Ain't that right, Zeke? I mean does anyone give a fuck about my problems?"

"Fuck no."

"Exactly. Hey, Sammy, wake the fuck up. Can't you ever say hello to this special friend?" Castalone balled up a piece of paper and bounced it off the forehead of Fat Sam, who barely blinked. "Lookit this place. Every fucking day with that cigar until I can't hardly see through the haze." Castalone grunted, ashed his cigarette, and recounted the stack of twenties. "Sorry about this, Speed."

"It's no problem."

"I don't mean to cost you waiting on my dead ass." He pushed a single twenty across the counter and Zeke said thanks.

"Here. Have a Coke."

"Cool." Zeke popped the top and swallowed the contents in five gulps.

Castalone stuffed three stacks into a canvas bank envelope and zipped it shut. "You and me ain't missed a day in a while, huh?"

"Fuck no."

"I can't believe you were riding around in that shit yesterday." Castalone smiled, reached over the counter, and playfully slapped Zeke's cheek. "This fucking guy. Ain't he something, Sam? A hard fucking worker, boy, I'll tell you that."

"Whaddaya got?" Zeke asked.

"Three large. That your beeper?"

"Yeah. It don't matter." Zeke slipped the envelope into his bag and said, "Listen, I might be taking a half day tomorrow."

"Why?"

"Because it's so slow I'm going out of my fucking mind."

"Well, you know the deal. I don't trust any of those other rats on wheels. If I have a run, I'll make it a nooner."

"Cool."

"All right, kid." Castalone smiled and held out a hand for Zeke to shake. "You are all fucking right."

"Talk to ya." Zeke nodded at Fat Sam who did not not return the gesture. Outside, he took a right onto Causeway Street. Like Beacon Hill and parts of the Back Bay, the Italian North End pointedly retained the character of pre-revolutionary Boston, with narrow cobblestoned roads beneath imitation gas lanterns as streetlights. Zeke cruised under the monstrous roar of I-93 and passed into an older world of butchers and grocers who hung gutted carcasses in the windows and shelved crates of prime vegetables on display like decorations. There were fresh cheese shops, dessert stores, and scores of Italian restaurants seeping delectable aromas throughout the neighborhood.

Gearing down, swinging right onto Commercial Avenue, he passed a relatively empty Columbus Park, where two busloads of tourists straggled along the sidewalk like lemmings marched through a kiln. As he braked to a stop, the Norwest Bank clock read 1:31 PM, 101°. With humidity, Zeke figured the heat index to be 110 inside the steeped veil cloaking the city. His arms were already slick as he pulled in one putrid breath after another, the eddying exhaust from the traffic and construction diesel like a carcinogen-filled lung bath.

Inside the bank, he ignored the curious looks until a pretty teller asked, "How is it out there?"

"Are you kidding me?" Zeke eased the sunglasses up to his forehead so he could wipe his sweat-stung eyes. "It's like vacationing in the Congo."

She laughed, counted the deposit, and handed him the receipt. "Take it slow. It's supposed to be even hotter this afternoon."

"Are you trying to make me cry?" He stored the receipt with the slip for tomorrow's turn-in and quickly said good-bye.

Outside, the heat was like a living presence.

"Split Minute."

"Stuey."

"Zeke? Where have you been?"

"Miss me?"

"Please tell me you're at Hanover."

"Commercial. Whaddaya got? I'm heading to Rosemont as we speak."

"Hold on." There was a rustle of dispatcher sheets. "Rosemont's a Back Bay. Let's see. Pickup at Circumspect, 232 Broad, heading back here for a car ride. And Cross Digital, One Financial, has a Back Bay as well."

"Cool."

"Turn some pedals and call me from One Financial."

"Ten-four." Zeke cradled the receiver, slipped into his sunglasses, and thirty seconds later peeled down Congress Street. After a right turn on Atlantic Avenue and quick left onto the Summer Street Bridge, he looked down into the swirling brown contamination of the Fort Point Channel. Locking up outside the converted warehouse of 345 Summer, he plodded up the four flights like a prisoner marching to an uncertain fate. *I look like shit*, he thought, and, sneaking a quick whiff at his armpits, cursed because he usually carried deodorant. *Maybe she won't be here*, he thought and cursed again, already chickening out. What was worse, he knew, was only yet to come. The fumbling, stumbling, scatterbrained attempt at what others always seemed to find so easy.

On the final landing, pausing at the door, Zeke wiped the sweat off his face and tried on a pressure-jerked smile before pulling open the door as if he owned the place.

"Oh," she said, and Zeke, like a specimen held up to the light, felt pincered between the huge blue saucers of her gaze. "Isn't this a coincidence?"

"Hi, Liz." Zeke closed the door. "A nice one, right?"

Like a mouse, he thought, savoring the timid grin. She quickly glanced back at the computer screen as she said, "Hang on one sec."

"Sure." He reached back for his case, the sunglassed eyes granting access to a thorough full body sweep that ended only after she turned back and he said, "I was hoping to redeem myself."

"Yes?"

Zeke nodded. "Remember yesterday's entrance? How I went tripping to the floor like a drunk?"

Rewarded with another smile, his eyes fell along the descending neckline of the long-sleeved dress and over the creamy skin leading to her—

"I was never real good with first impressions."

"Could you take off your sunglasses?" she asked.

God, I'm fucking dying here, he thought, perching the Revos onto his forehead. *I never should've—*

"I'd offer you coffee but it's a little hot out there."

"Yeah. For real."

"Isn't that crazy?" she quietly asked. "How it could be fifty degrees and cold, then one hundred degrees the next day?"

"Fuck yeah. I mean, yes." He fumbled with the case. "Obviously, I spend a lot of time in the gutter."

She watched him sweating, standing there with a hesitant gaze and awkward movements in a T-shirt that was nothing more than a soaked film over darkened nipples.

"I kind of like it," she said.

"What's that?"

"The gutter."

"Oh yeah?" He smiled. "Thatta girl."

After it appeared, he feasted on her blush before cursing the extended silence.

"Um …" He looked at his case. "Guess I'm here for the 115 Berkeley."

She handed it to him, so he logged in the information. As he peeled off the pink receipt, his mind flew through the possibilities, something, anything to say, except, "Guess that'll do it."

"Okay."

About to turn for the door in defeat, he abruptly decided self-esteem was overrated, and so turned back to quickly say, "Listen, Liz, I'm sorry. I know how forward this is gonna sound. And I don't usually poach on customers, but I'm not here just to pick up any package."

"Huh?"

Flustered, he locked onto her eyes directly. "Go out with me. Tomorrow night. We'll do anything you want."

He thought her expression a mixture in between horror and flattery, the blush now a full crimson explosion across both cheeks.

"I … I'm busy."

"Please, Liz? Just another cup of coffee then?"

"Zeke …"

"I've had all my shots. And I shower every day."

"It's just … this is not a good time for me."

"Me either." He pressed onward, wedging himself into her hesitation. "How about a walk then? It'll be easier. That way, if you decide I'm a total loser, I'll stop at the nearest corner and you can just keep on going."

"You're not a loser."

"I know. And you're smiling. Which means you want to say yes."

"Zeke—"

"Don't say no."

"I'm sorry. I really am. But …"

"That's okay." He tried on a half-hearted grin. "I didn't mean to put you on the spot. I'm sorry about that. Have a good weekend."

He turned for the door as if the place were going up in smoke. Cursing his idiocy with every step, he had a hand on the knob, then heard, "Wait, Zeke!"

He turned back to see her checking over a shoulder for witnesses, anxiously spinning a pencil in her hands.

"I … tomorrow night'll be okay."

"Oh yeah?"

"Yes." She nodded as if still trying to convince herself. "Yes."

"Cool." He let go of the doorknob. "Then can I call you? After work?"

"Yes."

God, he thought, *she looks absolutely mortified.*

"What time do you get home?" he asked.

"Usually around six."

"I'll call you then." Holding open the door, he paused. "Guess I should ask you for your number."

"I … it's just that I kind of live with my father." She was wringing her hands and fumbling for words.

"How about you take my number? And call me whenever."

"Okay."

He recited as she scrawled it out and said, "Six-ish?"

"Six-ish it is. And Liz, I promise, you won't be sorry."

"Okay."

As the door clicked closed, he decided it was unbelievable, this miracle, just like one more thing women commanded. *Gotta be careful with this one,* he cautioned himself. *She's freaked out as it is.*

Taking the steps two at a time, he pushed open the door and found it was like stepping from one oven into another. Squinting, re-aligning his sunglasses, he walked towards his bike and adjusted the bag, storing the U-bar lock in its worn pocket. Pointing north, he clicked in, checked left, and jetted back downtown, his mind on the twenty-four-hour cheat and already answering that Friday night phone call. Ahead, One Financial loomed like a giant rectangle reaching for the sun.

Dead as it was, Zeke spent the rest of the afternoon killing time before the thought of counting his receipts made him ill. Even Stuart Rigby, always desperate for riders until 6:00 PM, closed the phones at five o'clock. Sun-stained and malodorous, Zeke accepted the low-count day and gladly stretched his legs towards home.

Cruising through Kenmore Square, traffic was heavy as he decided summertime had its moments. Besides the stink a few million people could create, those without air-conditioning would gather on porches, parks, and street corners citywide, fighting the night like the unbearable day just ended, and tossing in the sheets despite ice-cold showers and fans like daisy heads oscillating in the breeze.

Eventually, he pulled up outside 125 Easton and slowly smiled. The house was called the yellow submarine because of the same bright paint layered on year after year by an owner Zeke decided was either colorblind or just plain sadistic. Made legendary by a succession of Harvard undergraduates with a penchant for curfewless blowouts, the submarine had decidedly seen better days. It had three front porches, one for each floor and all sagging into oblivion. The yellow paint was like a leprous skin peeling up from the itch of the elements. Zeke shouldered his bike, wiped the sweat from his eyes, and saw the face of his first-floor neighbor abruptly poking like a target from a thrown open window.

"Zeke!"

"Not now, Rob."

"Please?" A thin torso was attached to a balding head with bespectacled eyes ablaze. The thin face was just one of many signals Zeke thought someone should have picked up on long ago. A postgraduate at MIT, and in the last year of five spent working on his thesis, Robert was the downstairs obsessive, wired on caffeine, valiums for sleep, and the occasional baggie for added dementia. *Like clockwork,* Zeke now thought, as Robert had only one way of socialization and that usually entailed him bursting onto the porch with some complaint or bothersome gossip of people and things Zeke could in no way care about. *Where was this guy's family?* Zeke had groaned on the many mornings he passed by the one-man rant at 6:00 AM, the day before him now prefaced by the loon's cry from self-exile.

Currently, Robert's arms were shooting in different directions as he yelled, "You've got to tell Booger, no more afternoon parties! Please, Zeke, this is the only quiet time I have here to work."

"I have no idea what you're talking about," Zeke's shoes began clacking up the worn wooden stairs.

Robert yelled out, "I don't want to call the police, Zeke, but I will!"

Abruptly stopping, Zeke stared back down the staircase and lifted his sunglasses. "Hey, man." Zeke shook his head. "Not even in jest."

"I mean it, though."

"Mean what?" He turned his whole body, already annoyed before smacking the rear wheel against the wall. "Mean what, Rob?"

"That I'll ..." Robert swallowed thickly. "Please. Don't make me do that."

"You're my fucking neighbor, moron. I sell you bags—no, I won't shush. You want to start screaming this bullshit at me after the day I've just had, so I'll scream right back. I'll talk to the other idiot. He's a fucking drunk, man, you know that. But if it's pissing you off, I'll make it go away. Is that all right with you?"

"Yes."

"And Rob. One more thing."

"What, Zeke?"

"Lookit me." Zeke waited and then said, "No cops. Not ever. You know my history, man, Jesus Christ."

Robert blinked. "You're right. I was just mad. It was stupid of me to say that."

"This ain't no desert island, you know? We've all got to live here. You don't go calling the cops on neighbors, man. What the fuck?"

"You're right."

"Cool." Zeke waited in the extended silence. "Everything cool?"

"Yes." Robert smiled timidly.

"Good. Then I'm going up to take a shower." Zeke began climbing the staircase. "I'll talk to assface right now."

"Thank you, Zeke."

At the third-floor door, Zeke banged it open and set his bike against the wall, then tossed the sweat-soaked courier bag and T-shirt into a corner.

"That you, Z?"

"Yeah." Zeke turned left into the television room and paused. "Jesus, what the fuck, Boog?"

Zeke scanned the few dozen empties littering the coffee table and floor, the puddle of what he guessed was puke below the windowsill, and the lamp smashed into a hundred jagged pieces by the wall. He let out a loud scoff. Booger, who was stretched out on the couch, peeled open his bloodshot eyes and said, "How was work?"

"Spare me." Zeke kicked a beer can across the room. "You know I ain't about this."

"Zeke—"

"Nah, man."

As Booger's tongue flopped around his lips like a dehydrated eel, he tried locating Zeke through the hazy film fermented across his eyes. A good six inches taller than Zeke, Booger, at the age of twenty-six, already had the lined seams and burst capillaries of an alcoholic twice his age. Gifted with strength because of his size, he was nonetheless a gelatinous slob averaging forty-eight Marlboros a day. The sandy-brown hair was unwashed and matted as he tried a smile. Seeing Zeke's expression, he said, "What?"

"Guess."

"Ah, Zeke, c'mon, man. I'll get to it."

"Fuck, I know that." Zeke kicked at another can. "It's just, you got the schoolboy all spazzed out."

"What?"

"Rob, Booger. I pull up and he's all about calling for the meat wagon."

"For what? Me?"

"What the fuck were you doing up here?"

"Hell." Booger ran a hand across his unshaven face, then scrunched up a pillow behind his head. "Santos and Dinky and me and Philla-toesious—"

"What the fuck happened at work? Did you all get fired?"

Booger laughed. "Nah, man, one of the fryolators caught fire. Burnt the fuck out of the whole back wall."

"So what?"

"So …" Booger coughed up a giant phlegm ball and grabbed a can for deposit. "So we got every line in the joint running through there, man—electric, steam, gas—Christ, the whole fucking place got shut down."

"So you all came back here and got fucked up."

"Pretty much."

Despite having no desire to, Zeke grinned and said, "Fucking bunch of drunk cooks."

"No shit." Booger yawned. "What time is it anyway?"

"Who knows. Six o'clock?"

"Where's the bowl for the bong? You seen that thing?"

"Naw …" Zeke stripped out of the soaked shorts. "Where's the remote?"

"Over there. Somewhere."

Zeke tossed through the mess until he found it. Clearing himself a space on the floor, he began stretching out his body.

"Fuck, dude, I don't want to watch the news," Booger said.

Zeke ignored him, and minutes later listened to the intoxicated breathing of Booger resuming his coma. Grabbing onto his right foot, he slowly let the hamstring unwind until his chest pancaked on top of his thigh. Inhaling deeply through the stretch, as he heard a newscaster describe the details of a revoked parolee, Zeke's own nightmare became re-triggered once again.

Three short months. That was all it took to see the possible lifetime yet to come. Norfolk, Shirley, Walpole—the names of where the cursed paced away the hours and days of weeks and months before a single year notched through. At eighteen, and already on probation without ever being forced inside, Zeke remembered his public defender telling him things could have been much worse. The intent to distribute and school-zone charges were dropped for a guilty plea on the felony possession of a Class B controlled substance, the assault and battery, his third, would run concurrently. The district court judge, his attorney said, had been exceptionally lenient. Either way, with the additional probation violation to also run concurrently, Zeke recalled every breath, each single second in that courtroom—the smell of his laundered suit, the impossible white of the assistant district attorney's dentures, and the late afternoon light shining across that mahogany throne atop which a single person smashed a gavel and said, "Six months House of Corrections, year and a half suspended." No matter how many had sat in that same seat before him, Zeke felt the thousands of years it had absorbed to be an insurmountable hex.

Running a hand across the worn armrest, and later superstitiously counting back his sentence each morning of every day inside that Suffolk County shithole, Zeke thought he had found inside himself the resolve never to allow that madness back into his life. The weekly piss tests and employment checks had been a mild torture compared to the suspended eighteen months dangling above his head like an anvil. It was, he knew, what you got when you made yourself a target.

Now, living below radar, skirting outside their periphery, he had forged a new life on the bottom rung, in camouflage and smoke, only crossing into society's border intermittently like a bandit or thief or fool. Which he knew he was as well. Expecting nothing, contributing nothing, his new life now a weekly paycheck sandwiched around the same seven days forever.

Happy days, he thought, and stared at the ceiling. *Happy fucking days.*

A pair of six-foot two-by-fours were bolted through the center forming a giant *X*. Two smaller boards attached parallel to the ground off the top allowed him to hang his bike for maintenance. Sitting on a chair, head level with the cranks, Zeke performed the ritual by rote. He ran the chain through the Parker Chainmate as three days' worth of debris dripped oily and black onto the newspaper spread below. Once clean and dried, he lubed the entire drivetrain as the back wheel spun suspended in the air. Checking the brakes, he tightened the cables until the pads arrested the rim at even the slightest tweak of the handlebar-mounted levers. Satisfied, he stored the bike by the door and folded the homemade X-brace into the kitchen corner. He cleaned up the soiled newspaper and zipped his tools into the small black leather case, which he then put back into his messenger bag. Salt-streaked and soaked, the bag was hung on a nearby doorknob to dry.

Now, he thought, *what to do?* A Thursday night and he had no money until tomorrow. His roommate was still couch-surfing, his slumber like thunder from the devastated living room. Stepping into the bathroom, Zeke ran the shower while watching his image gradually fade into the creeping mist and fogged-out mirror. The road-weary legs, thick and flexed, the cut stomach and underdeveloped upper torso with its smattering of ink, and the green eyes sparkling amidst the sun-torched valleys creasing his face. *God, he thought, I look exhausted.* Dialing back the hot water, he slipped beneath the still scalding spray as the greasy runoff slowly swirled about his feet. Propping each hand against a tiled wall, he thought about Elizabeth Downs and the promise of tomorrow night, wondered where Cammi was and if she still carried this morning's confrontation like an ax waiting to be ground against his skull. Over their sporadic years together, Zeke knew consistency and fidelity had often fallen into the martyrdom one could later foist upon the other. The summer three years back when she ran with some local promoter who had a speech impediment. Or his two months living in Charlestown in the apartment of a physical therapist honest enough to admit she had a penchant for slumming. And through it all, like opposite charges, they would eventually collide again for periods of stability and chaos until one or the other simply said enough and walked away. While those breakdowns could not be avoided, he knew she remained, as always, the one person turned to inside the loneliness three million people could facelessly provide.

Letting out a long sigh, he raised his head into the spray, let the shampoo and soap rinse from his sun-dried skin, and, as he stepped from the shower, decided this time the martyrdom might be hers.

Chapter Three

Friday, July 22

THE MORNING DAWNED AS Thursday had, with the humidity a new and improved form of torture. Zeke worked until noon, cashed his check, and ignored an irate Stuart Rigby, who, despite acknowledging the possibility of yet another low-count day, did not necessarily want to lose his top earner, if only for an afternoon. The fact that Zeke had not even asked for a day off in months meant almost next to nothing.

Returning home after lunch, he found it covertly slipped beneath the locked front door like a secret. RAT FUCK was assembled on the outside of the envelope in letters cut from magazines. At first, he thought it might be a prank or just another manifestation of Cammi Sinclair's true sickness. Shouldering through the door, he tossed everything aside, grabbed himself a Coke, and ripped the envelope open. Sipping cola, he spread out a single sheet, which said, in the same cut lettering,

> WE HAVE NOT FORGOTTEN. CONSIDER YOUR
> BROTHER, THE TRAITOR, DEALT WITH.

He actually read it three times, as the old nausea returned as if stored for safekeeping. For some minutes, he could only stare out the window until the threat became insurmountable and, viciously balled into a crumpled missile, was launched towards the wall. *Goddamn him*, he thought, but it didn't disappear since his brother, alongside two friends, had unleashed something none of them, even those left behind, would ever escape. Just thinking of it, of how long it had been since Zeke last visited, provided an exquisite burst of guilt. It had been, he knew, a first year with only correspondence, the then fourteen-year-old still too young to visit his big brother on his own. He remembered the letters' original vigorous return while slowly, with each ensuing pause, the gap began to grow. From twice a month, then cut in half before subsequently dividing in on itself to nothing. The neighborhood hero, as Zeke knew him, retreating into some other greater struggle Zeke would not fully comprehend until that first Saturday a year and a half later, after finally having the license and guts and car commandeered. Joshua, at six foot, and having grown up working in their father's concrete business, sat across from Zeke, jacked and fearless. His black hair was the same, clipped close and bristled. Facing through the eyes deadened over, reaching out in that certain younger-sibling awe, Zeke found his greatest fear in between the lapsed silences, strained conversation, and mundane briefings of close friends yet to stumble: the politics of separation.

While listening through the receiver as Joshua blandly offhanded his surroundings, made light of the appeals, and promised a swift return, Zeke remembered the unmet gaze and clipped tones before realizing it was all for his benefit, the lies and faked nonchalance like camouflage Joshua wore as smoke. The initial joy of seeing one another after so long quickly dissipating into a wordless discomfort. Standing at the end of it, saying good-bye after all kinds of promises, Zeke recalled tapping the window twice as Joshua slowly nodded, the beckoning guard behind him stone-faced and grim. And then, well, then the months became a year, then two without a visit, as both understood what neither would admit, and soon after his eighteenth birthday, Zeke acquired the felony conviction that would make any ensuing visits legally impossible.

On the strength of faked identification two years after his own six-month incarceration, Zeke, weathering Cammi Sinclair's loud remonstrations and forced entreaties, finally dragged her with him as both faced the glass like masochists in a zoo of exotic punishments.

Jesus Christ, he presently thought, and stood to retrieve the note. Reading it again, heading for his room, it was, he decided, something he could in no way deal with right now.

I need to talk to Lotus, was all he thought before squashing the entire affair into the back of his mind like a terrible curse reborn for a sequel.

When Liz Downs called at a little past six o'clock, Zeke was thankful for the distraction. Agreeing to meet at South Station in one hour, Zeke was choked for time. Always the optimist, he cleaned the bathroom and bedroom just in case, placed a clean shirt, deodorant, and a pair of Tevas into the courier bag, and then grabbed his bike before banging closed the door.

Not wanting to be a sweaty mess, he took the hill up Cambridge Street at half-throttle, smiling down at the jammed outbound lanes of the Massachusetts Turnpike. He took a left the wrong way down Linden and passed Pratt, Ashford, and Gardner Streets, which were currently quiet but would, he knew, later be alive with a few thousand off-campus revelers wreaking havoc towards the dawn. At the intersection of Linden and Brighton Avenues, he clacked over the tracks of the long-deceased A-line and pointed himself downtown.

Kenmore Square was a bottled-up nightmare with another Red Sox game only minutes away, so he split the lanes and cruised within inches of stopped traffic on either side. Passing the unnumbered masses streaming from the T-station below, he observed the suburban devotees with their red-and-blue ball caps, excited children, and handheld radios for the play-by-play. In contrast, the outdoor cafés on Boylston Street were stocked with the after-work crowd sipping mixed drinks as the orange sun slowly sank out west.

Friday night in the big city, he thought, barely making the yellow at the Berkeley Street stoplight before a cab shot directly towards him. The hatred, he knew, was more than mutual. Cabbies and couriers, couriers and cabbies. Two warring factions that earned a living based on precious seconds between points A and B. Fighting over road space, blowing through stop signs and red lights, the most dangerous of each sect juggled a precarious balance of greed and tempted fates while pedestrians were like barely dodged obstacles in a citywide drag race. Sideswipes, unsignaled turns, and abrupt dead stops to pick up possible fares were how the majority of the yellow demons spent their days. And while they sat behind their steering wheels like obese, lazy parasites, Zeke was out here pedaling through freezing winters and summers so bad most people would collapse from heatstroke or exhaustion or a combination of the two before noon. This provided a small source of pride, he knew, in a profession where little could be had.

Passing the Boston Common, he saw couples and families throwing Frisbees, sitting on benches, and quietly talking out what Zeke guessed were the day's events. He caught Essex Street and downhilled through what was left of the Combat Zone, and five minutes later locked up outside the mammoth South Station. Below ground, the Amtrak, commuter rail, and red-line subway interweaved like snakes on shared tracks, while above, in the recently completed three-tiered bus station, national carriers all had depots. Inside, to keep away the transients, the entire great hall had no air-conditioning and reeked of sweat and diesel. Making his way to the men's room, Zeke splashed water on his face and hair, which immediately spiked to attention. He applied a stick of deodorant before changing into a plain white T-shirt and, putting his Specializeds into the bag, he then slipped into the Tevas as a wall-mounted clock hit 6:53 PM.

Back inside the terminal, he sipped iced coffee and watched the commuters ebb and flow like tides released according to schedule. He said a silent prayer of thanks that he was healthy enough to have his bike instead of being trapped inside these heat-oppressed tubes that wound beneath the city's stanchions where, for a dollar, people got the pleasure of crowded cars and temperature-baked platforms rancid with all that dripped down from above. Luckily, as far as he could figure it, he had not been on any part of the subway in months.

It was quite a mosaic, he idly thought, cataloguing the throngs of commuters passing by. Construction workers on their way home after happy hour, immigrant families hauling their lives in dufflebags, and hippy students with backpacks bigger than their bodies. He was watching a young couple arguing when Liz suddenly appeared, rounding the corner to stop and search the sea of occupied benches. He waved and saw her gaze catch the motion. He stood and walked to meet her halfway, not entirely sure how to proceed.

"Hey," he said and awkwardly stuck out a hand. "Hope you're as hungry as I am."

"Oh yes."

Her hand was moist, her grip tentative, the enormous blue eyes bouncing nervously within the confines of the crowd.

"Let's get out of here," he said.

"Yes."

Taking her by the elbow, he marveled at how she seemed to favor long-sleeved dresses, even in this heat. She was a full head shorter than him, and he allowed himself a peek down at her modestly parted brown hair and the slight jiggle just beyond definition beneath the linen.

She let him lead her through the automatic doors and out into the tailing sun sinking over Allston. Spotting the bag over his shoulder, she said, "Did you ride here?"

"Yes, ma'am." Zeke guided them up Kneeland Street as she looked up at him with those blue eyes and said, "You really love it, don't you?"

"What's that?"

"Your bike, the job …" She shuddered at how stupid that sounded.

"I enjoy it, yes."

"You've got great legs."

"I know," he said, strutting along playfully.

"It didn't take too long for that go to your head."

"Watch it," he said and jerked her back onto the curb as the 23 bus roared past. Two blocks later they entered Chinatown where the restaurants, grocers, and retailers were on the cheap. On days with time to kill, Zeke might find a corner to quickly dine on egg rolls, dumplings, or rice. And while knowing next to nothing about Chinese culture or history, he nonetheless observed the work ethic with awe as even the elderly off-loaded trucks, maneuvered hand dollies, and pulled fourteen-hour days inside steam-filled kitchens.

They took a right on Harrison Avenue and found the Shanghai Garden mobbed. Giving his name, he then caught her frightened face scanning the pandemonium.

"Do you want a drink? We've got reservations, but it's gonna be a minute."

Despite her discomfort, she gave him a smile and said, "Sure."

At the bar, Zeke wedged her onto the one available stool and then flagged down a bartender with a twenty. Once the drinks arrived, she raised her Mai-tai and said, "I know it's kind of geeky, but I always make a toast."

"Cool." Zeke raised his Black and Tan and clinked her glass as she said, "Here's to us … and a beautiful summer night."

"You got that right." Zeke sipped the beer and automatically broke out a pack of Marlboros. "You smoke?"

"Uh, no, not really." Elizabeth Downs looked away and then back again, her grin somewhat sheepish. "I do, but only when I drink."

"Good." He held out the pack. "Cancer's more fun in pairs."

She laughed and leaned forward as he lit her cigarette, her fragrance inches away from his nostrils which twitched in pure delight. *Don't be a pervert*, he reminded himself, but scanned her nonetheless. The brown hair framing the oval face and wide blue eyes, the nose a delicate line. Her lips were small but perfectly curved, and pursed around the straw. Leaning an arm on the bar, he felt someone repeatedly bumping into his back but chalked it up to the crowded conditions.

"This was some week. Glad it's over," he said.

"Tell me about it." She punched at the ice in her drink with the tiny umbrella. "We had two contracts lost and one of the partners out sick for three days."

"Sounds like fun."

She grimaced. "I wish."

"I'm just guessing, but you guys are an architecture firm, right?"

"Yes."

"Commercial, industrial, residential …?"

"All of the above."

"No kidding?"

"I've only worked for them since last November, but believe me, they've got more work than they can handle."

"Sounds like it."

"You sound like you know something about it."

"Ah." Zeke batted a hand. "My old man was a contractor."

"Really?"

"Yep." Zeke drained the beer. "Used to spend after school and a few summer vacations with the miserable bastard."

"Oh."

He saw her gaze and said, "It wasn't that bad. We just never saw eye to eye."

"Huh."

"How's that mai tai?"

"Incredible. Want a sip?"

"No. I want my own. You ready for another?"

"Well …"

"That's a yes. Barkeep!"

After they were set up, Zeke nearly spilled his drink as a bump from behind came once again. Turning, he said "Hey …"

Four businessmen glanced over in unison. The closest one said, "Yeah, and …?"

"Well …" Zeke put his drink down. "Can't you at least say excuse me?"

"What's your problem, buddy?" one of the others asked. It was the tone more than anything else that immediately caused Zeke to think of her, and what it would mean to even choose otherwise. The guy looked geared up, heavyset but forty pounds overweight, his gray suit a baggy wrinkled sack, the brown eyes angry and red-rimmed over what Zeke thought might have been his eighth highball. Still, he knew she would be gone, so he said, "Nothing, man." Looking away, he added, "Nothing at all."

"That's what I thought."

Turning back, Zeke saw her blinking at him sympathetically and it made him sick.

"Zeke."

"Yeah?"

"Hey. I'm over here."

His eyes found hers and he gave the cheeriest smile possible.

"This is pretty good," he said. "I don't think I've ever had a mai tai in my whole life."

Putting a hand on his arm, Liz said, "They're not laughing at you."

He gave her a halfhearted smile. "So, I'm just guessing, but you went to college, right?"

"Yes. But not to be a receptionist. Why?"

"Don't take this the wrong way, but you seem way too smart to be answering someone else's phones."

"I'll take that as a compliment. I went to Simmons for two years."

"What happened? Did you get sick of it?"

She pursed her lips, staring down into the glass. "Well, it was more like I ran out of money."

"Oh."

"Yeah." She smiled. "Live and learn. Oh gosh, what a mess. Here you go."

She pushed cocktail napkins at him, seeing his gaze film over as he wiped the spilt drink off his hand.

"Zeke …"

But he was already turned and tapping the guy's shoulder, saying, "You did it again."

"What's your problem now?"

"You. You've bumped into me thirty fucking times in ten minutes."

"Boy, you really don't learn, do you?"

The heavyset guy stood up as Zeke squeezed off a grin and said, "Uh-oh."

"You know, you've got a big fucking mouth, buddy."

Zeke squared himself, all hope for the evening lost as he could almost hear her say good-bye. "I sure do," he said. "And you better sit back down before I ruin your fucking weekend."

"Zeke—"

"Hold on, Liz. This ain't nothing but a misunderstanding. Ain't that right, fellas?"

"Like hell it is." The heavyset man put his drink down. "Why don't you shed your bag in this crowd, moron, if you're so worried about your precious personal space?"

"Listen, fuckhead, take one more step towards me and your girlfriends here won't ever recognize you again."

The man's face froze into a perfect *O* as he said, "What was that?"

The guy closest to Zeke scanned the jammed bar and quickly said, "Jack, don't. He ain't worth it."

"Fuck no, he isn't," Jack said, grinning maliciously. "A mousy-looking chick and a bike courier, no less. Hey kid, I make more in an hour than you gross all week."

"Oh my God." Zeke applauded. "As if I give a fuck. Why don't you take some of that money then and get two of those chins sucked out?"

The guy lunged as his friends grabbed him at the last second while Zeke stood there sipping his drink. She had a hand on his shoulder, which he patted as the businessmen dragged their irate friend towards the door, his wake an obscenity-strewn tirade swiveling curious heads. Satisfied, Zeke turned, then saw her expression and thought *Goddamn it,* but said instead, "Fuck, Liz, I'm really sorry."

"That," she said, "was a close one."

"I'm sorry. You didn't need to see that. I tried—"

"I know."

"But that guy was just driving me crazy—"

"Zeke."

"I'll understand if you want to leave."

"It's really okay." Running a hand through her hair, Liz said, "Don't forget where I was born and raised."

"Fucking A."

"Do I really look like a mouse?"

"Are you kidding me? Man, fuck that guy."

"And you. Weren't you scared?"

"It's all relative." Zeke shrugged and finished off his mai tai.

"What does that mean?"

"Hey. The maitre d's waving. You ready to eat?"

"Absolutely."

Zeke grabbed her hand and followed the maitre d' towards a two-top against the window. Pushing her chair in behind her, Zeke thought, *I could get used to this gentleman thing.*

"I'm starving," she said.

"So am I."

A waiter came by and Zeke ordered another round of mai tais.

"Are you trying to get me drunk?"

Grinning, he flipped open the menu and said, "I have nothing but the most honorable intentions."

"Oh, I'm sure."

They ordered dinner while outside, Harrison Avenue sank towards dusk. He said, "I lived in Dorchester for a bit."

"Where at?"

"Ambrose Street."

"Uphams Corner." She nodded. "That's pretty close to where I grew up."

"Cool place. But lean."

"Yes …" She stirred her drink. "Too many people, too little room …"

"And too many kids with nothing to do."

"You could certainly say that." Liz grinned frankly. "My father worked for A&G Gas."

"His whole life?"

Liz shook her head. "He's been with the phone company for the past fifteen years."

"What about your mom?"

"Well …" She leaned her head, looking towards her fingers, which nervously clasped and unclasped as she said, "My folks got divorced when I was pretty small. She moved to Walla Walla, Washington, when I was in third grade."

"That's a long haul."

"Tell me about it." Liz grinned self-consciously. "It was kind of hard to deal with growing up, you know? I mean, it seemed the only thing that stopped her was the Pacific Ocean."

"That sucks."

"Yes, well, after a time we just had to write her off."

"Wow."

"I'm sorry. I don't mean to sound—"

"No, no."

"It's just … well, I'm sure you can see parts of who you are in your folks. I only had my father, and I can't see any part of me in him."

"Why's that?" He watched her blue eyes smart. "Don't mind me," he said. "I'm sorry about the fifty questions."

"It's okay."

"As you might have already figured out, I'm not too good with small talk."

"Is that all this is to you?"

"Uh … no. Of course not. I …" He hoped he was not sweating. "Ah, fuck. That's not what I meant at all."

His discomfort and blush raised a smile to her lips. "You're pretty cute when you're flustered."

"Yeah? Then how do I look with my foot jammed into my mouth?"

"Like you've been there before."

"Amen." He raised his glass and met hers halfway, toasting shared inadequacies.

"What about you?" she asked as the egg rolls arrived. "Are your folks still together?"

"Ah, not really." Zeke served them both. "My mom passed when I was younger."

"I'm sorry."

"So am I."

"Was it sudden?"

"No …" He tried not to squirm. "She had ovarian cancer." The silence hung between them so he added, "She was a cool mom."

"I'm sorry, Zeke."

"Yeah." He stabbed at his egg roll. "Anyway, they were both second generation. My father was Norwegian, she was Colombian. He was loud, she was not. You know how that goes."

"Where did they meet?"

Zeke grinned and said, "On the corner of Commonwealth and Harvard Ave. He was in his early twenties, a laborer for a concrete company. She was on her way home from her job as a domestic downtown. He nearly ran her over in the Bobcat mini-loader he was driving."

"Sounds like love at first sight."

"I guess it was. He had to help her home with the groceries, though, because she had twisted her ankle trying to get out of his way."

"Lucky she didn't sue."

"Why do you think he carried those groceries twelve fucking blocks?"

She smiled around a steaming mouthful, chasing it with the mai tai before she said, "And where is he now?"

"Not sure." Zeke dipped a fork's worth into the hot sauce. "Haven't seen him in years."

"Oh."

"He's a decent guy."

"So you said. What about brothers and sisters?"

"I've got one brother."

"Older or younger?"

"Older. By five years."

"He live in town?"

"You could say that."

"Downtown?"

"Uh, no. He's … he's been in Walpole since I was thirteen."

"Oh."

"He comes up in a month or two."

"For parole?"

He nodded, thankful to have the egg roll to jam into his mouth.

"Guess it's typical," she said, switching the subject. "I don't think I have more than one or two friends whose parents are still together. Of course your case is different."

"I know what you mean," he said. "Seems this last generation was nothing but a disaster. I think I heard half of them are divorced."

"Yep."

"Makes you wonder."

"What about?"

"If it's even worth it. Fifty-fifty is still a hell of a risk."

"It sure is."

The waiter appeared to clear away the appetizer plates, returning soon after with platters of crispy orange beef, chicken and pea pods, and shrimp fried rice. They helped themselves as Zeke ordered still another round of Mai-tais while she grinned helplessly and said, "If this keeps up, you're gonna have to roll me home."

"I'll just put you in my bag. I'll have to charge an oversize and overweight—"

"Hey!"

"But I always deliver."

"We'll have to see about that."

Thinking he may have misjudged her, he laughed despite himself.

"And you," he said. "Any brothers or sisters?"

She shook her head, chewing down a mouthful. "Just me."

"Huh."

"Have some of the chicken and pea pods. It's awesome."

"Nice." He dug in and they ate for a time in silence. Finishing his mai tai, Zeke decided he was pretty fucked up.

"You want another?"

"Drink?" She looked at him incredulously. "Uh, no thanks."

"Waiter!" Zeke tapped his glass. "*Por favor.*"

Setting down her napkin, Liz grinned and asked, "You speak Spanish?"

"Nope."

"Think he does?"

"Good question. You want any more of this?"

"No thanks."

Zeke spooned out the remainder of the crispy orange beef, and after it was finished he began hawking the chicken and pea pods with a crooked eyebrow until she got the hint and said, "I'm done with that as well."

"Sorry."

"No need. By the end of the day, you must be starving."

She swirled the ice in her drink with the umbrella. Shook her head emphatically when the waiter came by to clear away the carnage and inquire about dessert.

"Think I'm stuffed too," Zeke said, finally putting down the fork. "Just the check, please."

After the waiter departed, Zeke glanced across and saw her blue eyes slightly sleepy. "What now?" he said.

"It's early."

"I know. Friday night at nine o'clock and I'm ready for bed." Realizing what he just said, he quickly added, "I meant—"

"I know what you meant." She smiled pleasantly and said, "I'm not that easy."

"Damn it!" Zeke said in mock disappointment as the check arrived. He placed four twenty-dollar bills on the tray. "What's your fortune say?"

"Hang on." She cracked open the obligatory cookie. "Be aware, you are in position to reap substantial financial rewards."

"Huh."

"And yours?"

"Let's see." Zeke unrolled the script. "You will have dinner with an intriguing hottie and she will agree to see you again."

"Oh really?"

"Hey, man, I'm only reading what it says. But that Confucius, is he on top of his game or what?"

After she used the facilities, they met by the maitre d' stand and wedged through the crowd, which was now lined up halfway down the block. Back on Kneeland Street, he said, "What now? Hold on. I got you."

"Oh my God."

"What did you trip on?"

"My own foot," she said, grinning apologetically. "I hate to say it, but I'm pretty drunk."

"Likewise."

"I don't mean to be a party pooper, but it's been a long week."

"That's cool."

"Any other time—"

"Liz, it's okay. You want me to get you a cab?"

She shook her head. "The T's fine. Feel like walking me back?"

"Sure."

"You're mad, aren't you?"

"Liz ..."

"I'm sorry."

"Stop saying that." He paused them on the corner of Hudson Street while a line of traffic shot past. "Just tell me you'll see me again."

"I'll see you again."

"When?"

"Um ..."

Here it comes, he thought as they crossed the street. *She got her meal and now she's gone.*

"How about Sunday afternoon?" she asked brightly. "Maybe we could go down to the Common or something."

"Are you demoting me?"

"Excuse me?"

"From dinner to a walk in the park?"

"Zeke ..."

"I'm just bustin'."

She stopped him in the middle of the sidewalk and tilted her head to look him in the eye. "You know, I don't think I've ever met anyone quite like you."

"I'm not even sure that's a compliment."

She squeezed his hand and said nothing. As people passed on either side, Zeke decided to just go for it. He leaned down and in as her eyes lit up in surprise before closing all together. She was a good sport, and after a minute, as their lips disengaged, Liz Downs raised a hand to her mouth, blushing furiously. "Ahhh ..."

"Sorry about that," he said. "It's been the only thing on my mind since Wednesday."

"You too?"

"Let's get out of here before we get arrested for public indecency." As they headed for South Station, he said, "Can I ask you something?"

"Sure."

"It might be kind of personal. If it is, just tell me to piss off."

"Okay."

"It's just … I kind of noticed tonight that you don't seem real comfortable in crowds."

"Yes …" She was looking at the pavement as they walked. "I … I don't know how to answer that at this point."

"That's cool."

"What do they say about that? When someone's got things going on?"

"Issues."

"Yes," she said forthrightly. "I've got issues."

"You ain't kidding."

Biting back a smile, she said, "Do you take anything seriously?"

"I don't know how to answer that at this point."

"Fucker," she said and immediately grinned. "See what you're doing to me?"

"Say it again."

"Fucker."

"Once more."

"Fucker. Fucker, fucker, fucker."

He laughed and said, "Nice." Shuffling his feet as they waited to cross Atlantic Avenue, he said, "You know what's coming next, right?"

"Please do."

Placing a hand on her cheek, he leaned in for a quick one. Ten seconds later she pulled back and said, "If you keep doing that, I'm never gonna be able to leave."

"Sunday, right?"

"Yes." She reached up to pat his cheek. "Thanks, Zeke. I had a great time. And dinner was awesome."

"Cool."

"Talk to you soon."

He watched the white dress retreat into the gathering dark. She paused for one final wave beneath the fluorescent lights of South Station. Waving back, he saw her looking small under the lights and smiling before the doors swooshed closed behind her. Still tasting her on his lips as he unlocked his bike, he slipped into the Specializeds and, without looking back, wished tomorrow was Sunday afternoon instead.

In Lower Allston twenty minutes later, with alcohol impairing his good judgment, Zeke took the turn onto North Harvard at thirty-five miles per hour. On Easton Street, he braked to a stop in front of the yellow submarine and saw only darkness. *Booger must be on a double*, he thought and two-stepped it up to their apartment. Setting his bike in the hall, Zeke hit the lights, grabbed the phone, and punched in a string of numbers. He barely had time to pack the green Graphix and exhale before it rang back and he scooped it up to say, "Yeah, hello."

"Z. Thought that was you."

"Lotus." Zeke lit a cigarette and could hear crowd noise in the background. "You sound busy. Too busy to even pick up a phone?"

"Man, I ain't seen you in months. What's up? Where you at?"

"Home."

"That ain't gonna work."

"I need to speak with you."

"I'm at the Sixty."

"Is it packed?"

"Naw, man, still early."

Grinning, Zeke could picture the standard-issue black jeans, black T-shirt, combat boots, and ponytail, with Lotus chain-smoking in between gin shooters at what was, essentially, a wine bar for the professional class.

"You making new friends?"

Lotus gave him a cigarette-graveled laugh and said, "As if. On my way up to the Mo-dell."

"When?"

"Now. Meet me there, deadbeat."

"Cool."

The Modello Café was on the corner of North Beacon and Cambridge

Streets, the interior old-style booths and modest wood paneling adorned with a rotation of local painters. It took Zeke only eight minutes to get there, and once inside he found a somber-faced, late-twenties crowd milling through the shadows. Adjusting to the gloom, Zeke saw a wave and headed for the far left corner where Lotus abruptly pulled him in for a hug that ended with a clap on the back.

"Too long, man, you know?" he said.

"I know." Zeke shrugged. "It's fucked, isn't it?"

He followed Lotus to a booth where two stouts already sat. Sliding onto the smooth pine bench as he unslung his bag, Zeke caught Lotus in mid-smirk and said, "What?"

"Nothing." Lotus perched thin eyebrows over black eyes shrunk like dimes. As he smiled, the taut skin stretched across bony ridges and muscles beneath like an anatomical mask. He was six feet tall, his arms and chest created in stink-filled gyms and jails. Raising the stout, he swallowed twice and said, "To Ambrose Street."

"Yeah, man."

"You look fucking cooked, kid."

Zeke grinned and said, "Speaking of which. Ran into Kelly last week."

Lotus shot a sour look towards the table as Zeke recognized the expression and said, "Yep. Fucking kid barely knew who I was."

Lotus shook his head. "Goddamn."

"How long's he been out?"

"Hell, I don't know. Maybe two months?"

Zeke shrugged, rotating the glass in his grasp. "Some fucking rehab."

"Last time I saw him," Lotus lit a cigarette, "I was finishing up downtown. Turned the corner on Washington Street and there he was, winking out against the wall like a dead man."

"Good ol' Kelly." Zeke smacked his lips and set down the stout. "Had an ounce of kind bud broke into four bags just hanging out of his front pocket. I'm talking like right in the middle of Harvard fucking Ave."

"Jesus."

"Yeah. So I pulled him into a doorway, didn't even bother with any advice, not anymore, you know?"

Lotus shrugged. "What can you do?"

"Nothing. So I evened up for one of the bags, told him to put the rest of that shit away for real, and just watched him stumble on down the road."

"Man."

"That kid used to be my best friend."

"Mine too. Fuck."

"The old neighborhood."

Lotus nodded. "Probably jacked the weed for his precious packets any damn way."

"Had to pay him." Zeke shrugged. "Should've seen him. It really sucked."

"Let's change the subject."

"His left arm was tracked out and completely fucked with pus—"

"*Zeke.*"

"Yeah. Okay."

They drank in silence as the music kicked in and Zeke finally said, "It's just got me thinking." He held up six fingers. "There ain't many of us left."

Lotus looked miserably into his drink. "I thought we were going to change the fucking subject."

"Pussy."

Lotus grinned and said, "Of all the luck. Out of any street in the whole city, and I end up next door to the fucking Sandaman brothers."

"That's right. Eighty-three was the best year of your miserable life." Zeke smiled, easily recalling that summer day when the Ryder truck pulled up to the neighboring duplex, the father and son all that remained after a violent divorce from a woman Zeke knew Lotus did not blame or hate for leaving, because the father, a man not shy with anger, was also a reckless alcoholic. Two years older than Zeke and three years younger than Zeke's brother Josh, Lotus quickly found a spot reserved at the neighbor's table before Gabriella Sandaman's infirmity worsened. Thinking of it now, Zeke saw it like a grainy photograph, the handful of friends and his brother too, not yet lost inside the madness.

"Hang on, Z." Lotus turned towards the pool table. "Hey! Redoubt! C'mere."

One of the players detached and approached as Lotus held out a twenty and said, "Two more. And say hello to Z. Z, Redoubt."

Redoubt wore baggy jeans over half-exposed boxers. *Can't be more than eighteen*, Zeke thought, tossing him a somewhat apathetic nod. Redoubt pocketed the money and headed for the bar as Zeke said, "Lemme guess."

"Don't." Lotus frowned. "The carnival rages on."

"Must be getting desperate in your old age."

"Fuck. It sure ain't like the old days. Half these kids think they're fucking niggers."

Zeke grinned and said, "That his partner?"

Lotus nodded and finished his stout, backhanding the foam. "Safer in pairs. At least they think so."

"How late you run 'em?"

"Depends. Two, three o'clock on weekends?"

"Nice."

"Got six more downtown and another pair up here. Mad ounces, dude."

"Jesus."

Lotus smiled, watching Zeke finishing his drink and watching him, the pale green eyes awaiting more. "They run on twenty-eighty. You can guess which number's mine. I kick another thirty downtown."

"You arrange the fakes?"

"Sometimes. You remember Choco?"

"Yep."

"He's still around. Mainly out of Chinatown now."

"He used to make the best fucking licenses."

"Talk about a godsend. Half these pukes barely look eighteen, much less twenty-one."

"Choco."

"The one and only." Lotus lit another cigarette. "Could always use another partner, Z. You know that, right?"

"Man—"

"I know, I know. Just lettin' *you* know." Lotus craned his neck across the increasing crowd and said, "Here they come."

"Suckers."

"That what we are?"

Zeke blinked and said, "Fuck. Guess so."

Redoubt replaced the empty glasses with fresh stouts, then Lotus clicked

Zeke's glass and took a long pull. Zeke drained a quarter of his own and said, "So what's up?"

Lotus batted a hand, setting down his drink. "You know what I'm gonna ask, right?"

"Nope."

Lotus tapped ash from his cigarette before taking another drag. "Joshua Lynn."

Zeke froze for a moment before slowly nodding as if impressed and said, "That's exactly why I called."

"Ain't he up, like, now?"

"November sixth."

"That the hearing?"

"Yep." Zeke reached for his bag and leaned forward, tabling both elbows. "Check this out."

He spread the crinkled paper and Lotus read it, saying, "Are you fucking kidding me?" He re-read the sentence again before looking up at Zeke with an incredulous expression. "*You* got this?"

"Yep."

"At your place?"

"Right under the door."

"Jesus … just out of the blue?"

"Not really." Zeke reached for his drink. "Ran into Lindy creeping up Newbury two days ago."

"Oh man." Lotus picked up the paper. "So when did you get this?"

"This afternoon."

"Fucking pathetic." Lotus winced disgustedly. "Do you believe their balls?"

"I have to. I got no choice now."

"I can't believe this. Honest to God, man, ain't the kid been through enough?" Lotus worriedly tapped the paper and saw Zeke shaking his head. "What, Z?"

"I just can't believe they're still on the block. They must be like thirty fucking years old by now."

"And just dumb enough to wait eleven years to pull this shit too." Lotus pointed at the note. "Rat fuck?"

"Who knows? Fuckhead yelled something out the window, saying C.B. and Ju-Ju came home in coffins and blah blah blah."

"And what's that got to do with Josh?"

"How the fuck should I know?" Zeke blinked, regretting the tone. "It's been five years since I saw the kid."

"Man."

"What a mess." Zeke rubbed both temples before looking up helplessly. "I ain't telling him."

"Yeah." Picturing it, Lotus nearly shuddered. "That wouldn't be good."

"I mean, could you imagine? With him all pinned up in there, just itching for his hearing? And then he hears this shit?"

"No, man. He'd hit that corner and end up with two life sentences."

"And if I don't tell him …"

Lotus leaned back and said, "Hey, listen, he gets out, finds you, and we take it from there."

"Man."

"Zeke, I'll make some calls. See who's still around. Believe me, you were right the first time. This …" Lotus picked up the paper. "This ain't nothing he's gonna wanna hear about eight weeks out, man. Don't do it."

"Goddamn." Zeke ran both hands through his hair before grabbing the back of his neck. "It ain't fair. After so long, too."

"Zeke."

"You're right. I'll wait."

Lotus pushed the paper back and lifted his glass, seemingly still preoccupied, until Zeke said, "So what about Triple X? You even part-time?"

"Barely." Lotus's hands encircled the pint glass. "We got like thirty fucking guys now. Louie runs me and two others between the bikes and vans."

"That your Ninja out front?"

"Yep."

Disgusted, Zeke frowned and said, "Fucker. How much did that thing cost?"

"Check this out …" Lotus grinned. "Louie fronted it."

"What? Is your boss a sucker or just stupid?"

"Swear to God. I cut him fifty a week. Fucking thing's sick as hell too. Zero to sixty in four seconds."

"That's ridiculous."

"I know it."

"Fuck. We don't even have any motorcycle guys."

"What do you expect with Team Faggot?"

"Hey."

"For real, Zeke, Christ." Lotus held out a hand in exasperation. "I've offered to pull you in at least eight thousand times. Could set you up on one of those meat rockets bagging by the hundreds."

Zeke reached for a cigarette and said, "I like feeling the pain."

"Yeah, well, bike or motorcycle, ain't no one out there for free."

"But Stuart—"

"I know." Lotus held up a hand. "Say no more. He must be taking care of you. Besides, without you and that other freak show, Split Minute would be history."

"I don't know about that."

"Oh yeah? Look at the cast of fuckups that polesmoker's got. Among others, Fudgie, Spike, Larry, and Mother fucking Hubbard?"

"Looks worse than it is."

"Really." Lotus respectfully looked away. "That may be true. But see, I know you. Sometimes this loyalty thing you got."

"Yeah?"

"I don't know." Lotus shook his head. "You need to look out for yourself more."

"Who're you talking to?"

"Hey, easy. It's just, who gives a fuck about Stuart except you?"

"Let's change the subject again."

"Cool. That's cool." Lotus sipped his stout and smiled. "It's just a bitch to be right is all."

"Fuck. I hate it when they crank the music this loud."

"What?"

"Fuck you."

Lotus grinned, feasting on the pain before saying, "So what up with you and Miss Congeniality?"

"Ah, man …"

"Love and hate?"

Zeke frowned. "More like hate and war."

"Yeah, right. The two of you should just end it and get married."

"Oh my God."

"I'm not kidding."

"Then you must be drunk."

"You wish."

"I was … I was kind of on a date tonight."

"Kind of on a what?" Lotus put a hand behind his ear. "I'm not sure I heard you right."

"Yes you did. I met her a couple of days ago."

"Zeke …"

Zeke shrugged and said, "Me and C have been having problems, man, you know? And then I hit this office and there *she* was and I … well, she's got these huge blue eyes and a killer little rocket body—"

"Whatever, man." Lotus grinned as if it was nonsense. "Even though she hates me, that chick can kick some serious ass."

"Cammi doesn't hate you." Zeke rubbed his forehead. "She just gets worried whenever you're around."

Lotus laughed and took a long draught of the stout. "You need to start thinking with some other part of your body, man."

"Bullshit." Zeke shook his head. "It's always a fucking trauma, you know? I mean, what the fuck? Isn't this shit supposed to make you happy?"

"Yeah, Zeke, if you live in Wonderland and your name is Alice. You wanna be happy, buy a puppy. Otherwise, welcome to adulthood." Lotus looked towards the pool table and said, "One sec. I gotta take a squirt."

"Yep."

Zeke sat in the empty booth in a crowded bar on a Friday night and only wished he was at home. Maybe it was the town or just the repetitive scene replayed in every nightspot until the clichés just wrote themselves. He thought of Lotus, a.k.a. Brian Altamont, and figured it must be the same the world over. How people came and went from each other's lives only to reappear unannounced at intervals determined by coincidence or self-interest. Sadly, he knew, it was the latter that had forced this evening's rendezvous with a near half-brother he might see six times a year. *Boston,* he regretfully thought, *was not that big.*

Zeke watched Redoubt by the pool table, palming fifty bags and making change like a store clerk instead of a conscientious drug dealer. As a profession, inside a club or bar, Zeke knew it was not what others might suspect that got one busted. By then, drawing the increased surveillance, it was already way too late. Beyond brazen, Zeke almost stood up before deciding the problem belonged to someone else. He looked down into the remnants of his stout, Ambrose Street on the creep again as he watched Lotus gab into a cell phone near the bathrooms.

The two of them had only had a handful of years together before Zeke's relocation from Dorchester to Allston, the death of Gabriella, Zeke's mother, a stain worse than blood across every inch of that house. The three who had been left behind faked the first six months badly. With their core abruptly excised, his older brother and father were barely speaking when the inevitable broke one and sent the other to prison. And Lotus, well, he became a part of everything else abandoned in Uphams Corner. Having found his niche at a young enough age, and as deeply wrapped up in the lifestyle as Lotus was, running white and steering teenagers became the compromise at upwards of five thousand dollars a week. And not that he wanted to hex one of the only true friends that Zeke had, but Lotus's turn was coming. Knowing it firsthand, Zeke also knew the luxuries wouldn't mean much if he got locked up or killed.

He watched Lotus stalking towards the booth in his black jackboots, eyes tightened into a steady sweep like someone waiting to be attacked. Sliding onto the bench seat, he reached for Zeke's Marlboros and Zeke said, "Listen, I haven't spoken with big bro, but you're right. I need to start lining something up."

"Z, hey, no worries." Lotus ran a hand through the black ponytail. "When the time comes, believe me, I've got plenty of things to do."

"He'd appreciate that."

"Like I said, whatever the two of you decide."

"Cool." Zeke finished his stout. "What else you got on tap for tonight?"

Businesslike, Lotus consulted his watch, nibbled a lip, and said, "Fuck, it's still early. I'm gonna take the fellas over to the Chamber in a few minutes. Wanna come? Have you ever been to that place?" Lotus whistled appreciatively. "They got chicks in cages, bro, just tearing it up."

"Come on."

"I ain't lying. Check it out."

"All right. But if they're coming with us," Zeke nodded towards the pool table, "they need to calm the fuck down."

"Oh yeah?" Lotus paused. "That obvious?"

"With my paper?" Zeke frowned and pocketed the cigarettes. "Something needs to be done."

"Let's get some shots." Lotus stood. "I'll straighten them out, and then we'll DD."

"Yep."

Reaching into his wallet, Zeke tried laying a ten-dollar bill on Lotus, who recoiled as if offended. Ahead, at the bar, surrounded shoulder to shoulder amid people he could not care less about, Zeke Sandaman did not blend in.

Chapter Four

Sunday, July 24

BENT INTO A CROUCH, Cammi Sinclair took the corner onto Easton with her left knee practically scratching asphalt. Coasting up onto the sidewalk, she came to a stop standing sidesaddle on the left pedal. Clicking out, she tossed a U-bar Kryptonite around the frame and through a chain-link fence, unconcerned about tire theft because, like Zeke's, both her axles had been switched out from quick-release to Allen's head requiring a specific wrench for removal.

Glancing up at the yellow submarine, she wiped away the sweat from the morning sun and thought, *Can't believe I'm the first to cave.*

She found herself looking down at the white T-shirt and hacked-off jeans, her Izumi shoes cracked and burst from overuse.

The hell with it, she thought, and cursed this vanity. Blinking through the heat, her brown eyes were surrounded by veiny webs spun overnight in red. Adjusting the omnipresent courier bag, she pushed open the gate and said aloud, "He sure as shit better be alone."

Hungover, she took the stairs while praying for Zeke's moron first-floor neighbor Rob to even poke his perverted head out the window. On the top floor, she used her key but knocked twice before entering. Unslinging her bag and shaking her head at the forty or so beer cans tossed about the TV room, her bike shoes clacked across the scarred wood floors. The bedroom door was ajar. Tapping it with an elbow, she saw him face down on the queen-size mattress squared into the near right corner, the sheets like entangled tentacles about him.

God, she thought devilishly, *I could seriously fuck him up.*

Kicking a pile of dirty clothes off the lone chair in front of a desk cluttered with compact discs, bike parts, and a smudged picture tacked to the wall, Cammi sat instead. There were two shadeless windows pouring in sun, and even from this distance she could see the sweat dotting his forehead like jewels.

Breaking out a pack of cigarettes, she flicked her Zippo and took a long drag, watching him sleep. Nudging aside room on the desk, she propped and crossed both legs, exhaling twin streams into her lap. Her eyes wandered across the dozen or so autographed posters from his days at the Rat's Nest. Rancid poses of Fugazi, Twisted Bitch, Suicidal Tendencies, the Butthole Surfers, and, her personal favorite, a six-foot life-size tour promotion of Lou Reed in full shock mode, circa 1976, when the New York Dolls and Sex Pistols prowled Manhattan's Lower East Side and she was all of four years old, her true era past and gone in time for an adolescence of cheese-filled '80s' crap.

Wandering up the wall, her eyes found the familiar photograph and her smile quickly vanished. How many times had she looked at it? In seven years, it was the only picture of any family member she had ever seen. She knew that Gabriella was her name, and besides the beautiful green eyes, Cammi had long figured Zeke looked nothing like his mother. Such a pretty face, Cammi judged, exhaling thoughtfully. And a cute little plump thing, with her black hair, toned skin, and gentle smile belying the exotic. Knowing Zeke as she did, she thought the picture seemed irrational. Light-haired, miserable, scraggily-ass Zeke and his nice Colombian mother. If the whole story hadn't ended in such disaster, Cammi knew she might have had an endless cache for torture.

But since the steeped venom she had originally nurtured for this visit was now devolving into sympathy, she abruptly turned away. Finding a new target, she was about to kick his feet when an eyelid slipped slowly open, tested the unwelcome light, and closed with a disgusted squint.

"Hey," she said, grinding out the cigarette. "Wake up. It's almost noon."

He did a slow roll, the pillow across his face swallowing a pain-filled grunt. After another wounded moan, he lifted it enough to say, "How'd you get past security?"

"I showed them my tits."

"Awesome." He started coughing and put a fist to his mouth, leaning off the mattress. Seeing his hand wave in desperation, Cammi passed the coffee cup she had ashed in, saying, "Gross, Zeke."

He let droop a giant wad of mucus. Grinning, he started coughing and belching. After he came to a teary-eyed stop, Cammi said, "Thanks for not puking."

"Jesus Christ."

"Little too much to drink last night, Z?"

"Ugh."

"Want a smoke?"

"God no."

She smiled, watching him run a hand through a vicious case of bed-head. His upper body was shredded from all the cycling, the tattoos a scattered mosaic.

He said, "I'll give you a dollar if you get me a glass of water."

"Make it five."

He nodded, coughing again as he pointed to a wallet by her feet. Reaching down, she found it completely empty. "There's a surprise."

Returning from the kitchen, she handed him the water and said, "I'll just put that on your tab."

"Thanks." He gulped the entire pint, checked to make sure it was not about to reverse direction, and leaned back with a grateful smile.

"So I ran into Dr. Detroit and Telly at the Playkill show," she said.

"Last night? Telly's back in town already?"

Cammi yawned and said, "Yep."

"Man, New York must've kicked his ass."

"Not according to him."

"Of course not." He propped a pillow behind his head. "Yeah, so we got a little roasted."

"I can see that."

"What about you?"

Cammi batted a hand and said, "After the show, me and Liza boozed at The Silhouette till close."

"Nice."

"Yeah, she's cool."

It was now, she knew, feeling the pressure of his gaze like a giant question mark she could not answer.

"So?" she said.

"So," he said.

"This what I think it is?"

He shrugged and said, "Maybe. For a bit."

Sneering derisively, Cammi lit another cigarette. "God, you are such a pussy."

"Cam—"

"Naw. Don't even bother."

He clutched his head in his hands and said, "This is exactly what I'm talking about."

"What's that? The fact that you want to play a heavy-handed round of apologize or get lost?"

"Unbelievable."

"You're right. It is." She ashed on the floor. "Fuck, I came all the way over here, didn't I?"

"And for what?" Zeke raised up onto an elbow, the bloodshot eyes twitching like a barely contained aneurysm. "So I could apologize to you? Are you out of your fucking mind?"

"Zeke—"

"Bullshit! That whole thing was bullshit. We had a great night together and then, because your psycho mom and sister are gearing up to pull another disaster on you, I get fucked like a toothless whore."

"Gee, Dr. Dumbass," Cammi rolled her eyes, "is that your professional opinion?"

His defeated sigh sounded like a pin through a balloon.

"Poor Zeke."

Leaning back, clasping both hands over his face, he said, "Whatever, Cam. Okay? Fucking whatever."

Standing up, she dragged on the cigarette as she swung her courier bag over a shoulder.

"You know," she said, "for someone who prides himself on what a bad motherfucker he is, you sure are a nutless liar."

"You are so—"

"What's her name, Zeke?"

"What? Whose name?"

Cammi Sinclair would have smiled if her wild guess had not been so accurate. *Look at him*, she thought, *squirming like a bug that's about to be smushed.*

"I take that back," she said. "You lie about as good as you fuck."

"Hey! What the fuck!" He quickly backhanded her lit cigarette off his chest as she gave him the finger and stalked out. Wrenching the front door closed with enough force to dislodge the jamb, she stomped down the steps, swearing, "That was the end of *that*."

Unlocking her bike, picturing him sidling up next to some bitch in one of his drunken escapades, she wondered at the freshness of this betrayal. Saw him leaning against the bar with that insipid grin he always thought was just so unintentional. That miserable *prick*, she nonetheless groaned and, setting pace, shouldered what hurt because now this was his to bear.

"But I guess I'll just try calling you back if—"

"Hey!" Zeke fumbled with the phone, the answering machine screeching feedback until he killed it. "Hey, it's me, Liz."

"Hi, Zeke. Did I catch you at a bad time?"

Standing, barely able to balance from the previous night's pickling, and with Cammi's exit ten minutes earlier still echoing like a gunshot through his lacerated brain, he merely grinned and said, "Ah no. Of course not."

"Good."

"What time is it?"

"Almost 12:30."

"I'm psyched you called." Zeke pulled some extra cord and kicked aside beer cans, collapsing onto the sofa. "Did you have a good weekend?"

"It was okay. Didn't do much last night. How about you?"

"Same thing. Just chilled out. What're you doing?"

"Oh, I'm sorry. I'm in the kitchen just banging some pots—"

"I meant today."

"Oh." She laughed. "Nothing. That's why I called."

"Let's hang."

"Okay."

"What do you want to do?" he asked.

"I thought I'd come up your way. I've got some errands in Kenmore Square, but it shouldn't take too long."

"Maybe we'll toss a Frisbee or get a coffee or something."

"Okay," she answered brightly. "I'll call you in, like, two hours?"

"Cool."

"Talk to you later."

"Bye, Liz." Hanging up, unsure of whether he needed to vomit or just go back to bed, Zeke slowly shook his head in wonderment, saying aloud, "A normal chick. Fuck me."

But the mind was cruel, and his own quickly looped backwards until there was Cammi again, at the foot of his bed, her cigarette arcing towards him. He knew he would have pursued her, carried this battle downstairs into the street where they usually ended up, nose to nose, the hate like twin streams of gasoline across the flints of their well-honed tongues. Except … except that this time she was right. Feeling dirty for even admitting it, Zeke leaned back and replayed the door slamming closed with that building-rattling concussion and angrily thought, *God, what a fucking psycho.*

Reaching for the Graphix, he decided to get high to readjust the horrendous start to what was otherwise the last day before Monday and Stuart Rigby and all the usual trauma. Slowly, after three more hits, Zeke Sandaman headed for the shower.

———————————

They met on Harvard Avenue at a small coffeeshop called Sugar and Cream at half past three that afternoon. Liz Downs, though a lifelong city resident, did not often get out towards Allston. She had been up and down the block twice before finally recognizing his bike locked up in front of a store that had a tiny sign. Slanting an eyebrow, she quickly checked herself since she had worn her brand-new outfit straight out of the store. The skirt was blue and hemmed at mid-thigh, the shirt a white long-sleeve that she had, at the counter, in front of a horrified clerk, instantly clipped into a neat little belly shirt. Her legs, she knew, were very white, but more than shapely enough. Staring across the street, fighting against the same old predictable surge, she told herself it would be okay. But the saboteur, already on overdrive, counseled otherwise.

He thinks you're worth nothing more than a dumpy little coffeeshop, the voice warned. *Didn't even come out to see if you were wandering around in that godawful outfit. And those black pumps, how eighties. And what is with your hair?*

Crossing the street, Liz removed the sunglasses and, upon entering, saw him reading a newspaper at a two-top table against the wall. The place was otherwise empty. Canned jazz filtered down from unseen speakers. The tinkling door chime announced her presence as he looked up and said, "Well, all right."

"Sorry I'm late." She put down the shopping bags she had been carrying for too long and said, "I would've been here sooner, but that sign—it's hard to see."

"Oh man." He winced. "Fuck, Liz, I'm sorry."

"It's okay." Sitting down, she said, "I finally saw your bike."

"Thatta girl."

She thought he seemed impressed, so she said, "I wasn't that drunk Friday night."

"That's not what I was thinking."

"I know." As if she were a gift he wanted desperately unwrapped, she caught him feasting on her legs and exposed belly.

A waitress, who Liz thought looked about as hung over as Zeke, approached the table and said with a sigh, "Can I help you guys?"

"Two coffees." Zeke looked at Liz. "They got everything here. Bagels, donuts, sandwiches …"

"Coffee's fine."

The waitress left. She watched him fold up the *Boston Globe* as he said, "Did you flip a coin?"

"Excuse me?"

"On whether or not to call."

"Twice." Looking down at her clasped hands, she grinned somewhat bashfully and played along, saying, "Unfortunately, it came up heads both times."

"See? I think the gods are trying to tell you something."

The waitress arrived with two cups and a steaming pot, which she placed between them. Zeke poured and Liz added cream and sugar to hers and said, "You look like you had a rough night last night."

"Really?" Zeke grinned. "How could you tell? The vodka breath or shaking hands?"

"Both."

He laughed and it pleased her, the sound of pure amusement instead of the half-sneer or forced smile, and it came at his own expense, something that made her grin as well.

"Yeah, I ran into some old friends last night," he said. "On top of that, I just got off the phone with a buddy who moved to New York like three months ago. At the time, he told us what suckers we were for staying in lame old Boston."

She smiled, still somewhat nervously, but finding herself increasingly intrigued by his distraction. "So what happened?"

"Apparently, he hopped off the bus with his bag and bike at the Port Authority like a total hayseed only to find his cousin's place padlocked for back rent. So he looks in the paper, finds a shoebox two-bedroom looking for a roommate, and a week later comes home to find all his shit gone. Turns out his new roomie had a bit of a drug problem."

"Oh my."

"Yep."

Liz sipped at her mug and said, "Have you ever been there?"

"New York? Couple of times. Usually just to party."

"Would you ever think about living there?"

"Maybe." Zeke shrugged. "But I figure you have to really care. You fight for everything. Guys like me, with my income, a place like that is death."

"I love New York."

"It certainly makes things interesting."

Scanning the coffeeshop through the stagnant air, Liz said, "Is it hot in here or is it just me?"

"Naw, it's pretty fucking hot. Can't believe they don't have AC."

Trying not to disclose her increasing boredom, Liz looked around the place for a second time. "So what do you want to do?"

"Check it out …" Zeke leaned into his bag before hoisting up a Frisbee. "Feel like hucking the disc?"

"Sure."

She watched him search for the absent waitress, lay a five-dollar bill on the table instead, and shoulder into his bag. Standing, he said, "Gimme two of those."

"I can carry—"

"Yeah, but it's easier for me." Holding open one of her shopping bags, he asked, "Do you mind?"

"Nope."

She had some undershirts and socks and panties, which he consolidated into two neat stacks before sliding the bag into his courier sack. He hopped once to readjust the load to center on his back and held a hand out towards the door. "After you," he said.

She picked up the remaining bag and pushed out into the kiln of Harvard Avenue as heat-rippled waves shimmered off the asphalt. After he unlocked his bike, Liz walked alongside him and lowered her sunglasses. "So where're we going?"

"Dunn's Park. We'll take a right up on Comm. Ave."

It was a quarter-mile walk, the Sunday streets half empty as people headed for Revere Beach, Wright's Pond, and South Boston's Carson Beach, polluted though it was. A veteran of many summers, Liz knew the options were few, unless of course one wanted to bob around in the bacteria bath of an even rarer open city pool. As if reading her mind, Zeke said, "When I was a kid, and on the weekends when my old man didn't have to work, he'd pack us all up and head for Plymouth Beach."

"Isn't that place beautiful?"

"Hell yeah."

"I love Plymouth," she said.

"I used to see a girl from there. She was kind of an idiot."

"Are you now?"

"What?"

"Seeing anybody?"

She waited through the delay, growing anxious until he finally said, "Um ... no, not anymore."

"Hmm ..."

Liz looked towards the sidewalk as Zeke quickly said, "Believe me, I don't play like that."

"Like what?"

"Like Johnny Romance. Women … let's just say I can only manage one at a time."

"So you're …"

"I am definitely not. What about you?"

"Nope." Adjusting her grip in his hand, she said, "I was up until about two months ago." She shrugged. "It's just not easy for me."

"Tell me about it. Usually everything's fine until I open my mouth."

"And then what?"

"They start running."

"I know what you mean," she said. Piecing together the few moments they had shared, Liz began to see the contradictions more clearly, the profane hood usurped by a seemingly timid graciousness. *What must it be like,* she thought somewhat jealously, *to be so pathologically honest, vulgar, and, well, fearless? God, how vain,* she thought, and figured her interest might only be fueled by the fact that so far he ran in direct opposition to what most men she had met found sacred.

"It's pretty fucking hot." He looked down at her parentally. "Are you okay? One more right and we're there."

"I'm fine." She watched their tall shadows hand in hand upon the sidewalk. "I'm guessing you know Allston pretty well, huh? With your job and all, this city must be like your own backyard."

Zeke grinned and said, "Let's just say I don't have to break out a map all that often."

"The things you must see."

"And each day's completely different from the last."

"Well—"

"I wish I had that. You know?" She looked up at him with this hope. "I mean, I know what you do must be incredibly difficult, but that's gotta be a perk."

"It certainly helps."

"I just find it so interesting."

"Why's that?"

"The challenge of it. And dangerous to boot."

Zeke frowned and said, "It's really not. I mean, it has its moments, but like anything else, it also has a certain flow to it."

"Flow?"

"Yeah. I'm not sure I'm explaining this right, but it's probably like skiing or surfing or whatever. Once you get zeroed in, you become oblivious, and you're only just another part of the rhythms around you."

"Sounds like Zen." She tried to picture it, being surrounded by all that hurtling metal, and almost laughed aloud. "I guess I would be too scared to move."

"Liz, it ain't nothing like that, you know? It's all about position, seeing a spot and taking it before someone else can. And then it becomes a matter of trust. Of course the cabs and trucks and cars behind can kill you. Will they?" He shrugged. "So far so good. It's like a pact, you know? I don't ride like a crazy asshole, and I respect the rules. Whoever gets to a certain spot owns that spot until they switch lanes or stop. Period."

"And if you can't flow with the flow?"

"Then you better get a fucking job at Wendy's and call it good."

She grinned and saw the park up ahead. "Is that it?"

"I know. I'm sorry. As long as it's got grass, I pretty much consider it a park. Just don't fall on any empty bottles or syringes."

Up top, there was a corroded backstop and overgrown baseball field. A handful of miserable kids were throwing rocks at an abandoned car where first base should have been. Heading for the outfield, following him, she snuck furtive glances at his toned calves and tan thighs peeking out from beneath the shorts; the compact backside tightened to the point where she flushed from this possibility. *I work out too*, she thought morosely, and ducked her glance after he turned.

"Good enough." He dropped his bag and bike.

She added her parcel to the stack and watched him whip out the Frisbee.

"You any good at this?" he asked and she almost laughed again, her coordination not exactly something she was in a rush to boast about.

Unslinging her purse, Liz stepped back ten paces and said, "We'll see."

"Here we go." Zeke lofted a floater, which she snagged. Her return throw was a little wobbly but he said, "There it is."

"I like the way you snap it."

"It's all in the wrist. Quick snap and see ya. Here ya go."

He released the Frisbee, which traveled in a straight line toward her chest. Her return, though, sent him running.

"I like this," she said and felt the sun like a bright dot through her sunglasses. "Step back a little farther."

Ten minutes later there was thirty feet between them. Over by first base, she saw the kids had switched from rocks to a baseball bat, smashing at the hapless car.

"Ready?" she called out.

"Bring it. Toss it out in front so I can make a run at it."

"Like this?" She hucked the Frisbee and saw him in full sprint, going behind his back for the catch.

"Showoff!" she shouted, clapping nonetheless. "Let me try that."

"Are you sure?"

"Bring it!"

He led her by fifteen feet, her arms outstretched as she followed it in like a wide receiver in full concentration. Within inches, though, she abruptly tripped, grinding herself into the ground.

He called out, "She goes end-o!" And then, after a pause, "Liz, are you okay?"

She was sitting with her back to him, numbly holding an arm. She knew she did not have to look because the wetness was coldly spreading.

"Liz?"

She jolted when he put a hand on her shoulder, clutching the left arm tightly. Then she looked away. *This is what you get*, she thought. *Please, not like this.*

"I have to go," she said and stood up.

"What is it? Your wrist? I should've warned you. This field ain't exactly too—hey, wait a second. Liz?"

It felt like a fast burning panic as she said, "I'm sorry."

"For what? Liz, at least let me check it out."

Nice try, she bitterly thought, *it's way too late for that*. She was making quickly for her bag of clothes and purse when Zeke caught up.

"I'm sure it's just a sprain," he said, but she was clutching the arm to her chest as if it would otherwise fall off. "Goddamn it," he said and roughly grabbed it.

"Please!" she screamed.

"Hold on. You're fucking bleeding to death."

Her white shirtsleeve was spreading into a field of red as he quickly shoved it up to her elbow and gasped, "What the—"

"No!" She tried pulling away. "Zeke—"

"What is this shit?"

But now she was angry. Embarrassed, humiliated, and determined not to show it—not to *him*, anyway.

"How did this happen?"

As she struggled, she saw him staring dumbly at her forearm, which was filled with scabs, some that ran the entire length of her arm.

"Let me see the other one."

"Zeke—" Unable to stop him, she felt him grabbing her right arm, exposing the same network of wounds.

"What the fuck?"

She busted out of his grip and fled but heard him immediately give chase. Once caught, she fought and kicked until her arms became a lifeless sag. She felt herself turned around and, quietly sobbing into his shoulder, noted the kids were now watching with concern. Sensing him move from confusion to something worse, she knew he would be courageous.

"Who did this to you?"

Like fucking clockwork, she thought, knowing how typical men were. Not wanting to play a role in this drama, she hiccupped and turned away. "I'm sorry about this." She released from the embrace and sat down. In her peripheral vision, she saw him flip off his shirt and rip the bottom six inches into a rag.

"I need to blow my nose," she said and hiccupped again. Removing the now crooked sunglasses, she wiped her eyes and nose with a small piece of shirt.

As if asking permission, he said, "Okay?" then gently lifted her arm.

She waited as he wrapped it, her grief gradually dissipating until it left the two of them in an abandoned outfield surrounded by questions.

"Please," he said. "Talk to me. You're fucking freaking me out."

She did not even know where to start. "I can't …"

"Liz."

"You don't know …"

"No," he quickly said. "You can't say that. Not when it comes to shit like this."

"Don't be so dramatic …"

"Was it your old man?"

Oh God, she thought, but said instead, "Zeke—"

"A boyfriend?"

She dodged his gaze as her bottom lip began to quiver, and the tears spilled freshly over.

"It wasn't anybody." The more she tried to compose herself, the worse it became. *He doesn't fucking get it.*

"You don't have to cover," he said. "Just tell me who it—"

"Me!" she blurted out. "It was me, okay? Now would you please just fuck off!"

She pulled away and this time he offered no resistance, a look of disbelief as he stupidly said, "You? But how?"

She fell over sideways into the grass, sobbing, leaving Zeke to add it all up, the riddle of the constant long-sleeved outfits all the proof she did not now need to offer. It was told in the paralysis of his glance, though, which she caught looking down at the bandaged left arm and the grisly sliced white skin beneath.

"Liz," he said. "Come on. We're gonna get you fixed up."

She felt herself lifted up by the armpits as she immediately fell into his shoulder.

"What did you say?" he asked.

As she peeled away, her blue eyes might have been puffed and tear stained, but their expression was plainly resolute. "This isn't your concern."

"Nothing ever is, right?" He gave her his best smile, forced though it might have been. "Believe me, I've seen worse."

Really.

Liz watched him jog over to reclaim their gear, shouldering the bags as he turned and saw her watching him, the look on her face a purposeful razor across whatever resolve he might think he had in reserve for them both.

Undaunted, he came upon her and put an arm around her shoulder. Allowing herself to be steered towards the street, she quietly said, "Where're we going?"

"My place."

Out on Allston Street, hailing them a cab, Liz felt a familiar fear like a chisel scraping down the day.

The cabbie was Vietnamese and barely spoke English, so Zeke loudly shouted directions. Already disgraced, Liz laid her head against the window, observing the stifling scenery. The bleeding arm was pinned to her chest. *My knight in shining armor*, she thought sarcastically, knowing that this particular wound was little more than a scratch. No one knew anything, except her father, and he lived, had always lived, in a world of work with entire evenings spent speechless in front of the television. From the third grade on, when her mother finally left, Liz was taught to clean, taught to be responsible, and let herself in after school to do chores and homework before eventually being instructed in the kitchen. She remembered relishing the role at first, doing her share for her suddenly abandoned father. Her mother, as Liz recalled, had been a quiet but loving person. As young as she was, Liz could still remember finding her alone most nights in the kitchen, sometimes flipping through a magazine or having coffee, while in the next room the flicker of the television washed the darkened walls. In the months leading up to the end, when Liz would peek around the hall corner even though she should have been in bed, there were no more magazines and a favorite talk radio station remained unlistened to. Her father never raised a fist, nor did he explode verbally in rage. Doing only what he thought was expected, spirit ground to nothing, those around him shrank to supplemental bits of advertisement lost to the surrounding programming.

"It's coming up on the left," Zeke instructed the driver, turning towards her with an empathetic expression. "Two minutes, babe."

Some hero. She gave no answer. Outside, the triple-decker row houses of Lower Allston reminded her of the opening scene from *All in the Family*. *What a disaster*, she morbidly thought, and found her hopes destroyed in a single stroke. *I should've known better. He's gonna put a goddamn Band-Aid on me and send me packing.*

Over the years, during the dozen or so times she got carried away and needed hospitalization, the reactions had varied. Either they were so overwhelmed by her circumstance that the doctors stitched her up and said nothing, or they had her put in restraints in the psych ward on suicide watch, an action that never ceased to amaze her because the actual situation existed completely in reverse.

"This is it," Zeke told the cabdriver.

As they pulled to the curb, Liz stared up at one of the ugliest houses she had ever seen. Painted a startling bright yellow with sagging porches and half-attached gutters, it was the epitome of the term "eyesore." Outside, Zeke pulled his bike from the trunk, paid and thanked the cabbie, and then popped into her window like a trick.

"You good?" he asked, and the thought of what was coming next made her feel even sicker. It was nothing new. Roommates, friends, all those caught by mistake and soundly repulsed, their masks of concern exactly that and easily shattered.

Stepping from the cab, Liz let him shoulder all the bags and bike while she slung her purse and followed him up. At the top, he cursed as he fumbled for the keys, finally yanking clear the two-foot chain snap-locked to his belt.

"Sorry about the mess," he said over a shoulder, and deposited the bike against the wall before dropping the bags onto the couch. As he turned back, she saw him hesitate, glancing at her in the entryway, her expressionless blue eyes and the blood-slicked arm dangling like a threat.

"Let's clean that thing." He seemed clearer with this purpose. "Follow me."

In the bathroom, he set her on the closed toilet seat. Reaching out, he waited until she offered her left arm before gently laying it across the sink. From beneath, he pulled out what looked like a white steel briefcase with a giant red cross decaled on its lid.

"Wow," she said.

"What?"

"That looks pretty official." She nodded at the crowded rows of gauze, instruments, ointments, and bandages of every size. On the sink, he placed a pint bottle of hydrogen peroxide, an antibacterial aerosol can, iodine, a roll of gauze, and tape.

"Should be. I lifted it off a construction site. Hang on. This might stick."

But her sleeve, still moist, slid right up. He blinked when he saw that her entire forearm was different shades of dried blood around the exposed flesh of what looked like a six-inch cut ending near the wrist. Never mind the dozens of other scarred-over pathways; he focused on the newest installment and said, frankly enough, "That's pretty deep."

"So?"

"I could butterfly it, but you'll blow those open in a second."

"Zeke—"

"I could also stitch it."

"You could what?" She hoped her look communicated this impossibility.

"It's not that hard," he said with a shrug. "I got the cat line and eyehook. Fuck, I do it all the time."

"What're you talking about?"

"My job, Liz." Zeke snapped on a pair of latex gloves. "You learn to adapt real quick when the ER costs five hundred just to hit the fucking door."

She frowned and said, "You blow off your worker's comp for that?"

"There's no such thing."

"Oh my God." Liz blinked. "You're kidding, right?"

"This might sting a little." He ran her arm under cold water, gently massaging off the blood. Leaning in as well, she noted a slim layer of fatty tissue like tapioca beneath the skin. A first course of muscle peeked out from deep within the cut like a string of chicken tenderloin. Using both palms, he carefully spread the gash and said, "Hold on."

Her fingers twitched immediately but she bit back against the pain. She saw his fleeting expression, as if somewhat impressed by her tolerance. Veins, arteries, tendons; long practice had maneuvered the blade like a laser within micrometers of each.

"All right," he said and turned off the water. "Here comes the peroxide."

"Great."

Angling her arm down, they watched the diluted pink runoff swirling round the sink.

"Now the antibacterial."

He quickly sprayed the cut and Liz only lowered her head, gasping at the floor while her arm momentarily spasmed.

"That's incredible."

"What?" she meekly asked, eyes red-rimmed again as Zeke shook his head and said, "Believe me, I know. This shit hurts like hell, and you barely moved. That's fucking incredible."

Her arm, though, actually felt as if it had a smoking red-hot poker shoved up inside the marrow. The scene was so ludicrous—the two of them here in this hideously tiled bathroom huddled over the bloody remains of their second date—that she did not know whether to cry or laugh hysterically.

"Moment of truth, babe."

"No offense, Zeke, but I think I'll take the butterflies."

"Whatever."

She watched as he half-peeled six of them, becoming gradually impressed by his systematic demeanor. "I think you missed your calling."

"Don't we all."

"You were kidding before, right? About the stitches? I don't care what you say—I know they don't sell that stuff over the counter. And it's certainly not in any jobsite first-aid kit."

"Yeah, well, you're right."

"So where'd you get it?"

"I know a concerned friend who likes to barter."

Confused, she furrowed her brow and said, "For what?"

Disturbed from his work, he glanced up and gave her a simple look that seemed to say, *Don't know you that well yet.*

"I used to skateboard a lot when I was younger," he said instead, turning back to gently apply a moistening antibacterial gel along the cut. "Phlegm, Kelly, Lotus, Tater Boy, the whole crew. I sucked at first—we all did—but as we got better, board-sliding the rails at Government Center, downhilling through Charlestown, skying crazy 180s, then 360s and blah, blah, blah. We were all like twelve, thirteen, bored out of our tits. Fuck, you know what I'm talking about. You grew up right there."

"Yes." She found herself nodding in agreement. "Lots of street time."

"Exactly." Zeke fully peeled the first butterfly bandage and paused to say, "Anyway, we used to wreck ourselves something awful. Split knees, broken elbows, brain busters, road rash by the acre—cut after cut after cut. It got so bad my pop finally freaked out about the bills and took my board. All right, this might pinch a little." Starting near the elbow, he squeezed the cut and set each side of the butterfly to hold it closed. He then placed two small pieces of tape on each end of the bandage for reinforcement. Peeling back the next, he said, "So one afternoon, like a week later, I ripped my shin wide open on a concrete stair. Kelly and Lotus came up with the bright idea of using fishing line so I wouldn't get in trouble."

"No, sir."

"It got infected as fuck."

"Nice story, Zeke."

He smiled, finishing up with the third bandage and dabbing at the blood boiling up through the seam. "Yeah, we needed some hobbies."

"I just can't believe you have no workers' comp."

"We're 1099. Independent contractors. Hang on. Three more and we're done here."

"And your boss has no group health plan?"

Apparently not wanting to be rude by laughing outright, he simply grinned. "My boss is a businessman."

"And the health of his workers is bad business?"

"Yes." Zeke smoothed the fourth bandage flat. "I mean, who are we kidding? A trained monkey could do what I do."

"Oh my God. I can't believe you just said that."

"Liz, think about the rates on that shit. It would be like a second fucking rent if I went solo. And because of this job, even more for him, if he had the heart. How does this feel so far? Anything pinching?"

"No, sir."

He applied the fifth and sixth in silence. Taking a roll of gauze, he wrapped the arm until it resembled exactly what it was, a half-cast created by a bike courier instead of a doctor.

"Test her out."

Liz lifted her arm, flexing her fingers several times before she said, "Nicely done."

"You sure? If it's wrapped too tight—"

"Zeke …" She put her other hand on top of his. "It's fine."

She saw him look down at the sink, at the swirl of blood and the mess of backing from the Band-Aids. Knowing there was something that must come next, she heard him say, "Stay." And it was towards the sink that he looked, the rejection, if it came, that much easier to deposit. "I've got some cocktails. Doctor's orders."

Liz pulled her hand off his, held the bandaged arm directly under his stare, and said, "Zeke, look at me."

She watched him gather up his nerve to answer her gaze, which he did slowly, panning up the arm and to her eyes which held no hesitation. Gauging its sincerity, she double-checked the green-eyed glance before she said, "I'm not into heroes."

"What does that mean?"

She pulled her arm away, tucking it against herself as she said, "It means that this is mine."

"I know it."

"Entirely and completely."

"Liz, believe me, I'll be the last motherfucker handing down lectures."

She smiled then, pausing a moment. "Okay."

"Cool. Let me clean this up and I'll meet you in the kitchen."

She stood and stepped out into the hall. Flexing her arm once more, she marveled at his finesse before stumbling upon the disaster somehow missed on the way in. The counters and sink were clustered heaps of teetering dishware. A handful of flies buzzed over them like fighter pilots with too many targets. *Just like school,* she thought, recalling some of the more heinous MIT fraternities the women of Simmons College mistakenly frequented.

"Sorry about the mess," he called out from the bathroom. "We don't get many visitors."

"We?"

He entered the kitchen and said, "Yeah, me and my roommate Booger. I think we got two clean glasses somewhere."

As he dug through the cabinets, she said, "What's Booger do?"

"He's a cook." Zeke took down a half-full bottle of gin. "A very large, very drunk cook."

"How nice."

"The house specialty is gin and lemonade. Feeling adventurous?"

"Sure." She caught herself leaning against the counter and involuntarily shuddered. "Where's he work?"

"B.U. West Campus. Hope you don't like ice."

"Why's that?"

"Because our freezer's fucked. I tried chipping out the ice instead of defrosting it and put a screwdriver through one of the coolant lines."

"And you wanted to stitch me up?"

Grinning, he handed her a cocktail and said, "Follow me."

She supposed it was a miracle that the TV room was actually clean. She noted the wall-to-wall blanket of posters and said, "Geez. Some of these groups I've never even heard of." She nodded at the walls and ceiling, where Ozzy Osbourne grinned down at them like the father of dementia. "Is he holding a bat in his teeth?"

"Yep." Zeke gestured towards the sofa as he cranked the window fan onto high. "Luscious breeze."

Joining her on the couch, they clinked glasses in silence. Liz sipped her concoction and said, "Surprisingly good."

"It's all part of my master plan."

"Is it now?" She found herself grinning. "Judging by the condition of your apartment, you couldn't have been all that confident."

"The stink is just part of the overall atmosphere."

"I'm sure it is. The girls must love it."

"They really do. Hey, you wanna hear some tunes?"

"Sure."

He stood and put a mix tape on low. Pounding the rest of his drink, he said, "Uh-oh. I'm empty. Back in a sec. You need anything?"

"Nope." She watched him leave, the alcohol a pleasant hum and, considering this afternoon's disappointment, readily appreciated. *Great, Liz,* she thought, *drinking on a Sunday afternoon.* After his return, she asked, "Who's this?"

"Skinny Puppy." His grin grew broadly. "Too much? I got mellower shit."

"No, it's sort of nice. I think he just screamed out something about cutting off his mother's head."

"What respectable rock star doesn't?"

Scanning the walls, Liz said, "I can't get over all these posters. Did you work in a record store?"

"You know the Rat's Nest Bar? Kenmore Square?"

"Vaguely."

"I worked there for a couple of years."

"When?"

"Hell, I think '90 was my last year? Who knows?"

"Did you bus tables?"

"What?" Zeke looked horrified. "Ah, no. In the beginning, because of my real job, I ran things for VIPs, packages. Eventually I worked in the office. Promos, ticketing, bank ..."

Liz sipped her cocktail. "You're twenty-four now?"

"Yep."

"So you were, like, nineteen when you quit?"

"Something like that. Why?"

"Well, you were just so young is all. Sounds like a lot of responsibility."

"Huh." He lifted his drink. "Things were a lot different back then."

"How so?"

"Let's just say I was kind of rebellious."

Nearly gagging in mid-sip, she quickly coughed into her hand. "I'm sorry. That's pretty funny."

He smiled. "I'm not kidding."

"Well then … what's the difference between then and now?"

"Um …" He gave her a look that politely regarded her ignorance as something of a godsend. "That story we'll save for later."

"Really …"

She watched him nearly kill his drink before she decided to tackle her own. *Keep it up*, she thought, *and you're gonna add puke to that shirtful of blood.* Lowering the glass, Liz scanned her chest and said, "Believe it or not, I just bought this top today."

"I love what you've done with it."

She laughed despite the flush of embarrassment and thought, *I can't believe that's actually funny.*

"You're a sick one, Mr. Zeke."

"So they say."

"Tell me, what's a package for a VIP? You said you ran them."

Zeke shrugged. "Like I said, it's a real long story, Liz."

"Then can you fix me another drink before you start it?" She smiled brightly until he realized his fate. Returning minutes later with two full pints, he sat down beside her, lit a cigarette, and said, "I told you most of it already. After I dropped out, I needed a job. I started on the pedals and after work had nothing to do. I was way into hardcore back then, and the Rat's Nest was one of the few places where the best bands showed up. Well, so did I. I was always trying to weasel inside, spewing lie after lie until finally the door guys took a shine. After that, I was pretty much there every night. And I remember being young enough to think it was like a permanent Christmas, you know, just the coolest place on earth. The owner, this huge Samoan named Ramos, Jamison Ramos, really loved me because I was already inked up and mohawked and pretty soon I guess I became a mascot for the whole place. I didn't have anywhere to really live, so I pretty much couch-surfed.

You've got to remember, I was still a kid, so a few of them really looked out. Especially the waitresses. I always had something to eat, somewhere to crash, blah, blah, blah. Anyway, because of my real job, Ramos found a use for me. Most of the time, I'd be running tickets last minute. Ramos was so cheap, he didn't hold nothing at the door, VIP or not. You wanted in, you paid at the door or had a ticket already. No guest list or waylaid tickets for people who didn't even bother to show. Whatever. But a lot of times I was moving more than that. Bands would hit town, entourages needed feeding, and I'm not talking about food." Zeke tapped his cigarette into an ashtray and said, "Believe me, the stories are endless."

"Sounds like fun."

"It was. There were some great people at that place."

"What made you quit?"

"Things …" Zeke took a long, uncomfortable drag on the cigarette. "Things got a little fucked up elsewhere."

"How so?"

"Anyone ever tell you how nosey you are?"

"All the time." Liz wound some hair around her left ear. "So what happened? You can't leave me hanging like that."

"I was stupid. Got busted freelancing blow." He faked interest in his glass, stubbing at the decal with a thumbnail. "It's funny, but you go through—I guess I should say *I* went through—life thinking I knew who I was until I screwed up and let people, fucking complete strangers, walk into my life and completely destroy it. I know there are laws and all, and I'm not saying what I did didn't deserve it. I'm just saying it will never be allowed to happen again." He shrugged. "It was only three months in Suffolk County, but I got the point; make yourself a target and this is what you get."

"Zeke—"

"I think that's where we should end it." He nearly begged with his eyes. "Seriously, I'm just glad you're here." He raised his glass and she took the hint, sipping her drink as well.

"Can I get one of those?" she asked.

"Sure." Zeke shook another two cigarettes from the pack. The tape ran out so he rose to flip it. When he returned, he sat down beside her and pulled over the ashtray. "Is it too hot in here? I got another fan in my bedroom I can bring in."

"Nope." Liz smacked her lips, the gin and lemonade going down easy. She blew a perfect smoke ring and caught herself feeling quite at home. Crossing her feet on the coffee table, she leaned back and said, "One more of these and I might pass out."

"Nice. And I didn't even have to break out the roofies."

She punched him on the left bicep.

He grinned. "Can't blame a guy for trying."

Exhaling, she gave him a coy smile and said, "One more refill and even you might become attractive."

He laughed immediately. "Nice one."

As they leaned for the ashtray at the same time, she felt it held inside the music and today's near catastrophe. Three drinks in, Liz rode the pulse and sped the green eyes towards collision, which then came next in an awkward clash of lip and tongue before the gentle rhythm found its groove. Blindly struggling to table their drinks, things ratcheted up with both hands free, entangling into pairs like lost mates fiercely reacquainted. She had him by both cheeks before dropping a hand to his chest and then beneath the shirt and onto the sweat-sticky skin. Given the green light, Zeke did the same, running a finger up her arm and across the gauze before snaking away from sight. She began pulling off his shirt before he gulped, finally breaking away. "Liz, listen, today was pretty intense. And we're both kind of ginned up—"

"Zeke." She could see he felt stupid, until he glanced up to where she waited, and they kissed again before tugging off each other's shirts.

Almost panting, Zeke said, "Come on."

She was led by her good arm as they practically jogged into his room, where he found her again, kicking closed the door. Liz felt deliciously overwhelmed until she launched her own offensive, backing him into the wall as if escape was not an option. He was a good kisser, and even better at the sleight of hand, because she found her bra already bunched at the wrists before letting it fall towards the floor. She opened her eyes, seeing his close immediately, the full investigation of her body something he was not quick enough to hide. Knowing it was out of her control allowed her not to care at all as she decided he had met his match. She slowly disengaged, her tongue trailing down his cheek to caress the chin before his neck became her feast. Hearing him groan, her hand searched for denim and the bulge she had created, worked, the buttons popping open like doors sprung in greeting. Descending, her tongue encountered both nipples before he shivered and the boxer shorts and shorts as well, lost amid the scuffle. Face to face, she gently teased the tip with lips and tongue until he groaned again, her hand a comfortable grasp about the shaft. It was not something she always did, but when he warned her some minutes later, his caution proved unnecessary. Drinking him in, loving the fact that she was the cause of this spasm, she felt herself pulled to her feet.

"Let me get some water—"

She was not allowed to finish. He was on her now, practically tossing her onto the bed as her laugh caused him to grin like a carnivore set to pillage, which he then did, diligent with his touch. Gently spreading her with his tongue, she felt a finger rhythmically prodding and massaging before his wet lips clamped down. Seeking the spot, he found her until she squeaked and panted and panted and yelped and minutes later it was just his tongue lapping at her tremors. Staring at the ceiling, her cheeks were flushed and moist. She felt that part of him nudge like a hint, so she spread her legs without hesitation, watching in the awkward space as the intimacy became suspended in the fumbling formality of a torn-open packet. Guiding him in, she hung onto his gaze as both hungrily smiled, as if together they had discovered this incredible expression which now seemed theirs alone to perfect.

When late afternoon came, she had his arm around her waist while feeling the gentle exhale of his sleep against the back of her neck. Liz blinked, slowly caressing his hand. Taking a moment to gather it all in, she grinned, thinking, *That* was pretty ladylike.

She wished he was awake to hear it. *He's dragging me down to his level*, she thought and almost laughed out loud. Compared to what became expected, she felt a slow fear gather as a voice gleefully said, *Pity fuck. That's all it was.*

And if so? In the great cosmic balance, when it came down to what and who and how many instances she would have, there could be no more apologies.

Her shoulder began to ache, so Liz rolled over and found his green eyes open. Momentarily self-conscious, she glanced down and found their nakedness somewhat appealing. As she realized this, delicately running a hand over the smooth rise of his naked hip, she wondered at the comfort near strangers could provide, inside moments, when what was now became forgotten.

Chapter Five

Monday, July 25

JUST AFTER 6:30 AM, stopping his bike on the Cambridge Street overpass, Zeke jammed a toe into the chain-link fence for support. Below, three inbound lanes of the Massachusetts Turnpike limped sadly along. *Must be an accident ahead*, he thought, while sipping a bodega-bought coffee. Behind him, from out over the Atlantic, an already fierce sun stained the horizon like a bloodshot eye.

Lighting a cigarette, he balanced on his seat killing time until Stuart Rigby paged him with the morning inbounds. Since her departure by cab an hour before, he had been thinking of Liz Downs and yesterday and what was now between them. He took a long drag. On some level, it was still simply incomprehensible. Reworking the point of view, he tried to imagine dragging a razor or knife through his own body and could not empathize in the least. Even half awake, his mind was sponging in the details of this new reality, and what cost his share of it would now be. *A cutter*, he thought, and decided it would take something that fucked up to make Cammi Sinclair's psychosis actually preferable.

Remembering how he had awakened to see her quietly dressing in the dark, he now found himself craving her absurdly. She had said thanks for everything and to call her and he was surprised, after and despite all of his own quick fades, that being used never felt quite so good. Smiling at the recollection, he called himself a girl, took another drag, and wondered where the fuck Stuart was with his page.

The smile ended when he thought of the day ahead. On deck was an unavoidable skirmish with Cammi Sinclair, another hundred-degree scorcher, and a city full of assholes playing dodgeball with his life. As if on cue, his beeper abruptly sang out. Tossing the half-full coffee cup into the gutter, he pulled in one last drag, flicked the smoke over the railing, and thought, *Welcome to Monday.* Rolling up on an empty pay phone near the corner, he picked up the receiver and the number nearly dialed itself.

"Good morning. Split Minute."

"Stuey."

"Richie! It's luscious Zachariah on the phone! Hi, Zeke, and how was your weekend?"

"Too good to last."

"Well, we were just sitting here having our morning café and wondering if you would be so kind as to pick up at Foster, 1032 Comm. Ave. #5, going to Fennimore Developing, 320 Mass. Ave., also pick up at Kenmore Dentistry, they've got three X-rays heading downtown to Mass. General, and then …" Stuart flipped through the dispatcher sheets. "And then let's go to our old friends at Hazard with a deuce heading to Ferrelly Publishing, 145 Oliver."

Zeke finished writing out the three tickets as he said, "Leftovers?"

"Yes, Zeke. If you hadn't taken a half-day on Friday, maybe these would've already been delivered."

"Don't tell me your problems."

Stuart tittered quietly and said, "Now, now. Let's not be jaded. Could you also be so kind as to tell Cammi—"

"I'm not at home."

"What? Where are you?"

"Corner of Cambridge and Harvard Ave."

"And where is she?"

"Don't know." Zeke coughed up a ball of mucus. "Haven't seen her."

"Oh dear." Stuart Rigby sounded concerned. "Are the two of you still circling inside this dance of death?"

"No comment."

"Richie! I owe you ten bucks!"

"Stuart—"

"This should be an interesting day," Stuart mused. "Should I tell her to fuck off for you? Or maybe I can tell you to fuck off for her—that way we can get this out of the way."

"Yeah, fuck me."

Stuart purred like a cat and said, "Zeke, you devil you. What will Richie say?"

"Stu—"

"I've been waiting for those magical words to come from your luscious lips since—"

"Stuart!"

Chuckling suggestively, Stuart Rigby said, "You're on the speaker phone, Zeke-a-licious, and Richie looks sooo jealous."

"Hi, Zeke," Richard Parks deadpanned in the background. "Don't pay any attention to this little fairy. He's had too much coffee already."

"I don't know how you do it, Richie."

Richard Parks audibly sighed. "It's just not easy, Z."

"Well, God bless you, buddy. Tell fairy boy I'll call him from Kenmore unless otherwise paged."

"Sure thing, Zeke."

"Hey!" Stuart Rigby screamed. "I am not a fairy boy! Do either one of you see any wings on my back!"

"Good-bye, Stuart."

"Zeke! I've got my tongue—"

Hanging up, Zeke closed and stored the contractor case before pointing his bike towards Commonwealth Avenue. Because of the ever-present humidity and soaring temperatures, summer mornings usually found the dewy streets coated with a stink somewhere in between old gym shoes and unwashed armpits. Up ahead, the light was his, so Zeke took the outside line on a tight left turn inches from the curb.

He arrived at 1032 Commonwealth, a modest nondescript four-floor walk-up. With nowhere convenient to lock up, he hoisted the bike to shoulder height and wedged the U-bar Kryptonite around a tapered lamppost column. Adjusting his pack, he hopped the stairs to a door with a single buzzer next to a slot with no name. After depressing the button, he took out a piece of gum while the tiny camera overhead relayed shots of his arrival. When the lock finally disengaged, he pushed through to another door where a large, immaculately, dressed black man awaited with a benign expression.

"Hey, Ronnie."

"Zeke." Ronald Dunlap slapped Zeke's hand. "What up, kid? You tear it up this weekend or what?"

"Fuck. Tried to."

"Right on."

"Am I heading up or staying put?"

"They're finishing up right now." Ronald Dunlap re-engaged the three deadbolts, clicked on the alarm, and turned for the stairs. "After you," he said.

Zeke's Specializeds clacked up the wood staircase to a second floor with a single door and nothing else. Ronald Dunlap produced a key and a second later they strode into what looked like a huge studio apartment. The setting and decor, Zeke knew, changed day to day. Currently, a four-poster Victorian bed stood in front of a blue wall. Around it, at intervals, were lighting stands, microphones, and cameras with separate technicians servicing each. The windows were draped over and duct-taped. To the left, Zeke saw a handful of women in various stages of undress around a table crowded with coffee and donuts. To the right, a muscle-bound white man with a blond ponytail sat naked in a chair reading the *Globe* sports page as a fluffer girl readied his tree stump-sized cock.

"Want some Joe?"

"What?" Confused, Zeke looked at Ronnie, who grinned and said, "Coffee, Z."

"Yeah, sure. For a second I thought you were talking about—"

"Naw, man." Ronald Dunlap laughed and said. "Besides, his name's Johnny. Johnny Nine Iron. Dude's got a sixteen-inch prick."

"Hope these chicks got health insurance."

Ronald Dunlap grinned, heading for the coffee table. "Excuse us, ladies."

Trying not to be a pervert, Zeke nonetheless found himself harvesting the sights, the spectrum of the rainbow represented by a pretty Asian, two blondes, and an incredibly well-endowed black woman who, although she got paid for much worse, cinched her robe tighter until Zeke finally looked elsewhere. Handing Zeke a cup, Ronald Dunlap said, "Arnell should be out in a sec. Have a seat."

Which Zeke did, slinging his bag to the floor. Watching the others working around him, he inevitably returned to yesterday's macabre revelation, wondering at its cause. Shading away from disgust, he began to see the act as something much deeper, like a form of tribal mutilation. He remembered lying next to her in bed, his finger tracing along the raised hieroglyphic scabs rendered with such care. He had found worse between her breasts, where the seams became an uncountable pile of snakes. *So much damage,* he had thought, knowing as well that she was right. From where this urge might come, and to what end it attained, he was nothing more than a clueless bystander fascinated by someone else's reason why.

Distracted, Zeke saw a thin man with a frazzled expression check each camera, consult his clipboard and yell, "Okay, let's have Sandra and Monique and Johnny, please. Let's go, we're almost on schedule here."

A blonde and the Asian approached the bed as Johnny Nine Iron tossed aside the paper and strode towards them with a swinging boner and a nonchalance that almost caused Zeke to burst out laughing. A technician moved in with a lighting gauge as the participants arranged themselves. The fluffer girl resumed her duties as a door opened to reveal Arnell Stepps yelling at a subordinate. With long gray-streaked black hair and a near permanent squint from years behind the camera, Arnell Stepps was, Zeke knew, like Lane DeSanto of Graphic Art, just another hard-luck-story-turned-millionaire. Having started with an 8mm camera twenty years earlier, Arnell Stepps had gone from independent films to documentaries until stumbling upon the fertile, highly competitive and financially rewarding avenue of hardcore pornography. Over fifteen years, SubLife Films had blossomed into one of the largest mail-order adult film distributors on the East Coast. And while Arnell Stepps was busy transforming himself into a pornographic institution, he was also a successful businessman who happened to be gay, a precarious combination that left him actively involved in all the various social and political responsibilities men of his position do not take for granted. This was how he met Stuart Rigby a decade before, at a rally trying to raise funds for the hospitalization of a man beaten nearly to death in a predominately homosexual part of the South End.

"Ronald! Is he here yet?"

Zeke grabbed his contractor case and stood up. As he always did upon entering, Zeke let his eyes travel the walls across the B-film-like-posters filled with scantily clad people fondling cartoon-sized body parts under appropriate titles, such as *For Whom the Balls Toll* and the widely regarded Arnell Stepps classic, *Forrest Pump*. Otherwise, besides a huge mahogany desk and antique Greek furniture, the office was as sparse as the smile Arnell Stepps proffered as Zeke said, "Hey, Mr. Stepps."

"Zeke," rolling his eyes, Arnell Stepps batted a hand, exasperated. "Arnell. My name is Arnell. This obsession with manners for someone in your profession is quite frankly remarkable."

"Yeah, well, I'm a real go-getter."

Arnell Stepps smiled broadly, his eyes puffy and ringed from the all-nighter he was minutes away from completing. The black shirt was opened to the waist, his cut chest and stomach tightened vainly to perfection. As the plain blue eyes found his own, Zeke decided the unnerving sensation came from the curious observation Arnell Stepps seemed to unleash equally, in both life and work, upon those he encountered. *Like being catalogued,* Zeke thought, returning the concentrated gaze Stepps abruptly broke by saying, "And how's our delightful friend Stuart?"

"Demented as always."

"Excellent. Zeke, say hello to Aphrodite. She's my new secretary."

Zeke nodded at an attractive brunette who did not return the gesture. "Why's she sitting in your chair?"

"Ah, Zeke." Arnell Stepps batted another hand. "Who is ever really in charge?" He nodded at a bulging manila envelope on the desk. "If you would be so kind, *Monsieur* Zeke, to inform our Mr. Rigby that that is a priority round trip. I've got a return ready after one hour."

Zeke noted the essentials on a slip, which he then handed Stepps for a signature as Zeke said, "Might not be me, though. Stu's loading me up for downtown."

Arnell Stepps gave him a wry look, handed back the contractor case along with a twenty-dollar bill, and said, "I'm sure you'll be able to work something out."

Ever the capitalist, Zeke said, "Gimme two hours. Monday mornings're always fucked."

"Done."

Taking the package, Zeke detached the receipt, shook Arnell Stepps' hand, and said, "You need to get some sleep."

"Do I look that good?"

"Fuck …"

"They're coming after me, Zeke." Arnell Stepps looked out through the window and shrugged as if nothing else could be expected. "I won't trivialize it, but sometimes I think I'm going to be in court forever."

"Huh …" Zeke shifted his feet.

"Do you know about the subject I speak of?"

"Only rumors." Zeke pursed his lips. "Gossipy bullshit—you know."

"I do."

"Besides, there isn't anything they can do to you."

"If only that were true."

"Truth?" Zeke raised an eyebrow. "Seems to me, the truth is what the best attorneys eat for breakfast."

Arnell Stepps folded his arms and squinted. "You may be right, but when it comes to a person's name, especially in the business I provide, lurid rumor and hideous innuendo feed the hounds."

"I hear ya."

"Zeke, please tell Stuart I said hello."

"Absolutely."

"See you in two hours."

Pulling the door closed, Zeke saw the bedside combatants still readying themselves in final preparation. The Asian was applying lotion to her own breasts as the fluffer girl, robotically stroking the Nine Iron, stared at his penis as if no other analogy could better sum up her life. Storing the parcel, Zeke shouldered his bag as Ronald Dunlap met him at the door.

"I like that suit, Ronnie."

"No shit?" Ronald Dunlap flapped the lapel. "Half price, B. Brooks Brothers."

"Sweet."

Dunlap followed Zeke downstairs.

"I'm usually a big fan of naked chicks," Zeke said, "but at seven o'clock in the morning …"

"After all night too." Ronald Dunlap popped the gum he was chewing. "I tell ya, Z, it all just blurs together—titties and all."

"I guess it must."

"There ain't nothing I ain't seen. No hole I ain't seen plugged half a million different ways."

"Jesus ..."

"It's fucked."

"I bet your friends think you're the pimp of all pimps."

"Man, if they just knew the half of it."

Zeke stepped aside so Dunlap could disengage the alarm and locks.

"You still got the same cell?" Zeke asked, wiping his sunglasses before sliding them home.

"Yep."

"I'll ring you on the return."

"Check it."

Heading for his bike, Zeke forced himself to think of his next stop instead of porno actors and moist holes and, in its growing importance, the face of Elizabeth Downs. Already jammed with hurtling metal, Commonwealth Avenue was in full commute mode and stalking the single instant when lapsed judgment might leave one smashed across the street. Gearing down, he checked left and white-lined the middle lane, whipping through the usually pedestrian-filled minefield of Boston University. The light was his, so Kenmore Square flashed by until he hit the brakes and leapfrogged two lanes towards the curb. Kenmore Dentistry Associates was in the last building on the left, and when Zeke re-emerged minutes later, his bag remained open to accommodate the three X-rays headed for Massachusetts General Hospital. Five minutes after that, he was locked up outside the Jessica Hazard Modeling Agency on Newbury Street. In the front door alcove, Zeke rang the buzzer until a familiar voice tiredly said, "Hazard Inc."

"Hey, Cherise."

"That you, Zeke?" the voice sighed. "Is it unbearable out there yet?"

"It's on the way."

"God, it's been so hot these last few weeks."

"Yes, it sure has."

"I suppose you want to come up."

"Not unless you want to throw the package out the fucking window."

"No, I don't think Linda would like that."

The lock disengaged with a singing clatter as Zeke pushed through and jogged upstairs to the lobby where Cherise Maxwell, as Zeke soon saw, once again struggled beneath another long night's wreckage. Huddled over the omnipresent coffee mug like a battered survivor, she gave him a weak smile that candidly echoed this disease.

"Don't even say it."

"Didn't have to." Reaching back, he found the contractor case and said, "But, Jesus, Cherise …"

"What did I just say?"

"I know it."

She watched him as if this admission was too easy. The lectures had recently been coming from all quarters. Roommates, friends, family, even former colleagues from her days in front of the camera, whose own cannibalistic motives and homogenized sincerity belied the pleasure they found watching an aspiring competitor self-destruct. Yet, by exercising the same stubbornness that had fueled her rise, Cherise Maxwell was likewise losing her life, a proposition only faced when someone equally as obstinate said, as Zeke did now, "You look like the ass end of a bad April Fools' joke."

"Fuck you, Zeke." She shook her head as if amazed. "Like you've got any room to talk shit?"

"Hey, I ain't lecturing—"

"'The ass end of a bad April Fools' joke.'" Cherise scratched her chin in mock deliberation. "Hmmm, what exactly does that mean? Are you telling me you're concerned because you're my friend?"

"Cherise—"

"You know what? I'm not even listening to you anymore."

Blinking, he refocused on filling out the slip.

"You're right," he said without looking up. "I shouldn't be talking shit. I spent half the weekend in a sling."

"I know."

"What?"

"I ran into your friend Lotus Saturday night. He said the two of you got wrecked on Friday at the Chamber."

"Dear God, did we." Zeke smiled, handing her the case for a signature as he said, "We're a couple of classy guys."

"The *Chamber*, Zeke? I mean how cheesy can you get? A bunch of wannabe hookers dancing in cages?"

"Well, as they say, one man's art is another man's porno."

"Really." Despite her splitting headache and volatile innards, Cherise Maxwell grinned sarcastically. "You an art buff now too, Zeke?"

"Who isn't?"

"Here." Disgusted, she handed back the case. "Tubes are in the corner."

Spotting them, Zeke passed her desk as she said, "What's in those huge envelopes?"

"X-rays."

"Really?" She abruptly sounded intrigued. "Can I see them?"

"*What?*"

"Please, Zeke?"

"Don't be a weirdo." Squatting down, Zeke double-checked the addresses before storing the three-foot cardboard tubes. "Besides, they're dentals. Just a bunch of teeth."

"How cool."

"If you say so."

"What's the strangest thing you've ever carried?"

Zeke frowned, pondering. "Huh. I once carried an engagement ring and proposal. I also picked up some guy's toupee from a girlfriend who was dumping him. But I guess the weirdest thing was fish."

"Are you kidding me?"

"Nope." Zeke reslung his bag and stood up. "Some grandpa guy sent a bag of them to his grandkid in Cambridge."

"A bag full of live fish? How sweet."

"Yep. False teeth, purses left somewhere the night before, an urn full of ashes—"

"No way."

"Yep. Feldspar Funeral Home used to be one of our regulars. Not for ashes, obviously. That only happened twice."

"Gross."

"And one guy downtown was so lazy he'd have the morning paper dropped off. Which, by the time we were done with him, used to cost him seven dollars."

"Why didn't he just get it delivered?"

"Because rich people are stupid."

"Zeke …"

Shrugging the load to center on his back, he said, "Who knows? He said he was in and out of town on business."

"Imagine that." Cherise Maxwell shook her head in wonderment. "Thirty-five dollars a week for the paper."

"Hey, can you ring Stuart real quick?"

Cherise hit one button and handed Zeke the phone.

"Split Minute."

"Zeke at Hazard heading for Fennimore."

"Nothing right now, Zeke-a-licious. Make the drop and head on into my waiting arms!"

"Yep."

Cherise took the receiver and cradled it before sipping her coffee and scanning him from over the brim. He caught her intense look before he uncharacteristically turned for the stairs without another word.

"Hey. Hey, Zeke," she said, and he stopped with one hand on the railing. "Maybe it's not so bad."

Wondering if she actually believed it, he could not look her in the eye. "I'm sure it's not." Digesting his own lie, he lost all heart and said, "Be cool, Cherise," before stepping down and away and into where the rest of Monday might take him.

Outside, the humidity was already an unpleasant shroud around the scowl Zeke could not contain. Unlocking his bike, he pushed it all from his mind, checked left, and cursed his luck as the light ahead went instantly red.

———————————

Having dropped the Foster roundtrip, with no new pickups, Zeke headed for the office to dump Friday's receipts. Passing the overwrought extravagance of the Christian Science Center, he banged left on Huntington Avenue and hit the straightaway at top speed. The Hynes Convention Center and the towering Prudential Building flew past as Zeke saw the green light and floored it. Huntington ended at Dartmouth Street, and as he blew through the intersection onto St. James, he crossed lanes and jumped the opposite curb. After locking up, he hit the front door and saw the lobby clock read 7:36 AM. On the eighth-floor, entering Split Minute, he headed towards the back office where Stuart Rigby was apparently holding court. Richard Parks and Father Time were seated across from Stuart, who was all fingers and phones.

"Hey," Zeke said, pulling up another chair between them.

"Good morning again, Zeke," Richard Parks said. "Coffee?"

"No thanks." Slinging his bag to the floor, Zeke nodded at Father Time, who was already wearing one of his patented frowns. With graying lamb-chop sideburns, sun-worn skin, and an attitude even worse than Zeke's, Donald Parsons had been pushing pedals for almost sixteen years. A dishonorably discharged navy veteran who had been a baker before his pastry shop burned down, Parsons had been at Split Minute nearly since its inception. And while the effects of age may have slowed him to the point where Stuart basically kept him in one zone downtown, Zeke knew Donald Parsons was taken care of, handed plum assignments, and allowed to work the dispatcher position when Stuart wanted a three-day weekend or long lunch. And in a destabilized profession marked by chaos and almost constant employee turnover, where work ethic and five-day riders were as rare as a complaint-free day, Zeke was not sure which was worse—the fact that he and Father Time got along so well or that one day soon he himself might be pushing forty years of age on a goddamn bicycle. Which was the funniest part of all. In a world of thirty-five hundred dollar mountain bikes and spike-haired posers, Donald Parsons could usually be found in crumbling denim shorts and K-mart helmet wobbling through intersections on a twenty-year-old Schwinn while screaming at jaywalkers as he pushed the envelope at five miles per hour. Just thinking of it now caused Zeke to swallow a grin he was not quite yet, at least at this ungodly hour, prepared to share.

"FT." Zeke held out a hand. "How they hanging?"

"Wet and stuck to my leg." Parsons let a smile escape through an equally overgrown mustache. "If Mary here would get off the phone, maybe we could make some money."

"Amen."

"Yes, sure thing, Mr. Turnell." Stuart Rigby snapped his fingers at Donald Parsons. "Pickup at 270 Washington, going to 10 Chauncy. We'll be right over … Uh-huh, bye-bye now." Stuart hung up and said, "Did you get all of that, *gramps?*"

"Yes, Stuart." Parsons quickly scribbled out the proffered information.

"Sure? Maybe you should turn up your hearing aids."

"I sold them for crack." Donald Parsons smiled wickedly.

"And you …" Stuart swung his gaze onto Zeke and snapped his fingers. "Got my Friday?"

"Right here." Zeke slapped down two dozen slips. "Got four on me for downtown and the Foster's now a roundtrip for a 9:30 return."

"Damn it." Stuart nibbled a lip as he made a note on the dispatcher sheets. "Did you speak with A.S.?"

"Yeah." Zeke leaned back and crossed his legs. "They were in between fucks when I got there."

"And how is he?"

"Frazzled." Zeke shrugged. "Who wouldn't be?"

"Did you see yesterday's *Herald?*"

"Nope."

"I saw it." Donald Parsons chuckled enthusiastically. "Sounds like he's gonna make a lot of new friends in prison."

"Donald!" Stuart Rigby clutched a hand over his heart. "How can you say that about such a dear friend of ours?"

"Who said I had any friends?"

Stuart Rigby sipped coffee, nodded his head, and said, "Point taken. Zeke, take a good look at this old frumpy-dumpy little fireplug of a man and make sure you never let yourself go, you sweet, delicious, chocolate-coated, ass-cheeked—"

"Stu …"

"Oh, sorry, Richie." Stuart winked at Zeke while Zeke was picking at his nose. "I do like them young, ain't that right, Zeke?"

Making sure Stuart saw it, Zeke smeared the snot beneath the armrest and said, "What?"

"Gross, Zeke."

"Were those chicks really sixteen?"

Glancing back at Parsons, Stuart said, "What're you babbling about now, *gramps?*"

"Arnell. The paper said that's what the indictment—"

"Now, now, Donald, no client gossiping."

"Me?" Parsons grinned.

"He's fucked." Zeke leaned forward to reload his case with fresh slips from the giant stack on Stuart's desk. "Three counts of child endangerment, accessory to statutory rape, exploitation of a minor—"

"Zeke, please." Stuart held up a hand. "Nobody knows who's telling the truth. Besides, eighteen, sixteen, a whore's a whore."

"Yeah, I'm sure the jury will see it like that."

When Richard Parks grunted his concurrence, Stuart quickly turned on him and said, "Don't be agreeing with the help!"

"Independent contractor," Zeke said, standing up. "Help is for the helpless."

"And what do you think you are?"

"Hopeless, not helpless." Zeke put his sunglasses back on, reslung the bag over an already damp shoulder, and said, "I'll call from Oliver."

With one last glance at his sheets, Stuart Rigby frowned and said, "I wish I had more going. No matter. I'll let grandpa stew here a while longer before sending his geriatric ass downtown with any *freshies*."

"Whatever."

"Wait, Zeke, I almost forgot. Where, pray tell, is your better half?"

"What're you talking about?"

"Take one guess."

"Fuck, man, you got me." He gnawed a lip, somewhat concerned. "For real? She ain't even called?"

"Nope."

"I think that's a first."

"Let me know if you hear from her, please. Currently, I'm as concerned as I am pissed off and not sure when I'll be more of one than the other."

"Right, Stuart." Donald Parsons sneered sarcastically. "I'm sure she's real worried."

"As you all should be!" Stuart extended an arm and swung it like a sword. "Any one of you could be next out that door!"

Donald Parsons laughed as Zeke shook his head and said, "A trained gerbil could do this fucking job."

"Then maybe that's what I'll do! Gerbils on bikes instead of listening to this insolence!"

Heading for the door, Zeke called out, "Gerbils have more than one use then, huh, Stu?"

"Zeke! Come back here! I'll show you my own gerbil, you sweet little man-pleaser!"

Hearing the roomful of laughs, Zeke pushed out the front door, elevatored down, and as he walked towards his bike, thought of Cammi Sinclair against every impulse that he owned.

Chapter Six

Saturday, October 21

LIZ HEARD THE SMOKE alarm before he did and so nudged him from behind. Gurgling as he rolled over, Zeke awoke and said, "What …?"

She smiled, watching him blink sleep-puffed eyes in confusion. Naked, slinking deeper beneath the comforter, she nodded towards his bedroom door and said, "I think the house is burning down."

"Great." He swung both legs to the floor, belched, and stood to readjust his boxers. Swinging open the door, gray smoke unrolled across his face and he coughed, fanning uselessly at the tumult.

"Booger!"

"Sorry, man." Booger's giant head popped into the doorway. "Hey, Liz."

"Hi, Brian."

"All right, all right, enough." Zeke winced through the haze, abruptly shoving his roommate. "What the fuck, man, she's naked."

"Nice!" Booger, miraculously, seemed hangover-free this morning. His blue eyes were clear and twinkled with mischief as he feigned barging in but met Zeke's shoulder instead.

Zeke nodded towards the kitchen and asked, "What the hell's going on?"

"Torched a crepe. Hope you two are hungry."

"In a minute." Zeke closed the door and opened the window. Turning around, he caught her there, the head cleanly sliced at the neck by the comforter, the brown hair a spilt tossed circle on the pillow framed behind.

"Zeke?"

"Yeah, baby."

He dove headlong across the mattress, chewing at her neck until she squealed. Morning breath forgotten, they kissed and groped, groped and grinned, and soon after Liz straddled him while feeling for position. As they were grabbing one another, she unwrapped it, then wrapped him, slowly descending while his eyes rolled back before her own did the same and she became a piston bearing down upon him.

Afterwards, collapsed into the nook of his shoulder, she felt his touch somewhat oddly tracing between her breasts until she was unnerved enough to say, "Stop."

But he could not, because this latest edition was particularly atrocious. It began near the top of her left breast and hugged its downward curve. It was not sliced or thinly injured, but instead shallowly hacked into a crusted zipper-like formation. There were times, she knew, when this sight, even through the hottest passion, left him both concerned and repulsed without the heart to hide it. Or it was that they were drunk or it was dark and what he could not see did not matter until something happened, like what was happening right now and, reaching for a Kleenex, he quietly said, "Baby, you're … it's bleeding again."

"Gimme that." Clamping it to her chest, Liz saw what might have been a pained expression and knew from experience that when it came to others' involvement or even their opinion, her own sanity came first. Among her ex-boyfriends, there was Oscar Lopez, an intern at her old job, who smothered her with such concern that the mere sight of him caused her to shudder claustrophobically. Or Dennis Laugherty, a bartender she dated for a month before shedding her shirt one steamy night when he told her it did not bother him, which was apparently the truth because he then practically raped her between slaps to the face and, once finished, he slapped her again and said he liked the freaks. It was, she knew, a dangerous feeling being here next to him now and so completely at ease. She was staunching a bleeding scab in his own bed and he was actually helping hold the Kleenex.

"Hey." There came a knock at the door as Booger said, "Stop humping and let's eat."

"On the way." Zeke propped his head onto his hand, looking at her directly. "Hungry? You know Booger and his crepes."

"I do." Peeling away the bloody clump for closer inspection, she found the situation in hand and said, "For someone with his talents, I can't believe he cooks at West Campus."

"Tell me about it." Zeke stood and tossed her his bathrobe. "Fucking kid was a French-trained superstar before he became a drunk."

"I heard that!" Booger yelled.

"Dormitory food for college brats." Zeke shook his head while yanking on sweatpants. "At least we're both wasting our lives together."

"Zeke." She threw him a look.

"It's a joke."

She cinched the robe tight, fluffing at her sleep-strewn hair in the mirror. He made a move for the door and she soon heard him and Booger exchanging raucous insults.

Nudging a thick book with her foot, she sat back down on the bed, looped some hair behind her left ear, and hoisted the tome onto her lap. It had come as a surprise over dinner last night, and after one too many chardonnays, she had been too drunk when they returned home to investigate these claims. She remembered they had been speaking about the future and how she had seen a picture of herself in the near present re-enrolling at Simmons College. Having worked in an architecture office these last six months, surrounded by what pencil on paper could create out of concrete and steel, she judged the entire process to be both necessary and worthwhile, dreaming up where others might live and work in tomorrow's somewhere else. After she had finished telling him this, she had said, "What about you?" And, characteristically, he wrote off this next part of his life with a dismissive shrug before realizing that she was waiting, and realizing also she might be saying, no matter how surprising these past few months had been, whatever developed eventually had to stand for something.

"I like taking pictures," he had said before glancing away, embarrassed.

And here they were, in four giant albums stacked inside his closet. Thumbing through the nearest, she saw the layout to be in no particular order, the composites in both color and black-and-white, the subject matter fiercely eclectic. Pictures of churches and historic landmarks, parks and street corners overrun with tourists in ridiculous garb, headlights blurring along Storrow

Drive, and a shot of an alley where ambulance lights played disco with the night. Other couriers in various poses, a child crying disconsolately, and an elderly man whose furrowed face reminded Liz of a grinning, wrinkled Shar Pei puppy. Shots of blizzards, a man sleeping in a cardboard box; an exhausted female participant vomiting curbside during the Boston Marathon. A Back Bay brownstone fire blazing into the night; sunsets facing Cambridge; a single Harvard eight-man crew boat sculling through the dawn. She saw lead singers screaming, crowds writhing, and photos of friends pulling bongs and much worse. There was a shot of a political rally at the State House as a man with a bullhorn and veins near bursting became frozen in time forever. She also found an inordinate amount of photographs of one female in particular who could be seen time-lapsed through the years: her in bed, her in the kitchen, her giving the camera the finger half a dozen times, her smiling and holding up a sign which said, OUR FIRST PLACE; her at Christmas opening presents beneath a single tree branch shoved into a forty-ounce beer bottle somehow strung with lights. She came and went, this new face Liz did not know but now jealously feared, for where was this, this *exhibitionist* now?

Regardless, as the last page turned, she decided it was a story told by random urges, the camera like a bat swung blindly. Realizing she was no expert, he seemed adept at catching nondescript people at inexact moments, and if that was not the precise definition of freelance photojournalism, it was at least a point towards which to aim. Outside the ridiculous risks he daily tempted, it just seemed so malicious, because he wasn't stupid or undisciplined or afraid of forging his own way. After their second date, when she almost let a simple game of Frisbee destroy what the last three months never would have been, they were no longer new to each other and had progressed this far, thankfully, without those horrible games.

Except his past. There was nothing there. She knew little more than she ever had, which was basically nothing. Piecing together a timeline of coincidences, there was his move to Allston somewhat coinciding with his mother's death and the older brother he pathologically avoided discussing. It was as if his life had begun twenty minutes before he walked through her employer's door and a day later asked her out. Yet if she complained, there would always be that day in his bathroom, her clutching the freshly bandaged arm and practically telling him he need not ever ask. By doing so, she had set a clear precedent that each could now abstain from what it was that made any achievement or relationship even worth a damn.

"Liz!"

"Yes?" She placed the book down with a thud. Her feet were freezing, so she pulled on socks. Glancing at the condom wrappers scattered about the floor, she recognized the paraphernalia of the junkie she'd become. Striding in from the kitchen, Zeke held out a glass of orange juice and said, "Why're you smiling?"

"No reason." She gulped a mouthful, grinning at him as if he might be her next meal.

"Easy, killer." He tweaked her left boob through the robe. "Guess it's true what they say."

"What's that?"

"It's always the quiet ones …"

She laughed and took his hand as he pulled her into the kitchen where Booger, in boxer shorts and a T-shirt that said Budweiser Men's Bikini Team, worked his magic at the stove. Taking a seat at the counter, Liz watched Booger ignite brandy in a saucepan.

Zeke set out three plates and silverware before turning back to clean a pot-filled sink. Seeing them busily attending to their duties, Liz thought it almost comedic, the lumbering giant and his surly accomplice in domestication. Despite his size, Booger was basically harmless save for the fact that he was a horrendous alcoholic. On more than one occasion, at the point where they might be turning off the lights, Booger's arrival home became a symphony of miscellaneous thuds and crashes, TV or stereo cranked way too loud. It was then that Zeke would curse and grab a towel to cover his nakedness before standing in the door to curse again and yell, but usually only once, because Booger would then apologize, unseen but somewhere near, and some nights might even cry and Zeke would feel bad. Booger had tried to quit more than once and seemed genuine enough, but he would then lose himself every night inside the case of beer he dutifully punished. Still new to their scene, she saw a drama that had its roles and predictability like any good soap opera going nowhere. Sipping her coffee, she watched as Zeke attacked the pots.

"So how'd you two meet?"

"Who?" Zeke half-turned. "Us?"

She sat perched on a stool, the coffee cup in both hands near her lips as she said, "Yep."

Zeke grinned and said, "Work release, right?"

"Not likely." Booger's expression became morose, as if he was sickened by the mere idea. "There's only one convicted felon in this room."

Zeke said to Liz. "Yeah, tall, dumb, and stupid here, me and him met at a weekly poker game a few years back."

"Tell the truth, dude." Booger dipped a finger into the saucepan before freezing a moment to taste. "This, if I do say so myself, is an incredible *sabayon*." Nodding silently, he then cut the flame and said to Liz, "Be careful. This kid can stretch it like a porn star."

She watched Zeke wince and dump out what looked to be three-week-old macaroni before he scrubbed the pot. Zeke said, "Yeah, so Johnny Vegas over here, he wasn't really ever too bright with the cards, but he goes through a particularly rough spot, like I'm talking he's losing big every week for months."

"That is such bullshit." Booger finished rolling the last crepe and arranged them on the plates. Drizzling the sauce on top, he dressed the plates as well. Licking his lips, he said, "God, I'm good."

Zeke said, "So anyway, he starts going into everybody, you know, twenty bucks here, fifty bucks there, until finally he's got nothing left and actually starts shoving his furniture at people."

"I didn't shove." Booger rolled his eyes at Liz as if she might better understand. "I *suggested*, you know, since it wasn't like I was expecting a windfall anytime soon, that maybe what I had could be used as payment instead."

"Some bargain." Zeke nodded at the television room, arms busily submerged. "A puke-covered couch, two half-broken end tables, a lamp that sometimes works, and a TV with a black line that slowly rolls up the screen like a fucking suicide test."

"How dramatic," Booger laughed. "It really bothers you, doesn't it? That line just crawling up the screen."

"Awful." Zeke placed the last pot on the drying rack. "So, after about a month of this, I've got, like, the kid's whole apartment. He'd even forked over a killer set of kitchen knives—"

"Henckels," Booger said with an eyebrow arched distinctly. "Germany's finest."

"Whatever." Zeke wiped his arms and hands before tossing the towel behind the rack, which Booger instantly retrieved, spreading it open to air. Filling a coffee cup, Zeke said, "I had some other moron living here at the time and we didn't really get along."

"Can you imagine?" Booger deadpanned from the stove. "Go figure."

"So you pretty much won Booger's furniture in a poker game and then he moved right in behind it?" Liz Downs grinned. "Talk about justice."

"Tell me about it."

"Here we are." Booger served the plates, handing them out like gifts. "These are actually after-dinner crepes, but, well, I like to play with fire."

Sniffing at the steam rising from hers, Liz said, "Mmmmm …"

Zeke said, "Looks great, man, thanks."

Booger just smiled, professionally obsessed, but could not disagree.

Later that afternoon, she saw him waiting stopped at the corner even though the light was green. Somewhat shakily, still getting adjusted, Liz clicked into third gear while cursing her glaring ineptness. Outside the eighth grade, this might have been her first time on a bicycle in twelve years. Knowing this, she should have insisted on taking the bike path along the Charles instead of playing High Noon on Commonwealth Avenue. Counting it as one more stupid thing she would never have done had she not met him, she saw his approaching smile and belatedly felt it then, the wind and sun and cloudless sky, blocks and streets with people jaywalking like targets or smaller prey for the motorized streaks whipping by her shoulder. Smoothly braking to a stop, she looked to her right and playfully asked, "What's the holdup?"

Zeke grinned, extending an arm like an invitation. "After you."

Clicking back to first, she checked left and took the lead like the old pro just two lengths behind her. She was wearing one of his old skateboard helmets, the sides a smattering of stickers bearing insults and bands she had never heard of. Together with the blue jeans he had duct-taped at her right ankle to avoid the chain and the white blouse over wind-teased nipples, she considered herself a strange and indecent sight.

"There!" he screamed out from behind. "On your right!"

She nodded and began to brake, shouting, "What number?"

"Two thirty-six. The first on the corner."

Making the turn onto Cummington Street, she immediately pulled over and followed him to a sign that said, No Parking. He stuck a key into the massive locked chain encircling his waist. Holding it out, he said, "Take that for a sec?"

As she did, it pulled her like an anchor directly towards the street.

"Oh my God." She hoisted it with both hands. "What is this thing?"

"Motorcycle lock." He sandwiched the pole with each bike before kneeling at the rear wheels. "It's big enough to lock up a deuce."

"How much does it weigh?"

"Here." Carefully, he threaded the cumbersome chain through the spokes and around both frames and pole. "Twenty pounds?" He stood and pulled two U-bar locks from his bag, securing the front wheels. Evaluating the scene, he seemed satisfied and said, "Done deal."

Taking off her helmet, she followed him up stone steps past a sign that read O'Neill Photography Building. Inside, milling about, were aficionados, locals, Boston University students, and staff. They were clustered in quiet groups near tables in the hallway sampling cheese cubes and wine. Her eyes ran the wall, over posters and notices of upcoming exhibits, across bulletin boards filled with fliers and provocative photos before realizing she had missed it, this undercurrent of experiment and thought like a gentle hum inside the brain.

"Babe …"

She turned and saw him in front of double doors propped open. With his hacked-off jeans, disconsolate frown, and courier bag others her age wore only for show, she figured he pretty much fit right in.

"This is it," he said, then paused. "What's the grin for?"

"You." Liz bent over to pull the tape off her pant leg and wondered how many people had already noticed it. "You look excited."

"Yeah. This should be cool as fuck."

He took the helmet from her and clicked it around his strap. Putting an arm through hers, he steered her in, where it began almost immediately, the two ways in opposite directions labeled North and South Vietnam respectively. Zeke grabbed two programs off an attendant left waiting until Liz turned to call out, "Thank you."

Scanning the brief pamphlet, she found the event a chronological history culled from armed forces photographers, regular civilians, and freelance journalists from either side, and like the divide, the room was split in two. Twenty-foot-high ceilings were in shadow as tiny spotlights, screwed into opposing walls, framed each picture succinctly. The images were sliced out of war, and she quickly discovered the enemy's pain inside the North Vietnamese exhibit. An orphan with round eyes incapable of knowing the impact sat innocently atop a pile of ashes while behind her a village burned down around the dead. A legless boy on crutches; a soldier's face seared by napalm. Skulls of collaborators lined up like bowling balls. Another showed acres of rice paddies sparkling in the sun before the thick, twisted maze of the battlefield jungle rose up green and dense and exploding with trees and wild flowers in forbiddance. There were guerillas digging tunnels, a young woman with a beautiful face and an AK-47 slung over a shoulder on post and sipping tea; people picking through the skeleton of a downed American fighter while US POWs in a barracks with cots and little else wore blank eyes hiding something worse unpictured. There was Ho Chi Minh returning from Paris in the 1930s, assuming power in 1945 and, like Castro, belligerent enough to throw rocks at a giant, except this time the giant struck back.

Zeke lingered a moment more before feeling her gaze, and said, "What do you think?"

"It's unnerving." She crossed her arms as if chilled and whispered, "It's really quiet."

"I know."

"I'm kind of freaked out."

"Well, it's probably not gonna get any better from here."

And he was right, because the first pictures on the American side were of marines in 1963, smiling at cameras on ships heading west, while one step to the right came scenes of green fatigues crashing the beach before the true horror of two medics covered in blood over a prostrate Ranger with his chest blown wide open, not dead, not yet, but clearly in his eyes the embers yawned. The faces were thoroughly American, and though they had been transported ten thousand miles away, she thought them common and plain and with that certain light, like the blond kid smiling while holding up a letter from home, or the black guy with a pick stuck sideways into a modest Afro and laughing at someone or something said to his right as he reassembled his M-16. Shots of

Bob Hope; soldiers playing cards, digging trenches, waving from helicopters and repelling by rope. There was General Westmoreland at the microphone addressing the green-clad thousands listening intently to their fate. Then there was the haunting scene of flares arching over a mangrove forest burnt like broken bones stuck into the earth. NVA-killed being stacked by two soldiers in masks as behind them bulldozers prepared a lime-drenched pit. Fighter aircraft screaming off carrier decks, and a somewhat confused GI glancing at a clipboard marked Duty Sheet while rolling a cigarette. They were all horribly human, Vietnamese and Americans alike, and she had to wonder if such a misunderstanding might arise again to claim another generation lost amid the rhetoric. She was thinking about the ramifications for all involved as they reached the end and finally saw that black wall unwind itself across a patch of Washington DC, and she was embarrassed by her tears as she thought, *God, those poor boys.*

"Hey," he placed a hand on her elbow, "let's get a drink."

She followed him into the lobby, where they were both pressed for identification before receiving stock wine in a thin plastic glass.

"Brutal," he said, and Liz was unsure, so she said, "Which?"

"Both. But our guys, man … so many fucking guys." Zeke finished his in one gulp and grimaced. "And this is some horrible shit too." He held out his glass towards a food service worker who did not seem impressed.

Liz sipped at hers, surveying others emerge from the exhibit in that obligatory way people behave, with an outward show of solemn respect, in case someone else might be watching. Zeke saw her concentrated focus and asked, "Feel like a smoke?"

Outside, they sat on the steps amid a brisk and blowing wind. After corralling her hair behind one ear several times, she watched him tuck and struggle before emerging with two lit cigarettes glowing in the breeze. The sun was bright but losing strength into the stretch of fall. Inhaling smoke, she said, "Can you believe that was thirty years ago?"

"No." Zeke shook his head, staring at his dangling cigarette. "What a nightmare."

"It was haunting." The wind was sharp but it wasn't why she had the chills.

"Makes me proud, though."

She studied him curiously. "What does?"

"I mean that was their job, you know? All those soldier guys. I know it sounds obvious, but part of their job description was dying."

She tapped off some ash and said, "You're right, but I don't think they'd see it that way. Neither would the civilians. They were living, Zeke."

"Yes, they were."

She found his hand on impulse and took it in her own as they interlocked fingers and smoked as people came and went.

"What now?" She looked at her watch. "It's only two thirty."

"Feel like coffee? There's a great place a block down. We can even leave the bikes."

"Okay." She stood and brushed at the seat of her pants. Taking his hand, thinking of the exhibit, she thought she might have a better appreciation of this beautiful Saturday afternoon and so, looking up at him through the bright sunshine, Liz Downs embraced the day.

Chapter Seven

Thursday, October 29

EVEN THOUGH HE WAS doing her a favor, Zeke double-timed it into Allston. Cammi would be waiting and pissed at the delay. It was almost 6:00 PM, with nightfall just inches away. As he braked for an upcoming light, traffic slowed with him in tandem. While the crosswalk on Brighton Avenue spilled over, he thought of her and anxiously drummed a foot. During the last three months, as this most current separation became indefinite, the core of their friendship, like a scaffold or skeleton, provided support while also being daily threatened by collapse.

Tonight's chore was the removal of a couch ruined at a recent weekend blowout. He knew she had borrowed a friend's pickup truck and could almost picture her now peeking out the window with a frown, his tardiness unappreciated. Three blocks later, still smiling at the image, he turned left and locked up outside 110 Parkvale where she shared a three-bedroom on the second-floor of a giant house.

Upstairs, after hitting the buzzer, he saw her through the screen door quickly dodging from sight.

"Cam?" He entered and closed the door. "Sorry I'm late."

From somewhere unseen, he heard her blow her nose. Unslinging his bag, he loitered in the kitchen to pound three cups of water. Thumbing through a magazine, he finally called out, "Cammi! What the fuck?"

When she reappeared, her hair was pulled into a ponytail, her expression unamused and plain. Sensing trouble, he watched her back at the sink before carefully asking, "Are you okay?"

"Yes." She filled a glass of water and turned, sipping at it. "Why do you ask?"

"Because it looks like you've been … why are you crying?"

"I haven't—"

"Cammi," he shook his head, "are you fucking kidding me or what?"

"I got a phone call," she said with forced nonchalance, "from New York."

"Oh, great." Zeke frowned. "What's the latest?"

"Thanksgiving, or so she said."

"After blowing you off last July?" Zeke shook his head again. "And now she wants to fuck up Thanksgiving too?"

"Zeke …"

"I'm sorry. But what else am I supposed to say?"

"Nothing." She put the glass on the counter and wrapped her arms around him. Nestling into his shoulder, she said, "I'm just real tired."

Holding her, imagining what he must smell like, he said, "I'm probably too stinky for this."

She laughed quietly, detaching from the embrace to wipe her eyes. "I just had time enough to shower."

"Yeah, let's do this." Zeke glanced around. "Which sofa is it?"

"In there."

Ten minutes later they were breathing heavily by the curb. Leaning against the Toyota, Zeke patted the couch and said, "You and I had some long nights on this thing."

"Yes, we did." Cammi stood and grinned seductively. "You amongst many others."

"Hey!"

"Ha-ha!" She tossed her bike onto the couch and jingled a set of keys. "You want some dinner? I'll be cooking when I get back."

"You don't need a hand unloading this thing?"

She shook her head and said, "He's gonna dump it in the morning. His place's only a couple of blocks away." She opened the driver's side door. "Back in a few."

He's gonna dump it in the morning? Zeke thought and turned for the staircase. Sure she was on the loose and free to date whomever, and although he was in a relationship of his own, the thought of this someone else made him ball a fist and curse this unknown *loser.*

Upstairs, he looked around her quiet apartment and felt instantly out of place. He stole a Coke from the refrigerator and meandered aimlessly, finally ending up in her room. On the bed, he found an ornate dress seemingly half-finished and guessed it must be her costume for the upcoming Halloween ball she and her roommates annually hosted. There was a stack of patterns next to a Singer sewing machine, and different outfits hung from hooks. On the floor were scattered fashion magazines and individual pictures of models honoring the latest trend. It was a passion she had revisited over the years, and she took great pride in studying this craft; nonetheless, Zeke was startled by the FIT application at the foot of her bed and wished he had not seen it.

Deliberately ignoring it, he sat at her desk and craved a cigarette but had none to light. Bored, he ran his eyes over the pictures she had tacked onto a board—Cammi as an infant, in preschool, and then inside the first of many Catholic school uniforms. Zeke smiled, as he always did, because she came from a place far removed. There was a picture of Mr. and Mrs. Sinclair— judging by her bouffant hairdo and his horrible plaid suit, Zeke guessed it must have been the seventies. They were hand in hand, on a wide green lawn, and the house behind them was huge.

Born and raised in upper-class Newton, Cammi was the youngest of two daughters separated by three years. Zeke had met the mother and older sister occasionally and found the dislike equally distributed. The mother, of old blood in a new design, with her sleek suits and punctuated jewelry, seemed more like a weapon itching for release, the chiseled beauty balanced by the awful threat of her heedless tongue and a thousand years of breeding. Having witnessed a few prime encounters between Cammi and her mother fearlessly squaring off, Zeke quickly learned to take cover from the crossfire before inching towards the door.

As for the sister, looking at Josephine's picture now, Zeke recognized the mother's obsessive vanity and taste for wealth but knew she lacked the heart to earn it. Educated at Tufts, still subsidized by a monthly allowance, and night clubbing like the debutante she was not, Zeke thought of Josephine as a parasite consumed by gossip and a completely practiced wit, with borrowed opinions she sold as her own. It was, he had to admit, just about everything someone should never be—vacuous, bland, pleasing, and stupid—all rolled into one, and barely considered her worth his time.

Spotting Mr. Sinclair, Zeke noted the downcast eyes and symmetrical baldness, the face a fatigue-stretched lump. *Must've been towards the end,* Zeke thought, because the expression seemed entirely defeated. He had never met him, but he knew that Cammi's father had been a rising star on Federal Street before his abrupt firing and subsequent humiliation. As proud as she was, it remained a subject of disgrace and hostility, and to tread where those two words collided with Cammi Sinclair required a courage Zeke simply did not possess.

Hearing the front door open, he glanced to where she leaned against the doorjamb and cocked a hip.

"Comfy?"

"You weren't kidding." He stood up and rubbed at a stiffening lower back. "That didn't take long at all."

"Told you. It's right around the corner, sweetie." She turned for the kitchen.

"Hey," he said.

She looked back to see his foot nudging at the paperwork. "Oh," she said and smiled sadly. "Yeah, that. I was gonna tell you."

"Fashion Institute, huh?" he said, trying to sound enthusiastic. "You've been threatening this for a while."

"Zeke—"

"I'm being serious."

"Come on." She nodded towards the kitchen. "I left the rice on."

"Is that what's burning?"

"Keep talking," she said. "And you'll be eating dinner at McDonald's."

Minutes later he was watching her julienne vegetables for a stir-fry. She caught him sipping at her half gallon of orange juice and said, "Use a glass, pig."

"But it's almost done."

"Zeke …"

"All right!" Withholding further incitement, he sensed the ominous shift in her mood and said carefully, "That for the Halloween party? That dress on your bed?"

"Yes." She sliced through a green pepper quickly.

"It's fucking beautiful. Who are you gonna be?"

"Queen Anne the Horrible."

"Nice." The tartness of the juice caused him to smack his lips. "Sounds like a woman after my own heart."

"You have one of those?"

"One of ... oh God, real funny, Cammi."

She smiled, then did not, and said, "I was gonna tell you ..."

"I know." He looked out the darkened window uncomfortably. "New York's not that far."

"Sweetie—"

"Do we need to talk about this now?"

"Yes." She maneuvered an onion into the path of her knife. "We should start. Because this guy I'm seeing, this Roger, he's from there, and then I've got my mom and all her connections ..." Cammi paused, the knife stuck poised for a downward cut. "It's just ... lately I've been feeling a little fucked up."

"About what?"

"In general? Should I pick a number? I mean, is this it, Zeke?" The forthrightness of her gaze, swung on him abruptly, caused him to glance away. "Could it be that it's just the same fucking thing every day? That I'm fucking twenty-four sliding into thirty, and I'm still pushing pedals, for what?" She shrugged and began slicing again. "Or maybe it's just that I'm in love with someone who's wasting my time?"

"You're what?" Zeke almost laughed. "You've been dating this, this *Roger*, for two months and you're—"

"Zeke." She shook her head in disbelief. "I'm talking about *you*, you fucking retard."

"I ..." His mouth worked emptily, as if the words refused direction. "Cammi—"

"Don't." She held up a hand. "Thanks, but knowing you, you'll only make it worse."

He smiled at the slight, knowing it was true. But seeing her standing there, boldly laying it down, stirred a passion that almost caused a shudder. "And I'm not?"

"We can't talk about this." She shoved the onion and pepper into a wok sizzling on the stove. "I thought we could but maybe we shouldn't. Nothing's definite. About New York, that is."

"If you did apply," Zeke asked, trying to act only mildly interested, "when would you go?"

"Summer?" She shrugged. "Maybe fall?"

"Oh."

"Do you want carrots in this?" She held one up.

"Yeah, sure." He caught himself staring at the refrigerator, his thought one giant looping circle of college and New York and her fucking this goddamn Roger. She had been down this road before, with other guys and thoughts of her future, but never the two in combination. After earning her GED at eighteen and swearing that would be it, maybe this time she was actually serious about continuing with school. Still, he remembered those evenings in bed, her head on his shoulder as the high world of fashion became her next design. This from a girl who wore Mickey Mouse T-shirts and safety pins for earrings.

Stirring at the vegetables, she winced at the oil snapping onto her forearms and said, "It's ..."

"What?" Zeke watched her at the stove. "It's what?"

"Never ending." Turning, she cocked an eyebrow. "You know?"

"Cammi—"

"Six AM," she said. "And that hellish alarm clock and me racing around this fucking city all day, for what?"

Zeke shrugged and said, "Fuck, I don't know."

"Exactly." She briefly turned back to stir the vegetables before saying, "Where's our slice of the pie, Zeke? You know? I mean, we can't even keep a fucking relationship together."

"You can't say that."

"Why not?"

"Because we're just ... we're ... it's just always like this. Shit goes good for a while and then it's off but we always make it back."

"Really?" She turned towards the stove. "Is that what you tell *her*?"

"What the fuck does that mean?" Zeke shook his head, amazed. "Are you blaming me for this?"

"Well ..."

"Well what?" He stood. "I want to hear this. This should be good."

"Seriously." Cammi faced him. "Is that what you tell her? That you and I are on some kind of fucking spring break from each other?"

"That's not what I meant—"

"And that, at some point, whenever his royal highness decides upon his wench, she or I'll be sent packing?"

"Fuck you, Cammi." He finished his drink.

"Where do you think you're going?"

"Home." He grabbed his bag. "You're a fucking mental case."

"Zeke—"

"Naw. I ain't about this, this pain and fucking suffering. You looking for someone to rescue you? Call 911. Either that or learn to stop whining."

"Fuck you!"

Opening the door, he turned back and said, "You know what I like most about her?"

Cammi crossed her arms, her expression decidedly revolted. "I can only imagine."

"I just have to deal with one of her personalities at a time." He ducked as a glass came sailing into the door, which he quickly closed, scurrying down the steps.

"You forgot your dinner!" she screamed from the window above. "Guess I'll just have to make it to go!"

"Jesus!" he screamed, dodging the steamed rice and incoming vegetables scattering across the street.

"Wait! Don't forget the soy sauce!"

She was surprisingly accurate despite the range, the bottled explosion hitting in stride but three feet off to the right. Saddling up on the run, desperate to get out of range, he heard her scream, "Fuck you, Zeke!"

Once he made the corner, he decided McDonald's didn't sound half bad.

It was some time before she closed the window upon the gutless retreat Zeke had left hanging like a vapor above the street. Looking at the blue flames licking up through the now empty burners, realizing there was nothing left to cook, Cammi closed them down and said, "Fuck me."

Staring at the wreckage of dinner, she tossed the debris from the cutting

182 | *Tom Trabulsi*

board and started to clean. Wiping the stove, she succeeded in pushing Zeke from her mind only to have him replaced by the earlier conversation with her mother, and she knew where it always got her. The grudges, like carefully cut diamonds, were worn with pride. After all, that was the Sinclair way, she dryly noted, and regretted how little had changed.

Her mother, the once dutiful housewife, had singlehandedly ground her stalwart father into pulp. Marrying above his station, plucking a woman from old money with expectations, Charles Sinclair rose from firm to firm until his co-workers openly wondered when they might be leaving with him to start his own financial consulting agency. With both daughters already enrolled at the prestigious St. Catherine's School, he might have felt a small measure of success before paying the tuitions and for his wife's extravagant vacations while re-mortgaging the brick palace in the neighborhood he knew they could not afford.

And then there were her friends, from equally established lineages, with their pricey lifestyles and ridiculous obligations, one of which, Cammi eventually knew, was mocking him as a ladder-climbing irrelevant. A cannibalistic circle of socialites, Cammi remembered that scene with a distaste she would not rationalize until much later. Still, she marveled at how her mother and older sister played their roles spectacularly, and how her father, finally, became nothing more than a portable ATM for them to abuse. At the time, she just felt out of place among all the angst and grew to savor the instances when her father would take her downtown or to the mall or to just about anywhere they were not. In tandem, the mother and older sister became two ghouls whom the youngest slowly grew to hate. Gradually withdrawing, her father would work eleven-hour days before coming home to a quiet scotch in a room he promised himself he would one day convert into a study. Then the scotch became two and sometimes three, before one night, there he was at the door, trying not to cry, facing his wife with dread. Something had happened after work, he said, and could not look her in the eye.

The next day, as if none of the sacrifice during the preceding years could save him, he was fired, and his wife, hearing that he had exposed himself in the hatcheck room to an assistant of the executive vice-president, exploded what remained. Rendered *persona non grata* on Federal Street, Charles Sinclair eventually rented a one-room office above an antique store in Newton and quietly forged ahead. An accountant by trade, he squared a living, but not like before, and his wife's displeasure became volcanic. Nearly wiped out by the settlement for his perverted misstep, unable to provide her and the girls with the way of life his wife demanded, he suffered the worst humiliation of all as she went behind his back to her own family for assistance. With prior advertising experience, along with her family's considerable pull, she landed a lucrative position with Knightson and Hiller and never looked back. Socializing late into the night, barely concealing even the biggest hint of her infidelity, she caused her husband to retreat further still, until, with only his youngest to relate to, the rest of his family was squeezed from sight. It was two years after that, Cammi remembered, after having one too many highballs at his office, that he forced her into opening the front door at fifteen years of age to face a pair of state troopers who seemed horribly muted by this upcoming imposition.

"Is your mother home?" one of them said, and life was very different after that. Yet within weeks of the accident, both mother and daughter were carrying on in public while at home it was as if he had never existed. As they rode out another year on the life insurance payout, the extravaganza continued.

Thinking of it now, covering the sink in Ajax before scrubbing like a machine, Cammi recalled the ensuing twelve months like a sickness. Suspended at school, ostracized at home, she was eventually left with Josephine so her mother could start over in New York. This arrangement was an unmitigated disaster for everyone concerned. No longer outnumbered, and having studied her opponents as they took her for granted, Cammi finally struck back when prodded, sought out weaknesses to exploit, and basically, systematically, destroyed any trace of who or what she had planned to be. Their example, she decided, called into question every theory adulthood held as hallowed, and those lies were now put to bed for good.

She loaded up the dishwasher, remembering that last awful fight. After getting caught making out with a guy her peers considered socially inept, what had started as meaningless teasing from Josephine and her friends had snowballed into a three-day exchange of hostilities before exploding into full-scale war. The Sinclair sisters, after years of escalating tension, traded atrocities until finally, while Josephine was still in class at Tufts downtown, Cammi, after hearing Josephine had raided and broadcast excerpts from her journal to what friends remained, worked her way through every room, knifing pillows and disemboweling cushions, trashing paintings and smashing mirrors and heaving anything she could through the windows. It took over an hour until the tumult climaxed with her gathering all of Josephine's clothes into a gas-soaked pile in the middle of the front lawn before lighting a twenty-five-thousand-dollar bonfire.

That night, she stayed at a downtown hostel and was arrested four days later. She was transferred to Newton, where the police were incredulous that an occupant, a sixteen-year-old girl no less, was the cause of this destruction.

Her mother, despite Josephine's protests, would not press charges. Instead, there came ultimatums; straighten up, coexist with your sister, pull a B average, or move in with Aunt Sarah down in Greenwich, Connecticut. Cammi remembered the conversation, remembered sitting in that coffee shop on the corner of High and Federal streets, her mother immaculately dressed across from Cammi who had not showered or changed clothes in days. "How could you do this to me?" her mother had said. "Has anyone *seen* you in this condition?"

A stuffed head covered in makeup, Cammi remembered thinking, knowing in fact that she probably would have returned home in an instant if only her mother had taken one second to hear her side of the story.

Afterward, on the pavilion outside One Financial, she watched the bike messengers gracefully swooping in from all parts of the city, and by the end of the week, on a bike proffered by a rapacious dispatcher, had fallen in love with every aspect of the job. She met a guy named Bob from Somerville who had a room to rent and quickly found out what every young woman fears, when an offer for assistance actually turns into a demand for something else.

The following day, she moved into an Allston apartment shared by four of her co-workers who partied every night. But gradually, as the venom towards her sister leaked into the base of her demeanor, she found her anger before it found everyone else and watched it take its toll. Like a child with a handgun, she had no boundaries, and she loved the shock wherever she pointed. Quick with an insult, riding like a lunatic, and self-abusively promiscuous, she used her body as a vessel aimed directly towards a cliff.

Six months later, she and Zeke collided on one of those brutal hung-over mornings. At first, of course, there had been no time for attraction—she attacked him when he was barely conscious. Thinking of it now, she smiled, because even then, rolling away from the blows, he had that certain look people share in chance meetings, when someone equally insane crosses their path. *God*, she thought, *it's been so long.* She remembered their menacing staredowns in various brief encounters after the collision. Yet within weeks, she ran into him at the Rat's Nest, where he worked, and that's when everything changed. Up on the roof after the show, they drank malt liquor until dawn and compared strange histories. She would often regard their initial encounter to be something more than mere happenstance, and as they quickly fell into that blissful period of inseparability, where they even shared the same mohawk haircut, it seemed things would last forever.

Now she could see herself, usually after he stormed out, knowing exactly why she poked and tortured in this giant game of *What If*, and why seven years allowed such leeway. It was because they had grown to use each other as a last resort, and everything else now suffered.

She wiped down the microwave before attacking the countertop, knowing she was equally to blame. Despite the claustrophobic closeness of the initial three years, they waged war through the first breakup, realized there was absolutely no one else out there, and had spent the next four years trading preemptive strikes when one or the other grew too close. Admitting it, she knew, meant the situation had run its course. She was happy he had seen the FIT application, could almost picture the gears shifting through his suddenly preoccupied mind. And as much as it seemed like a mistake she could not reverse, the thought of spending the rest of her life at his side was something she just could not shake—even if it never happened. Whether or not he realized it yet, he had been put on notice.

Chapter Eight

Wednesday, November 22

CONSULTING A PEDESTRIAN'S WATCH, Zeke squinted into the chilly November breeze and nodded his thanks. 4:45 PM.

Fuck, gotta get moving.

After dropping off at Chase, he was downtown on Federal Street during one of those moments right before five o'clock when the whole city seemed poised like a cocked trigger. This being Thanksgiving eve, rush hour, at least for those commuters unlucky enough to stay the full day, promised to be a bumper-bruising nightmare. Cigarette burnt to a nub, Zeke watched office workers buttoning coats and ringing their own necks with scarves while fleeing for the nearest T-station. *Like watching the trickle before the dam breaks,* he thought, and pushed off from the curb.

Little more than a row of skyscrapers glinting polished steel and glass, the three-block canyon of Federal Street was home to Boston's banking district. Parking, save for underground garages, was strictly prohibited. Instead, especially at this late hour, the street was a slew of darting cabs, limousines, and delivery vans of every sort. Each building had a loading dock in its bowels, and the vans came screeching out like carrier planes off unseen catapults. From experience, Zeke knew to avoid the curb. And for those suicidal enough to ride the sidewalk, luckily, New England Medical Center was only ten blocks away.

Finding a pay phone outside a Burger King on Summer Street, Zeke punched in the eight-hundred number but got a busy signal. Hanging up, deciding he was exhausted, Zeke rubbed at a grease stain on his knee-length denim pants. Beneath them he had on a pair of skin-tight black Izumi leggings, while on top he wore a T-shirt, turtleneck, sweatshirt and a one-ply black windbreaker. He knew it was important, and would become even more so as the long teeth of winter set in, to balance layers for ventilation without necessarily freezing to death. Experience dictated a dark outer layer to absorb what heat the unreliable sun could provide until late December produced gale-force storms, sub-teen temperatures and all bets, Zeke knew, were off. *Gotta get my mountain bike up and running*, he reminded himself while trying the number again.

"Gobble-gobble!" Stuart's voice immediately sing-songed.

"It's Z downtown on Summer with absolutely nothing."

"Zeke! How goes it, *mon frère*!"

"I just told you."

"What time you got?"

"Hell, I don't know. Five o'clock?"

He heard Stuart Rigby flipping through the dispatcher sheets. "What say we shut it down? The only thing I've got is a Cambridge round trip, and even I am not that heartless."

"Wow."

"Consider it a gift. Let you get a head start on the holiday."

"Yeah, great."

"I'm sure it's gonna be a load of fun. Cammi called it at three o'clock just so she could start cooking."

"Don't remind me."

Stuart laughed delightedly. "Of course, you could always come over to our place, Zeke. We play such wonderful games, like hide the salami in the stuffing—"

"Stu—"

"Or the Tongue Olympics. Ever cover yourself in mashed potatoes, Zeke?"

"God, that's so gross."

Hearing Stuart's laughter almost caused Zeke to grin, so he said, "Talk to you Friday."

"Yes, Zeke. And please, no hangovers."

Cradling the phone, he checked left and dodged pedestrians before launching from the curb. He geared a leisurely pace as people darted from cabs, shops, T-stations, and supermarkets, the whole city alive with unfinished errands. Thanks to daylight savings, by 4:30 PM there was none left, so Zeke reached back to click on the small pulsing red light bolted into his shoulder strap. Hunching through the biting wind, he powered west towards Allston. *Thanksgiving at the Sinclairs*, he thought with a shudder. It was going to be a bloodbath. On top of the sister she was barely on speaking terms with, Cammi had also invited her long-absent mother, a woman who shared no love of Zeke Sandaman. Having met sporadically over the years, a palpable animosity had developed between them like a mutual disease. Cammi's current boyfriend, thankfully, would be out of town. As for Liz, Zeke knew she was fielding her own paternal nightmare, an event she in no way wanted him to witness.

He came to an abrupt stop on the corner of Charles and Beacon Streets. Two ambulances, six cruisers, and a pair of fire trucks had the intersection completely blocked. Four cars were twisted into a crumpled mass, and Zeke, having experienced enough of these moments, watched the ensuing activity with dread. Wheeling around the obstruction, he glimpsed three firefighters calmly pleading with a woman trapped in one car's passenger seat as a horrific head wound openly bled. Judging by the relatively light traffic jam and the fact that people were still being pulled from cars, he figured the whole scene was less than ten minutes old. Finally wedging out onto Beacon Street, Zeke tried to forget her bloodied face and fifteen minutes later he was on approach for the yellow submarine.

Despite pulling up and noticing every light in the place ablaze, even after the harbinger of the awful accident just witnessed, he decided he was just too tired to care. Shouldering the bike, he hoped Booger had merely stumbled home inside the permanent inebriated haze he called consciousness.

Inside, tossing his bike and bag against the foyer wall, he heard the television and stepped around the corner.

Their eyes met, and as Joshua Sandaman stood up, Zeke's relief and happiness quickly faded. Overcoming a momentary dizziness, Josh held out both arms, which were immediately filled by his little brother's awkward hug. Thirty seconds later, disengaging, Zeke bit back four and a half years of absence to say, "Joshua."

"Hey, man." Clasping Zeke's face in his grasp, Josh Sandaman began smiling and crying at the same time as Zeke laughed until he felt his own eyes spilling over and said, "Jesus."

"It's so good to see you."

"Goddamn." Zeke hugged him again, felt the bony ribcage beneath the dirty white T-shirt, and said, "When did you walk?"

"Man …" Joshua released his brother and wiped at both eyes.

Zeke began cataloguing something much worse but only said, "Sit down. You want something to drink?"

"I'm already set up …"

"Chill for a sec, will ya? I need to get some water."

Turning for the kitchen, proceeding normally despite having no way out, his only thought was, *What am I supposed to say now?* The yellow skin, sunken eyes, thinned-out, emaciated torso, the obviousness of catastrophe beyond apparent to the point of insult if not addressed. With hands braced on either side of the sink, Zeke could picture the only image he had ever known and wondered who the fuck that was supposed to be on his couch. Growing up as his opposite, Joshua had been thick-chested and strong-armed like their father, quick with a joke and comfortable inside his own skin, unlike the gangly Zeke. There Zeke was, at ten years old, watching from the cab of their father's pickup as Josh pushed wheelbarrows full of demolitioned concrete and swung a sledgehammer as the older fellows gently ribbed the boss's son. Put to work that next summer, two years before Josh would be imprisoned, Zeke quickly learned what working for a concrete contractor meant, mainly sweating out a gallon of water every hour as his lower back became individual strings of pain-torn muscle. Combined with the bark of their father, a man who purposely misunderstood the meaning of the word "nepotism," Zeke still recalled those summers like visions out of hell. Five years older than Zeke, and not averse to leaving work in an exhausted stupor, Josh made sure their old man paired them up on the daily labor list. Shouldering any slack and taking blame for every fuck-up, he provided Zeke the only cover from the wrath of Robert Sandaman, who thought his youngest son an undriven weakling addicted to his goddamn skateboard.

Turning now, he saw Josh leaning against the counter as if it was the only thing holding him up. His black hair, formerly short and spiked, was now long and disheveled. The once fierce black eyes, deadened over, ran amok amid the permanent ex-con scan.

"I was gonna tell ya, but …" Josh pursed his lips and shrugged. "What was the point?"

Swallowing as if it was a question he could barely ask, Zeke said, "What is it?"

"ESRD." Boosting himself onto the counter, Joshua shared a flicker of the old devilment as he cracked a smile and said, "End-Stage Renal Disease. Otherwise known as chronic kidney failure."

"What the fuck are you talking about?"

"Zeke—"

"Nah, man." Zeke shook his head. "I ain't trying to hear none of this." Reaching into a cabinet, he pulled down a bottle of vodka and found a semi-clean glass for three fingers' worth, which he immediately shot, gagging, swallowing, nothing added to the sickness he felt already rising up. "You son of a bitch."

"Zeke—"

"Nah, fuck you."

"All right. Whatever." Holding up his tremulous hands, Joshua said, "Maybe now ain't the time."

Pouring another shot, Zeke listened idly to the phone ring until the answering machine revealed Cammi Sinclair's frantic voice. Picking up the portable, Zeke winced through the screeching feedback until he made it into the front room and slammed a fist onto the machine's stop button.

"Yeah, Cam."

"Hello? Zeke? What the fuck? Where are you? I thought we—"

"Cammi."

"And it's already like six o'clock. Please don't screw me on this."

"I was gonna call you." Frowning, not wanting to deal with any of it, Zeke rubbed his forehead and said, "I'll get the potatoes. It's just … I got to call you back."

"What? Goddamn it, you're ditching out on me, aren't you?"

"Cammi, I just walked in the door and found my brother on the couch."

"Huh …?" Cammi paused. "Josh? He's out! Oh my God! Bring him over too! I've got drinks and we'll have plenty of food and both of you deadbeats can lend a hand. I can't believe I agreed to cook for all of these idiots. Tomorrow's gonna be *such* a disaster."

"Gimme an hour and I'll call you back. I gotta talk to this kid."

"Well, yes, of course. How cool is that? Home just in time for Thanksgiving too."

"Tell me about it."

"Call me."

"Yep."

Zeke heard the line go dead and smiled as he returned to the kitchen.

"Who was that?" Joshua stretched an inquisitive eyebrow, sipping at his glass.

"Cam."

"Who?"

"Cammi Sinclair. You remember her, man, she came with me that last time?"

"Jesus, that was like five years ago."

"Almost."

"And you two are still putting it to each other?"

"Not really."

"Why're you smiling?"

"Because she's over there losing her mind. I'm supposed to be helping her cook."

"Whoops."

"Yeah, no kidding."

"So you're not hitting it and still you guys are friends?"

"Ah, man ..." Zeke shook his head and refilled the glass. "Not now, Josh. My brain's totally fucked as it is."

The silence crept up behind them as Zeke stood at the sink and stared out the window, the guilt a thousand pounds an inch.

"Hey."

"Yeah." Zeke felt the vodka begin a slow crawl outward, so he shot another inch and a half and gasped.

Josh said, "Anyone ever tell you you look like a fucking cartoon?"

"Huh?"

"I'm serious. The fucking elf shoes, hacked-off jeans, black tights, fingerless gloves ..."

"Are you finished?"

"Maybe." Josh grinned again, his teeth yellowed sticks. "What the fuck, kid? After how long you been on those pedals, it's a miracle you're still alive."

"Look who's talking," Zeke said and instantly regretted it. "Fuck, man, I didn't mean—"

"Zeke," Joshua nodded, and his smile somehow seemed at ease, "it's been some kind of fun, all right."

Turning back to the window, Zeke did another shot as the minutes ticked away.

"So," he finally said, addressing the black outside.

"So," Joshua answered, "can a guy get a refill or what?"

"Of what?"

"Booze, man, shit."

"You're drinking?" Zeke turned, his face an unpleasant grimace. "With End Fuck Rectal Disease?"

"That's renal, Zeke." Josh smiled and reached for the bottle. "My ass is fine."

"But your brain isn't." Zeke shook his head, glancing up with a forthrightness the other did not expect. "You're telling me your kidneys are fucked up and I'm supposed to just sit here and watch you get hammered?"

"My liver's only enlarged, not fucked."

"Your liver." Zeke slowly closed his eyes, grinding his jaw muscles mistakenly in release. "What else? Huh? You got cancer, AIDS, what?"

"Nope." Smacking his lips, Josh sipped at the room-temperature vodka and said, "Since you've had like six shots in three minutes, I guess we need to talk."

"You think?" Zeke scoffed, grabbed the bottle, and headed for the couch. "You got a lot of balls."

Muting the television, Josh took a seat in a recliner across from Zeke. Lighting a cigarette, he eased back, set the glass on a knee, and said, "It's poison."

"Gee, no shit. Have another shot."

"Not the booze, moron."

Pausing, Zeke squinted and said, "What're you talking about now?"

"You and me, right?"

"Yep."

Leaning forward, Josh swallowed the grin and said, "Then please, for once, just shut your mouth and listen."

Surprised at how politely he was asked, Zeke fell back in line, as they all did—the head menace unchallenged. *But look at him*, Zeke thought, *skin and bones beneath soiled jeans and shirt and jailhouse ink scrawled across the toothpick arms which used to be jacked. This is a fucking nightmare.*

The next twenty minutes offered no new details—the trial and sentence, daily life at the Pole, an eighteen-year-old living among men.

"The three of us had been separated at first," Joshua said, eyeing down into his drink. "I had no one, except for maybe Chino, but I barely knew him. Besides, he was rolling with La Familia, and they didn't want shit all to do with my white ass. Ended up with my back to the wall against everyone— Asians, niggers—pilfed all my shit no matter how many fights I took. Believe me, I finished every one of them off but still … "

"Jesus."

"And I quickly realized, without a grip, I was gonna be turned into a fucking lifelong appetizer. That's when I ran into Tully. Remember him?"

"Tully?" Zeke frowned. "Columbia Road?"

"Yep."'

"What the hell was that loser doing in there?"

"He wasn't." Joshua sipped his drink. "Cedar Junction had a contract with Phillips. Bread drops three times a week. I was assigned to the kitchen on two of those days."

"Lemme guess."

"You don't have to. On the ass end of a dead-end job like that? I barely had to ask him."

"I'm sure."

"So one day we tried it out and it was just too perfect, you know? What boot is gonna spend half his tour checking five hundred fucking loaves of bread?"

"Yep."

"Anyway, soon enough the Aryan Brotherhood was down, and instead of trying to jam my teeth into my skull, the price got set and things couldn't run any smoother. For a while."

"How soon was it?"

"Shit ... three years in? Maybe?" He took another sip. "So with this new juice, I got Cancer Boy and Ju-Ju put up on either side of me."

"Go on."

"So whatever. I wasn't the Brotherhood's only connect but a few years after that I was, fucking A. Tully was no moron. As long as he kept stuffing that loaf with smack, I was squaring him off with a deuce a week. And I wasn't worried about him stepping all over it, because it would have been both our asses."

"But ..."

Smiling, he lit another cigarette and said, "But I guess I got greedy."

"Jesus, Josh."

"I mean, I worked in the fucking kitchen, bro. There was baking soda and other shit and pretty soon I was hitting the packages, and then all three of us got hooked, so I stepped on it even harder and then one day the gig was just up."

"How?"

Glancing at the floor, Josh's smile ran vacant. "Ju-Ju."

"Ju-Ju what?" And then Zeke's eyes brightened in awe. "No way."

"He ... he, well, he just never forgave me, you know? Even though I set both of them up with a split on the juice I had comin' in, he just ... he couldn't accept the fact that I was gonna one day walk, you know? And he would never be free again."

"*Ju-Ju*, man?"

"He flipped me, Z, me and C.B. By then I was past three-quarters through, too." Josh shook his head as if still amazed. "You know how he used to get, with that bitchy little temper if he thought anyone was fucking with him? Well, he just never got past our fucking trials."

Zeke nodded grimly. "People were talking outside too."

"I mean, what was I supposed to be? Sorry? That my fucking attorney got me a pass?"

"I hear ya."

"So Ju-Ju saw his opening and he decided to take it." Joshua smiled ruefully. "Thought he could just hand us over and take control of Tully, and to be honest, inside that cesspool, even fucking over your best friends becomes acceptable—you know what I'm talking about?"

"Barely." Zeke shrugged. "Fucking Suffolk County wasn't nothing like the Pole, J—that's for sure."

"I understand that. But I don't have to waste my breath explaining it."

"Naw, man." Zeke paused, his expression one of a shared unpleasantness. "I ain't trying to relive none of it."

"Exactly. Anyway, after all of the horrible shit that was to come for C.B. and Ju-Ju finally arrived, they came for me." He stared at Zeke directly. "At first, I didn't know what was going on. I would get sick as a dog for a day and then better, and then the next week I'd get sick for two days and blah, blah, blah."

"Blah, blah, what? You're telling me the Brotherhood found out you were stealing from them so they decided to smoke Ju-Ju and C.B. and fucking *poison* you?"

"Yes. That's exactly what I'm saying."

"You're out of your mind." Zeke stood and unzipped the forgotten windbreaker. As he peeled off the turtleneck beneath, he heard Josh say, "Exactly what part don't you believe?"

"What is this, fucking Hitchcock?" Dismayed, shaking his head, Zeke re-took his seat and poured a quarter glass. "Then tell me why, why would they even waste their time?"

"Instead of just ganking me?" Josh's sneer was filled with possibility. "Or renouncing my rights as a white and whoring me out to the fucking niggers? Gee, Zeke, I never thought to ask."

"Because it's bullshit."

Josh immediately stood up, sick or not. "If you call me a liar one more time—"

"Goddamn it, Josh, sit down."

"Naw, fuck you! You're really gonna sit there and tell me my own *history*?"

Staring down, stilled in flashback, it was all recycled again. "Goddamn it," he said, then looked at Zeke. "I panicked." Josh pursed his lips as if he wanted to spit but slowly, reluctantly, collapsed onto the recliner instead. "Gracie."

"Huh?"

From the beaten look Zeke received, he knew Josh apparently could not, even after this long, give up the name without facing its meaning.

"He was it, you know?" Josh almost grinned. "I mean, I was fucking eighteen when I hit those gates. And every motherfucker in there knew it. And Gracie ..." He swallowed thickly. "He watched me, you know? Because I didn't sign up with them and handled myself like I didn't need to and well, back then, before all this ..." Josh ran a hand over himself as if he were a malfunctioning product on display. "I wasn't about making any friends, man, you remember."

"Yes, I sure do."

"In there, I made a point of anyone that even twitched at me, and Gracie, well, he just respected the fuck out of that. I racked up so many D-reports for fighting that I pretty much made a second home on 10-block. Hi-power, motherfucker."

Zeke squinted and said, "Who the fuck is Gracie?"

"The Brotherhood, man, the head fucking psycho over fifty other freaks."

"Jesus."

"Yeah. Even before I came to them with my Tully connection, Gracie, when I would run into him, he was always just looking out, you know? Fuck, I was so young, I thought he was the man, you know? He told horrible stories about the DOCs in New Hampshire and Maine and I'm pretty sure there wasn't a prison within four hundred miles he didn't see the inside of at least once. He was a biker, something like fifty years old, but you could never tell it. From all that time, in all those weight rooms, his body was built like a fucking dump truck."

"Great."

"Yeah ..." Josh shrugged. "It was also because of what we all did to get in there in the first place, you know, that's really why he noticed me. I mean, what fucking Aryan wouldn't?"

"I hear ya."

"So anyway, once Ju-Ju ratted me to Gracie, a day later, Ju-Ju, after all his scheming and last fucking betrayal ... he, well, they carved him up first, the stupid fuck. As if Gracie was gonna deal with *him*? When he'd been in on it the whole fucking time?" Josh scoffed at the suggestion before refocusing on some unseen point. "And then C.B. and I ... well, we were scared, man, I mean totally freaked out. Stealing from the Brotherhood?" He wore a look that relayed the exact outcome this proposition undoubtedly represented. "I just figured we were next, you know?"

"What, Josh," Zeke nearly whispered. "What did you fucking do?"

"Goddamn …" He shook his head. "I really figured we had nothing left to lose."

"Josh …"

"I … I passed some money."

"No."

"To Chino."

"Oh my God."

"And they fucked me." Josh threw up both hands as if what else was to be expected. "La Familia fucking fucked me, those goddamn tortilla-eating motherfuckers—"

"They rolled you. Why?"

"Why not? What was I to them? I mean, they fucking hated Gracie, but everyone did. That's why I thought it was our only shot, you know? We're talking about a guy hauling three life terms plus a hundred and twenty years thrown in just to make sure. At the time, he was waiting on another trial because within, like, five years he basically killed his way to the top of the Brotherhood, and once he found out about the contract …"

"Jesus Christ." Zeke felt like he needed to puke. "What the fuck were you thinking?"

"Is that what junkies do best? For real, Z, I was already punched out, you know? What was I gonna do?"

"So what then?"

"C.B." Josh took a deep breath and exhaled defeatedly. "They ran him to Med-Wack with eighteen holes and two screwdrivers sticking out of his chest."

"What the fuck?"

"It was awful, man." His expression deflated even further. "Within a week, too. And then, well, and then I just waited. Every second of every day, every shadow, every sound, any person within thirty feet of me—I just waited. And the days turned into a week, then two, then a month and still, nothing. Honestly, I just figured it was too much heat, you know? Two in six days? Fuck, we were locked down twenty-three hours a day for a month."

"And then …"

"And then, like I said, one day I just got sick. And I'm not talking about a fever. I'm talking about vomiting until I thought I was gonna be wearing my stomach for a goatee. Delirium, tremors, sick as I've ever been. Day later, I can eat, barely, but definitely better. This goes on for a while, once a week, for like months. Now, I know what you're thinking. How can you not notice this? Well, I did. But like I said—and telling my kid brother this ain't exactly the high point of my life—everyone knew I was hooked by then. Screws, nigs, fuck, even the doctor said I probably got a bad hand. But see, I didn't share none of that. Never. A kid two squares down was diabetic, so I had my own rig, hell, ten, twenty if need be. I wasn't like those other animals, passing that evil dick from vein to vein. And fucking Gracie … To set me up even further, word passed through that my life would be a day-by-day what-if, and that either way, once his trial was over, he was personally gonna make my acquaintance."

"What the hell …"

"So, shit goes on, months go by, his case goes nowhere, and then it's worse—twice, sometimes three times a week. Got so bad they had me in the infirmary on IVs for a week. And let me tell you how creative a junkie has to be. Fuck, I was juggling God knows how many illnesses. But like some miracle I got scared. Scared enough to go clean. Which I did. And guess what?"

"You still got sick."

"Worse. Once the motherfuckers heard I went clean, I got dosed left and right. Food, sheets, clothes—"

"Wait, wait, hold on a second. Sheets? What the hell was this shit?"

"Napathalene."

"Napa-what?"

"And paradichlorobenzene."

"Huh?"

Glancing at the floor, Josh wore a look as if it was still so odd, the names like old friends sealed inside forever. "Supposedly, it was a trick Gracie got off the grapevine from a level-four max in Kansas." Extinguishing the cigarette, he simply said, "Mothballs."

"*Mothballs?*" Zeke paused, waiting for a punch line until it did not arrive. He looked at his brother in amazement. "Those things are that toxic?"

"The doctors think they were either reduced back into powder or liquified."

Joshua shrugged. "Doesn't really matter either. Shit gets you through the skin, swallowing, inhaling …"

"But didn't you just say you worked in the kitchen?"

"Yeah." Josh lit a cigarette. "You listening to anything else? Two fucking eye drops' worth is all it took, Zeke, and like I said, it was once a week, not every meal."

"Jesus …"

"Throw a few sprinkles in the bed sheets or underwear or those god-awful fucksuits … you getting an eye on this yet? We're talking about fifty-odd strong, with motherfuckers in every department."

"Man …"

"And I'm not a moron. In the beginning, when I finally got a doctor freaked out enough to believe me, they ran all kinds of tests, toxins too, but found nothing. Apparently, that shit needs time to kill the organs that flush it. It was still too early. Didn't matter. I ate only the meals I cooked in the kitchen and went commissary my two days off until I was still getting worked and started eating whatever and believing the doctors when they told me I was just a sick man and not the object of some fucked-up conspiracy. Besides, asshead's trial was dragging on and, believe me, they were in no rush when it came to expensive tests and specialists, and I was just told to be a patient patient."

Zeke almost smiled as he asked, "And how long did that last?"

"Fifteen minutes at best. Towards the end, I was like a crazy rat in there, screaming at the fucking doctors, who at first thought I had a stomach condition, and then it's an inflamed ulcer, and then colitis, and then next it's Crohn's disease, and I'd take shitloads of meds for a month until I told them, 'Look, you stethoscope-sucking bitches, take another goddamn look.' And on and on and on. They thought I had twenty different things until one brain surgeon finally found that shit loading up my blood."

"And of course by then …"

"Way," Joshua blew a smoke ring, "way too late."

Blinking, Zeke tried digesting the facts and consequences before cursing the stupidity of it all. "Jesus, Josh."

"Yep." He let fly another squadron of smoke rings. "Finally, the morons diagnosed this shit called hemolytic anemia, which basically means red blood cells die early. That's the good news. Bad news is that the long-term exposure pretty much killed my kidneys."

"Just like that?"

Josh nodded slowly, glancing at Zeke's horrified expression. "Believe me, bro, I know more shit about this shit than most GPs. When they tell you you are going to die without a transplant, you start reading. Especially in there. You have no choice, because you're sick and getting sicker and more scared every single day."

"Jesus Christ."

"It was awful." Josh gulped his vodka, staring at the floor as if looking through a window. "I thought the worst part was not knowing what was killing me. But actually finding out who was on the other end … and then realizing it was just to see if this sick fucking toxic bullshit actually worked? I mean proving a goddamn *rumor*?" He batted a hand disgustedly. "My lawyer finally got an appointment with another toxicologist who figured the napathalene level to be a thousand times above the safe exposure limit, which is pretty much zero. It was in my muscles and skin and tweaked a bunch of other shit, like my liver, heart—and eyes. Glaucoma's another nightmare I've got to look forward to."

Each time Zeke thought it entirely unbelievable, he took one look at what they had so skillfully done and thought, *A killing in science fiction.*

"I've got dialysis scheduled three times a week at Mass. General." Josh let the cigarette drop into a beer can. "And I'm on SSI until my lawyer straightens everything out."

"You're going to sue?"

Something in his tone, he soon saw, caused Josh to lance him with a look. "Are you listening to any of this? Or just nodding your head like a moron?"

"Hey, I only—"

"We're talking about ten months before detection. Another nine until release with me staggering around that fucking sewer like Gracie's fucking lab rat? Exactly when do I stop being a nice guy?"

"That's not what I meant. At all. And what about this lawyer? Once they found out all this horrible shit, they couldn't at least have moved you to Shirley?"

"Medium security? With a fifteen-year bill and D-reports out the ass? You're kidding, right?"

"But—"

"And for another, you can't deal shit and not attract a certain amount of baggage. None of which they could prove, of course, but once they started dangling Ju-Ju and Cancer Boy, I just about lost what was left of my mind."

"Yeah, well, I got more good news." Zeke stood and left the room, returning a minute later with an envelope. Handing it to his brother, he said, "Found it under my door two months ago."

Reading the threatening sentences contained therein, Josh scoffed at the individual letters cut and pasted with such care.

"The Burgess fucking morons," he said and tossed the paper aside.

"Josh—"

"Hey, spare me." He pinned his brother with a gaze. "C.B. and Ju-Ju knew what was up. To me, that's all that matters."

"But I thought you just said you were the one stepping on—"

"So what? Ask fucking Ju-Ju about *this*." Staring straight at him, Josh held out a thin, yellowed arm. "And I owe those fucks an explanation?"

"Fuck, Josh, those guys were our bros—"

"And! What was it gonna be, Zeke, for any of us?"

"They sent those kids home from Walpole in *bags*, man." Zeke held out both hands as if the answer rested palm-side up. "Can't you see how that looked? Especially when no one, including me, ever heard a word about Ju-Ju ratting you out or … or this other horrible shit with Gracie?"

"And?"

"And?" Zeke fought the exasperation. "On top of already thinking you left those guys—"

"Watch it!"

"But it's what they think, man, can't you see that? That you dodged felony murder and they got life?"

"Listen." Josh pointed at Zeke. "We'd been collecting off that old man for months. Ju-Ju didn't need to bring that fucking gun into the store, and as a matter of fact, since we already had that other shit in the car, I specifically told both of them to jump in clean. Period. I had just bought that Mustang—remember that beast?—so I wasn't about to let either one of them drive it. They went in and next thing I knew I heard sirens screaming and then the window exploded and two turned into four turned into eight and when no one showed, I fucking jetted." Josh scoffed. "I love that argument, too. That I should've hopped out and run in to help them? With what? Bad language?"

"It just didn't look good—"

"Let them hate me then." Josh's eyes grew tighter. "That day, that fucking store was the least of our priorities. The man in Southie was looking for younger talent, and through his other guy we were just starting out running his shit but ..." Josh slowly shook his head. "Only Ju-Ju could destroy the whole fucking thing I created in ten goddamn seconds."

"It's just how it appeared is all."

"They need someone to blame." He looked at Zeke. "How the fuck could that have ended any differently?"

"I totally agree, okay? But that doesn't mean people aren't stupid."

"That's not my problem."

Zeke held up the threatening letter. "Really?"

"I ain't worried about the fucking Burgess Street Mob, Z. Believe me, those wannabes can take a fucking number."

"Yeah, well, they found me and my name ain't listed anywhere. Not on a lease, a bill, a single fucking credit card—"

"But it is with the department of parole and the probation people and on and on. Come on, Zeke, nobody's invisible."

"Exactly my point."

Josh bit back a reply, sullenly gnawed a lip, and said, "Who do we still got?"

"Fuck, man, who knows? I haven't been back since." Zeke shrugged tiredly. "I saw Lindy on Newbury a few days before they played cut-and-paste with this bullshit," he nodded towards the note, "but Lotus, he says Lindy and Boxer are still around, supposedly pulling strings."

"You saw Lindy?" Josh tried to feign nonchalance, reaching for a cigarette. "How'd that go?"

"Pretty much as you'd expect." Zeke tossed him a lighter. "Besides putting on thirty pounds and balding, he looks stupider than ever."

Josh grinned through the smoke and said, "So what'd he say?"

"What, from the car window?" Zeke shrugged. "A whole bunch of hateful shit ... The guy's a fucking tool, man. Fuck him."

"And good old Lotus?"

"Kicking it. Moves shit at night, works part-time for Triple X, but that's just for taxes."

"Can he get a pulse on these clowns or what?"

"Probably." Zeke tabled his empty glass. "I'll talk to him. Also says he's got a job if you need one."

"I always liked Lotus."

"We'll see what he can do." Zeke took a deep breath and found the alcohol, combined with the conversation's weight, spreading heavily across his shoulders.

"Lindy and Boxer—what a couple of retards," Joshua said derisively.

"Yep."

"And to think we helped start that whole fucking scene."

"Like I said, no one knows, Josh. I mean, look at what they fucking did to you." As he waited for his brother's caustic reaction, he was surprised to see him grinning. "What's so funny?"

"What isn't?" Half-drunk, Josh raised his glass, laughing despite himself as Zeke's annoyed expression only furthered his enjoyment. "Ah, c'mon, Zeke. It ain't like that."

"Suck it."

He laughed again, giving his brother a sideways wink. "I still know which buttons to push."

"Yeah, you're a real genius all right."

Letting the smile linger, Josh said, "I missed you, missed this."

"Yeah."

"That ain't no shine, either."

"Come on, man."

"What?"

"Don't get all faggy on me."

"Jesus, look at you. All squirmy and shit?"

"You're just drunk."

"That maybe so." Josh grinned as he drained the glass. "Some welcome home party. Piss-warm vodka in a goddamn pigsty."

"The freezer's broke," Zeke said, trying to hide the smile as he stood. "I gotta take a leak."

"Yeah, good luck with that."

After changing into sweats and a T-shirt, Zeke turned the corner to catch

Josh wincing, both hands a delicate cup feathering the left-side distension. Zeke said, "What's up? You all right?"

"Yeah."

Zeke frowned. "It's the booze, isn't it? Your face is bright fucking red, man."

"It's nothing."

"And ... Jesus, you're sweating like hell."

"Easy, nurse." Josh swiped his face again, sitting up straighter. "Just a little flushed. Nighttime kind of sucks."

"It's not even seven o'clock."

"So?" Reflexively brushing at himself for no reason, Josh said, "I'm fine. Believe me."

"Whatever." Zeke sat back down. "So when did you walk?"

"Two weeks ago. Actually, it was November 6, at 8:36 AM."

"Two weeks?" Zeke blinked. "And you just come strolling through now?"

"Hey, hey, exactly how was I supposed to find you? You talk to the prick since the last time we spoke?"

"No."

"And, like you blabbed out before, you ain't listed anywhere."

"Well ..." Zeke grinned. "Okay then. So how did you?"

"After getting nowhere, I finally called every company in the book, hoping you were still alive."

"Who'd you talk to?"

"Some guy named Stuart. Talked to him this morning. Told him it was a surprise."

"I'll be damned." Zeke shook his head. "Loverboy kept a secret for the first time in his life."

"You really haven't spoken with him?"

"Who, Stu? Talked with him at—"

"No, idiot, Pop."

"Oh." Zeke leaned towards the coffee table for a refill. "Nope. See the trucks sometimes, but ..."

"But not him."

"To be honest, if I do see one, I'm looking anywhere but driver-side."

"Huh."

Watching his brother glance away, Zeke stomached a growing concern. "You're not gonna … are you?"

"Zeke—"

"Christ, what a sucker."

"I'm just asking."

"Really." Zeke saw otherwise. "I gotta say, that kind of makes me sick."

"Oh, please."

"I want no part of it, Josh. You talk to him, you ain't seen me at all."

"Yeah, well, he has a right to know. About this." Josh nodded down towards his body. "Besides, you never know."

"Kid yourself all you want. He doesn't give a fuck."

"You just got it all figured out, huh?"

"Fuck that guy."

"Nice, Zeke. Between the three of us, it's no wonder—"

"That's two of you. Keep the math straight."

"He's still family."

"Is that the last thing you got left to hold on to?"

"You're amazing." Josh massaged his temples. "Fine, you win, okay?"

"For real and for good."

"Fuck yeah, killer. So I guess you can handle it. Especially in the next twelve months, when the medications and even the dialysis shit the bed. I'll just throw myself around your neck and drag us both down into oblivion."

"I thought you just said you were suing—"

"Like I've got eight fucking years on appeal! C'mon, Zeke, I swear, I've been here an hour and you're getting stupider by the minute."

"Me?" Zeke laughed in surprise. "Are you insane?"

"I knew this was a mistake." He stood up. "Where's the john?"

"Around the corner. Two doors back." Sitting there numbly, Zeke heard him shuffle towards the bathroom. It was, he knew, a compromise he could not make. Even to think otherwise would cripple the self-wrought history, erode away eight long years of endless torment, although he would not ever admit it. *As basic as human beings get*, he thought and drunkenly raised his glass.

When Josh reappeared, he was cinching a belt that had nowhere else to go. Reaching for an imitation leather jacket, he said, "I gotta roll."

"What?" Zeke stood up. "Where? Why?"

"Gimme your beeper number."

"You know …" Shaking his head, disgusted, Zeke went for his bag. Hastily scribbling across a Split Minute slip, he rose and thrust it into his brother's chest as he passed by. "Don't forget to lose it."

"I'll call you tomorrow."

"I won't be here." Grabbing the remote control, Zeke flopped onto the couch. "It's Thanksgiving, remember?"

"Late night then."

"Gotta work early." Zeke flipped through the channels. "Next week's good for me."

"Don't be a fucking baby. I can't stay here."

"Who's asking you to?"

A moment later, out of his periphery, Zeke saw him standing in the doorway, too tired to fight, and completely ignored. Turning for the door, Joshua gave him the finger and made sure to slam the door.

Chapter Nine

Thursday, November 23

PLACED INTO THREE HAPHAZARD stacks on the counter, Cammi Sinclair cleared the last of the dishes. She then helped Zeke bring in decimated platters of mashed potato, stuffing, and a turkey's shorn carcass. He fixed another rum and Coke as she stood sink-side in a Bullwinkle apron, sud-smeared arms submerged.

"The happy homemaker," he cracked, and sipped at his drink.

In honor of the occasion, Cammi had her hair pulled into two pigtails that popped up on either side of her head like misplaced ears. Her strapless black crepe dress was, as she had proudly informed the gathering, just recently completed. She also wore a pair of stiletto high heels that caused Zeke to say, "You need to do this more than once a year." And whistled until she blushed.

Cataloguing his perversions, she then turned and caught him standing idly by. "Is that table cleared?"

"Yes, ma'am."

"Garbage out?"

"Yes, ma'am."

"Well, grab a towel."

Outside, the hum of the Boston night was like a white-noise serenade.

Working in silence for a time, he re-stacked clean dishes in the cabinets she described.

Taking a sip of his drink, Zeke said, "So we made it. And there wasn't even a single fight."

"Miracle."

"You can really cook."

"Another miracle." She paused to rub an arm across her perspiration-dotted forehead. "Next year, it's your turn."

"Again?"

She smiled, recalling the burned potatoes and the turkey he had ripped in two to cook faster—memories of their last holiday sojourn left to burn as both got wickedly shitfaced. "When was that, by the way?"

"What's that?"

"That Thanksgiving, when you lost it with the hacksaw?"

He smiled. "Is there anything in the last seven years that you couldn't enter into evidence?"

"Probably not."

"Besides," Zeke laughed. "I saw that on Julia Child's show."

"Sure you did. Was Julia also doing whiskey shooters in between lines of blow?"

"What good cook doesn't?"

She smiled again, picturing the two of them spun to the gills, the meal forgotten, the sex one long session doubling as dessert.

"Yeah," she said nostalgically. "That was one for the books."

"I thought your sister was pretty well behaved tonight."

"Yep." Cammi dumped the last of the potatoes into a Tupperware bowl. "No name-dropping, no bragging."

"And no bitching."

"It was yet another paranormal event. At least for Josie."

"And your mother too. She didn't call me drug dealer even once."

"I know. She still hates you, though."

"Who doesn't?"

"No kidding. How about some music?"

"Yep." He turned for the common room. "Man in Black?"

"Sure."

Standing at the sink, she had a moment to recall the evening. Despite a number of incredibly awkward silences, she allowed herself a minimal pat on the back. Her mother, the Manhattanite advertising executive who now lived with a boyfriend two-thirds her own age, had appeared at the front door with bottles of wine, a smile, and, of all things, a hug. In the midst of this ambush, as they embraced, and despite Cammi's best efforts, the tears nonetheless threatened every grudge and misdeed four years' absence demanded. Not wanting to let her off that easy, convinced her mother could appreciate none of it, she had turned for the stairs in a quick and businesslike silence.

Hearing Zeke cursing from the next room, Cammi smiled and said, "What's the problem, spaz?"

"This fucking stereo, man, is fucking fucked up."

"Jiggle the plug around. Sometimes it has an attitude."

A minute later, they heard Johnny Cash addressing a large crowd before strumming into a ballad about adultery and death. Zeke entered the kitchen holding his beeper as he said, "I think it's Josh."

"Tell him to come over."

Zeke grabbed her phone. Hanging up a minute later, he told her, "He's just around the corner."

"Where's he staying?"

"Who knows?"

"Well, you're not off duty yet. That pot's not gonna dry itself, now is it?"

As they worked, she saw what it was, and what it always turned into, that made their latest separation seem so shortsighted. Three months and still, despite the current relationships each pursued, one to the other was like comparing a best friend to a blind date. The floundering awkwardness of pretending to care as her new boyfriend prattled on about his painting, a form of portraiture that Cammi thought of as second-rate at best, and which made the fact he did not know this devalue his appeal even more. As for Zeke, all Cammi knew was that she did not want to know a single thing about her replacement. That satisfaction, she knew, he could never have.

As the last of the dishes were dried and stored, they had time to mix another round of drinks before the door buzzer rattled.

"Fuck."

"Take it easy," Cammi said, depressing the button.

"Remember what I told you. He looks completely tweaked."

Nodding at what she still mistook for exaggeration, she opened the door before wishing she had not. Having met only once before, and through a telephone between three inches of reinforced bulletproof glass, this might as well have been the first time, so meager was the resemblance. She found the greatest difference in the upper body, the once prison-pressed slopes shrunken down to nothing. Other than the now-unkempt black hair and sullen black eyes, little else remained the same. Gaunt to the point of concern and stained that horrible yellow, Josh gave her a beaming smile.

"Hey, Cam," he said and held up a brown paper bag. "I brought a little something to wash down the bird."

It may have been the alcohol, but with arms outstretched, she enveloped him in a hug that appeared to catch him off guard. Despite the winter jacket, the destruction beneath could be clearly discerned. *What the fuck ...?*

Disengaging, she cursed herself and wiped an eye. "Come in."

Glancing around the apartment, he nodded as if impressed. "Nice place, Cam."

"Thank you."

"It's not all yours, is it?"

"No. I've got two roommates. They went home for the holiday."

Joining his brother at the table, he gave Zeke a pointed wink and said, "Still digesting?"

"Fuckin' A." Zeke rubbed his stomach in satiation. "That was the best meal I've had in six months."

"I wouldn't go that far," Cammi replied.

Josh nodded. "Must've been something special if you got this clown into slacks and a dress shirt. You look like you just got back from court."

"Thanks for reminding me." Zeke peeled off the oxford to reveal a worn out T-shirt. "What's in the bag?"

"Only the best." Grinning, Josh pulled out a 50-ounce jug of Thunderbird wine.

"Oh no." Zeke laughed. "Back from the dead."

"You guys are absolutely disgusting." But Cammi filled three glasses and passed them out. "Can I fix you a plate, Josh? Did you eat yet?"

"Thanks, but I'm good." Taking off his jacket, Joshua scratched at both arms repeatedly. "Glasses? Baby, you got to swig this shit in order to appreciate it."

"Uh, no, thanks." Cammi proposed a toast. "To the end of pain."

"Right on." Smacking his lips, Josh said, "Eleven years like it was just yesterday."

"Big bro here always had class," Zeke told Cammi. "We used to drink this crap out behind the old Emerson Junior High almost every summer night."

"Remember the Vietnamese guy?" Josh winced. "God, we were assholes."

"That poor bastard." Zeke turned towards Cammi. "We never had any ID and at first, when he wouldn't sell us booze, we'd straight up gank it."

Josh grinned. "He quickly decided it was better to take our money than get ripped off."

"For this crap?" Cammi cracked and raised her glass. "Looks like he got the better end of that deal."

"Here's to being a pillar of the community," Zeke said and they all laughed.

Josh scratched at his face and neck and asked, "Remember Holtzman?"

"Jesus." Zeke frowned. "I haven't thought about that kid in years."

"Me either." Josh looked at Cammi and said, "We used to have this friend, Ronnie Holtzman, who would do almost anything if you got him drunk enough."

"All you had to do was dare him," Zeke added.

"Thunderbird was his kryptonite. Remember that night he jumped off Kelly's garage roof? On that piece-of-shit BMX he was so proud of?"

"Oh God. And the ambulance guys?" Zeke laughed softly. "They were horrified."

"Fucking kid fell two stories, busted a bunch of bones, and they still had to put him in restraints."

"Sounds like a real brain surgeon," she said. "So whatever happened to him?"

Their smiles froze. Josh picked at his glass and said, "Well ..."

"He got tatered one night," Zeke said, "and passed out on the B-line tracks."

"Poor bastard," Joshua sighed. "What a dumbass."

"He never felt it, though."

"Here's to Holtzman," Josh said. "And Monkman too. Did you hear about that? Got stuck up at that liquor store on the corner of Columbia and Boston …?"

Inside the next half hour, as the reminiscences came tumbling forth, Cammi nodded at the appropriate times and refilled their glasses while analyzing each like a fingerprint. Recalling the picture of Zeke's mother, Cammi figured Josh, with the black hair and eyes and pre-jaundiced skin tone, was nearly her identical twin. Taller, better-looking than Zeke, she noted, although both had noses broken and re-broken into misshapen hooks. And as siblings will, intertwined inside the shared mannerisms and speech, who came first or said what became almost impossible to delineate. The sly grins and impish eyes were like an eerie reflection in duplicate, while both found humor in places no one else should. Glancing at their arms, she acknowledged the craftsmanship of Zeke's tattoos, in particular a crested mountain range backlit by an orange sun. As for Joshua, no such compliment could be given. From wrist to elbow and God knows where else, the black and blue ink from pirated ballpoint pens littered him like sleeves of the damned. There were the obligatory naked women, a clown with a gun to his head as the opposite temple exploded, a four-inch knife cutting the throat of a robed judge beneath the caption JUSTICE in old English type, multi-headed demons with octopus arms clutching body parts, and a clock with both hands stuck at midnight as another caption screamed, TIME. With so much of it on his hands, locked inside an environment Cammi would not even pretend to comprehend, his body read like a tombstone highlighted by the buildup of yellow waste beneath the painted skin.

Only this morning, from what little Zeke had reluctantly divulged, she knew something about the circumstances surrounding the illness and that, whatever he had done to cause it, had been graciously repaid in triplicate by people incapable of anything else. Guilt or no guilt, staring at him now as he scratched compulsively at his skin every few minutes, and comparing his face to the one she barely recalled, Cammi felt a growing nausea replacing what little goodwill remained towards humanity. *Like fucking animals*, was all she thought as the two of them broke out laughing after the conclusion of yet another story. And while Cammi Sinclair did not necessarily hate men, she attributed most of the world's evil to their thinly veiled stupidity. As he once again raked his skin, she finally had to ask, "What causes that?"

"What?" Caught in mid-act, he self-consciously pocketed his hand. He stared at his glass, trapped. "My phosphate level is all screwed up."

Intrigued as well, Zeke said, "And that means …?"

Taking a deep breath, Josh looked into the void opened by the question and tiredly scratched his face. "Zeke already knows about the dialysis. Since my kidneys are fucked, I go to Mass. General three times a week because it's the only way to clear the wastes from my blood. But the kidneys also regulate a bunch of other functions, like red blood cell production, hemoglobin, fluid management—a ton of stuff. The doctors figure what they call a dry weight, which is where my fluid level would normally be. The dialysis aims for that number, but sometimes I'm either parched or swelling from too much liquid. None of this shit is exact. Too much phosphorus means the body takes calcium from the bones, which can lead to another beauty called chronic bone disease, where the bones become brittle and the pain … let's just say it fucking kills. So I take this stuff called aluminum hydroxide, a phosphate binder. The potassium level is also critical. Too little causes weakness; too much can mean heart palpitations or even cardiac arrest. I take Kayexalate for that. Dialume for the phosphate, ferrous sulfate for an iron supplement, a shitload of vitamins like B and C and niacin and B6. No salts, no dairy, and my diet reads like an old man's nightmare."

Staring at the horror-stricken masks surrounding him, Josh allowed himself a grin. "We'll be having a test on that later."

Cammi said, "Coming from your lips, you sound like a fucking doctor."

"The ex-con doctor," Zeke echoed without humor. "Jesus Christ."

"How do they do the dialysis?" Cammi asked.

"Right here." He held out his left wrist. "They made a fistula here, which's basically a vein and artery sewn together. And in case that blows out, I've got a graft sewn into my neck."

Running her hand across the wrist-side bulge, Cammi said, "And you have to do all this until the transplant?"

"Transplant …" Zeke whispered, abruptly perking up. "Yeah, Josh … goddamn, I never even thought about that—"

Holding up a hand to stop them both, Josh finished his glass of wine. "Forget it."

"What …?"

214 | *Tom Trabulsi*

"They don't just hand those things out."

"But they're kidneys, right?" Zeke looked at Cammi as if she were somehow the deciding voice. "Don't family members give those things away all the time?"

"Zeke …"

"Take one of mine." He laughed. "They ain't doing me any good."

As Cammi Sinclair shot him a rage-filled look, Zeke had a second to audibly swallow his own ignorance. "Man, I'm sorry about that."

"Zeke—"

"I'm an idiot."

"You sure are." Cammi stood up and refilled their glasses. "But what about that idea, Josh? I mean is it possible?"

"Not really. And I don't blame them. Ex-junkie ex-cons don't rate too high on their lists. I appreciate the love, but right now I got about a million other nightmares to worry about."

Not wanting to exacerbate what she judged to be a growing irritation, and wondering what could be more important than replacing two failed kidneys, she returned to the table and let plop a single cube into her glass. "As if it's gonna make a difference. This crap tastes like bull piss."

"The working man's cocaine," Josh said with a playful grin, and completely drained the glass. "What hick is this?"

"Johnny Cash," Cammi replied indignantly. "I love this disc."

"It's live?"

She nodded while swallowing a mouthful of Thunderbird. "It was recorded at Folsom Prison."

"Great. You got a gun with a single bullet in it?"

"Relax." Grinning, Zeke said, "Might be a little too soon for prison songs, Cam."

"Oh my God," Cammi said. "How stupid. Sorry. You can thank Zeke for that."

Retreating into the next room, she hummed quietly until the industrial hatred of Ministry spewed forth. Rejoining them at the table, she asked, "So where are you staying now?"

"I got a monthly on Fordham," Josh said, nodding in the general direction of Brighton Avenue. "A one-room box and a bathroom I share with fifteen other morons."

Zeke half-grinned. "Sounds exotic."

"Why don't the two of you get a place?" Cammi suggested, but neither said a word in answer. "What? I think it'd be perfect."

"I already got this lease," Zeke said lamely.

Josh nodded. "I'm square too."

"Whatever." Reaching for one of Zeke's Marlboros, Cammi gave them both a hostile squint through the smoke. *Like two wet cats*, she thought and, watching as they avoided eye contact or even the slightest act of intimation, she smiled and shuddered simultaneously. Sadly, inside their frozen play at what life had been, lurked the impossible obstacle half a lifetime apart represented. And while it was classic Zeke to bask in that patented cavalier nonchalance, Cammi knew too much, had been involved beyond the point where parts of people, over the long years, could possibly be misconstrued. It was the bead in his eye that betrayed it, his quick smile and willingness to laugh in lieu of the sneer and misery he truly thought of as a way of life. All of it, including the structured excuses she knew by rote, momentarily vaporized to expose exactly what they were when all of what was yet to come for each would eventually leave them here, in Allston, Massachusetts, drinking gutter-strength elixir at her kitchen table. As Cammi allowed herself a lazy smile, she decided she was pretty fucked up.

"What's so funny?" Zeke asked.

Cammi dismissed him with a shrug, holding out her empty glass. "It's your round."

Hoisting the near-empty jug, Zeke said, "Roger that."

"Yeah." Josh belched. "Bottoms up."

"I don't know how much I like this," she said, folding her arms crossly. "Feeding alcohol to a sick man?"

"Believe me," Zeke said. "It's like talking to a wall."

"Yeah," Joshua said, glass extended. "Save your conscience for church."

"Oh no." Zeke winced. "I just saw what time it was."

"Zeke …" Cammi blew smoke directly into his face. "You can't ever leave good enough alone, can you?"

"Supposed to be snowing out the ass, too."

"Zeke, shut the fuck up!" Cammi and Josh high-fived. "You can be such a pill."

"Whatever, lady."

"Hey, the tunes," Josh said as the CD repeatedly skipped and Cammi sprang to her feet, slipped, and nearly ate the countertop face first as the others laughed.

"Looking good."

"Yeah, nice moves," Zeke cracked. She gave both the finger and disappeared into the next room.

While changing the CD, she overheard Josh say, "She's a piece." There was the sound of a lighter being flicked. "Seven years, huh?"

"Gimme one of those."

"Where'd you meet?"

"At the corner of Milk and Oliver."

Pressing the play button, Cammi grinned at the recollection.

Josh said, *"Where?"*

"No shit. She blew right through the goddamn—"

"Yeah, okay, Zeke," Cammi called out. "Whatever you say."

"Hey! No eavesdropping! I'm trying to tell a story here."

"Your brother," Cammi said, re-entering the room, "hosed a stop sign before flying out into the intersection like a *total* hayseed."

"Bullshit—"

"So I ran him over like a turd."

Josh laughed until Zeke grinned, humbled. "Yeah, I guess she's right. It was actually worse than that because …"

And as Zeke held court, man enough to disgorge every humiliating detail of their abrupt and violent introduction, Cammi had a second to savor his disgrace. She was surprised to find herself thinking that in moments like this, tonight's surrender for tomorrow's burden was no choice at all. Sipping the rancid wine, the fool's smile plastered across her face, Cammi only listened.

Chapter Ten

Friday, November 24

IN THE MIDDLE OF the kitchen, the mountain bike hung suspended on the six-foot-by-six-foot homemade X-brace made out of two-by-fours. As an AM radio station crackled out the details of the day ahead, Zeke heard none of it as he sat at the derailleur furiously working a socket wrench while his beeper chirped again. Barely able to focus, reliving the Thunderbird mistake with every fetid breath, the vomit was like a shotgun cocked and aimed up his esophagus. Outside, there was four inches and three more on the way as the weatherman took center stage, apparently beside himself at the possibility of a citywide paralysis.

Over-torquing his grip, Zeke ripped open an index finger before flinging the pliers at the wall. After his beeper went off for a third time in five minutes, he saw a flash of murder, took a deep breath, and reached for the phone where an instant later Stuart Rigby said, "Split Minute."

"Beep me one more time and I'm quitting." Slamming the remote phone onto the countertop, he saw a one-inch slice across the first knuckle, stuck the entire finger into his mouth, and was sucking grease and blood as both the beeper and phone rang simultaneously. Kicking at the pliers, he stalked the kitchen in his boxers until Stuart Rigby's symphony of pain finally spiderwebbed his already beleaguered resolve. He grabbed the phone and moaned, "What, what, what?"

"Za-cha-ri-ah!" Stuart sing-songed. *"Que es su nombre!"*

"No es fucking bueno, Stuart." Clutching his forehead, Zeke weathered another burst of nausea, frantically swallowing the precursor liquid slime that ominously squirts in warning. "Oh God, back in a sec."

Hanging over the sink, gulping in hitches, the vomit exploded, hitting the sink bottom before ricocheting up in a splash that left him screaming through the acid. Thrusting his head sideways beneath the faucet, desperately blinking to see, he puked again and this time hit the sink wall inches from his nose. Having puke shoot up both nostrils made him retch again, and he groaned as Stuart Rigby laughed hysterically on the still-open line clutched in his abruptly dampened fist.

"Oh, Jesus." Zeke slipped down the cabinet until his backside hit the floor. "I can't believe I'm not dead."

Putting the phone to his ear, he found not one but three different people convulsing with laughter. Unable to share in their merriment, Zeke coughed once and said, "Hope you girls are enjoying the show."

Which only served to send a new paroxysm through the crowd.

"Oh jeepers," Stuart finally gasped, and Zeke could just picture it, the three of them all snuggled around coffee cups barely waiting to make a nickel off his dime. Running a hand across his face, he heard Stuart Rigby say, "Thank you, Zeke. How I do love the speakerphone. Say hello to Richie and F.T."

"Poor Zeke," Richard Parks said empathetically between hiccups of tapering laughter. "That was incredible."

"Yeah, Zeke," Father Time chimed in. "How's your stomach taste on your fucking tongue?"

"Oh God ..." Grimacing, Zeke fought back another gag.

"We just got off the phone with your better half," Stuart cracked. "At least she wasn't spewing her guts out."

Zeke groaned at the mere suggestion. "Just wait."

"What in the Lord's name happened last evening? Did the two of you hop into a giant vat of Jack Daniels?"

"I wish."

"And what time can I expect you?"

"Stuart, it's not even six thirty."

"Two minutes till, *mon frère*, but we won't wrestle with semantics." Stuart paused. "Do you like to wrestle, Zeke?"

"Oh, God …"

"Because I've got the cutest outfit for you and we can cover ourselves in virgin olive oil—"

"Stuart! You're gonna make me barf again!"

There was another explosion of laughter as Zeke grew tired of the delay and said, "Listen. I'm wrenching like crazy. Ten more minutes, and then another ten after that."

"What!"

"Stuart! Don't even start with me! Half your spokes probably already cancelled, the fucking pussies."

"Zeke—"

"Am I right? How many bang-outs you got?"

"That's not the—"

"It sure is, Stuart. Christ, I just finished puking all over myself, the derailleur's half-attached, and we're gonna go to war over twenty fucking minutes? On the Friday after Thanksgiving?"

"Oh, it'll be busy."

"More like *I'll* be busy because every loser you hire doesn't even have half the sack for this."

"Are you quite finished patting yourself on the back?"

"Twenty minutes, Stu."

"Fine! Wait, Zeke! Did someone get in touch with you Wednesday night?"

"What?" Zeke took a moment in recall. "Oh yeah. Thank you."

"So …?" Stuart paused. "So how'd it go? How is he?"

"Hey, Oprah, I'm not about to talk about this shit on the fucking speakerphone. Let me get moving. We got all day to gab."

"The high today is thirty. WBZ's saying blizzard conditions until early afternoon."

"Stop trying to cheer me up." Clicking off, Zeke Sandaman felt the creep of his own disease, wobbled to his feet, and stumbled immediately for the shower.

———————————————————

Humbled by the weather and his shaken coherence, Zeke cautiously ran the just-fixed derailleur up and down the five-gear cogs. Feeling a slight hitch coming out of third, he shrugged it off while avoiding the mountain of slush angled curbside by the plow blade. At high speed, even a small mound could send the entire day sideways.

Visibility was poor, the snowflakes wet and huge blown broadside against his left cheek. Knowing the headwind came in off the harbor, he grimaced at the thought of eating this crap face first for half the day. He wore a twenty-dollar knockoff pair of Elvis sunglasses, the wide side arms and oversized lenses offering about as much protection as the ski goggles some of his peers preferred. With the temperature at exactly thirty-two degrees, it was still too warm for the sub-zero tights, so he wore the usual black one-ply beneath green fatigue pants cut at mid-calf to avoid the chain. He had traded in his Specializeds for a pair of black leather Hi-Tech trooper boots that would nonetheless be soaked by noon. Up top, he was already breaking a sweat under two T-shirts, a turtleneck, and a hooded black EPS Gore-Tex jacket. Gloves, as always, were the biggest headache. The fancy winter biking alternatives were not made to be snowed or rained upon for ten hours at a clip, so he carried two sets of regular black leather in rotation and one pair of ski gloves, which, although the warmest, were the last resort and dangerously bulky, hindering his response time.

Making a slow right turn through four inches of slush, he saw Cambridge Street was a bumper-to-bumper crawl even at this early hour. With most schools and government offices closed and the storm only growing worse, these must have been the lower-management types, one step above working class yet two steps below having the day after Thanksgiving off.

As he crossed above the Massachusetts Turnpike, a howling wind blasted the exposed overpass. He cinched the hood closed while battling one-handed for control. A true hybrid, the KHS mountain bike frame had swapped-out ten-speed handlebars. Like the road bike, the gearing was five-speed only, with the same Shimano S-10 braking system. The three-quarter-inch knobby tires had been last year's gift to himself, nearly two hundred dollars even with a 30-percent discount. *Money well spent*, he thought, while fanning a two-foot wake as he made the left onto Commonwealth. Even with the front and rear fenders, Zeke knew his feet were in for a cold and sloppy daylong torture.

The Casement Bank clock flashed the time at 6:55 AM. Heading east, the shadowed towers of downtown were like distant fenceposts obscured by the snow and wind fighting him directly. Gearing back to third, he eventually coasted into Kenmore Square and locked up outside 522 Commonwealth. Two-hopping the steps, he kicked an inch of slush off each boot before hailing an elevator. Upstairs, he trudged along an empty corridor of closed offices until a single rectangle of light framed the opposite wall across the hall from Pierce Specialized Investigations. Knocking once, Zeke swung open the door and caught Donald Pierce with half a finger drilled up inside a nostril.

"Hey, Zeke."

Pulling off his steamed-up sunglasses, Zeke pushed aside his hood and readjusted the Carhartt knit cap. Clearing the lenses, he gradually acclimated to the stink of an unemptied garbage can and half a dozen Styrofoam containers reeking of forgotten Chinese and Thai takeout. Glancing at the brown slacks, pink shirt, and stained tan tie, Zeke decided the stench was always less offensive than Donald Pierce's outfits or his horrible baldheaded comb-over.

"That's some storm out there, huh?" Donald Pierce said, lighting a cigarette. "Did you have a good Thanksgiving?"

"I guess." Zeke slipped the glasses onto his forehead. "Ate some bird, got loaded …"

"Yeah, here ya go." Donald Pierce sifted through the desktop carnage until he found a pack of Wrigley's. "I'm getting drunk just sitting here."

"Thanks." Zeke unwrapped the proffered stick and could not believe his breath was actually noticeable above the surrounding stink. Reaching back for his slipcase, he said, "What about you? Got any family in town?"

"Nah, it's just me. I got a plate down at Riggio's."

"Yeah?"

"Then headed for the Glass Slipper."

"Nice, Don. Thanksgiving spent at a cafeteria before perving out in the Combat Zone."

"Only the best." Donald Pierce smiled broadly, revealing twin rows of yellow teeth. "I tell ya, Zeke, I just love the ladies."

Maybe on your porno tapes, Zeke thought, *or possibly on the other end of a twenty-dollar blowjob gummed out by some crackhead in the Slipper's notorious back alley.*

"What's not to love?" he said.

"Thatta boy." Leaning forward, Donald Pierce nudged an envelope and said, "Just one for Fitzroy. He should be in by eight."

"Nothing for the court?"

"Court?"

"Jesus, they closed the courts already?"

"Already?" Donald Pierce smiled again. "These are lawyers and judges, Zeke—you know, normal people that usually try to stay home during a blizzard that's got half the city shut down by 7 AM."

Zeke's beeper went off as he slipped the parcel into a garbage bag for added protection. Holding out the slipcase for a signature, he then stored both items in his courier sack and said, "Do me a favor—if Stuart calls, tell him I just left."

"No problem. Do me one in return. Fitzy might have my Sheppard domestic finished."

"And now since there's nowhere to file it ..."

"No rush. I'll be here till noon."

"Consider it done."

"If not, it'll probably be your first one Monday morning."

"Oh God ..." Zeke clutched at his suddenly shifting stomach. "Not again ..."

"What?" Donald Pierce's sallow eyes abruptly widened. "Are you gonna puke, Zeke?"

"No." Taking a deep breath, he swallowed twice, steadied the vertigo, and stood upright, momentarily triumphant. "I gotta go."

"Yeah, sure. Here." Donald Pierce held out a five-dollar bill. "For coffee."

"Thanks, Don." Stuffing the bill into his pocket, Zeke decided Donald Pierce's eccentricities and questionable hygiene were still not beyond the reach of five bucks. "I'll catch you on the way back through."

"Good luck out there."

"Yep."

Exiting, Zeke closed the door and wondered what was worse: the blistering ache chiseling through his brain or the fact that the hangover might actually be an easier punishment compared to what Mother Nature had brewing street-side. Downstairs, repositioning the sunglasses, he yanked the hood closed and stepped outside like an astronaut stuck surveying a wind-blown asteroid.

———————————————

Storing the U-bar lock, Zeke had just straddled his bike before the previously threatened eruption reappeared to leave him dry-heaving from the saddle. Long past the point of having anything to eject, he backhanded spindles of dangling mucus while wondering how anything could be this disgusting. Someone honked a horn at his misery, so he let fly an extended middle finger. Blinking to clear the tears from his eyes, he checked left, pushed off, and took the inside line against parked cars as Commonwealth squeezed into a mere two lanes. Surprisingly, the intestinal insurrection gave him new energy and a clearer focus.

The plows had been busy, the snow already jammed in an ever-growing wedge against door panels and wheel wells. Approaching Massachusetts Avenue, he watched a car skid halfway through the intersection without getting T-boned. *Miraculous*, he thought, turning right as the shaken driver frantically reversed in a sliding spray of slush and road-slime. With only the Pierce, and no new calls, he was aiming for home base to dump Wednesday's receipts when his beeper chirped again. *Gotta take it*, he decided, and slowed to a stop at a bank of phones across from Tower Records. Still seated, he leaned a shoulder against the booth and, while dialing, watched an old man swing a cane at a cab before turning his rage towards two oncoming lanes bearing down.

"Split Minute. Hello? Is anyone there?"

"Yeah, yeah, Stu, it's me. Sorry. Just watching someone else's day hit the shitter."

"Ah, Zeke-a-licious, ever the wordsmith."

"What's up? I was heading in when you paged."

"Hazard, *mi amore*, has a deuce that will go nicely with your Pierce."

"Goddamn it, Stu—"

"They're not tubes! I already checked, so just calm down!"

Zeke grinned and said, "Perfect. I'm even at the top of Newbury."

"Zeke?"

"Yeah?"

"Tell me. Are you wearing those lovely black tights today?"

"Stu—"

"Because, as you know, yesterday was Thanksgiving. And I've got some leftover stuffing I'd just love to slip inside your bird."

"Gross, man." Zeke could hear the laughter of those loafing in the background. Stuart continued, "But it'd be the perfect hangover cure, your little gobble-gobble all covered in my sweet potato pie!"

"Good God, that is so fucking wrong." Cradling the receiver, Zeke couldn't help but grin at the harassment. He waited, then shot across the intersection at the next red light. The unshoveled sidewalk left him powering through four inches while the back tire lost traction to momentum in a dangerous clash of physics. Approaching 254, he slammed on the rear brake while hucking the backside ninety degrees and watched the slush, like a gray-speckled tidal wave, gracefully arc six feet through the air.

Locking up, feeling suddenly nauseous, he stumbled up the stairs and hit the buzzer as the reliably uninspired voice of Cherise Maxwell said, "Hazard Inc."

"Cherise. Guess who?"

"Zeke? Listen, they're not tubes, so don't freak out!"

"I know, I know. Open up, will ya?"

"Some weather. You are just a monster, huh? Nothing stops Zeke Sandaman, apparently not even common sense."

"Cherise!"

Cherise Maxwell chuckled through the intercom before the door buzzer rattled its invitation. Woundedly, he stalked upstairs towards the third-floor lobby.

Already on her second cup of coffee, Cherise Maxwell flipped casually through an industry magazine, cherishing the silence as only three employees were yet on site. Film techs, she sighed, before thinking about last night and the holiday crowded with family and an exhaustion that actually left her at the bedroom door by 10:00 PM. Hearing the booted clomps ominously ascending, she grinned at the ray of sunshine headed her way and decided few things were more enjoyable than encountering Zeke Sandaman on a bad-weather day. Readying her insults, she was caught off guard, because his appearance, even from this distance, was easily diagnosed. Putting a hand on each knee, he took a deep breath and looked up as she said, "Whose carnival ride were you last night?"

"Man …" Pulling back the hood and removing the sunglasses, he watched the moisture drip from his nose to the floor.

"Are you okay?" she asked.

"In some cultures." Finally standing erect, he trudged towards her as Cherise Maxwell observed the horribly bloodshot eyes and scowl, which seemed even more venomous than usual. Taking a seat across from her, Zeke leaned back to rest his head and said, "Maxie, I think I'm fucked."

"Here." Cherise stood and disappeared into a back room, returning quickly with a towel and steaming mug. Handing him both items, she said, "Careful, it's hot."

Sipping at the coffee, he ran the towel across his face and neck while backbiting against another surge. Once it had passed, he was able to thickly swallow and post her a bleary-eyed gaze that barely passed for human.

"Go ahead," he said. "I deserve it."

Tilting her head with a sympathetic smile, Cherise circled back around her desk.

"I don't know," she said, and as she sat the smile quickly dissolved. "On top of riding a bike through this nightmare, you're apparently, by the stink, still half-drunk. I mean, what the fuck? The worst of the storm is yet to come." She paused as if the math of this equation should have been elementary. "Seriously, if this keeps up, you'll be lucky to be alive by lunch."

Two-handing the coffee cup like a tentative child, he gave her a weak smile and said, "The statistics prove you wrong."

"No, actually, your ant-sized brain is clouded with alcohol—and stupidity." Picking up the phone, she hit one button and soon said, "Stuart? Yes, it is. Well, I'm fine. Yes, he's right here and looks completely fucked up."

"Cherise," Zeke said but she held up a hand.

"I know that, Stuart, but even FedEx has halted their trucks … Because I just called them for a pickup."

"Hang up the phone," Zeke said in a voice that lacked conviction.

"Stuart, don't be silly. A courtesy for your customers? … Are you kidding me? You stopped your vans and cars, so how could it possibly be safer on a *bicycle?*"

Sitting up, Zeke abruptly said, "Cherise, gimme the phone right now."

Frowning, her obsidian eyes conveyed their objection, but she said, "Hold on a sec, Stu."

Taking the receiver, he said, "Everything's fine. I'll be there in ten minutes."

Hanging up, he caught a flash of her anger but said, "You got a deuce heading for Ferrelly?"

"Zeke—"

"I'm fine, Cherise." Standing, he downed the coffee in three scalding gulps. "It's nothing."

"Such a fucking tough guy."

"This is my job, Cherise."

"Yeah, whatever. Here." Holding out the manila envelopes, her gaze showed no concession. "I don't know what's worse, his greed or your idiocy. You stink of booze and puke. There's eight more inches on the way and every time the weather report comes on it sounds like something out of the Bible."

"Good. Maybe we'll break a record."

"For the lowest IQ?" she scoffed, her smile caustic. "I mean, is he for real? *A courtesy for his customers?*"

"Why are you so pissed off?"

"Because you're not."

"Easy, mom."

"Just … take these." She shook the envelopes until he obeyed, handing her the slipcase. Double-wrapping the envelopes with the Pierce, he readied himself in the stilted pause, the pressure of her displeasure like a weather system pushing him out.

"Did you have a good Thanksgiving?"

"Fuck you."

"Cherise …"

"Zeke, please, enough." She made busy with paperwork and looked up a minute later to say, "You're still here?"

"I am." Storing the items, he said, "I didn't mean to piss you off."

"You didn't. I don't even care. I hope you splatter yourself all over downtown."

Slipping back into the sunglasses, zipping up before he turned for the stairs, Zeke said, "I appreciate it. Seriously."

She watched him go and shook her head, aghast at her selection of friends. Pushing aside the papers, she turned and looked outside to where the snow was blowing sideways, and waited until the picture of Zeke Sandaman likewise floated from her mind.

———————

It was just past 10:30 AM when he saw a vicious blowdown on the Summer Street bridge. Fifty yards back, still on land, he watched a wind gust instantly flatten a messenger over the exposed Fort Point Channel. Battling between sheets of snow and blasts of frozen air, he approached the stilled shape which had yet to move. Dismounting, he tossed his bike and looked down through the hood and glasses like an arctic explorer. Nudging a thigh with his boot, he reflexively took a step back when a voice yelled out, "Hey!"

The body rolled to reveal a girl Zeke guessed might have been eighteen at best. She had a trickle of blood oozing from an already egg-shaped welt rapidly swelling out the left-side eye socket. He saw the bright blue eyes squinting up at him threateningly, a gloved right palm ready and fisted until she recognized his intentions.

"Come on." He held out a hand. "You need to ice that thing before your eye swells shut."

"Who are you?"

"Mother Theresa. Come on. I'm freezing my nuts off. Let's hit the coffee shop at One Financial."

She scanned him suspiciously, but nonetheless took the offered hand, brushed herself off, and claimed the lead as both then geared down through the storm. Three blocks later, they were locked up and seated at a table in the vaulted-glass pavilion where Zeke guessed there must have been twenty couriers drinking coffee and warming up in one of the few places that allowed them to do either. Without the usual flood of businesspeople on this partial holiday, the place had the feel of a loosely controlled riot watched earnestly by resentful security guards just beyond the fringe. Returning to the table with two coffees and an ice-filled sandwich bag, Zeke nodded nonchalantly at the boisterous greetings his passage aroused. Sitting down, he saw she had taken off her layers to reveal a wiry torso beneath a pink T-shirt that proudly exclaimed, in bold black letters, DIRTY GIRL. Recalling her instant hostility when she initially rolled over, and now as she again faced him boldly, it was all Zeke could do to blink away a superimposed image seven years left over.

He handed her the ice. "Here."

She tenderly poked at the bruise and asked, "How's it look?"

"Like someone hit you in the forehead with a baseball bat."

"Damn it."

"What're you doing? Keep the ice on. The first fifteen minutes decides whether or not you walk around with that thing for a month."

"So you say."

"What's your name?"

"What's yours?"

"Zeke."

Worrying a lip, she finally decided and said, "Lucy. Lucy Flynn."

"Right on, Lucy."

"I'm okay. You don't have to stay or nothing."

"No kidding. What're you holding?"

She grimaced and looked down at her beeper, seemingly amazed it was not yet ablaze. "Ten slips."

"Really." Sipping at his coffee, he pretended to be unimpressed and said, "Who for?"

"Global."

Poor girl. Watching as she winced beneath the ice's bite, he said, "How long?"

"This is my fourth week." She ran another tentative hand over the distension. "What about you?"

"Split Minute. They're on St. James."

"No, how long have you been out here?"

"Seven, eight years?"

"Holy shit." Lucy forked her unwounded eyebrow appreciatively. "You're an old one."

He grinned and saw her trying to decide if it was genuine before she reluctantly did the same. This curious tradeswoman, with her right pant cuff chain-chewed and stained, glanced over his outfit as if making note of the short-hem green fatigues. He watched as his black Hi-Tech boots, compared to her own oversized ducks, were catalogued as well. Moving the ice to a new spot, she listened as other couriers arriving and departing shouted greetings.

"You know all these guys?" she asked.

Frowning, Zeke said, "Most of them, unfortunately."

"Huh."

"Listen, no offense, but your company blows."

He saw Lucy Flynn nearly counter his forthrightness with a blast of her own, but instead she said, "How do you mean?"

"Their rates, the zones ..." Zeke shrugged. "They got it all stacked in their favor."

"What're you running?" she hostilely accused.

"Fifty-fifty," he said. "With expresses, oversizes, overweights doubling all that shit. What's your base?"

"Five bucks per."

"We start at seven-fifty. Cross-zones go up from there."

"Man ..." Lucy Flynn's brow furrowed as she did the math. "That's almost ..."

"With our volume? Two hundy a week more for you." Reaching into his bag, he pulled out the contractor case and wrote down Stuart Rigby's name. Handing her the slip, he said, "If you ride hard and take the first two weeks of his bullshit, he'll set you up."

"Sweet."

"Believe me, those fucks at Global ride their immigrants into the ground because they can. Driving rickety secondhand crap with Hefty bags slung over their shoulders ..." Zeke shook his head. "And because most of them barely speak English, they have no idea they're risking their lives for half of nothing. It's enough to make me sick."

"I had no idea."

As his beeper chirped, Zeke let loose a string of obscenities and said, "I don't know about you, but I'm about ready to pull the plug on this whole fucking day."

"So just call him up?"

"No." Zeke stood and adjusted his gear. "Go by there today and tell him you know me. On a day as fucked up as this, dispatchers love the diehards."

"Okay."

Zeke swigged the rest of the coffee, frowned as his beeper erupted again, and said, "Don't worry about the age thing either. Stu's got the whole bag of tricks."

Pulling away the ice bag, Lucy Flynn shot him an indignant look and said, "What makes you think—"

"Hey, take it easy." Zeke zipped up his jacket. "I was sixteen when I started and spent the first six months getting totally fucked over. Nobody lends a hand because they don't want you biting into their slice of a good thing."

"So why are you?"

"Why?" Zeke shrugged into his bag and pulled on wet gloves. "Because you need a new job. And because you've got ten on you in the worst fucking snowstorm I've seen in the last three years. Be cool."

Heading for the door, he heard his name and turned to see her waving. "Thanks, Zeke."

"And do yourself a favor. Trade in those baloney skins for a set of three-quarter-inch knobby. Traction's your only friend 'til spring."

Aiming for the door, Zeke pulled on the Carhartt knit cap and pulled up his hood, the nirvana of five o'clock buried inside the wind-torn avalanche raging just beyond the glass.

Gradually re-emerging from the previous night's poisoning, by noon Zeke was finally eating and pushing through the last of this morning's biological rudeness. Seated at a Dunkin' Donuts counter near Downtown Crossing, he stared out the window, feet propped on the baseboard heater. On any other day, twelve runs by lunchtime would have been an insult. Yet now, with thoughts ricocheting between Josh, Cammi, and Liz Downs, and in the middle of the swirling storm stalled somewhere overhead, he decided that his life in the last forty-eight hours had grown immeasurably more complicated. Having looked forward to his brother's release since nearly two seconds after the marshal's van left the courthouse, the once indestructible ringleader of a forgotten neighborhood had now apparently come home only to die. Trying to bear what this stark admittance signified, Zeke finished his coffee and glanced at the clock, which now said 12:15 PM. Liz Downs was expected by 7:00 PM for dinner, and he idly wondered how he would ever be able to explain what changes the last two days demanded.

Flattening the empty cup with a fist, he stood and zipped up, stomping the boots to shock his feet. His second pair of gloves, along with the jacket, were already soaked.

Stepping outside, he saw three-quarters of an inch on the bike despite having only stopped for thirty minutes. Shouldering through the wind, he found a payphone on an unusually vacant corner and soon heard Stuart Rigby say, "Split Minute."

"It's Z. I'm downtown with nothing."

"Zekey! And how is our abominable snowman doing?"

"Fantastic. Whaddaya got?"

"A big giant zero, friend. Where are you?"

"Summer, near Washington." Zeke watched a cab skid sideways, the snow shooting from its rear end like twin geysers. "It's a circus down here, man."

"So I hear. They're about to shut down the buses. WBZ's reporting the airport won't even be open till tomorrow noon, earliest."

"I'm looking at eight inches on the ground, plow or no plow."

"Yes, well, this whole operation's become entirely too dangerous. I've pulled the plug on everyone except you, F.T., X-man, and Cammi." Stuart clucked his tongue in contemplation and said, "Yes, let's call it a day."

"Yep. Oh, hey, Stu, did a chick named Lucy stop by?"

"Yes, she did." Stuart did not sound impressed. "Exactly what, may I ask, were you intending?"

"Don't be a pervert." Zeke turned his back on a piercing gale. "She's wheeling for Global with ten on her while half the shitbags you hire don't even have the stones to show up for work."

"Zachariah, I don't think so."

"What? Why not?"

"Because, and correct me if I'm wrong, but the last female you pulled into our employment turned out to be a raging psychopath."

Grinning, Zeke said, "I'm gonna tell her you said that."

"No! Zeke, please, she'll kill us both!"

"Hire Lucy, Stu, or enjoy your weekend," Zeke teased. "Because it might just be your last."

"Zeke!"

Hanging up, picturing Cammi's face, he could almost sense Stuart's pain. Taking one last look around at the empty streets, thinking about the eight-mile trek home, Zeke raised a hand and flagged the first cab he saw.

———————————————

With techno-remix Christmas carols blasting from a custom Rockford Fozgate, and singing joyously along in a thick accent Zeke did not recognize, the young cabdriver swung them through downtown like a pair of suicides looking for a wall. Initially annoyed, Zeke finally answered the harmless questions, hoping the driver would then just face front. Six months in-country from Indonesia, he was twenty years old, named Isram, and taking night classes at Tufts while also somehow sending money home.

"Snow!" he exclaimed with both hands thrust towards the windshield. "Is like I never seen before!"

Involuntarily grinning as the man's enthusiasm became contagious, Zeke marveled at the pure smile and pleasantness as Isram slammed on the brakes and slid them to a perfect stop at Kneeland and Tremont. Not wanting to call himself a pussy, Zeke nonetheless leaned forward and said, "This is your first time driving in snow?"

"Is first time I seen it ever, my friend! Ha-ha, yes!"

Peeling out as the light went green, Isram fishtailed it as Zeke wondered whether he should say a prayer or just give up and egg him on. Excitedly, Isram yelled out, "Smoke?"

"Huh?"

"For you, yes, is okay?"

"Ummm ..."

"Ha-ha, yes, Frosty!"

Cranking the decibels until even the windows pulsed, Isram sang "Frosty the Snowman" out of tune while thrusting a finger-thick bone through the divider as Zeke decided the surrealistic trauma of careening through the city with a burnt cabbie screaming out Christmas tunes in the middle of his first blizzard immediately required him to be just as stoned or even higher. Huffing madly, Zeke grabbed the hand strap above the window and eventually passed the joint, sitting back, relaxing even though the yellow death rocket seemed destined for a chronic case of rapid deceleration disease. Putting on his seatbelt as Isram continued to serenade, Zeke watched the massive clog-ups entering and exiting Storrow Drive. Even the brownstones along Beacon Street wore sticky beards of windblown snow. Tree branches, lampposts, every available edge was white-finned and picturesque above the brown-black soup churned inches thick and cresting either curb. *What a mess*, Zeke thought morosely, knowing the cleanup ahead for his hybrid would be extensive. Isram was gabbing about something as the joint returned for more abuse and Zeke occasionally nodded, hearing nothing other than Nat King Cole sampled and butchered into a hip-hop rendition of "White Christmas." *Like a little kid*, Zeke thought, watching the innocent delight as his driver took in every flake. Ten minutes later, they were skidding to a stop at 125 Easton Street.

"Yes, my friend!" Isram dialed down the music. "Big yellow is yours, no?"

Glancing at the fifteen-dollar charge, Zeke dug out a twenty, grinned at the horrified appearance of his house, and said, "Yes. Big yellow is mine." He curled the twenty through the divider. "All set."

"I thank you, Zeke."

"Don't thank me." Zeke grabbed his bag and opened the door. "That smoke was killer."

"Killer, yes!"

"Be cool, man, good luck."

"Yes, my friend."

Exiting with a final nod, Zeke dug his bike from the trunk, tapped on the closed lid, and then got thoroughly road-slimed as Isram bolted forward in his rolling disco of death. Finally surmising that idiots like this were on the other end of nearly every job-related nightmare, Zeke stared down at the glistening slush trashing his clothes and enthusiastically cursed the five-dollar tip. Stalking up the steps, pausing at the third-floor landing, he saw the television washing the walls in shadowy shapes and pushed inside to greet them.

———————————

Closing the door, Zeke tossed his bike and bag against the wall and said, "I guess your breaking and entering skills haven't dulled."

"Are you kidding me?" Josh replied from the couch. "Did you roll around in that shit or what?"

"Nah." Kicking off the drenched boots, Zeke peeled off his socks like a dead skin and said, "Fucking cabbie, man."

"I can't believe you were even conscious this morning."

"Who said I was?"

Josh watched him shed the EPS jacket and noted the turtleneck and pants beneath were completely soaked as well. Recalling how long his brother had been on the pedals, he considered Zeke's longevity a lifetime of luck that was wearing thin by age twenty-four. *Some fucking existence*, he thought and grinned because he was thankful, thankful that time, *his* time, no longer had any play in this, not when it came down to picking up with who or what had always been when everyone else, after so long, became nothing more than rumor.

As Zeke worked off the layers of shirts, each one equally waterlogged, Josh remembered them once at Carson Beach in Southie, after Josh's twelfth birthday, just him and Zeke, who might have been seven years old. It was autumn, not yet dark but close enough, and the beach was all but empty. They were skipping flat rocks across the meager surf greenly lapping at the shore. Ahead, they eventually saw three shapes beating a fourth, who was slouched over, arms clasped about the head. The guy was pleading with them to just take his wallet but they would not, and the beating recommenced even after he had fallen.

Side by side, he and Zeke watched from some distance as the shapes stopped when the guy no longer moved, his body like a reef facing out towards Dorchester Bay. As one of the attackers bent over, Josh could hear him say, "Now I'll take your wallet *and* your watch, motherfucker."

"Hey," Zeke had whispered and tugged on Josh's arm. "Ain't that Lindy's older brother and—"

"Shh!" Josh pulled away, because all three were now approaching, laughing, the body behind them like a mere speed bump in their path. Finally seeing them, one called out, "Ain't that the Sand-a-bitch brothers?"

"Ha-ha, yeah, man," another said and Josh recognized them all from the block, Lindy's older brother and Lark from two doors down, and their buddy was called Boots because he puked virtually on command. As they swaggered in, Josh was scared, but he knew enough not to break eye contact. As they passed, Lindy senior held up the wallet while jiggling the watch in his other hand.

"Are you two fags," he had said, "one day gonna take what's yours or what?"

"Probably not," Boots cracked. "That little one ain't never been too bright."

"Look who's talking!"

"Zeke ..." Josh palmed Zeke's face as he writhed and fought, setting him loose only after all three had passed. He remembered Zeke's expression as they both then stared towards the body, which had not moved in minutes.

"Do you think he's …"

"Let's go." Josh grabbed his arm. "He'll be fine."

"But shouldn't we call some—ow, Josh, you're pinching me!"

Spinning him, Josh grabbed him by both biceps and hissed, "We need to get out of here, okay? So just shut the fuck up and start walking."

Shut the fuck up and start walking.

"Hey." Currently, Zeke scooped up the mountain of soaked clothes and broke for his room. "You daydreaming or what?"

"Naw …" Josh stared at the empty space, his gaze like flattened stones. There were, of course, other memories, but over the years, only a few were left sticking up like mile markers on a long forgotten road.

Zeke quickly returned in fresh sweats and socks. "What're you watching?"

"Some talk show. That freak there banged his own sister."

"Great." Zeke bent low at the waist, sinking into a stretch until his nose nudged a kneecap. "What happened to you last night?"

"Huh?"

"Where'd you sleep?"

"Nice blackout, Zeke. I slept right here. Woke up early."

"What?" Zeke stood. "You mean I was awake at 6:00 AM and you were already gone?"

"Yep."

"What in the hell for?"

"Errands." Joshua nodded vaguely while staring at the screen. "Had dialysis too."

"You're a freak."

"Hey, Stretch Armstrong, you're blocking the fucking show."

"You sure you weren't raised in a trailer park?"

"Hey, I like this stuff. The stories are whacked, the chicks are dirty, and if you weren't here right now, I might even be rubbing one out."

"Aw, man, that's horrible."

"Seriously, dude, get the fuck out of the way."

"Cousin Cooter and his talk shows," Zeke shot back as he headed for the kitchen.

Josh waited until Zeke returned swilling a Gatorade and then he killed the television. "So where were we?"

Zeke slowly pulled the bottle from his lips. "Not again, man, no way."

"No shit, Z." He nodded at the empty La-Z-Boy. "Take a seat, man. This won't take but a second."

"After the day I just had?"

"Stop fucking whining." He paused. "You know, I've never asked you for a fucking thing ..."

"Dude—"

"Listen! Stop fucking talking. It ... You're not making this any easier!"

"Goddamn, I fucking knew it." Zeke ricocheted the empty plastic bottle off the wall. "Fucking sideshow, man ..." He massaged his temples. "What? What else is there?"

"You really are an asshole."

"Excuse—"

"Just shut the fuck up! Okay? Fuckin' A, Zeke, I swear, sometimes it's like you got no memory at all."

Zeke digested the threat and sighed. "Talk to me."

"I wish, you know? I'm so ready to just walk the fuck out." Easing against the seatback, Josh took a deep breath and said, "This ain't Disney. And I ain't gonna turn into a blonde with big tits."

"I'm sorry, okay?"

Scratching at his throat and left shoulder, Josh ignored the apology. "I didn't just get to walk out of there."

Zeke nibbled on the corner of a chapped lip. "How do you mean?"

"I mean the fact that two weeks before I had my papers for release squared away, Gracie caught me slipping on the way back from chow and, well, he was half strangling me and I really thought that was gonna be it, you know?" He blinked. "I just felt it all coming to an end, dying with that evil dick's b.o. and foot-thick bicep wrapped around my neck ... and I was just kind of relieved, you know? God ..." Josh paused, the black eyes retracting into points. "Just before I passed out, though, he stopped and laughed and asked if I was looking forward to seeing you all and that ... that was when I wished I was dead. Because it was only beginning again."

"Josh, what the fuck are you talking about?"

Josh batted a hand and said, "This moron Pony is my new connect, supposedly while I work off what I owe."

"What ...?" Zeke sat up straighter. "Oh ... *shit.*"

Watching the news spread like a blush across his brother's face, Josh nodded. "It ain't pretty."

"How much?"

"After interest like a vig out the ass …?"

"What the fuck, Josh, how much?"

Weakening, licking his lips, Josh could not hold the glance. "One hundred and eighty-seven thousand dollars."

"Oh my God."

"Zeke—"

"No." Standing, Zeke looked around as if unsure where to explode. "No way this is happening."

Watching him leave the room, Josh put his head into his hands. The Brotherhood. His eyes clenched into that closeby world where the big neighborhood tough guy was suddenly outnumbered by a thousand felons dividing up time and space like defrocked demons left to curse and kill one another. Cliquing up, ethnically clustered, and globally represented by the blacks in 20 Love and the Five Percenters, the Blood Red Dragons of the Southeast Asians, the Mexican Mafia, the Vietnamese dividing the feuding Brighton Boyz and Saigon Boyz, the Puerto Ricans in NETA, while the Hispanic heavyweights of La Familia and the Latin Kings were just two more names on a list of more than sixty active syndicates burrowed into and through the Massachusetts Department of Correction. Maximum security a vicious literal twist as nowhere, not even in 10-block—administrative segregation—could one find a single inch of safety if contracts and contacts exchanged their silent wares.

As all three were affiliated gang members, for the first two years Josh did not see Cancer Boy and Ju-Ju even once. And the Brotherhood, with their tattooed missionaries whispering up the new recruits about niggers and spics and the protection of one another as the lone minority, offered formidable arguments that some whites embraced, some did not, and others came to wish they had. Through it all, Josh nodded respectfully, observed others who had refused, and decided to do the same. Blessed by the severity of his crimes, he nonetheless found himself an instant target, an eighteen-year-old prime prospect for the waves of propositions, affiliations, and outright assaults stalking every unaware second. Gradually, with each turn in and out of ad. seg.'s isolation unit, and after administering a particularly brutal beating on an older inmate as final warning, Josh found himself at nine hundred and seventy-one days, still only twenty years old, but basically allowed a name. Thinking back on that afternoon, recently reassigned from Buildings and Grounds to the kitchen staff, he would remember seeing old Tully from Columbia Road in his blue polyester striped Phillips Bakery uniform before committing the second biggest mistake of his life.

Unsure how his own naivete had seduced him, and wanting protection without necessarily begging allegiance, he originally thought the Brotherhood would welcome another avenue for the importation of what was, decidedly, a fiercely guarded source of income and influence. This supposition, he would later find out, could not have proved more costly. Eventually cornered in a walk-in cooler by an Aryan lieutenant and two soldiers, he was told when and how much, what percentage he could pocket, or he was welcome to enjoy one final night before it became his last. Debating the terms, and seeing it as something he would yet like to keep, he traded in what was left of his life for something even worse, and now he sat on this couch eight and a half years later reliving every hideous second.

"Zeke?"

There was a long pause. Then a gasp and the sound of something hitting the countertop.

Standing awkwardly, he found Zeke with both arms propped sink-side as outside the window every inch of space seemed occupied with blowing flakes. A worn bottle of gin and shot glass stood guard to the right as Josh asked, "Where's Booger?"

"Connecticut." Zeke lifted and emptied the shot glass.

Josh stared at his brother's back. "Don't think they're ever expecting the full deal."

Zeke refilled the glass and said distractedly, "What?"

"Four grand every two weeks, eight Gs a month." Josh leaned against the wall. "It's just suffer money. Supposedly what I owe after ripping them off for so long."

"Yeah?" Zeke drained number three. "And ...?"

"And ... Well, now you're part of it too."

It was hard to watch. Zeke looked as if his gut had done a slow, sleazy roll. "Come again?"

"Zeke—"

"*Me?*" He punched his own chest. Punched it again, then once more before grabbing the empty gin bottle and shattering it against his bedroom door. "Tell me how? How the fuck did I get on deck? You all out of friends to set up?"

Collapsing slowly down the wall, Josh came to rest on the floor with a single drop crossing the yellowed cheek. "You … me … and Dad."

"*Dad?*"

"One missed payment—"

"How did that moron get dragged into this?"

"Or mark not wasted—"

"Jesus Christ, Josh."

"Anything." The tears were streaming as he held out his empty palms. "Don't you see? What Gracie did …? I'm their fucking dick-toy now, man." He was sobbing, eyes closed while slamming the back of his skull against the wall like a cuckoo clock driving itself unconscious.

"Josh."

Whack … whack … whack …

"Cut that shit out."

Whack …

"You're gonna fuck up the drywall."

Backhanding the tears, Josh glanced aside. "I don't know, man. What was I supposed to say? Was I just gonna call you up and hang out like it was old times?" He angrily palmed the snot across a jean-covered thigh. "Now you know why I didn't call or come over. At first, it was like, 'How am I ever going to tell someone this?' I mean what the fuck is that about?"

"Josh—"

"Transplants, lawsuits … As if … you know?"

"The money … we'll find some way—"

"Money?" Squirting tears around the laughter, Joshua wickedly sneered. "Are you fucking kidding me? Gracie pulled a number out of thin air and then tacked on twenty-five points a month. This ain't about money. It's about turning the screws slowly tighter while I do every fucked up errand they need until the time comes when I'm even too sick to earn, and miss a payment and … well …"

"Meat pie city."

"Exactly." Josh leaned back in defeat. "They're gonna run me like a rat on a wheel until I fall or don't provide amusement anymore."

"Jesus."

"Believe me. In the beginning I was like no way. Huh-uh. Fuck that, you know? The kidney shit was going to kill me anyway eventually, so when they found out I was being released, and ran word through about the new fate awaiting my arrival, I was like *Fuck it, I'll just end this shit myself.*"

"But …"

"But he's not that stupid. They could have smoked me fifteen feet outside South Gate. Could have gutted me a thousand times in ad. seg. This ain't about money or death. It's about making an example out of someone who went behind his back on a contract, who he had trusted, and the slow torture of knowing whether it's the kidney thing or suicide, the second my heart stops beating …"

"Josh—"

"No, man." Wiping his eyes was now useless. "You will never know a punishment worse than having your own mistakes pulled from the skin of the only people left, man, what the fuck!"

"I don't know—"

"Fuck!"

"We'll—"

"We'll what, Zeke? Haven't you listened to a single fucking thing I just said?"

"Nope," Zeke stood up. "Apparently, as usual, you've had your say."

"Excuse me?"

Zeke turned and rummaged through a cabinet before pulling down a handle of whiskey. Pouring three fingers' worth, he gagged while swallowing and turned a fume-burnt eye towards his brother. "I ain't about this. Not anymore. You expecting sympathy from me? Why don't you ring up Pop and tell him who's outside waiting and see what kind of shoulder you get to cry on."

"Fuck you."

"You already did." The sickened smile creased out into a thin line of malice. "Next time, use some gr—"

Josh punched at the same second Zeke's elbow flew into his face. Thrown to the floor, Josh was quickly overrun until there was a crack, and Zeke recalled the next blow because the blood, like a breached seal, squirted from the right nostril as words like hemolytic anemia and kidney failure abruptly came to mind.

"Great." Unnerved, Zeke quickly said, "Are you all right?'"

"Yeah." Josh turned his head and spit a wad of blood onto the floor. "I'll be even better once you get up off me."

"What were you thinking?" Rolling from his chest, Zeke quickly grabbed a dishtowel and tossed it. "God, that was stupid of me, man—"

"My bad." Slowly sitting up, Josh tentatively investigated his nose. "I think it's broke."

"Put your head back, man, Jesus Christ."

Clamping the towel to the leak, Josh felt the rest of his face already swelling and said, "Fourth time's the charm."

"Come on." Zeke held out his hand. "I'll get you another towel, too."

"Yeah, thanks. Nice first aid. You give me a fucking dishrag covered in—what's this, cheese?"

Turning the corner, Josh collapsed onto the couch. Before him, Zeke stood wordless and shaken, his own split lip staining his shirt. "I need to know."

Blinking through the fracture, Josh scrunched the towel over his eyes. "I'm so fuckin sorry."

"Hey …"

He had his head between his knees.

"This ain't right." Zeke swallowed thickly. "We need to fucking think."

"Fuck." Josh coughed, then reached for a pack of cigarettes off the end table.

"You never answered me."

Lighting up, Josh dabbed blood from his nose and said, "I promise." Exhaling, he looked Zeke in the eye again. "Side by side, okay? For whatever it is we decide to do."

"For real, right? From here on out …?"

"Yes."

"Because this ain't 1985."

"Zeke—"

"Hey, man. This is my fucking life we're talking about. You want my help, that's the deal. It's either that, or I'm gone, like, as of tonight."

"I said I promise." Josh felt him measuring his sincerity, as if the weight of what would now come next might just kill them both.

"It'll be okay," Zeke said. "We'll work it out."

Turning for the kitchen as his confident words already faded, Zeke quickly poured another shot.

Calling herself deranged for even attempting it, Liz Downs zipped her jacket and yanked the hood closed, tentatively stepping outside as if testing the still-lashing storm. The waiting yellow cab wore a second white skin three inches thick. She was in jeans and boots, her father's old bulky winter work jacket that said "A&G Gas" in gold lettering. After stating Zeke's address to the cabbie, Liz belted in and settled back, nervous but glad to be gone. The tension of yesterday, where she cooked an entire feast with barely a nod, was disheartening but obviously not unexpected.

The cabbie almost skidded through a red light, so she closed her eyes. Having just got off the phone with Zeke, listening as he stammered through an apology about the dinner he could not now cook, Liz decided he sounded pretty depressed. *It's been five days*, she thought, counting back to Monday night as the last one they had shared. *What was going on?*

Twenty minutes later, Liz ascended the three flights and knocked once as Zeke yelled out, "Come in!"

She did, stomping her feet inside the entry.

"Whew," she said, unzipping the jacket. "It's a mess out there."

"Hey, babe."

Peeking around the corner, she saw him sitting on the couch. The only light in the whole apartment came from a lamp over his right shoulder. Slipping off the boots, running a hand through her brown hair, she stepped into the silent room and said, "You didn't have to get all dressed up for me."

Smiling drowsily in his sweatpants and stained T-shirt, Zeke said, "Nothing's too good for my baby."

"Apparently." She sat next to him, planting a kiss on his cheek and smelling whiskey. She made a face.

"Yeah, I'm sorry about this. I had a few this afternoon."

"What's up?" She stared at his profile, lightly trailing a hand across his cheek. "Work? Please, tell me you didn't work."

"Only till noon."

"Is your boss a Nazi or just plain stupid?"

"What's the difference?" Chuckling as he took another sip, he said, "Can I fix you one? The house drink tonight is whiskey and Coke."

"Sure."

"Sweet."

"Can we put on some music?"

"Yep."

Hearing Neil Young strum into "Sugar Mountain," Liz waited as Zeke played bartender and reappeared with a full pint glass. Retaking his seat, he lit a cigarette and said, "I need to talk to you about something."

Oh God, here it comes, she thought. *I knew it was only a matter of time.*

"My brother made parole."

Stopping herself from exhaling in relief, she forked her eyebrows and said, "All right." Then she saw his somber expression and became confused. "That's good, right?"

"Yeah … yeah, it is. It's just … there's a lot of other shit brought along for the ride."

"Okay. And that means?'

Like a diver going down, Zeke took a breath and said, "I told you how we lived in Dorchester. Ambrose Street. We didn't move to Allston until I was fourteen. But there was a reason." Zeke ashed his cigarette into an empty beer bottle. "You know what I'm talking about. This was like '85, '86. Within four blocks three different flags were already trading shots. The Easties and Furies and all that crack garbage. Whatever. We had Thatcher and Hillsboro and Humphrey Street and part of Columbia Road too. It started as a bunch of delinquents moonlighting as gangsters. But there came a point when we couldn't even hang outside without facing down a wagon full of masks. And Josh, that's my brother, he finally picked up a gun and then we all did and the Burgess Street Mob was off and running."

"The Easties were in my neighborhood." Liz sipped her drink and decided it was hazardously strong. "That was a long time ago, Zeke."

"I know this ain't news to you, baby, just bear with me for a sec." He ashed the cigarette again. "Anyway, it wasn't ever the same after that. My brother … He just got carried away. Almost like he couldn't thug enough. And the older guys stoked it too, egging him on before even they became his targets. He was just lost, you know? We all were. Half of those fucking guys were never gonna know anything else and the other half had nothing better to do. Even by that point, I think I was the only one still in school. But pretty soon it wasn't about being able to hang outside. Posting corners, stomping unknowns … palming smoke and white and finally even that wasn't enough. So Josh, he came up with the bright idea of shaking down our own run of Columbia and Stoughton Roads. I'm talking about the same businesses our parents went to, run by our neighbors, people we had grown up with."

"Not good."

"Yeah. It sure wasn't. But I was, like, twelve back then. And there's my big brother standing up for our neighborhood and I thought he was a god, you know? We all did. No one ever questioned anything. The way we saw it, those people owed us something for us risking our lives every single day."

"Great."

"Yeah." Zeke stared off miserably. "What a fucking disaster."

"So?"

"So, one day, it was a Friday. I don't know if you remember, but there was an old Portuguese guy who ran a smoke shop on the corner of Columbia and Stoughton. Anyway, he fucking hated us. Looking back, it ain't hard to figure out why. When we weren't outright stealing, we were insulting him to his face. Getting extorted on top of it was more than he could handle. For six months, my brother would just walk in there with a baseball bat every two weeks and hold out his hand. But that day, that Friday, the whole thing turned to shit."

"How?"

"The guy's nephew, this ten-year-old kid, was there, in the back. Obviously, he had no idea what was going on. He heard his uncle yelling and thought they were being held up, so he called the cops. Once they heard the sirens, Ju-Ju and C.B. must've freaked out. Three shots blind. Out the window. The cruisers swept down and some guy started yelling on a bullhorn and … and … just like that it was over. The police told them to come out and a few minutes later they did."

"But …"

"But, Mrs. Beth Ann Wright was lying dead across the street."

"Oh my God." Liz felt her hand move reflexively over her mouth. "This was *that*?"

"Yep."

"Oh my God."

"Yep."

"I do remember it."

"It was like shooting Mother Teresa. I mean, that lady was a one-woman charity machine."

"A saint."

"Yep." Zeke rubbed his forehead with the row call. "YMCA, drug treatment, religious shit, soup kitchens, after-school activities, outpatient counseling—"

"A saint."

"And black on top of it. Gunned down by three white kids."

"I can't believe that was your brother."

"I still remember hearing it too, Lotus screaming from the street to come on down because all hell was breaking loose. A day later there's the crime scene on the cover of the *Herald* below the caption 'Gang Guns Down Dorchester Icon.'"

"I'm so sorry, Zeke."

"For what?" Zeke dropped the butt into the bottle. "For us? For how stupidly three kids ended their own lives and someone else's? Believe me, we were *all* responsible. Josh never took me on collections because I was still a punk kid, but I would've been right beside him." Zeke put down his glass, seemed to think of something, but then decided he could not even pretend. "It's because it wouldn't have made a difference. And because everybody's heroes are someone else's monsters."

"No wonder you had to move."

"Yeah." Zeke lit another cigarette. "Josh went to hell. And I got to go to Allston." Fidgeting with his hands, he said, "He's my brother, and I love the guy, especially now, because he has no choice and needs me, but prison—it was like the only next stop left for a guy like that. Do you believe I just said that? How fucked is it?"

"Pretty fucked." Liz stole his cigarette. "But also sounds pretty true."

"Yeah."

"Also sounds like you're a pretty lucky guy."

"What?"

She smiled and leaned forward to ash the smoke. "My policy is, never date monsters."

"Really."

When he did not return her flirtation, she put a hand on his arm and said, "Zeke, you were a kid."

"Uh-huh," he said, not blinking.

"And I'm an eyewitness." She inhaled another drag. "It wasn't like growing up in fucking Newton—that's for sure."

"Whoever thought."

"What's that?"

"All his demons." Zeke drained the glass and stood. "That afternoon destroyed his life. Mine too. All of us."

"Zeke—"

"Need a refill, babe. Back in a sec."

Liz sipped at the whiskey, listening to Neil Young sing about Marlon Brando and Pocahontas while still absorbing the unexpected revelation. *Gruesome*, she heard herself think. Just listening to his story triggered flashbacks— walking directly from the bus to her house while all around, like some teenage hallucination, the gangs recruited round the clock. Jimmy Denton, Brian Pershaw, acquaintances from high school all buried by eighteen.

"You need a refill?" he called out from the kitchen.

"Almost."

He reappeared carrying a bottle of Jim Beam and a two-liter Coke. Sitting down, he finally looked at her and said, "Anyway, that was it. Get tough and Reagan and all that nonsense had everyone in a panic. There was an eyewitness who saw my brother's car at the scene, but he arrived too late to see Ju-Ju and C.B. exit the car. He just saw Josh leave after the fucking store window exploded. The license plate went out over the wire, and while Josh was fleeing the scene, he got sideswiped and hit a pole on Columbia Road."

"Oh my God."

"The cops found just under a kilo of heroin in the car but couldn't prove anything else. Ju-Ju and C.B., they knew what would happen if my brother ever got word, so they coded up and didn't say shit. The cops were ballistic. They knew all about Josh, believe me. They scoured that entire fucking neighborhood trying to find anything to connect him to the scene but came up empty. All they had was the drug charge, so they extended the maximum to him on that."

"So the other guys …"

"Ju-Ju and Cancer Boy went down for the whole deal. Six felonies. Armed robbery, assault and battery/dangerous weapon, assault with intent to rob, extortion, possession of weapons, and first-degree murder."

"Oh my God."

"Yeah. You remember, right? The marches, speakers—I don't know who hated my brother more, the blacks or our friends and neighbors. I mean, people were fucking pissed. But his lawyer, man, that guy was a genius. My brother avoided a life sentence by inches and got ten to fifteen years instead." Zeke drilled a tortured look through the wall. "After the verdict, I thought the whole city was going to explode like Roxbury did that night. I mean, this is *Boston*, you know? And now this white kid, after all this other racist shit had built up over the years, was just gonna walk?" Zeke shook his head. "Not likely. As you know, the fucking blacks weren't having it. And as for Ju-Ju and C.B., those two didn't stand a chance at their trials. The fucking National Guard was almost called out."

There was a moment of silence, and Zeke frowned. "I can still remember blowing off school and going to court, meeting my brother's lawyer to get in and being so nervous sitting there I thought I was going to shit myself. I think I was in the eighth grade. I just remember thinking the whole thing was like a play or TV show or something, you know? Parts of it were so boring until I scanned the defendant's table and saw my brother, and I was still young enough to believe it was gonna be all right. You know? It'd been six months by then and pop had already sold the house and it was just me and him, night after night, listening to him curse my brother to my face." Zeke looked at the floor and slowly blinked. "I mean, everything was evaporating and he just couldn't handle it. Because of his income, he had to pay for Josh's lawyer, which bit into his business, and while it was always steady, it was still nothing to brag about. The worst part, to him anyway, a guy who had grown up and lived there his entire life, was what my brother did to our name. It was unforgivable to him. And towards the end of the trial all my father was doing was writing checks. It was a joke."

"He was probably humiliated, Zeke."

"Doesn't make it right." He stood and walked to the window, fidgeting anxiously with the blinds. "It was exactly when we needed each other most, too. I can see that now."

"What about your mom? Was she … was she still …?"

"Yeah." He glanced back out the window. "She's a big part of this too. She got sick when I was eleven."

"I'm sorry, Zeke, what was it again?"

"Ovarian cancer. She was … she was the strongest person I've ever met."

Liz looked at his back but saw only a vacant expression reflected in the darkened windowpane. "How old were you when she passed?"

"Thirteen." Zeke smiled at her memory, but it slowly drained away in the blowing snow outside. "It was so quick. That was the worst part. I don't know how much you know about this shit, but that type of cancer has four stages. When she was finally diagnosed, it was late stage three." He paused. "Like, overnight, too. They say it's the worst one to get because it's so quiet. And back then, there weren't even any tests for it either. Is that unbelievable or what?"

"Yes," she said and could barely nod. "It is."

"It took a year and a half. They scooped out her uterus, poisoned out her hair, stuck her full of tubes and false hope, until finally she was just a set of eyes beneath a blanket."

"Zeke—"

He held up a hand and said, "It ain't like that, I know. Still, when you're that young, surrounded by all these so-called experts and billion-dollar machines, like the court thing with my brother, you just assume it'll be all good. But when 'all good' means she just continues to get sicker and sicker without a single complaint, and finally has to spend the last three months in the hospital, and her husband is too busy and such a coward he can only show up for two hours on Sunday, and her oldest son is by this point neck-deep in the same shit that's about to destroy his life, and her youngest pedals up three times a week just to see her … I mean, could you imagine? I think about her sometimes, lying in that bed knowing she was going to die while all around her, the one thing she had devoted her life to was completely unraveling." Zeke paused. "It must have broke her heart." He slowly blinked. "God or whoever was somewhat merciful, though. At least she didn't get to see what Josh did."

"That's a meager bonus."

"Talk about searching for silver linings."

Saddened, she tried picturing Zeke's mother and then said, "You really know how to show a girl a good time."

His laughter was quiet, the smile warming until she said, "You're still angry. With your father."

"Absolutely."

"I can't believe it's been so long. I mean, to not even have spoken?"

"Eight years," he proudly stated. "My life didn't start until I could get away from him, Liz. You might have some idea what I'm talking about. Every word out of his mouth, every bullshit excuse he made to mom, the way he bullied and threatened my brother, who really went off the deep end almost out of spite. My father rarely raised a fist, and not because he couldn't—believe me. His mouth was such a fucking machine, you never had a chance. Besides that, we're talking about a guy who got out of the army and then went to work every day of his life. Him and his fucking concrete. I think he might have poured some of it into his head because the guy was just an incredible douchebag. And big too. Half a life swinging twenty- and thirty-pound sledges, dragging buildings down, a real Ford-truck-driving asshole. Whatever. That shit with my mother, though …" Zeke swallowed audibly. "Once a week for two hours, man? To this day, I still don't know what the fuck he was thinking. She was the best thing that could ever happen to a moron like that."

"Maybe he was scared. People sometimes mishandle their stress and grief, you know? Especially when it comes to those around them."

Incredulous, he turned and said, "What?"

"I'm serious."

"You can't be. Mishandling stress and grief? Are you *joking*?"

"Hey!"

"Is that what you call leaving your wife of eighteen years in a hospital to die? Or tossing away a kid after he commits a crime that makes the whole city sick? Granted, what Josh did was completely fucked up, but do you know he sent my father cards on his birthday and Christmas for years and didn't get a single thing in return? No visits, no phone, no commissary, no letters—nothing?"

"You can't compare the two."

"Yes. I can. That ain't what family means. Not to me, anyway." Zeke gnawed a lip. "I watched it happen twice and wasn't about to wait for my turn."

"How awful."

She saw him spin with an angry look and realized her words had been misconstrued. "Not that. I mean, the whole thing." She shrugged benignly. "It's just so sad."

"Yes."

Liz patted the cushion next to her. "Please sit down. You're getting all worked up over there."

Zeke did as instructed, leaning back his head and staring up at the ceiling. "I don't know what I'm gonna do when Josh goes."

"Goes where?"

He closed his eyes as if the real story was yet to come. "I'm really sorry about all this."

"What're you talking about?"

"It's just … I can't half-tell any of it. And if I don't tell someone, I'm gonna lose what's left of my mind."

"Tell me what?"

"Hopefully, I'm just drunk enough to do it."

Which he then did, every detail, and at the end she knew her face was a giant question mark for which he had no answer.

"I know what you're thinking." Zeke stared ahead blankly. "But just wait until you see him. Only my brother could piss someone off this badly. Can you imagine the planning that must have gone into this?"

"Zeke, I literally don't know what to say. I've never heard of anything so barbaric. Never. But your dad?" Liz felt a chill. "And *you*?"

"It won't come to that." He lit a cigarette. "What about you? Talk to me, Liz."

"I don't know." She ran a hand through her hair, pulled her knees up, and rested a chin on top. "What're you gonna do?"

Dragging on the cigarette, he squinted through the haze. "Is that really a question?"

"Is that gonna be your excuse?" She saw a flash of hostility before it hid like a moon behind another burst of smoke.

"Maybe you didn't hear what I said before."

"Well," she said, "then I guess you'll do what you have to."

"That's not what I asked."

"What am I supposed to say? That I'm excited, after so long, and now all that might be taken away?"

"Don't exaggerate."

"Well, what then, Zeke?" She stood up. "Frankly, the whole thing makes me sick. It makes me sick to think of that poor lady. It makes me sick to think of what they did to your brother. It makes me sick that he'll never be the same or healthy— but you know what makes me sickest of all? Having you sit here and practically beg for permission."

"Is that what I'm doing?"

Liz shook her head, as if embarrassed by the act. "You know what? Never mind."

"Liz—"

"I mean, how is that even possible? Eight thousand dollars a month?" She could only shake her head; it didn't take much to figure out what they would have to do to secure that kind of money. *You're gonna raise that cash,* she wanted to say, *and we are going to be finished.* Instead, she leveled her gaze and simply said, "Do what you want."

She left for the bathroom before he could reply. Sat on the toilet peeing while fighting back against something that was, apparently, already decided. *Asshole,* she cursed, and tore off a strip of paper. Zipping up, Liz checked herself in the mirror, ran a finger under each eye, and smoothed out the green-sleeved shirt.

She flushed the toilet and yanked open the door. Re-taking her seat, she knew Zeke had seen the dead-serious expression, because his gaze was suddenly troubled.

"Baby—"

"Don't." She ground her teeth. "Please. I don't want to talk about this anymore."

"I'm sorry. My attitude tonight … it's totally fucked."

She gave him a pleasant, devastatingly chilled smile which, more than anything else, made him all but give up.

"So …" he said.

"So …" she echoed with a yawn. "What time is it?"

"Probably like ten."

"I'm bushed." She stretched both arms and arched back like a cat. "It was a long week."

"Yep."

"Can we crash? Or is it too early?"

"Nope."

Leading him towards the bedroom, she closed the door and searched the dark, their hands busy with each other's clothes until Zeke abruptly stopped.

"Geez, babe." He sat on the bed. She approached him, invisible, and drew him near, pulling his cheek into her belly.

"Shhhh …"

Stroking his hair, Liz felt him kissing her stomach and up her chest until he hit the fresh scabs between her breasts with no further reaction. Tonguing each nipple, he stood and they were together as the window rattled against the worst storm in years.

Chapter Eleven

ZEKE TOOK THE INSIDE line heading west on Tremont, clicked into fifth gear, and saw a car door blindly swing open. Without even having time to curse, he juked left to miss it before leaning right to again parallel the curb. He had three on him and sensed the afternoon would be busy. The Hanley Building clock read 12:52 PM, 41°. The biting wind blowing in from the harbor was at his back before he made the turn onto Massachusetts Avenue. Knowing how hard it was to stay focused these past ten days, Zeke had a picture of himself eating that car door at twenty-five miles per hour and nearly flinched again.

After locking up, he paused outside a storefront window that read COMMUNITY ACTION NOW in bold black letters above a clenched fist thrust powerfully towards the sky. Reaching back over a shoulder, he yanked out the slipcase and envelope before heading into a minority tenants' rights group. Inside, the tiny office had hanging plants, slogans doubling as posters, and three huge women at different desks. His arrival caused each to look up as he smiled and one of the women said, "City Hall?"

"Yes, ma'am." Zeke perched his sunglasses on his forehead like a second pair of eyes. Re-adjusting the Carhartt knit cap, he said, "Got a package from HUD."

Detaching the pink receipt, he headed back outside. Storing the lock, and with only two left, he wondered where the hell Stuart was with his page.

He straddled the bike and checked left before nosing from the curb. As he scanned the intersections ahead, his mind churned back through the past week and he decided it was a lost cause. Braking to let an elderly man scuttle along the crosswalk, he recalled the previous Saturday night like a contest with no prize.

In a total act of desperation, the four of them had huddled around his kitchen table hatching ridiculous schemes between shots of vodka and angry shouts as one by one the alternatives dwindled to none. Lotus, angling from inside, suggested they start targeting mid-level dealers. When that idea failed, he somewhat suicidally proposed a turn-and-tape for the state, the Brotherhood be damned. Cammi Sinclair explored the option of committing a parole violation to go back to prison, thereby escaping the exorbitant debt and street gang's added threat. And Josh, working with the end of the law, sought a way to set up both factions in a double-cross so preposterous Zeke could not take it seriously. Through it all, he watched the excitement fade as the hours dragged on and each idea became stupider than the last. And while his brother's well-being was foremost in his mind, Zeke did not necessarily think the remainder of their lives was worth half the risks these plans demanded. The bottom line was that they owed eight thousand dollars a month, indefinitely. It was as simple as that.

He turned left on Commonwealth and geared down, pedaling furiously to sidetrack his wandering brain. The questions seemed to be piling up like bodies. Even with Lotus donating his boys, and Zeke chipping in last week's paycheck, they still had a tap dance with the first deadline last Tuesday night. Swearing it would take only one more week to get organized, Josh already had Lotus spinning on command as Liz Downs' words proved prophetic and Zeke's apartment, despite meager protests, became ground zero. Booger had not been home in days. Cutting and bagging, scales and razors, the ghouls of the night faced down the dawn like zombies. With a felony possession already listed, Zeke was under no illusions as to what this joyride might ultimately cost. A second Class B possession with intent to deal might mean six to ten, depending. Lotus, too, was sweating in private as he told Zeke of the haphazard rush threatening the discretion of his and Josh's nightly tours. Abstaining because of his early work start, Zeke was spared the hustle-and-bust life club dealing demanded. Either way, be it bad luck or circumstance,

Zeke knew that, with interest included, there could still be three years of payments, an eternity in such a hazardous trade. *God forgive me*, he thought, *but what if his kidney thing really does hit the shitter?*

Seeing the red light at the last second, he squeezed both brakes and skid-hopped the back tire along the street in a final effort to stop.

"Jesus … *Christ.*" Ending up sideways in the crosswalk, he balanced precariously, feet still clicked into the pedals. *No more thinking*, he swore as his beeper went off and the light blinked green right after. Finding a payphone in Kenmore Square, he dialed the eight-hundred number and heard Stuart Rigby sing-song, "Season's greetings from your friends at Split Minute! And how may we assist you?"

"Hey, Santa, could you be a bigger loser or what?"

"Zeke! How merry! And where are we?"

"Kenmore with a deuce. Then I'm empty."

"Fine. Let's pick up at Sandstone Fine Art, 331 Newbury, going to Lynch, 150 State … and … let's see. Graphic Art going to City Hall, Department of Education, third floor."

"Swell." Zeke shorthanded the slips, the phone pinched between shoulder and ear.

"Zeke?"

"Yeah?"

"If you don't mind me saying, you seem a little more hateful than usual today."

Zeke grinned and capped the pen. "Are your feelings hurt?"

"Possibly," Stuart said, playing coy. "Would you care to massage them?"

"Maybe with a chainsaw."

"Zeke!"

"Or how about some broken glass?"

"You big meanie! See if you get another express the whole rest of the day!"

"Hey, wait a second. I'm sorry, Stu."

"You're just saying that." Stuart sounded hurt. "You big meanie."

Organizing his slips, Zeke said, "Does the Graphic for City Hall have a name or what?"

"No, sir."

"Great."

"Call me from Sandstone before heading downtown."

"Ten-four."

Zeke stored the case, checked left, and gradually slipped away from the curb. Immediately captive again, unable to shake any of it from his mind, he blankly steered ahead.

Chapter Twelve

Wednesday, December 3

It was a little after 6:00 PM when three crisp knocks interrupted the silence. Before that, Zeke had been chain-smoking on the couch for thirty minutes, home from work but unable to focus. As with everything else these last two weeks, it began and ended with his brother, who, thoughtful as always, was already half an hour late.

Through the door, he saw Lotus hunkered down behind the upturned collar of his leather jacket, the motorcycle helmet cocked on a hip like an extra head grown sideways.

"Hey, man." Lotus stepped inside. "Old man winter can kiss my ass."

"You ain't kidding."

"It's fucking freezing, man." He shoved the door closed and stomped his boots. "Anybody home?"

"Naw."

Lotus blew into both hands for warmth and said, "What time's she coming?"

"Not for another hour."

"Where the fuck is Josh?"

Zeke scoffed. "I don't have a clue. Either way, we need to be cleaned up in forty-five minutes, at the latest."

They converged on the kitchen, where Lotus ran a hand over the table as if inspecting it. He then placed his helmet, keys, and courier bag on one corner. Looking up, he waited a moment to settle in, grinned at Zeke, and said, "This shit is fucking unbelievable."

"Yeah?" Zeke turned on the light over the table, which hung like an upside-down spider lit up between them. "Blue sky?"

"Dialed in, man." Lotus pulled out a paper package wrapped like butchered meat. "Blue sky is right. Fucking three drops' worth and the shit went instantly off the chart."

"Nice." Zeke got himself a glass of water. "How many times can we turn it?"

Lotus pulled out a triple-beam scale, a container of vitamin B, and a pile of tiny Ziploc baggies. "We finally caught a break. I'm guessing we can go four to one on net, after everyone's cut is squared."

"You want something to drink?"

"Naw, man. Got an ashtray?"

Zeke placed an empty soda can on the table as Lotus shed his jacket. "What's up?" he said. "You look—I don't know—pissed off."

"Naw." Zeke turned for the refrigerator, replacing his water with a beer. He looked back at the semiautomatic tucked into Lotus's waistband, then noticed an ugly snout peeking from his bag. "You got a tip on a riot or what?"

"Aw, man." Lotus tapped his temple. "I'm slipping in my old age. It's …" Lotus razored open the package, watching the white powder spill out like a toxic dune. "I got some shitty news, man."

Zeke rubbed his forehead. "What."

"Got a late-night phone call." Lotus ran a credit card through the pile, snapping off four mounds. Pausing, looking up at Zeke, he said, "They're comin'. Tonight, tomorrow, this weekend …" Lotus shrugged. "I'm sorry. Believe me, I really thought it was bullshit. I mean the fucking pussies sent a *note* first?"

"Tell me about it." Zeke nodded grimly. "Fucking clowns watch too much TV."

Lotus grinned, but not for long. He said, "It ain't good."

"Who'd you talk to?"

"Holtzman's little brother."

"Snot Boy? Jesus, that poor kid. What's he doing with fucking Lindy and Boxer?"

"The same thing we all did." Lotus lifted an eyebrow. "Not only do they have your place and work; he says they got Josh's digits too."

"Fuck."

"They know about the dialysis—"

"Man …"

"And this ain't exactly something you're gonna wanna hear, but they got your girl's place too."

Zeke scoffed. "Cammi's not even—"

"Not her, gigolo."

"Oh man." Zeke put down the beer. "No way."

"I'm sorry." Lotus perched his eyebrows as if he did not know what else to say. "They followed her home from here. Like three weeks ago."

"Oh my God."

"What the fuck, Zeke? She lives practically ten blocks from them."

Nauseated, he yanked out a chair and glanced up at the ceiling. *Fucking Josh*, he cursed, but knew it did no good. Subconsciously or not, it was simply what happened to those close enough to care, when the good times crashed like glass upon a wall, and whoever remained got to wade through Josh's mess. With his head still tilted back, he said, "Am I insane, or is half the city trying to kill this kid?"

"Naw." Looking down with a sympathetic expression, Lotus lit a cigarette. "At this point, insanity would be a gift."

"Fuck."

"Zeke, they ain't gonna roll on her. Snot Boy said it was just dumb luck."

"And you …" Zeke did not want to have to ask. "They got you yet?"

Lotus slowly shook his head. "Wouldn't matter even if they did."

"Choosing sides? Pissing directly into their faces?"

"Hey." Lotus exhaled a large cloud of smoke. "Don't nobody need to hold my hand."

"Oh yeah? You all grown-up now?"

Lotus grinned and said, "Mom always said stay in school."

"Yes, she did."

"I'm leaving this here with you." Lotus pulled out the pistol-grip shotgun.

"There's five in it." He pointed to a switch above the trigger. "Green is good." He flicked it. "Red is dead."

"Thanks, Dad."

"Man, how long's it been since you handled one of these?"

It was cold to the touch, recently oiled. Zeke held it loosely, reluctantly, as if disgusted. With only ghosts and rumors for targets, wondering how far his recent re-enlistment might go, he stared down at the gun. *Here we go again.* It was like before, on that long past summer afternoon, when Josh returned from Chambers Street with the first firearm Zeke had ever seen. And in that alley off Snowden, where they had blasted at the rats brought by the bloodied dumpster of Petticomo's Butchered Meats. Guided into this new world, they caught the fever and thought he had done them all a favor. Yet now, considering the mood Zeke was in, and the way this plague was spreading across his life, he realized he was more likely to use it on Josh than any moron stumbling through the door. He handed it back.

"Bad idea."

"Zeke—"

"Listen," Zeke looked up at Lotus through the light, "I didn't ask. And this ain't what it's gonna be about."

Lotus's face froze in a half smile. "Are you for real?"

"What?"

"This *is* what it's about. Right here …" Lotus motioned around the apartment. "Right now."

"They won't come for me."

"Holy shit." He closed his eyes. "Sometimes you worry me, man, honest to God."

"This whole thing …" Zeke nodded at the gun. "It's just turning into fucking chaos."

"What is your fucking problem?" Palming the table, Lotus leaned in. "Is this about her? Huh? You half-assing this shit when you, of all fucking people, know exactly what this means?" Lotus straightened up and began pacing through the kitchen. "This isn't your choice."

"It can be."

"No, Zeke, it can't. It isn't. And the fact that I've actually got to stand here and listen to this self-righteous fucking—"

"This ain't about morals."

"Then what?" Lotus stopped pacing and faced him. "Huh? You want to tell me what I'm missing? Because I'll tell you, there wasn't a single fucking time we cased someone for free. Man, they were right outside your fucking *door*."

"Goddamn it."

"You know I'm right."

Zeke could feel the stare.

"Look me in the eye," Lotus said. "Call me out and I won't say another word."

Zeke looked towards the window above the sink and saw the black night like an escape hatch he could not reach. When there was nowhere else to put his glance, he picked up the gun and slowly stood, the movement awkward in this silence. Heading towards his room, he had no argument left to give and no real room left to maneuver. As he placed it behind his door, he thought, *I am going to regret this*, but knew he already did.

Back in the kitchen, Lotus had finished with the cut and was now working the beam and baggies. Sitting back down, watching the process, Zeke lit a cigarette and said, "I really just don't get it. I mean, those guys were our fucking bros, man."

"It's just been too long, you know?" Lotus sealed another bag, piling the scale again. "None of it, you know? There wasn't any ending. And fucking Ju-Ju and C.B., man—they got put on Josh's tab for the fuck of it." Lotus shook his head. "They just believe in it, like the Bible." He grabbed another bag. "Don't fucking lose it, Z, because I know we all did the same thing right behind him, but he did open up the door."

"Too bad." Zeke finished the beer in three gulps. "They're dead fucking wrong on all counts."

"Yep." Lotus nodded. "They ain't nothing, man, just a couple of leftovers begging to be dealt with."

Zeke looked up, watching as Lotus meticulously worked the scale. "Is that what you're thinking?"

"Me?" Lotus grinned, working the mix through the staccato chop of the card. "All's I'm saying is, pretend one day you got a house and kids; if there's a poisonous snake in your yard, and you're lucky enough to know it, are you just gonna turn away and hope it disappears? Or are you going to grab a shovel and go out there and hammer that motherfucker into the ground?"

"House and kids?"

"All right, bad example." Lotus grinned again. "Then you and Cammi, out in a park somewhere, when you have to be her knight in shining armor."

"Oh man."

"Wait a minute. What am I saying? She'd probably beat you to it, you fucking pussy."

As he laughed and gave him the finger, Zeke felt the tension briefly collapse, the moment like it used to be, he thought, until he heard a startled voice say, "Oh my God."

Immediately turning, hand hesitating at his waist, Lotus squinted and said, "Who the fuck is *that?*"

"Liz?"

Zeke, as if caught naked, saw her shape in the open door. He watched her for a moment, seeing the disappointment before the door smashed closed and Lotus, turning back to the triple beam, said, "Let her go, man."

But he could not, and grabbed a jacket on the fly.

"Liz!"

Leaning over the railing, he saw that she was already near the first-floor landing, so he quickened his descent.

"Liz! Please, let me explain!"

But she was moving fast, almost half a block ahead before he reached her shoulder. She recoiled, screaming, "No!"

"Liz, please …" Zeke, panting, stopped dead in his tracks. "Goddamn it, let me explain!"

She slowly halted, but did not turn around.

Zeke watched his labored breath hiss like smoke towards her unturned, black-capped head. "Liz …"

"Just say it." She paused. He saw her head shake as if already bored. Could almost picture her expression, because she only wore one when really pissed off.

"Well …?"

"I'm sorry."

"Right."

She took a step and he screamed, "Please! You can't just go. Not like this. It wasn't what you think."

"Really?" She turned, and the bitter sneer hurt more than what was coming next. "Then I guess I'm just stupid. So tell me, what was all that, that *shit* on the table. And the guy with the gun in his pants, is he an old friend too?"

His gaze fell towards the sidewalk. "Baby ..."

"Don't." She shook her head, unsure of whether she was more ashamed of him or herself for letting it come to this. "You didn't even lock the door."

"But you're half an hour early, babe." He tried on a shrug. "And I know what we said—"

"Zeke—"

"No, please." He spread both arms. "I told you about his ... his deadlines, man. How the fuck else can we exist?"

"Not like this. I can't, Zeke, you know?" She looked at him empathetically and shrugged as well. "I just can't."

"Please, you can't do this. It's just until we figure something else out—I swear."

"Zeke—"

"No. I swear, honest to God, may he strike me dead, just a few more weeks."

"Of what? That?" She threw a nod towards the yellow submarine. "Do you actually think I'm gonna wait around to watch you all get busted or killed? Is that what this is gonna mean?"

"Baby—"

"No. No more babies, Zeke, okay? I can't hear sweet talk from someone I used to respect."

"Liz!"

She stomped off towards the corner.

"Liz!"

As she made a right onto North Harvard, he yelled, "But it can't end like this!"

She disappeared from sight.

"What the fuck!"

He knew if he ran after her, she would see right through it. And if he didn't, he was as good as dead.

Turning for his house, surprised at how much it already hurt, Zeke did not look back.

Chapter Thirteen

Friday, December 5

Two days later they met after work at South Station with the crowded thousands streaming by for their daily commute home. Arriving first, Liz was at a corner table in the back of the pavilion, tightly clutching her purse. She was still wearing her black beret and a new brown overcoat, dreading his arrival. When she had at last spoken to him this morning, he sounded relieved. "Let's just talk," he had said, and she reluctantly agreed.

Which, of course, proceeded to ruin her day. She spent the next eight hours in a state of second-guessing, her mind unleashed upon their situation and expectations while knowing as well, in the short time they had shared, she really had no complaints. Walking away the night before last, she barely made it onto North Harvard before lingering on the hope of his pursuit.

Relaxing her grip on the purse, she thought, *God, what a waste.* An ex-con bike courier? With an ex-con, convicted murderer for a brother? Oh yeah, not a *convicted* murderer, just a ringleader who was dying after apparently pissing off so many people that they were lined up ten deep just to wait their turn. And Zeke? She smiled sadly, remembering his expression in between shock and horror, her standing in the open door as if the last four months had practically ended in that second.

When she spotted him scanning nervously over the tables, she forgot all of it. Here he was, Anxious Zeke, Concerned Zeke, the guy who had slipped past her defenses. Once he finally caught sight of her, she knew all of this had been in vain.

"Hey," he said and gamely smiled. "You mind?"

"Nope."

He shed his bag and took a seat, sighing as if his day and its many miles finally just ended. He pulled off his gloves, sunglasses, and hat, his face red and wind-whipped. They waited in an awful silence until she said, "So ...?"

"So here we are." He gave her a grin that she did not return, then seemed to regret it. "About the other night—"

"Zeke—"

"I'm sorry." He leaned both elbows onto the table, interlocking his fingers. "I was wrong about ... about not telling you the specifics, and I realize you must be pissed off—and you have a right to be pissed off—but you have to understand, this isn't something for the long term, you know? Believe me, I can't live much longer like this either."

"Zeke ..." She was unsure of what to say next. "It's more than that, okay? I mean, how am I supposed to sleep at night when someone I care about is surrounded by all that nonsense?"

"I understand—"

"No. You don't. Because if you did, we would be out to dinner tonight, like we've done every Friday night since this whole thing began."

"And ..."

"And instead, we're sitting here, waiting for something in the other to change."

"Change?"

"Yes." She leaned back in her chair. "If I asked you right now to walk away from him, could you?"

"It's not—"

"And if you asked me not to care about it, do you honestly think I would?"

"Baby, please." He clutched his forehead, squinting miserably. "I'm just asking for a little more time. Honest to God, I'm not saying you're wrong. I'm just ... I ..."

She watched the division occur—the fierce commitment to familial duty or the woman in front of whom he was now gasping for his life. Admittedly, it was a little of each that had caught her eye originally, the hard-working guy forging ahead, never missing a date or forgetting to call, the sense of duty unyielding. Except… *Except for his fucking brother*, she thought, and knew he could not choose. He was sitting right here waiting to be guillotined because he could not pull the trigger on himself.

"Zeke—"

"Baby, please," he nearly begged. "Doesn't this mean anything to you?"

"Me?" She blinked, startled. "You're going to put this on *me*?"

"No, of course not. I … I didn't mean it like that."

"Because if you think this is what I want …" She saw his eyes light up with hope until she said, "This was your decision, remember?"

"But what else am I supposed to do, Liz? Tell me how, how the fuck we are supposed to come up with that kind of money? I don't play the lottery and my last name ain't Kennedy."

"Zeke …"

"So," he leaned back and held out his hands, "you're just gonna walk away?"

She could not look him in the eye.

"This whole thing," he said, motioning through the air. "What was it, just practice?"

She looked at the table and quietly said, "You know that's not true."

He let out a deep breath, then rubbed his face, exhausted by everything he no longer controlled.

"Oh, man," he said dejectedly. "Your palm …"

She did not want to lose her poise, the advantage and defense she was trying to bolster. *This was going to be his fault,* she thought, and abruptly crossed her arms to hide it.

"I'm fine."

"I know you don't want to do this!"

"You don't know anything! You can pretend pretty good, Zeke Sandaman, but you just can't face that fact, can you?"

As if slapped, his face was in perfect shock. He started and stopped with two or three sentences before he stood to leave. He grabbed his gloves and hat. Observing this sudden sadness, she could see she had crushed his spirit.

"Okay," he said.

She watched him turn and leave, her tears already welling before he was even halfway to the door, re-affixing his hat and sunglasses, the courier bag slung low on his shoulder.

Chapter Fourteen

"OUCH … AW, MAN." ROLLING INTO the wall, Zeke cracked an eyelid, saw the room drunkenly shift, and clutched the pillow to his face in horror. The stink of his own breath made the artificial night impossible, so he glanced at the digital clock to see it was 12:17 PM. He tried piecing together his evening, recalled Liz dumping him at six o'clock and by eight-thirty, completely shitfaced, getting the boot from J. J. McCannister's. In Allston later on, he remembered running into Cash Monroe, all dolled up and hitting the town. Always the party boy, Cash enjoyed Zeke's pain and bought shots, trying to empathize, but Zeke could barely function.

Now, running a scaly tongue across chapped lips, the thought of ice-cold water made him abandon the night-stored warmth between the sheets. Darting quickly for a bathrobe, Zeke stepped into the kitchen like a mistake awakened by chance. Hearing the television, he yawned as he walked, his whole body one large ache. Running a hand through the daisy-like bedhead, he turned the corner and saw his brother, who, after crashing last night, was now sprawled couchside in only his boxers.

Wincing, he then noticed Josh staring straight at him.

"Sorry, I—"

"Don't worry about it." Josh dragged on a smoke, running a hand across the once formidable six-foot frame. "It's some shit, though, ain't it?"

"Yes." Having seen it bare-skinned for the first time, Zeke finally had to will his gaze elsewhere. The pencil-thin limbs were steeped in yellow dye to join at a gaunt torso made cartoonish by the bulbous distension his diseased gut had become. The menacing homemade ink crawled like dead vines across the devastation until what was left made them look inappropriate at best. Zeke blinked and glanced away instead, the black eyes and emaciated face like a ghost he could not shake.

"I need some water," he said numbly. "You good?"

"Yeah."

Pulling a U-turn, he saw his bike upside down in the corner by the door. Approaching it, he noticed the smashed rim and bent front forks.

"What the fuck?"

Joshua chuckled. "Take a look at your face, moron."

Stepping in front of the bathroom mirror, Zeke saw the forehead gash and cut neck. Whipping open the bathrobe, he found a hematoma hung along the outside right quad like a blackened tangerine.

"That's gonna hurt for weeks," he groaned, turning back to the mirror and gently pushing at the second set of lips sliced into his forehead. With arms bracketing the sink, he exhaled, exasperated, then glanced back at what he had somehow done to himself yet again and wondered at what age this might end.

Not wanting to deal with any of it, he got the water and joined Josh, shoving his feet aside for a seat. Observing his brother's smirk, Zeke said, "Enjoying yourself?"

"Thoroughly."

"Tell me, please, what happened last night? And how are you laying there in boxers? Aren't you freezing?"

Josh grinned without turning his head from the TV. "You puked out your window. I bet the thing's still wide open."

"Jesus ..."

"Yeah, you were a mess. Came stumbling in like an elephant at like two thirty and could barely talk."

"What ...?"

"I tried to get you to clean those cuts, but ..." Josh shrugged. "You were fucking tatered, kid. Said you ran into a tree or something."

"That's gonna be two hundred bucks at least."

"What?"

Zeke stood without answering, looked at what had once been his favorite work bike, and cursed its ruination. "I'm a fucking idiot."

There came a knock, and Zeke turned to see Cammi Sinclair scowling amid the blustery clouds surrounding her.

"Oh God … " His smile was pure despite the gashed open head. "Put something on, J, Little Miss Muffet just made the scene."

———————————————

Zeke unlocked the front door, giving her a wide grin and holding out both arms as his robe yawned open like drapes hung on his thin, scraped-up frame. He crooned, "Good morning, Miss Sinclair. How 'bout a hug?"

"Are you testing the strength of my stomach?" Cammi pushed past. "Good God, Zeke, you know?"

"Hey now—"

"Honestly …" Cammi saw the bike, glanced back at the crusted, ridiculous wounds, and decided she need not ask. "You forgot about today, didn't you?"

"Baby—"

She checked her watch and said, "We still got time."

"I just woke up. Come in and say hi to that kid right over there."

Cammi unslung her bag and shed the outer fatigue, revealing black leggings, a pink Minny Mouse skirt, and red T-shirt with white lettering that read, EASY WHEN DRUNK. Joshua grinned, tossed a salute, and said, "Paperclip earrings?"

She caught herself staring at him, and her pity made her feel ashamed. Hoping to cover it up, she smiled and said, "So what?"

"Wasn't it high heels and a dress only two weeks ago?"

"Bite me."

"Now you're talking."

Hiding a grin, she claimed the recliner and crossed her legs, her Izumis still on despite the boots inside the bag. Twirling her hair innocuously, she said to both, "So?"

"Don't ask," Zeke said from the entryway. "I got hammered at the Sixty-Six with Cash and J here. What? Were you and Lotus out on the rake?"

"Naw." Josh batted a hand while watching the football game. "Took the night off."

Zeke looked at Cammi and said, "Two minutes. In and out of the shower, I swear."

He left as Josh asked, "Where y'all going?"

"Animation fest." Cammi gleamed excitedly. "Gonna pull some tubes and watch cartoons."

"Where at?"

"The Brattle."

"Nice." Josh glanced back at the TV.

Already bored with the football game, she slid her gaze imperceptibly left to where the top half of his chest protruded from the sleeping bag like a jaundiced tongue. Watched him watching football almost serenely while her mind was still a thousand questions and even panicked because somehow he was not. Through the glass five years ago, she remembered seeing for the first time this brother Zeke had only spoken of in the broadest of strokes, and thought to herself he had been gracious to say the least. Because staring back, with black eyes a constant sweep from her breasts to her face then to Zeke, was a muscled animal sniffing predatorily, peppering questions like an interrogation, and with an attitude more like a slap than expression of thanks, even though Zeke had not been there in years. In the parking lot afterward, not wanting to be rude, Cammi decided the mystery was no more. Having finally met the infamous older brother, returning volley for volley as he poked about for weakness, she thought him to be petty, perverted, and dangerous. Added to that was the resemblance and speech and mannerisms in stereo as Cammi found Zeke not to be an original but more a project cut off in mid-experiment once Josh lost his hold from prison. Now realizing what might have been had Josh remained free to complete his masterpiece, she remembered staring at Zeke for the entire forty-minute drive home before completely fucking his brains out.

"Hey," she said and waited until Josh glanced over. "I brought some cocktails but I feel guilty."

"Why's that?"

"Well, you're ... I mean, this can't be good."

"Cammi ..." He stopped, appreciating her concern. "You're right. It's not. But that choice was already made, you know?"

"You're telling me to mind my own business?"

"Yes."

Still seated, she bent for her bag and took out the mixings. Fetching three glasses from the kitchen, she tried to imagine herself in his position, toward the very end, and knew what she would tell those offering unsolicited advice. Pausing, listening to her own words, she decided it was the only rationalization left as she mixed a Bloody Mary for a half-dead guy on dialysis.

Handing him his drink, she washed away the guilt in giant gulps until her glass was drained.

"Jesus," he said, beaming in admiration. "It's too bad you guys are taking off." He winged an arm behind his head. "Kind of wanted to steal him today."

"For what?"

"It's kind of a surprise."

"Oh yeah?"

He nodded cryptically. "You should come too."

"They do have show-times tomorrow …" As she fixed herself a refill, her curiosity won out. "Let's do it."

"For real?" Josh rolled his head along the armrest to put her in his gaze. "Cool. But he'll probably just whine like a bitch."

"Not while I'm alive, he won't."

Josh grinned. The phone rang and he picked it up. "Hello? … Uh, he's in the shower. Can I take a message? … Sure thing."

After he hung up, Cammi said, "Who was that?"

"Liz."

"Who?"

Trying to off-hand his fuck-up, he retreated into nonchalance. "Some chick."

"Liz," Cammi repeated, tightening her grip on the already half-gone drink. *So, it has a name*, she thought. "What's her story?"

"Who?"

"Don't play stupid."

"Fuck, Cam," he said, squirming. "She's a weird little thing. Works in some office somewhere doing something."

"Thanks, Josh."

"Talk to *him*, man." Josh turned back to the game. "I ain't getting into the middle of this bloodbath."

"Pussy," she said.

Josh grinned but would not take the bait.

Searching her bag, she dug out an aspirin bottle and shook out four pills. She walked two of them over to Josh, who said, "What's this?"

"Percs."

"Nice." He chased them with the cocktail.

Zeke came around the corner in blue jeans and plain white shirt, grimacing at the array. "Already?"

"It'll cure." Cammi shook out two more pills. "And so will these. Here."

"What's this?"

"Percocets."

"God, you are such a good girl." Zeke grabbed a drink and sat next to his brother.

"For those who couldn't be here." Cammi lifted her glass. "Like little Miss Liz, the office clerk."

With his glass frozen in mid-air as the insult washed over, Zeke pinned his brother with an angry glance. "What the fuck, kid?"

"Hey, man." Josh raised both hands. "All I did was answer the phone."

"She called? Just now?"

"Yep."

Shaking his head and tabling the drink, Zeke stood and stalked out.

"Geez." Cammi frowned. "Way to take a joke."

"Things ain't good." Josh licked his lips. "She's …"

"What?" Cammi knelt in close.

Josh reached by her for a pack of Marlboros. Keeping his voice low, he said, "Since I've hit town, let's just say she's not down with this scene at all."

"Oh."

"Yeah." Josh lit a cigarette, exhaling the smoke as if it were repugnant. "Like it matters."

"Josh—"

"I'm fucking up his whole life," he hissed. "His roommate's gone, this whiny bitch refuses to see him. I mean, what the fuck …?"

She punched his shoulder and angrily whispered back, "Don't even waste my time. As if you know?"

"So?"

"And wouldn't do the same in return. Is that what you're telling me?"

"Cammi—"

She pointed directly at him and said, "That's right. Guess what? He's the only one stupid enough, too. And you're the only thing he's got left. Connect the fucking dots."

"Fuck you."

"Really?" She stood, her eyes brightened by the challenge. "I haven't said a word, Josh, and do you want to know why?"

"Cam—"

"Because he wouldn't listen even if I did." She crossed both arms. "Because there's no way he would throw you out, even though I'm beginning to think he should."

"Really?" Josh appeared amused. "He didn't seem to have a problem showing you the door."

"You know …" Angered, Cammi stepped toward him. "As it is, there isn't anything left. And now, thanks to you, he's back at that ledge beside you again and just about ready to jump."

"Like I don't know that?" Josh rolled his bloodshot eyes. "Like I need to hear this shit from you?"

"Just remember, that's all." Cammi wanted to smack the grin from his lips. "Your pathetic fuck-ups have a habit of ruining his life."

"All right! Please …" He looked up at her as if fearing what they were about to unleash. "You don't need to say that, you know?" He shrugged. "Me and you … we just can't."

She stood there, watching him watch the game. "Pussy."

Buzzed from the alcohol, she stepped into his line of sight until his eyes wandered up to hers. "The fucking Sandaman brothers," she said. "What does that say? When you two retards are the best thing I got going on?"

Watching him laugh, Cammi turned for the bathroom before running squarely into Zeke. "Well, well," she impishly said. "If it isn't idiot number two."

"What?"

"Don't ask." Josh frowned. "Chick's flipped. What up?"

"You said she called from home?"

"I never said that. She just said to call her."

"Huh. There was no answer."

"Bust it out."

"Yeah."

Zeke left and returned with a Smurfs' mirror won at a carnival some years back. Sitting down, he ran a card through the pile before handing his brother a cut-down straw. Cammi rejoined and lifted both eyebrows, saying, "Can I play too?"

"Yeah, man."

Pinching off a nostril, Josh snorted as Zeke shook his head and said, "I'm not even gonna be able to see the screen."

"Zeke?" Cammi knelt on the other side of the coffee table. "Sweetie, there's been a slight change of plans."

"What?"

"We'll hit the cartoons tomorrow." Cammi took the straw and railed up. "Josh's got a surprise."

"And you're gonna fall for that?"

"Where's your sense of adventure?" Josh cracked and sniffed up loosened mucus. "Won't take but a second."

Zeke looked at Cammi. "Hey, it's your show. You obviously don't care."

"Not at all."

"Whatever." Zeke tugged at Josh's sleeping bag. "You might want to lose this, though."

"I'll shower up right now." It might have been the Percocets, the alcohol, or the cocaine, but when he stood for the first time in hours, the head rush buckled his legs.

"You all right?" Zeke asked.

"Yeah, just a freebie." Josh headed for the bathroom.

Waiting until he heard the running water, Zeke cut up two more lines and said, "He's not looking so good. And the fucking kid shouldn't be drinking at all."

"No." Cammi stared off towards the hallway. "But he's a big boy, Zeke."

"Yeah, right, and you're not exactly helping things, Miss Port-o-bar."

"Hey!"

Making one of them disappear, Zeke quickly sniffed a handful of times and palmed off the snot. Cammi did one of her own and said, "It's cool, right? They run the same show tomorrow at two."

"Whatever, man." Zeke sipped at the Bloody Mary. "But get set. Recently, Josh ain't really been too appreciated for his surprises."

Grinning, Cammi felt a warm buzz separate from the alcohol and narcotics while listlessly awaiting amusements no animation festival could ever properly provide. Zeke watched the game without caring, lit a cigarette he soon forgot about, and drummed his heel in a cocaine-driven twitch bereft of any thought whatsoever.

An hour later they were on North Harvard, buttoned up and hooded against the misting rain and thirty-four-degree temperature. Josh limped along, the alcohol already swamping his system with nowhere to go until tomorrow's treatment.

Trudging forward, Zeke's frown plainly stated he had better things to do other than getting soaked on his day off. Worse, a giant Band-Aid was stuck to his forehead like a reminder of the previous evening's debacle.

Two steps back, Cammi walked with Josh as he nodded towards Zeke skulking along, and he and Cammi shared the joke, taking turns from the bottle. Seeing an empty cab on the creep, they hailed it and swung the door open before all three tumbled in like a wave.

"We're headed to St. Mary's," Josh said. "You know where that is?"

The cabbie slowly nodded, speechless, and turned up an Hispanic AM radio station.

"Are you kidding?" Zeke leaned forward to look across Cammi's lap. "Today? Now?"

"What's going on?" Cammi glanced from one to the other. "What's the surprise? Church?"

"We're going to visit Gabriella," Josh said brightly, then looked at Zeke. "Ten minutes, in and out. I promise."

"You know …" Zeke shook his head. "Every fucking day, man, it's like a whole new nightmare inside this fucking funhouse."

Grinning, Josh left the insult unreturned. He watched the dreary afternoon, gulped down a burst of warm gin, and, while ignoring the cabbie's flash of disapproval in the rearview, said, "I was too chicken-shit to go alone, all right?" He looked outside as Cambridge Street passed by at forty miles per hour. "And I knew what your reaction would be."

"It ain't like that." Zeke said, sounding regretful. "It has been awhile."

"It'll be nice." Josh handed him the bottle. "With both of us there, too? You know her birthday's only three weeks away?"

Like a slow, crushing talon, Cammi's hand pierced Zeke's thigh until he said, "Yes. Yes, it is."

Fifteen minutes later they were almost through Brighton as gradually, in concentric rings expanding from the city center, the neighborhoods became more residential and prosperous. When the stacked rock wall appeared on their left, Josh saw just beyond it the acres of modest granite tucked like bookmarks into neat rows. Inside the main entrance, Josh found himself recalling the awfulness of that day ...

Broken into three limousines and a dozen cars, both families, the Sandamans and Marquezes, had traveled like a slow-moving centipede along this same road twelve years ago. Long gone from the house, having severed his relationships, Josh had shown up separately, watched his father from across the gathering, and sincerely wished it was him they were burying instead.

Unlike Zeke, towards the end of her illness, Josh's visits were perfunctory and businesslike, usually at night with a carload of hoodlums anxiously awaiting him below. Slowly pushed aside as her husband and oldest son waged war, she had, Josh knew, sympathized with his position while fighting to maintain her own. Seemingly pissed off every day of his life, running three crews and forced to babysit grown men lest he turn his back for one single second, and weekly stressing payroll while trying to do the books and raise a family as well, Robert Sandaman finally ended up coming home every night to face them like three more contracts yet to complete. Then there was Gabriella, tolerating the outbursts and insults with that quiet absolution Josh could never figure out. Robert Sandaman's entrances were without purpose, more like systematic ambushes, slinging disapproval like bullets towards all he saw, which was basically two kids and a wife forced to carve out what they could around his negativity and moody dominance. When she gained weight, he called her names. When she said something obvious, he told her she was stupid. And across the table, the eldest watched his father with a growing recklessness neither one could afford. Maybe it was for her kids or matrimonial duty or the deep belief she exercised weekly inside the Catholic church down the block. But this was, he knew, what only made it worse. Having had a mother he did not know allowed him to feel as if he had abandoned her, which he eventually did one night following his sixteenth birthday, her shape a sorrowful slump in the hallway as both cried while he made the choice instead of staying behind, his father's demands outweighed by what Josh already carelessly regarded, mainly his future and those who would help him destroy it. Her big black eyes, even early on in the sickness, unswayed by what her baby boy had become. It was, he knew, why people obligatorily said time healed all wounds. *Dr. Time*, Josh thought, and decided no greater lie had ever existed.

"*A donde?* Where?" the cabbie innocently inquired.

Josh nodded ahead. "Keep going. I think it's around that next corner."

"It is. Right over there." Zeke pointed at a stand of elms. "Gimme that." He took the gin bottle and punished it.

Pushing a twenty through the trough, Josh told the cabbie to wait. Then, even though it was his idea, he scanned outside like a paratrooper afraid to take that final step towards the door.

"All right." He stiffened. "Last stop, Graceland."

Ten seconds later they were standing in the drizzle. Taking Cammi's hand, Zeke pushed ahead as Josh paused roadside for one final swig before bringing up the rear. Eleanor Ray Thomas, Reginald Paul Hedrick, William Percy Flynn, the forgotten names of those they passed.

The elm trees were in clusters of three, scattered every hundred yards, and stretched like giant canopies towards the sky. Watching as Zeke and Cammi slowed to a halt, Josh soon joined them in silence. GABRIELLA LOUISA MARQUEZ SANDAMAN, the top line read, and beneath it, DEVOTED WIFE AND MOTHER, and beneath that, JULY 11, 1949–AUGUST 16, 1985, and beneath that, MAY YOU WATCH OVER US.

"Jesus." Josh felt all the old sadness and despair spring open like a switchblade. Taking a dull pull off the gin, he passed it to Cammi, then stepped forward to run a respectful hand along the headstone's arc. Tracing an index finger down the chiseled trenches of her name, he smiled sadly and said, "Hey, Mom."

Cammi abruptly hitched, knuckling an eye with her fingerless gloves.

"What the fuck " Josh knelt down, then swiveled back. "Wasn't none of this right."

"Yeah, J." Zeke could not hold the gaze because Josh's eyes were widely spilling over.

"I'm here," Josh said, turning back. "Finally, right?"

Kneeling as well, Zeke gently pulled until his brother lifted from the headstone. He put a hand to the back of Josh's skull and said, "It's okay. You got that, man. She's right here."

Cammi joined them, throwing an arm around each and there they knelt, in the sodden grass, a lone living cluster surrounded by stone.

"Josh!"

"Zeke, get him."

"I'm trying." Shoving open the cab door, Zeke yelled out, "Josh! Goddamn it, where're you going?"

"It's right up here!" Josh pointed drunkenly down the block. He gave Zeke his back and continued while Zeke looked into the cab. "Pay him," he said to Cammi. "I gotta stop this kid."

"Where's he going?"

"Fuck, man, I thought he was kidding." Slinging the courier bag containing the gin and assorted chemicals over a shoulder, Zeke chased his brother through the rain. He heard boots slapping through puddles on Snow Street, a side road off Washington Street in Brighton. The houses were comfortable two-floor colonials with their own driveways and garages. Boston College was just down the road in Newton.

"Josh!"

Zeke saw him jog up onto a porch. He broke into a sprint, but it was too late as his brother was already knocking. Nearly slipping on the steps, Zeke was about to grab him until a lock disengaged and the door opened to reveal a small child with straight blond hair.

"Hi," the kid said with a big smile, looking up at the two puzzled faces still trying to catch their air.

"Hey … little man." Josh knelt down as Zeke said, "C'mon." He tugged at Josh's jacket. "This ain't even it."

"Can I help you?" The voice was attached to a slender woman in designer jeans and a white turtleneck. Stepping in front of the child, her pretty face was filled with a sudden anxiety as she tried on a polite smile.

"Um, yes." Josh stood, trying to peek over her shoulder. "I was looking for 136 Snow Street."

"Well, this is it."

"Do you live here?"

She appraised again the haggard faces, smelled the alcohol, and reinforced her stilted smile. Sensing her fear, Josh stuck out a hand and said, "Joshua Sandaman." He nodded to his left. "And my brother Zeke."

They watched it like a slow-motion film, how her face became even paler as her expression ran somewhere between shock and outright discomfort, until she found herself shaking his hand and saying, "Phyllis … I'm Phyllis Sandaman."

"I …" Joshua's hand stopped pumping hers as his mouth worked a sentence that never materialized. He stared at her dumbly until the little head poked around her left buttock.

Zeke grabbed Josh by the elbow and said, "I'm sorry, miss. We were just leaving."

"No." Josh yanked free. "We were not. As a matter of fact, we were looking for Robert."

Seemingly trapped within a middle-class graciousness, she buffed another smile and said, "Just a moment."

The door swung closed. From the sidewalk, Cammi Sinclair said, "What's going on?"

"Hell if I know." Zeke punched his brother's shoulder. "What is this gonna prove?"

Josh was still staring at the door, seemingly oblivious to the protests as he quietly said, "He remarried."

"Did you hear me?"

"You think that's our half-brother?"

"Who gives a fuck," Zeke spat. "Fuck him. Fuck this whole thing, man. Let's *go*."

He was turning to leave when the door re-opened to cast a long shadow across the porch. It might as well have been just yesterday. Josh silently stood next to his brother before the man both had once looked up to, and now did so again, as neither one found a single thing to say. Topping six feet, with the robust build of a lifetime spent in a no-nonsense profession, Robert Sandaman ran a hand through his graying buzz cut, blinked the tight blue eyes twice, and said, completely straight-faced, "Hello, boys."

Unsure of whether he wanted to take a swing or just ask why, Josh said with a grin, "Hey, Pop."

The earnest gaze had lost little of its intensity, Josh decided, having already noted the graying hair and additional lines to the weather-beaten face as the only significant differences the missing decade had made. They were the same height, could have been the same person save for the disposition which had changed even less as Josh recognized Zeke's scowl like a genetic fingerprint upon their father's face.

"You should've called."

"Really." Josh grinned again. "We were just in the neighborhood." He held out his arms. "What? No hug?"

"You're drunk." Robert Sandaman looked at Zeke. "And so are you."

Zeke said nothing, the hate-filled glance barely containing his revulsion. Looking as if he might spit at their father's feet, Zeke met his gaze with serenity.

"I got nothing to say to you," he said, then nodded at Josh. "This wasn't my idea, believe me."

"Well, what then?" Robert Sandaman looked from one to the other and shrugged. "Money. Is that it?"

"Fucking incredible." Josh's sense of humor was gone. "Did you get my cards?"

Robert Sandaman shifted his weight as if already bored, saying nothing.

"Or my calls before you went unlisted?"

"Josh …" Robert Sandaman worked his jaw muscles. "This really isn't a good time."

"Really?" Josh smiled and nodded at Zeke. "Hear that?" He turned back and this time the grin was gone. "Make the time. I've been waiting twelve fucking years for this."

"Josh—"

"That your new wife in there?"

"She's got nothing to do with—"

"And the kid? That yours too?"

"He's too young to know—"

"Know what?" Josh paused. "Huh? That he's got two older brothers left for dead?"

"Josh—"

"Naw, don't worry. After you slip out the back door again, I'll make sure he gets the fucking message."

Robert Sandaman stepped outside and closed the door, taking a moment to choose his words. "Let's not make this any worse than it already is," he said in a measured tone.

"You should've thought about that before, Robbie." Josh grinned heartlessly. Despite his infirmity, the bully was back. "Yeah, that was a mistake. Did you think we were just gonna disappear into thin air?"

"Both of you ..." Robert Sandaman put a hand on the doorknob. "You need to leave right now."

"I don't think so, Robbie. I think you need help. And that's why we came. To help a grown man face his sins. Ain't that what you told me way back when? That I would have to face my sins?"

"Josh ..."

"And now I'm standing here, looking like a goddamn scarecrow, and my own father can't even ask why!"

"Why what?" Robert Sandaman whirled and caught him by the throat, backing him against a post. "What kind of balls," he hissed, "lets you show up at my house with threats?"

"Hey." Zeke took a step forward until his father shoved him back.

"The ex-con and the fuckup," Robert Sandaman said, squeezing tighter. "Two for the price of none. Way to make me proud."

"Let go of his neck!" Zeke yelled. "Can't you see he can't breathe?"

"Shut up."

"Fuck you!"

"Let him go!" Cammi screamed from the street.

"Robert!" Phyllis cracked the door. "This isn't—"

"Shut that door and don't open it again!"

She did, and he turned back to Josh, nose to nose. "You will never come here again. You will never call or write or so much as stroll by ever again. Do you hear me?"

Josh gasped, the spittle and increasing asphyxiation preventing response. Zeke watched the violent escalation until the adrenaline triple-beat his pulse. He saw Josh's eyes begin to bulge, finding Zeke's with a plea that finally brought the gin bottle down. Their father's head slung sideways, arcing a spray of blood across the pinewood siding. The hands unclasped from the forgotten neck as the glass rained down and the body went headlong for the deck. From the street, Cammi watched one brother fall to his knees to gasp while the other became a body attached to a boot.

"Zeke!" she screamed, but now they were both standing over the still conscious form and continuing their work, arms swinging for additional momentum. She broke for the porch, arriving as Josh finally put a hand on Zeke and said, between breaths, "Look out."

The bottle had torn open his scalp, which was flapping above a hemorrhaging right ear. His father's face was stretched and bright red from the boot heels, the tongue reflexively running across the gap where his front teeth should have been. He was coughing, blood spilling from both corners of his mouth as he tried to say something before Josh straddled his chest. Encircling the throat, he leaned over like a doctor examining a patient and said, "Confession time, Robbie."

"Josh!" Zeke took a step forward. "Naw, man, not like this."

Josh heard the collective gasp as he drove a thumb against a closed eyelid, his father's remaining eye bulging a simple request until it watered over and he gagged beneath the strain. "Yeah, that's right, choke on it." Grinning coldly, Josh looked into the frightened lone blue eye below and said, "You should be so lucky."

He pulled his hand away. Grabbing a piece of glass, he tapped the skull like a door. "You are dead to me now." He tapped a temple with his knuckle. "Think about what's right. Because if we get cited for so much as jaywalking, there won't be enough concrete on the planet to protect you—*or* them."

Gathering up a final ball of phlegm, he deposited it onto the broken face as Zeke grabbed his arm and said, "Let's blow. That bitch probably already called." He saw Cammi staring hollowly at the bloodied crab slowly moving its limbs and said, "Let's go, Cam."

Arming them both towards the stairs, Zeke paused for a last look back before shaking his head and likewise sprinting through the falling rain.

Chapter Fifteen

Monday, December 8

THE ROAD BIKE REMAINED unrepaired, so Zeke wheeled the hybrid up onto the pavilion outside the Thomas P. O'Neill Federal Building at half past ten on an already busy morning. The hematoma on his thigh from Friday night's drunken crash was a merciless, constant throb. Like an over inflated balloon, he felt his pulse push thickly through the purple-and-black swelled mass. The cut on his forehead, though, was taped and covered over by his hat.

After locking up in the designated area to the left of four front doors, Zeke saw the long line for the metal detectors and winced dispassionately. It was, he knew, an inconvenience that had no remedy. He had nine on him, and Stuart had been riding his beeper since dawn.

Heading through the carousel front door, he cleared his pockets and stood on line with lawyers, plaintiffs, deliverymen, secretaries, clerks, janitors, and defendants, the ever-present specter of Oklahoma City forcing all entrants and items through a maze-like gauntlet of body sweeps, obnoxious beeps, X-ray machines, and stand-alone doorframes targeting metal. Ten minutes later he shared a crowded elevator to the thirteenth floor. Once there, he found another line outside a window cut into the wall that had a sign above it which read, BANKRUPTCY. Ahead, he saw Jamison, who rode for Instant, wearing his omnipresent BMX suit—the shoulder pads, body armor, and full-face cage helmet like that of an NFL linebacker looking for someone to hit. Catching sight of Zeke, two brown eyes lit up like candles inside the helmet.

"Yeah, Speed, what up?"

"Jame-O." Zeke grinned. "Having fun yet?"

"Man ..." Jamison, despite the gaggle of people between himself and Zeke, grabbed his crotch and said, "Clusterfuck, my friend. On a grand scale, too. You know I've been in this fucking building for forty-five minutes?"

"Multiple, huh?"

"Fucking three of them, man, and forfeiture had like one chick at the window. On a Monday? Are these people part of the real world or what?"

"Supposedly."

"Amen, brother." Jamison went for the radio clipped to his shoulder as his dispatcher bemoaned some complaint and Zeke sank back into thought. Saturday's debacle had left him waiting for the police all weekend while Josh simply disappeared into the thirty-six hours since. Fielding a late-night call from Lotus, who had spent the last ten days in a feverish attempt to help out one of his oldest friends, he did not in the least appreciate Josh's absence. What was the deal? They had not been on the push since last Thursday night, Zeke, are we still on or what?

He had no answers. As with most things since he could remember, Josh's motivations and destinations ultimately remained unfixed. He watched Jamison finally hand over his document and receive a signature before passing Zeke to say, "I'll pray for you, man."

"Stay safe, J." Hearing his beeper erupt, Zeke palmed it and impatiently drummed a foot until his turn eventually came and, receipt signed, he instantly headed for the nearest pay phone.

"Split Minute."

"It's, Z. I'm at the Tip O'Neill with four downtowns, five Back Bays."

"Zach-a-riah!" Stuart sing-songed. "And how is your Monday going?"

"Swell. Talk to me."

"All rightey ... Let's see, pickup at Oliver, 123 Lincoln Wharf, going to QuikPrint, 220 Mass ... And Cross, One Financial, heading for Peak Construction, 335 Boylston ... and, ah yes, our friend on Hanover has an express to be picked up immediately at 422 Commercial."

"That it?"

"And what else would you like, Zachariah, the entire city at your beck and call?"

"Yeah, see if you can arrange that. I sure as hell ain't making any money in the same goddamn zone."

"Now, now, let's be truthful. I count five downtowns, seven Back Bays plus the express, after which you will immediately call me."

"Thanks, Stu."

Cradling the receiver, Zeke's Specializeds clacked through the stone lobby as he passed an even bigger line at the metal detectors before getting slapped by the wind outside. The temperature was near fifty, unseasonably warm but with a chilled breeze that knocked fifteen degrees off that at least. Straddling his bike, Zeke watched the roiling gray clouds, aimed himself eastward into the breeze, and decided it seemed more like fall than winter.

At half past three that afternoon, his beeper sang out, but he had no chance to check it. White lining the second lane down Boylston, there were cars on either side, inches away and surging. He got lucky with the lights, which were lined up in successive green dots strung above the street. Dartmouth, Clarendon, and Berkley disappeared in a blur that ended when he checked right, found a slot in the traffic, and darted towards the curb. Gearing up while braking, he slowed to a stop outside the Park Plaza Hotel as a valet in a bowtie pointed at a pole half a block away. Circling back instead, Zeke locked up directly across the street.

Inside, behind a polished mahogany desk, a man with a pie-shaped face frowned at the new arrival. Perching the sunglasses onto his forehead, Zeke shot him an equally unpleasant expression and said, "Room 402."

He yanked out a package and his slipcase, but the concierge said, "I can't sign for that."

"What? Why not?"

"That's Mr. Desmond's room, and he explicitly said to call him." The concierge picked up a phone and a minute later, with a smile stretched to the point of insult, pointedly said, "He'll be with you in just a short while."

"Is that right?" Zeke glanced at his pulsing beeper. "Then I guess you won't mind if I make a quick call."

"Certainly not. The pay phones are right over—"

Zeke picked up the house phone and dialed nine as the concierge. "Sir. Excuse me, that's for guests and employees—"

"Stop." Zeke punched in the number and faced a window through which Boylston Street rushed past. On the fourth ring, he heard Josh say, "Hello?"

"What's up?"

"Yeah, bro, where you at?"

"Park Plaza."

He heard Josh chuckle and say, "Do you happen to have any Grey Poupon?"

"You got Lotus's phone?"

"Yeah. He dropped me off." There was a pause. "I'll tell you about it later."

Zeke was not about to guess, so he said, "What's up?"

"Nothing. Just beeping you because I'll be here at Mass. General until six o'clock. Thought I might catch you afterwards for dinner."

"Can you eat after that shit?"

"Not really." Josh offered a perfunctory laugh. "But it's part of being human."

"Don't flatter yourself."

"Meet me at Phil's, douchebag. I'll be there by six thirty."

Zeke smiled and said, "I'm looking forward to it."

But the line was already dead. Hanging up, he saw a thin man approaching with all body parts in total synchronization. The brown hair was a combed wedge across his forehead, and the alert green eyes shone above a slight smile that was amicable yet unreadable. Coming to a halt in front of Zeke, he maintained an unwavering eye contact.

"Hello, sir," he said, and actually seemed to mean it. "I am Paul Desmond, room 402."

"Hello, Mr. Desmond." Zeke handed him the envelope and slipcase, which he signed with a flourish. Detaching the receipt, involuntarily impressed by the man's dignified and selfless demeanor, Zeke found himself asking, "Are you a priest or something?"

"Ah, no." Paul Desmond smiled appreciatively. "I am in antiquities."

"Do you mind?" Zeke pulled out the throwaway camera. "It's for something I'm working on." He aimed it without awaiting approval and quickly stole one more eccentric for his collection.

"Have a nice day."

Turning, Zeke felt the concierge's glance oozing with condescension.

Shaking his head, Zeke grinned sadly and said, "Keep on keeping on, ass-clown."

Yanking his bag into position, he lowered his sunglasses and headed towards the door through a silent lobby.

———————————————

Phil Martinez's Bar and Grill was located on the corner of Ridgeway and Cambridge streets, seven blocks east of Massachusetts General Hospital. As Zeke slowly cruised by the front window, he spied Josh in a back corner booth surrounded by dimmed lighting and a crowd of singles in their early thirties.

After locking up, Zeke entered and smiled at the hostess, pointing to where his brother already sat. He passed tables filled with hushed conversation and candle splashed guests. In the rear, Joshua had his head leaned against a wall, darkened circles racooning his eyes from the dialysis' exhaustion.

Approaching the table, Zeke smiled and said, "How you feeling?"

"All right." Josh straightened up, reaching for a cup of coffee. "Pretty good."

Unslinging his bag, Zeke tossed it onto the bench seat before sliding in to face him. He knew there were still moments when the devastation appeared brand new, like now, as Zeke took in the bone-thin arms and sunken face, the wounded gut like a basketball stuffed beneath his shirt. Zeke blinked, thankfully distracted when Josh said, "You hungry? They make a mean steak sandwich."

"Maybe in a minute." Zeke scanned the crowd. "You hang out here after treatments?"

"Sometimes." Josh lit a cigarette. "Philly usually takes care of me."

"Philly who?"

"The fucking owner, Zeke." Josh exhaled. "Phil Martinez? From Mayhew Street?"

"He's the owner?" Zeke grinned. "The local boy done made good."

"Yeah, man."

A waitress appeared. Zeke, noting his brother's choice of beverage, and not wanting to instigate a binge, ordered coffee as well.

"How was your day?" Josh asked.

Zeke shrugged, reaching for a Marlboro of his own. "Talk to me."

The waitress reappeared and dropped off a steaming mug as Josh watched her rear end turn and slip away.

"This morning …" He set his jaw and looked back towards his brother. "Lotus came and got me. We had an errand to run for tonight, a pickup, and like, coming off I-93 up in Somerville, this fucking van, man …"

Zeke tapped his cigarette into an ashtray. "Yeah?"

"Fuck, I mean four right turns?"

"He circled the block with you?"

Josh nodded slowly, as if convinced of what this meant. "We were freaked."

"Yeah." Zeke stared at his smoke. "What then? Did you hook up after?"

"Are you serious? How could we? I couldn't catch a single face, and besides, I still had some shit left over from last night and Lotus, well, he wasn't about to bring this down on his boy."

"Yeah."

"So he dropped me at Mass. General and gave me his phone." Josh glanced at his watch. "Should be calling anytime now."

"For what?"

"A ride, man, fuck. Are you listening to any of this?"

"Hey, take it easy." Zeke sipped coffee, the warmth a pleasing spread. "So who do you think it was?"

"Jesus, Zeke, I'm not making this up."

"Who said you were?"

"It's your tone, man, like I'm fucking switching heads or what?"

Zeke frowned and put down the mug. "A little defensive today, kid?"

Scowling, Josh testily rubbed his gut and caught his brother staring. "The ascites, man, it causes the swelling. I think they fucked up my levels."

"Great."

Josh ground out his smoke. "So what's up? She called you yet?"

"Who? Liz?"

"Yeah."

Zeke shook his head, the distaste an abrupt puncture through his mood. "Not since we last spoke. She won't return my calls."

"How are you?"

He did not want to talk about this, did not want to assign blame to the one person already blamed for everything else. "What's there to say? I mean, you think she's out of line?"

"Look." Josh thoughtfully folded his hands. "A chick like that, with that kind of attitude, ain't really looking out for you at all, is she?"

"Oh, c'mon …"

"Seriously."

"Looking out for me?" Zeke wanted to laugh. "Don't you think she has better things to do?"

"All's I'm saying—"

"No. You have no idea what we had going on."

"Besides a lot of whining?"

"Josh—"

"And fucking passing judgment on me?" Josh pointed. "And you too?"

"She was interested in *me*, fuckhead." Zeke counted on his fingers. "Not you, or your fucking debts, or this fucking misery you've created."

"Oh really now."

"Yeah. She's actually cool as hell, just looking for someone halfway normal, someone who doesn't go around thugging on family or friends or have an apartment filled with God-knows-what."

Paranoid, Josh glanced over Zeke's shoulder and hissed, "Keep your voice down."

"Aw, man, who gives a fuck?"

The cell phone rang. As Josh dug it from his jacket, he stared at Zeke as if this exchange was far from finished. "Yeah … What's up, kid? … Sure, I'll be out front." He clicked off, reaching for his jacket as he said, "I gotta roll. Lotus's up the street."

"What?" Zeke stared in disbelief. "You're just gonna lay this shit on me and split?"

"Zeke—"

"Naw, man, fuck that."

As if in spite, they both rose and threw five-dollar bills on the table.

"You've got a lot of nerve," Zeke said.

"Like I—"

But Zeke was headed for the door. Outside, they stood in silence as the last of the evening's commute passed by. Zeke saw his brother's expression, the old self-righteousness as if anyone who dared question him should now consider their point of view irrelevant.

"You promised me," Zeke said, then knelt to unlock his bike. "You said it would be me and you—"

"Z—"

"And you lied." Zeke stored the U-bar lock, taking his time. "You ain't been on the push since last Thursday, the next deadline's already coming, and I'm supposed to take a lecture about the one fucking woman in the last five years that—"

"What about Cammi?" Josh smirked. "Playing both ends against the middle?"

"She knows what's up."

"Really." Josh shook his head as if it were a shame. "That shit is sitting right in front of your face, and instead you want me to believe you'd prefer that razor-eating freak—"

"Josh!"

"Enough with the act!" Josh checked left for Lotus before continuing. "You're not in love with her, moron. You think you might be, but you're not. And Cammi … Man, I don't think there's anything she wouldn't do for you. On top of that, she's a fighter. Think this bullshit would ever make her run?"

"Whatever." Zeke clenched his jaw. "Like I'm gonna take relationship advice off a guy who's been showering with men for the last fucking decade?"

Josh laughed until Zeke found himself grinning as well. Putting up his hood, Josh said, "Nice one," and snapped his jacket closed. "I gotta catch up with him on the corner."

"Okay." Zeke stood there numbly. "You guys still rolling by later?"

"Yeah. Figure an hour or two."

"Call if you're gonna be late, man, what the fuck."

"I will." Josh turned and started walking, his breath like frozen broccoli puffed into the night. Zeke yanked his bike off the post and reset his bag on his shoulder as Josh turned back to yell, "You need to step up with C, man, you know I'm right!"

Zeke batted a hand in farewell and straddled his bike before seeing a black Lexus come screeching up Ridgeway, rear tires smoking as it blew the light. Lotus was suddenly hanging from the window, the words he screamed swallowed by a roar as a van from the opposite direction swung across three lanes with an open door, the explosions instantly lighting up the inside where two men wore masks. Zeke had a second to think this might be the end before it actually was, then watched Josh pirouette into a heap beside the curb.

————————————

The Lexus made good time, hitting the Charlestown Bridge barely three minutes afterward. Outside, the sea below was as black as the night above while somewhere in between, the far shore of Charlestown glowed and Bunker Hill, its highest point, was lit in historical tribute. Zeke was staring ahead, his pulse rate an adrenaline-spiked overdose, his hearing a vacuum where only his steady panicked breath labored to be heard at all.

Turning, he saw Lotus's lips moving as he changed lanes and looked directly at Zeke while saying something Zeke could not hear. Blah-blah. Blah, blah, blah.

He felt himself facing front, swaying slightly in this new rhythm. He tracked his breathing in and out, in and out, that and the scenery hurtling by letting him know he at least existed. Grabbed, he slowly turned to where Lotus was now screaming something while checking his mirrors and two-handing the wheel, the dark eyes fearfully focused.

Hi, Lotus, Zeke thought, blinking dully. He felt two punches hit his shoulder and looked back, confused, to where Lotus was shaking his head and making wild gestures that Zeke thought were slightly amusing. Gagging once, he croaked out an apparent warning because the Lexus suddenly swerved off Rutherford Avenue and into an alley behind a warehouse, where Lotus killed the lights, the engine, the passenger-side door barely opened before the vomit exploded into the gritted dust and Zeke was on his hands and knees, retching continuously, the tears adding to the mix eddying right below.

————————————

"Zeke? You're in shock, man. You gotta focus."

Zeke heard the voice's concern, recognized the hand on his shoulder before looking up and seeing it bloodied, each of his own as well.

"Who's bleeding?"

"No one." Lotus bent down and grabbed an arm. "This ain't good, man. We gotta keep moving."

Hoisted to his feet, Zeke looked down at his shirt and the horrible stain and nearly collapsed again.

"Goddamn it," Lotus cursed, strong-arming him back to his seat. "Watch your head, man."

The door closed and Zeke saw Lotus's darkened shape jog around the front end before reappearing behind the wheel. *Where's my bike?* he thought and put his head into his hands. *What happened to my fucking bike?*

The one-room apartment was located on Solely Street, part of the working-class quarter of crowded three- and four-decker buildings ascending to where the spire of the Bunker Hill National Monument oversaw the neighborhood. The black Lexus stopped in front of number 183 and both doors opened.

Inside, Zeke followed Lotus up stairways filled with refuse and the occasional burst of sound from random close-by people. Inside apartment 3B, Zeke found an unfurnished studio with a card table and four chairs.

Lotus locked the door, scanning the hallway through the peephole for a full minute before he turned and said, "Sit."

Zeke did, watching as Lotus closed the drapes over three windows while a single bulb from an unshaded lamp glowed like a lidless eye. Zeke was staring dumbly at his hands, the dried red instigating flashbacks as he remembered hearing the shots and running to where Josh lay; the slow motion of rolling him over and desperately applying pressure, not to a single wound but instead to two large holes gashed into the blistered chest.

Where Lotus had come from remained a mystery, because Zeke's next recollection began with them in the car and ended right here, where Lotus stood before him as if in careful deliberation to say, "You all right?"

Zeke blinked, wondering exactly how that question could be asked.

"No, man." He looked away. "I need a smoke."

Lotus pulled a pack from his jacket and set it and a lighter on the table. His boots were a thudded echo on the hardwood floor as he cracked a drape to scan the street below. Zeke lit the cigarette and inhaled as if he hadn't had one in a hundred years, and promptly started coughing.

"Fuck." He wiped the mucus from his nose. "Fuck."

In his peripheral vision, he caught Lotus leaning against the wall.

"What're we gonna do?" Zeke asked, and stared at the table. "Huh?"

Lotus checked his cell phone. "You're staying right here."

"Why?"

"Because." Lotus detached from the wall. "I gotta dump the car."

He began dialing numbers and disappeared into the bathroom as Zeke felt the embers of the forgotten cigarette creeping towards his knuckles. *Look,* he thought, *just look at my fucking hands.* He realized he was smoking with his brother's blood coating his fingers and almost puked again, standing suddenly and running for the kitchen where he retched nothing but air into the sink before grabbing a bar of soap.

"Goddamn it."

"Listen …" Lotus appeared in the doorway. "I'll be back in a couple of hours."

Zeke said nothing, gazing at the bottom of the sink.

"Zeke …" Lotus licked his lips. "You've got to give me those clothes, man."

My clothes, Zeke thought and mechanically stripped the turtleneck and jacket, standing there as Lotus nodded at his pants.

"Them too."

He ended up in black tights and a T-shirt as Lotus gathered up the blood-soaked garments. After adding his own shirt and jacket to the pile, he stood as if to leave. They caught each other's eye as Zeke pictured them as little kids, on Ambrose Street, and suddenly felt like crying.

"Z …"

"It's all good." Zeke coughed and took a deep breath. "I… I just can't believe it yet, you know?"

Lotus dropped the clothes and hugged him, one arm patting his back. "I'm so sorry, man."

"I know."

"You guys …" Lotus patted him again. "You were… you *are* my bros."

"He always asked about you, you know?"

"Yeah."

"He …" Zeke tried to form it better into words. "God, it's so fucked up. It's almost like he was never here at all."

"Z …" Lotus's black eyes caught an image. "Before that shit with the store got to him, he was a dedicated motherfucker. He looked out for us all."

Releasing from the embrace, Zeke wiped his eyes. He noted Lotus's lingering concern but said, "You better get moving. That fucking ride is getting hotter by the second."

"Yeah." Lotus pulled out the keys. "Listen, stay put. The car's first. Then I'm gonna make some calls."

"Okay."

"Even though we're in Charlestown, don't leave the apartment. You never know."

"Yeah."

"What else you got on you?"

"I don't know." Zeke looked around, confused. "My bag?"

Lotus placed a small revolver on the countertop and then bent down to scoop the clothes. He was poised to leave before he stopped at the door. "Z, please, promise me you'll be here when I get back."

"I will."

"I said promise."

Zeke sighed and said, "I promise."

"Then lock the door behind me and stay away from the fucking windows."

"Haven't you left yet?"

Like a doctor pleased by signs of life, Lotus grinned. "Thatta girl," he said and exited the apartment. Feeding the locks, Zeke turned and leaned against the door, blown out, and slowly inched himself towards the floor. *This was going to be a long night,* he thought, and warily closed his eyes.

Chapter Sixteen

Tuesday, December 9

THE BEEPER AWOKE HIM at 6:15 AM. Having used his bag for a pillow, the pager was trilling like an alarm clock beneath his head. Rolling over, he discovered his body was a blanket ache and cursed the hardwood floor.

When the beeper sang out again, he guessed the time at 6:25 AM. Having worked for Stuart Rigby as long as he had, the sequence was well established. On the rare occasions when Zeke got caught slacking, the first few cursory pages were like warning shots across the bow. Arriving every ten minutes, they served as polite reminders compared to what would happen at 7:00 AM, when, if unacknowledged, they would erupt at interval minutes until Stuart got enraged or bored enough to quit. Still, lying here now, the attention was oddly pleasing. *Sorry, Stu*, he thought and wished he could at least inform him. A no-call, no-show for Zeke Sandaman? Stuart would think he was dead.

He rolled over again and dug out the pager, silencing the coming madness until the mere thought of lying on the floor a second longer propelled him to his feet. Stiffly yawning, he surveyed the empty room and saw the jacket, jeans, shirt, and boots Lotus had brought by late last night. Having only shared a minute before Lotus quickly left, his paranoia, Lotus explained, necessitated a night of cleansing, especially if he was placed at the scene.

"And you should think about it too," he had told Zeke. "They're gonna wanna speak to you first."

Which Zeke knew, of course, was true. His picture was already on file, which meant eyewitnesses in the restaurant could place him at the table. Yet what had he done? Showed up to have coffee with his brother?

Then why did you run? he could almost hear them ask, in that small dim room, where what was said became a noose.

Sitting down at the card table, Zeke glanced around an apartment that was not his, on the other side of the city, and promptly sought an answer. His fingers formed a pyramid in front of his face as this new reality settled in. While wondering at what came next, the locks disengaged and the door swung open to reveal Lotus bearing two coffees and a paper bag.

"Got some bagels," he said.

"Nice." Zeke waited, noting the exhaustion on his friend's face, the squinted eyes dried and drained of sleep. The ponytail, though, was still wet and shining from a recent shower. Zeke ignored the coffee until Lotus shed his jacket, pulled himself a seat, and said, "The car's gone."

"Whose was it, anyway?"

"No one's." Lotus blew hot steam, his lips over the brim. "Every few months, you know? For work?"

"Nice."

"Yeah." Lotus took a tentative sip. "The guinea I kick up to has a DMV guy—fake registrations, VINs—the whole deal."

"Even better." Zeke waited, wanting to ask, but could see him already winding through it.

Lighting a cigarette, Lotus said, "The van was hot too, stolen off a Jamaica Plain bakery yesterday morning."

"Yeah?" Zeke reached for his coffee.

"Some kid named Fig from Nellon Street was driving." Lotus tapped his cigarette onto the floor, looking at Zeke. "Both of them," he said. "They were both in the back."

"How do you know?"

Lotus grabbed his jacket and pulled out a *Boston Herald*. Tossing it onto the table, he said, "They barely made it around the corner before the kid blew the light, swerved into the other lane to dodge traffic, sideswiped a BFI garbage truck, and rolled driver's side up into the middle of the street."

Zeke looked at the newspaper, saw the caption in the lower right corner screaming "Ex-con Gangleader Gunned Down in Drive-By, p. 6," and doubted if he had the stomach for this right now. The thought of Lindy and Boxer in masks shotgunning one of their oldest friends as his little brother looked on was an event Zeke was still digesting. *Should have got me too, fellas …*

"Zeke."

"Yeah?" Zeke looked up as Lotus said, "All three were cuffed at the scene. BPD got everything. Both pumps, a couple of 9mms." Lotus shrugged. "The kid will roll, cop to manslaughter, and the other two fuck-ups will be looking at premeditated felony murder."

"Maybe."

"Maybe nothing." Lotus inhaled smoke. "The DA's probably balls deep in 'em as we speak."

"And what about the other thing?" Zeke swallowed as if he could barely ask. "They probably already know, huh?"

"Probably." Lotus leaned back, winging his arms behind his head. "Josh's connect was some monkey named Biker Pony, who's a member of the Red Devils, a subset of the same Nazi motherfuckers who poisoned him inside."

"Gracie," Zeke said.

Lotus nodded. "Apparently, this Gracie guy runs not only the Pole but the storm troopers in Shirley, Concord—they all report to him. He runs the prison arm, while some other Red Devil all-star named Big Jones handles the street-side operations."

"So Josh's two-week drop guy was Biker Pony?"

"Yes." Lotus nodded. "And he kicked it up to Big Jones, who no doubt kept an account for Gracie."

"Great." Zeke felt his stomach shifting ominously. "This is fucking great."

"Z, you can't worry about them now."

"Really?" Zeke's smile was sickly and thin. "Is there ever a good time to worry about a prison gang death threat?"

"Yes. There is." Lotus leaned in. "Right after you worry about the pigs and what they found if they already pried your door."

"Don't say that shit, man, what the fuck?"

Lotus shrugged. "It was too hot to go by your place last night, man, sorry."

Zeke took a moment to gauge the various angles squeezing off the light.

Took a moment more to wonder if he would be able to step outside, in the days to come, without bleeding and buckling towards the curb. He glanced up and finally said, "Fuck the cops. But the other thing ... Tell me the truth." He licked his lips, hesitating. "If you were me, how worried would you be?"

"There ain't no scale to weigh shit like this." Lotus tried to meet his gaze. "They'll keep it in-house if they come, which means there won't even be a contract to hear about."

"Great."

"Just ... take it slow, okay?" Lotus's hand motioned calmly to accompany the words. "One thing at a time, man. That's the only way to fight this."

"We'll see." Burning his tongue with the coffee, Zeke let his mind return to a glimpse of Lindy and Boxer careening through the city in a stolen bread truck and figured, at least for them, the worst was hopefully yet to come.

"Goddamn it," Zeke said. "I'm so fucking tired, man."

"I'll get you some pillows—"

"Tired of *it*." Zeke blinked. "You know?"

"Yeah."

Finishing the smoke, Lotus ground the embers against a boot heel and said, "Maybe a little break wouldn't be a bad idea."

"To where?" Zeke scoffed. "My summer home in the Berkshires?"

"Fuck, man, anywhere, you know? I'll sponsor that shit myself."

Smiling towards the floor, Zeke said, "I appreciate that."

"No joke. Couple of weeks? Up to Maine or Vermont? Enough's enough, you know?"

"Yeah."

Lotus looked at his own hands as if only they provided cover from what he needed to say next. "We better get you a lawyer, Zeke."

Zeke said nothing, feeling like a loser cast for one last sequel.

"I will," he said, and could barely stomach the disappointment—in himself, in Lotus, and in the big brother freezing up in a cooler somewhere downtown. *It had come to this,* he thought, and reached for a cigarette blindly.

It was just past 8:30 AM, at the corner of Dartmouth and Boylston Streets, when a Lowe's Dairy truck nearly killed her in the crosswalk. As she had for the last hour and a half, Cammi's eyes made a panicked sweep across every corner and face, street sign, fence, or post—a one-woman dragnet for either him or his bike.

Randomly catching word of the disaster on last evening's eleven o'clock news, she had stared at the screen as if it were a joke. After finding no answer at Zeke's, Josh's, or even the last known number she had for Lotus, she then worked through a list of their mutual acquaintances. Focusing on those in the trade, she tracked down Faustis and Cash Monroe especially, since she knew they would be on the pedals by 7:00 AM.

At midnight, the phone was forgotten as she patrolled much of Allston and Lower Allston and rode by the yellow submarine five times. She worked through the Back Bay and bars off Lansdowne but knew she would not find him by chance. Still, she tried until 2:00 AM, with her silent beeper mocking this futility.

God, what a scene, she thought, and remembered the swirling emergency vehicle lights splashing across various personnel in stenciled jackets, the emptied restaurant, and a tan sheet apparently spread to cover her ex-boyfriend's older brother. Which is how it would be remembered, at least for her, a thirty-second piece narrated by an anchorman blandly off-handing the execution as "probably gang-related."

She wanted to peel that man's face off. Wanted to pretend they hadn't just segued into a feature story about the upcoming dog show at the convention center. That a human life could be taken from their collective midst and would be largely forgotten by tomorrow was an eventuality she would shoulder on his behalf. She thought of Zeke, somewhere out there on the run, and felt the end draw near.

This morning, when she told Stuart the news, the usual playful banter was instantly wrung with sympathy as he rose to hug her. "I need to find him," she had said, and promptly resumed her search.

Now, as her heartbeat skipped in the airhorn wake blasting off the Lowe's Dairy truck, she felt the wind rush by at thirty miles per hour and scolded this careless reverie. Aiming back downtown, her beeper pulsed a number she did not recognize, so she darted for the nearest phone. Fingers impatiently drumming, she waited through a third ring until his voice tentatively said, "Hello?"

"Zeke?" There was a pause as she could hear him breathe. "Sweetie, are you all right?"

"Yes." He sounded distant and deflated. She could almost picture the pinched expression when he said, "Did you hear?"

"Yes, of course." She frowned, gnawing on a lip. "I ... I'm so sorry, baby."

"I know."

"I really am." She wanted him here, in front of her this instant. "Do they know what happened? I mean, was he with anybody?"

"Yeah, me."

"*You?*" She closed her eyes. "Oh my God."

"We were—"

"Where are you?" she demanded, and in return came only silence. "Zeke, please, you're fucking freaking me out."

"I'm fine," he said, sounding unsure. "I'm good, okay?"

"Zeke! Tell me where you are or I promise, you will not only be dickless but dead."

He chuckled quietly, coughing into the phone. "Can you find out what they're gonna do with his, um ... his ... Can you find out what they're gonna do with him?"

"Don't change the subject!" She took a deep breath as people started to look. "Are you really going to ignore me?"

"Cammi—"

"No! No, Zeke, forget it. I do not want to hear it. I've been up half the night, spent the last three hours riding around looking for you, and now you're just calling to, what, say hi?"

"I can't tell you where I am, Cammi. Please." He sighed. "I just need to figure some shit out."

"What shit?" And then she saw it, saw him and that asshole Lotus creeping for revenge, and her rage rekindled anew. "Zeke, I swear to God, if you and that other moron so much as *cross* the Fort Point Channel—"

"Cam, please—"

"You will never be dead enough. Do you understand me? I refuse, Zeke, simply refuse to attend any more funerals other than the one you should already be here planning. Okay? I loved Josh too, not like you, obviously, but think about it. Think about him, and if you honestly believe he would want you dead or in jail, then grab your boyfriend Lotus, and the two of you can fucking cut your own throats together."

"I … I need to get a lawyer."

"For what?"

"What do you think they found on him?" he asked, annoyed. "Two tickets to Disneyland?"

"What does that—"

"He was always carrying, Cam, you know? Strapped, bags, and he's placed at a table with his brother, who was already convicted for possession—"

"That was years ago."

"Or what they might find at his place or even mine, when they serve paper and crash the door?"

"Zeke—"

"God, Cam, don't be so naive." She heard him light a cigarette. "What should I do? Walk into Area D command and just pull my fucking pants down?"

She closed her eyes and found the deep breath did not calm her in the least. From years of experience, knowing he would not be swayed, she stood at the payphone and decided to give it one last shot.

"We're leaving," she said, but no response came forth. She did some quick math and said, "Seven days should be plenty of time."

"For what?" he asked. "Lotus said the same thing. So what happens after I get back—?"

"Oh, there's no coming back. Not in a week, or a month … not ever again." She smiled at the thought and actually got excited. "Today's Tuesday. Figure the funeral's on what, Friday? We could be in New York by Monday night."

He caught himself in mid-laugh, incredulous. "*What?*"

"Good. Then it's decided." She smiled, because she knew he was doing the same. "Brooklyn will be a good place to start. We can ride over the bridge to work every day, and on your time off you can run around with your camera and I can take classes at FIT, and if we get jammed up, well, there's always Mommy Dearest and her deepest of deep pockets."

He was laughing, not in mock amusement, but as if they might be on a couch somewhere else, playfully scripting the future again.

"God," he said. "You are incredible."

"I am." She was twirling the phone cord with an index finger, swaying in this flirtation. "I promise I'll be a good girl."

"I don't want a good girl," he said. "I want … I just want all of this shit to be gone forever, you know?"

"Zeke?"

"Yeah, C."

"Sweetie, where are you?"

He exhaled and quietly said, "I'm in Charlestown. But I'll be in the city by lunch."

"And then what?"

"Then, well, then I guess we'll see. Honestly, I have no idea."

"Okay, that's fine." She paused. "But please, just think about answering their questions, okay? I might be out of my league, but none of this shit is gonna disappear just because it sucks."

"I know."

She untwirled her finger from the cord, wishing she could in some way transport herself across the still-open line, in the seconds that remained, before he said good-bye. When she made no effort to say anything further, he finally faced the silence. "Cammi, I really … I mean, I should tell you—"

"Zeke …" Her smile abruptly cracked. She did not want it said like this, strained like this, suffused in desperation.

"Seriously, I've been thinking—"

Her eyes spilled over. "Sweetie, please, call me when you get here."

"Cammi!"

"I have to go," she said and, marshaling her courage, quickly cradled the receiver.

"Hello, Split Minute. And how may we assist you?"

"Stuey, it's me."

"*Zeke!*"

Zeke could almost picture Stuart Rigby's sudden implosion.

"Zeke! Where are you? We've been so concerned. Richie!" he screamed. "Zeke's on line four!"

When Richard Parks immediately clicked in, the circus hit full stride.

"Zeke?" Richard Parks sounded calm but apprehensive, as if opening a door in the middle of the night. "Dear Lord, what is going on? Are you all right?"

"Yes, I'm fine. I'm sorry I didn't call earlier. Things … are a little fucked up."

"Oh my God." Stuart seemed coiled with dread. "We were positively *dying* over here, Zeke."

"Yes, we were," Richard Parks said.

"And how could you not call!" Stuart shouted. "Sick! We've been worried sick!"

"Yes, we have," Richard Parks said.

"All these bullets and bogeymen and your poor brother. Zeke, I can't tell you how sorry we are."

"Yes. Yes, we are," Richard Parks solemnly concurred. "An absolute tragedy. That's what it is."

"An absolute tragedy," Stuart echoed, as if no better words would suit. "That's exactly what's occurred."

"I appreciate that," Zeke said, and quickly swept both sides of the block. He was walking down Winthrop Street, his paranoia in full command. "It was fucking horrible, man."

"No doubt," Stuart sighed.

"I'm sorry I didn't call."

"Oh please! You poor thing. As if you didn't have other matters of grave importance?"

"What's going on over there?" Zeke asked. "I guess I'm gonna be out for a few days."

"Of course, of course." Stuart paused. "Zeke? I must immediately tell you. A detective came by here earlier."

"Fuck!"

"Now, now. He only wants to ask you a few questions."

"Oh, I'm sure he does." Zeke frowned. "What'd he say? Like *exactly*."

"Well …" Stuart clicked his tongue. "First, he said hello, and then I said hello, and then he flashed his badge and I noticed that his eyes were a pretty shade of blue, the blond hair worn in a buzz cut like maybe he was ex-military—"

"Stu!"

"Okay, okay! He asked if you worked here and for how long and if we had noticed anything suspicious in your doings, and if we knew about your brother or if you had ever mentioned him. Then he asked about your address, which he apparently already had because he was staring at a little black notebook and only nodded. Then he asked us if we knew about that unfortunate incident in your past, and we said we had, and that you were the hardest working convicted felon on staff."

Zeke smiled and said, "That's beautiful."

"Well, you are, sweet Zeke. And then that was it. He left his card and told me to call if I heard from you, which I most assuredly will not be doing."

"What's the card say?"

"One second."

Zeke could hear him shuffling through paper. "Yes, here it is. Detective Lieutenant Roy P. McInnis, Area D Joint Homicide Task Force, Police Headquarters, Berkeley Street."

"Okay."

"Zeke, what are you gonna do?"

"I don't know. I guess I'll get in touch with my old lawyer, you know? Let him make the call."

"What do you need us to do?"

"Anything at all, Zeke," Richard Parks added.

"I appreciate that." Though grateful, he could not use the offer. "If anything comes up, I may have to take you up on that."

"Poor, luscious Zeke." Stuart sighed again. "Surrounded by all this foulness and intrigue."

"Yeah, whatever that means." Zeke checked the street again. "I'll call you guys as soon as I can."

"Wait, Zeke! Before you go, there's one last question I must ask."

"Sure."

"This thing with your brother and the police coming by here …" Stuart was phrasing it delicately. "Whatever he was doing to have this awful end transpire, are you involved at all, little Z?"

"No." The lie sounded more confident than expected. "They're probably just fishing."

"We're worried about you," Stuart said.

"I know. I've been listening to the phone ringing in the background and you haven't put me on hold even once."

"What's a few dollars?" Stuart grandly asked. "When it comes to the well-being of a dear friend in jeopardy?"

"I promise, I'll call as soon as I can."

"Take care, Zeke," Richard Parks said.

"Yes, do be most careful," Stuart added. "And be in touch!"

"Good-bye, guys," Zeke said, and glancing over a shoulder, hurriedly snapped closed the phone.

He waited, seated at a table in a coffeshop called Espresso Express, on the corner of Milk and Congress in the Financial District. Outside, the office workers, in their post-lunch-hour shuffle, were bound in jackets and caps against the cold. The bright sun, canted in a low winter angle, was already sinking westward.

Observing the ebb and flow on the street, he recalled speaking to his lawyer, and the advice he had not heeded.

"Let me talk to them, Zeke," he had said. "And then I'll call you back."

That had been late this morning, and by lunch Lotus's cell phone rang as promised.

"They say it's only to chit-chat," his lawyer said. "There's no warrant, but you fled the scene, Zeke, and let's just say they're curious."

"You told them I was there?"

"They *knew* you were there. I said nothing in return."

What it came down to, by the conversation's end, was a considerable fee to "start this process."

Sitting here now after declining the lawyer's offer, he was second-guessing this hasty decision. Convinced of his innocence, fearing the Aryans, the police, and what remained of his old street gang, he was blindly spinning in eight different directions. Buying time, wanting at least this threat addressed and momentarily subdued, he had made the call. Ignoring years of instinct, common sense, and good judgment was not easy, so he quickly dialed up the switchboard and was connected to the lead detective.

Now, watching the inevitable black Crown Victoria slide into a No Parking zone out front, Zeke had a second to register the true depths of his own stupidity. The man exiting was thin, almost six feet, and busy on the phone. His blond hair was tightly clipped up the sides to where a two-inch plateau evened out on top. He set a quick pace, as if already late for another appointment. Over a red tie and white oxford, he wore a black leather mid-thigh sport coat. Suddenly anxious, Zeke saw the blue eyes flash across him through the window and knew he had been made.

Still on the phone as he walked in, the detective held up a finger towards Zeke before heading to the counter. A minute later, he set a coffee on the table and said, "Let me call you back."

Clicking off, taking a second to survey the restaurant, he next set his gaze on Zeke—heavy, as if recording his features for a composite not yet drawn.

"Where's your lawyer?"

Zeke dismissed the challenge behind the question and returned the hostile glance. "He couldn't make it."

The grin that followed, as if Zeke was an hors d'oeuvre about to be devoured, was chillingly effective.

"For the record," the detective said, and pulled out a tiny tape recorder before flipping open his wallet. "Detective Lieutenant Roy McInnis, at your service."

"Great." Zeke watched him shed his jacket and pull a seat. As McInnis removed three pagers and two phones from his belt, Zeke noted the grin was not an expression of amusement but seemed pre-cast in only two reptilian variations: cockiness and disdain. There were currently equal parts of both shining on Zeke as McInnis loosened the strap on his shoulder harness, leaned back with an opened folder, and said, "Zachariah Rios Sandaman. Date of birth: 5/6/71. Social Security number: 050-38-8131. Last known address: 125 Easton Street, Lower Allston, Massachusetts. Three previous misdemeanor arrests, one probation violation, one felony conviction for possession of a Class B controlled substance. Served three and a half months out of six on a two-year sentence, year and a half parole completed." McInnis looked up and this time the grin was in his eyes. "Where ya been for the last five years, Zeke? Living in a cave?"

Swallowing thickly, Zeke felt his pulse accelerate and glanced outside the window. "Do you have some questions for me, Lieutenant?"

"Besides the one you just avoided?" McInnis interlocked his fingers serenely. "Dozens of them, my friend."

"I've had a job, you know?" Zeke shrugged. "Just working—that's all I do now."

"Okay. I'll buy that one for the moment." McInnis pulled out a pen and scribbled something in his notebook. "Split Minute Messenger Service, right?"

Zeke nodded.

"Where were you last night, Zeke?"

"You tell me."

"Well …" McInnis gamely smiled. "See, that's not really an answer, friend."

"I know." *Coming here was a mistake*, Zeke thought, *a giant fucking mistake*. "I guess some of your questions won't be answered after all."

"Then allow me to answer it *for* you. You were at Phil Martinez's Bar and Grill at a little after six PM. You and your brother …" McInnis consulted back a few pages. "A Mr. Joshua Lynn Sandaman, had two cups of coffee at a back booth. A heated exchange ensued, the two of you got up and exited the premises, and a minute later one of you was dead." McInnis waited, ratcheting up the pressure. "We have four eyewitnesses that place you at that table. Surveillance cameras at an ATM across the street show the exact times of your arrival and departure. On top of that, we've got the entire exchange on tape—the van, a black 1994 Lexus, you and another individual fleeing the scene."

"Okay."

"We also have three people in custody. Currently, they are all being charged with felony premeditated homicide, assault, and grand theft auto."

"Okay."

"These men are members of a street gang we've identified as the Burgess Street Mob." McInnis lifted an eyebrow. "That's a catchy name." He waited a second longer. "It's nice when old friends get together, Zeke, don't you think?"

"I haven't seen those morons in over a decade."

"Okay. Again, for the moment, I will take you at your word." McInnis made some notes, and when he looked up afterward, he said, "Your brother was released from prison barely a month ago. Kind of sickly, from what I understand."

"Yes, he was."

"From what, exactly, may I ask?"

"He told me he was poisoned."

"Yes." McInnis again sifted through his notes. "A Dr. William Presbik, a gastroenterologist consulting for the MDOC, has a cause listed as 'severe and continued exposure to uncontrolled substances.' He says the end result of this was something called ESRD."

"Yes." The acronym stirred a hollow pit. "He was receiving dialysis treatment at Mass. General."

"I know. Three times a week. The admitting nurse said he left yesterday at 5:33 PM after treatment."

"Okay."

"And you met him afterwards."

It was said nonchalantly, but Zeke was not that absentminded. "If you say so," he said, and caught McInnis's momentary disappointment.

He exchanged his pen for the coffee, looked Zeke in the eye, and said, "Why'd they kill your brother?"

"They haven't told you?"

Sipping coffee, McInnis stared at him blankly. "This is getting old, Zeke. Are you going to answer any of these fucking questions, or am I going to plan B?"

"Which is?"

Seeming to relish the dare, McInnis's grin stretched sideways. "Well, it begins with your arrest and ends in me charging you with any and all applicably related offenses. How about conspiracy to commit murder, for starters?"

"Yeah, *right*." Zeke scoffed. "Why? Because you say I was at the scene?"

"Damn." McInnis shook his head, the grin dramatically saddened. "For a second there, you had me going. Honestly, I was starting to think you were an intelligent guy. Besides the fact you came here without a lawyer—which I think you're beginning to see was a somewhat stupid knee-jerk reaction—you were side-stepping quite nicely. Believe me, I'm glad you called. It means you're either trying to help or, and this is my main concern, steer me in the wrong direction."

"And why would you think that?"

"Because, Zeke," McInnis leaned in, tabling both elbows, "pretend it's me, right, and it's my big brother? Shotgunned right in front of my own fucking eyes? Do you think that's a natural reaction? To flee the scene like a bat out of hell?"

"We were just meeting for coffee—"

"Bullshit." McInnis's eyes were soaked in condescension. "Kid's got a 9mm at the waist, an ounce and a half of blow, several thousand dollars, and his chest is blown open like a fucking greeting card?" McInnis laughed but did not withdraw, still leaning on the table. "You set him up, didn't you? Something happened, some bullshit from way back when, your brother gets released, the two of you get into it all over again, and you decided to call up some old friends. Is that it?" McInnis perched both eyebrows. "It is, isn't it?"

"You haven't got a fucking thing out of those three, have you?" Zeke was about to smile until McInnis said nothing, and then Zeke could not believe it. "Seriously? They've actually coded up for each other?"

McInnis frowned, seemingly unamused by this revelation. "One isn't talking. The other two were still waking up from surgery as of noontime today."

"So you're creating the conspiracies as you go."

"Why'd you run, Zeke?"

Zeke glanced aside, itching for a cigarette. He thought of what would happen if he remained silent and let the already imprisoned assassins cut each other's throats. But having to deal with someone like McInnis indefinitely camped inside his life was a decidedly unacceptable alternative. He took a steadying breath, contemplated his half-drained coffee, and finally said, "I'm sure you already know, but that shit with my brother way, way back when, sent him and two others to prison for a very long time."

McInnis flipped through the sheets, scanning quickly. "Leo Wicks, age seventeen, and Morgan Dirst, age eighteen, both convicted for the 1985 homicide of a Mrs. Beth Ann Wright. Received life in prison without possibility of parole for one count each of felony murder, along with convictions on various other felonies."

"Cancer Boy and Ju-Ju," Zeke said, and the names, once stated, brought their faces into his mind. "Ju-Ju, along with some others back on the block, thought my brother somehow weaseled his way out from under the shit that eventually cost them those convictions." Zeke felt a small place inside still harden against the accusation. "He didn't, but it was never forgotten. Eventually, with none of our family left on the block, the neighborhood needed someone to blame for that whole disaster."

"Okay. And so ..."

"So, once they were inside, my bro, C.B., and Ju-Ju, apparently they started dealing."

"Dealing what?"

"Josh said it was heroin."

Without looking up, scribbling furiously, McInnis said, "Were they bringing it in?"

"Yes."

"And how were they doing that?"

Zeke thought of Tully from Columbia Road, a working guy who probably had a wife and kids, saw his chance for a spare buck, and did not need this heat in the least.

"I have no idea."

"All right." McInnis's pen stopped while he checked what he'd just written. "So they're dealing and what? I've got listed here both Wicks and Dirst—what did you call them?"

"Cancer Boy and Ju-Ju."

"Whatever. Douchebag and fuckface for all I care. I've got them exiting Walpole KIA in 1993."

"Yep."

"So what happened?"

Zeke described them importing for the Aryans, and how Ju-Ju pulled a Judas and Cancer Boy got stabbed, and how Josh was guinea-pigged by some new trick passing through the system. Told him also about the threat Lindy and Boxer had posted beneath his door months before, and in the end McInnis rubbed an aching hand. Setting down the pen, he glanced at Zeke and said, "Revenge? Left over for twelve fucking years?"

"Yes."

"Then tell me, what was all that shit we found on him for?"

"Who knows?" Zeke had been waiting for this lie, and now held the glance intently. "You've got his file. Think a guy like that was gonna get out of prison and what—work for IBM?"

"So he was dealing again?"

Zeke shrugged and said, "Like I said, my brother was who he was. That type of shit, that life, was the only thing he'd ever really done."

"A guy on dialysis ... A sick fucking guy who, according to his own doctors, was pretty much living on borrowed time." McInnis shook his head. "He was on SSI. His parole papers, because of his condition, made it so he didn't even have to hold a job or live in a halfway house—"

"Don't forget about the lawsuit."

"What?"

"He was suing the DOC. For all that poisoning shit. They were freaked by his condition."

"So he got a cakewalk for parole."

"I guess."

"Then why," McInnis asked, "would he need to deal?"

"SSI?" Zeke said with amazement. "A fucking one-bedroom with a shared bathroom and maybe a buck-fifty a week in bennies?"

"Why'd you run, Zeke?" McInnis stared at him with a hungry flash. "You were helping him on the deal—ain't that right, Zeke? After pushing all those pedals for all those years, your big brother came home and you finally saw a chance for a little piece and thought, what's the harm?"

"No." Zeke gathered up the courage for one last lie and calmly met the gaze. "I was scared, scared to death. Scared that they might circle back or had a second car, because that's the way it always got done." He paused. "I should know. My brother pretty much taught those morons everything they know."

Smirking incredulously, McInnis said, "At eighteen?"

"Josh was ..." Zeke did not even know how to describe it. "He was a real mess, man."

"Who was in the Lexus?"

"That," Zeke said, "is where we end the conversation."

"Oh really?" McInnis grinned at this boldness. "Says who?"

"Detective, I'll testify to everything I just told you. Help you in any way I can to wrap those assholes up forever. But that name I will die with."

"How noble." McInnis clicked the ballpoint pen, probing for another entry. "He's most definitely another old friend, ain't that right, Zeke?"

"He was just showing up to give us a ride."

"Then gimme a name." McInnis shrugged. "What's the big deal? Gimme a name, and if all this other shit checks out, maybe you'll never hear from me again."

"And maybe one day my ass will play the trombone."

McInnis smiled. "That is quite an image."

"I'm telling you the truth, Lieutenant." Zeke exaggerated his shrug. "As you can see, I have no reason to lie."

"You were just scared ..." McInnis tapped a finger on the table in contemplation. "The big bad bike courier, ex-con, ex-gang member, left his brother in the gutter to die."

"Actually, I was beyond scared. Like paralyzed."

Disappointed, McInnis flipped back through what he'd written, consulted the folder one last time, and said, "I can't think of anything else at the moment." He clicked the pen in consternation. "I want that name, Zeke. Presently, I'm gonna let you walk out of here, but make no mistake about it. The second you leave, I'm hitting the phones, sweating those idiots I got locked up, and if even one single part of this blow job is bullshit, I am personally gonna make sure you get a paid vacation, at taxpayer expense, inside the lovely Walpole Hilton."

"It's not bullshit." Zeke sat back as if ready to leave. "I'm sorry I left the scene, okay?"

"But what? Old instincts die hard?"

"Hopefully not." Zeke reached for his bag. "Without them, who survives?"

"Speaking of survival," McInnis closed the folder, "your future's hanging by a fucking cunt hair."

"I swear it's the truth, Lieutenant."

"Of course it is." McInnis smiled sarcastically. "No one's ever lied to *me* before."

"I'm not like other people."

"Yes, you are, Zeke. In fact, you're worse. And if you've played me for a fool today, tomorrow the rest of your life is mine." McInnis clipped in his beepers and two phones, then killed the tape recorder. "Keep yourself available, friend." He stood and slipped into his jacket. "If you have any sudden plans to travel, I'd think twice about leaving the city."

"I'm not going anywhere. You know where I live and work. And that's where I will be."

McInnis examined his face. "For your sake," he said, and gathered up his notes, "I sincerely hope so."

Zeke waited, watching McInnis toss his coffee into the can beside the door, step outside toward the black sedan, and pull away before allowing himself to breathe freely.

That guy's gonna fuck me, he thought, and slowly shook his head.

Chapter Seventeen

Thursday, December 11

IT WAS ONE OF those ideas, born in desperate corners, that led them to the Braemore Café. Beside him, concentrating on driving the recently procured Infiniti sedan, Lotus was glaringly silent. They were negotiating relatively light traffic through Somerville, and the lunchtime crowd was ebbing. In contrast, the unpleasant vibe in the car, Zeke decided, was rapidly on the rise.

"Stop drumming your fingers," he said, and Lotus grudgingly acquiesced.

Breaking a ten-minute silence, Lotus turned to Zeke and said, "For the record, for the last time, this is the dumbest fucking thing I've ever been a part of."

Staring through the windshield, Zeke said nothing. He did not feel good, had barely slept, and now they were on approach. His foot was twitching, his pulse sporadic, the anxiousness filled with dread.

"Once you're inside," Lotus threatened, "there's nothing I can do."

"It won't come to that." Zeke confidently shook his head. "You'll see. I'll be out in a minute."

Lotus exhaled tiredly in answer.

"For real." Zeke turned in his direction. "I really got a feeling they'll take it."

"They might." It was said like a question. "Or you might be dead before the door closes."

"Thanks." Zeke frowned, his anger quickening. "Thanks a lot, dickhead." He saw Lotus blink and pressed forward this advantage. "I'm still open for suggestions …"

Having been through this, Zeke knew no response would be forthcoming. He turned back and watched the scenery spill past, making a vain attempt to corral his nerves.

"I can't believe I actually set this up." Lotus's eyebrows furrowed, disgusted. "How could you talk me into this?"

"Because you know I'm right." Zeke lit his tenth cigarette of the day. "You'll see. Dealing on me gets them nothing."

"Yeah, well, you've got a hell of a lot riding on this, this *hunch*."

Zeke pointed and said, "I think that's it coming up on the right."

The car slowed to a stop in front of a squat brick building. The broken green sign spelled out the word Braemore with the Café part shattered through. Zeke counted five motorcycles lined up in repose, and looked at the battered green door.

"Jesus …" Lotus scanned the abandoned warehouses and surrounding loading docks, leftover from a previous boom. "For the record," he said, "this is the—"

"Dumbest fucking thing ever. Yeah, I heard you." Haltingly, Zeke found himself starting to concur. "If … if you hear anything, man, just bug the fuck out."

"Zeke—"

"I'm serious." Zeke hoisted a thumb towards himself. "This was my call."

"Just go, will you, please?" Lotus pulled it from his jacket, checked the chamber, and reset it into its holster. "You get one roll with these fuckers, Zeke, okay? They'll put you through it at the door, and then sit you down somewhere vulnerable. I don't think Big Jones'll be here, but Pony definitely will. State the deal, no bullshit, and let him make the play."

"Fuck me, man." Zeke glowered at the bar, visualizing scenarios of unimaginable suffering. He opened the door and got out in one motion, quickly palming it closed. Blowing into his already cold hands, he scanned the empty block one last time and stepped forward.

Yanking open the door, he saw a bar and fifteen tables to the right, all but one of them empty. After noticing two guys playing pool in the back, he was grabbed by a denim-covered gorilla three times his own size and spun into the nearest wall. "Get' em up."

Spreading himself without resistance, Zeke felt two hands start at his neck and thoroughly descend. Once searched, he was turned to where a fat bald man sat in sunglasses and a two-foot black beard trimmed neatly into a cone. With thick arms locked across his chest, Zeke judged the guy to be five and a half feet tall but close to four hundred pounds. The denim pants, black T-shirt, and leather vest were like tents stretched across his girth. Among the smattering of poor-quality tattoos along each plump arm, Zeke saw swastikas and SS helmets, the phrase NIGGERS SUCK like an addendum. At the same instant he began fearing a blow from behind, the small mountain at the table nodded at an empty seat and said, "You got five minutes."

Blinking once, Zeke forced down the horrific odds and carefully stepped ahead. Taking a seat, glancing at the sunglassed eyes, Zeke found himself focusing on the long ash drooping from the guy's cigarette, then said, "I'm assuming you're Big Jones."

The round bald head rotated down to look at a wristwatch. "Four minutes and fifty-two seconds."

"Okay." Zeke felt a sour sweat squeezing from his pores. "This won't even take that long." He glanced at the table, found the beginning, and said, "Way back when, my older brother, Josh Sandaman, ripped off your boss, a guy whose name I was told was Gracie." Zeke waited for a reaction that did not come. "Anyway, my brother wasn't working alone. He and two of his bros were in on it, and once this Gracie guy found out, he—"

"I know the fucking story, kid." Big Jones lifted the cigarette from his lips, ashed it on the floor, and exhaled directly into Zeke's face. "Your brother, thievin' *fuck* that he was, got exactly what he deserved."

"Fine." Zeke held up a hand. "That shit was between you guys and him. He fucked up, he got dealt out. I ain't here to argue that at all. But see, he got me wrapped up, me and my old man and I ..." Zeke tried keeping his stare evenly leveled on the invisible eyes. "I came to make a deal."

Big Jones grunted, coughed up phlegm, and spit a wet wad towards the floor. Looking at his watch, he said, "Three minutes and forty-seven seconds."

"Jesus Christ." Zeke shook his head before uttering the biggest lie of all. "They were ripping you off twice." He paused. "The guys my brother used to run with whacked the shit on the outside coming in, then my bro and the others stepped on it again, palmed it on Gracie, before sending the money back out into their hands." Zeke saw he had his interest now and said, "They were doing that shit for years."

The thin lips munched on the cigarette, the bulbous head cocked slightly to the right. "Whose hands?"

"It seems to me," Zeke quickly licked his lips, "on top of ripping you off, my brother, who was the only one paying you eight G a month on it, won't be making any more payments now, will he?"

"Whose hands, Zeke?" Lapped over his crossed arms like a rug, Big Jones twitched his beard. "I ain't here to play these fucking games."

"I know." Zeke pursed a lip. "I'm in no position, man—I realize that—but me and my girl—"

"Kid."

"Listen, we were planning on being gone by next Monday anyway, which means you'll never have to see me again."

"Or," Big Jones dropped and crushed the cigarette beneath his boot, "me and Pony here could just lock that door." Big Jones smiled and shrugged as if it should have been that obvious. "That's the game, Zeke, okay? You and your bitch and whatever the fuck all else, right now, that shit shouldn't even exist to you."

"Fuck."

"Believe me, if you don't give me those fucking names the instant I'm done talking, we'll start the hail of God-type shit, and then you're as good as dead."

"Billy Lindemere and Tim O'Falen. Lindy and Boxer. They share the lead on the Burgess Street Mob out of Dorchester. Currently, they're being held on a no-bail, charged with first-degree murder."

"We were wondering who the fuck these clowns were." Big Jones re-crossed his arms. He worked his mouth as if chewing this over, then looked to his right.

Zeke watched Biker Pony depart, heading towards a door marked Office.

"Convince me," Big Jones said. "It's a little too convenient."

"It's the truth, man. We grew up with those fucking guys." He shrugged. "My brother told me everything."

"And since your brother got smoked, you figure coming in here, spinning all this bullshit, will get those shitbags cut inside instead of you."

"Honestly, I don't give a fuck what happens to them." Zeke hoped he bought it. "Like I said, the way I see it, after smoking Josh, they're stealing from Gracie again, aren't they?"

Big Jones said, "What about the cops?"

"The guy I spoke with was named McInnis," Zeke said. "Detective Lieutenant Roy McInnis." Zeke paused. "As far as he knows, with all the shit they found on Josh too, this was strictly old gang blood gone bad."

"So you say."

"I've tried to be careful." Zeke held the gaze without hesitation. "I just want my life back, man."

Unable to face the blankness of the sunglasses, Zeke panned his gaze around the plain brown walls in this awful silence. Eventually, after Big Jones slowly stood up and lumbered towards the office, Zeke took his first real breath.

They're making a call, he thought, and could not begin to guess. The two other bikers playing pool, along with the bartender, intermittently checked his progress. One minute passed, then twenty more, the sporadic clack of the cue ball like a cadence through this torture. When the office door finally opened, Zeke felt the room sickly roll like the deck of a storm-tossed boat. Watching them walk towards him, he had a moment to wonder about the next thirty seconds, out of the thousands already witnessed, and how many more might exist after this. As Big Jones performed a controlled collapse into his seat, Zeke let Biker Pony fade unnervingly from sight. Pulling out a pack of cigarettes, and in no particular rush, Big Jones said, "Tell me," he lit one up, "where are you and your girl going?"

The question was unexpected, and Zeke barely had time to come up with a lie.

"DC."

"For what?"

Zeke shrugged and said, "She's got family down there. Figured we'd give it a try, you know?"

Big Jones remained silent, leaning back, the trash barrel-sized chest creaking the wood in sad complaint. As he munched on the cigarette, his arms were crossed like barriers straining against the weight. "It goes something like this," he said. "Your brother made your name." He exhaled the smoke slowly. "Our code pays no right on family, especially for thieves. Outside of a traitor, a thief ain't but a step above. And you, coming in here and rattin' out these other thievin' fucks, makes me wonder if you ain't too far behind." Big Jones inhaled more smoke. He lifted a pudgy hand towards the door and said, "You walk through that thing and keep on going, understand? Boston's over for you, like forever. And whether it's DC or East Fuckville, USA, your chip, for insurance, stays in the fucking bag." Big Jones lifted an eyebrow. "You need to start walking, like right now, before I change my mind."

Instantly on his feet, the adrenaline propelled Zeke towards the door and into the street where Lotus started the car.

Fumbling with the handle, Zeke finally hopped inside as the Infiniti shot forward. Smirking, Lotus said, "One day you'll tell me."

Zeke, forearming the dashboard through a reckless turn, blinked in disbelief.

"They actually bought it," he said.

"Fuckin A." Lotus gunned it. "Suck on that, motherfucker."

Chapter Eighteen

Friday, December 12

THEY GOT LUCKY WITH the weather. A high-noon sun beamed down before the afternoon's promised snowstorm. The sky, blue and frozen, was still clear save for the rounded cotton of scattered clouds.

"Eternal rest grant unto him, O Lord, and let perpetual light shine upon him. May he rest in peace. Amen."

The wind forced a collective shudder as those present retreated into upturned collars and hats wedged down in unison. Exhaust purred from the long black cars idling in close-by single file.

"And while we might be created in your image, Dear Lord, we know ourselves to be stalwartly opposed to sin, though in weakness we may stumble."

Zeke Sandaman, standing in the first of five rows, felt his entire body itch inside the new wool suit. Ran a hand beneath his chilled and dripping nose, the wind punishing in its abuse.

"Incline Thine ear, O Lord, unto our prayers, wherein we humbly pray to thee to show thy mercy upon the soul of thy servant, Joshua Lynn, whom thou hast commanded to pass out of this world, that thou wouldst place him in the region of peace and light, and bid him be a partaker with thy saints. Through Christ our Lord. Amen."

Feeling like a heretic as he stared at the priest whom Cammi Sinclair had fortunately arranged, Zeke considered the words useless and benign, like practiced apologies from slaves begging mercy. Yet watching as the elderly man wore only his robes despite the arctic breeze, and culled each sentence like a care-worn ritual, Zeke appreciated the stoic resolve shown towards the perfect stranger in the plain oak box before him.

"Show us the ways, O Lord. And teach us Thy paths. O that our ways were directed. To keep Thy precepts. The crooked shall be made straight. And the rough ways plain." The priest corralled his windblown hair. "And now, if you would all please repeat after me, the Lord's Prayer …"

Turning his head, Zeke examined the shivering few. Next to him, the red face of Cammi Sinclair gleamed like a wind-chapped button. On her left, Lotus stood in his Sunday finest, the face a grim mask pulled out for these occasions. Booger, Zeke's Gulliver-sized roommate, was awash in a pop-eyed and strained sobriety, while in the row behind the rapaciously dressed duo of Stuart Rigby and Richard Parks headed up the contingent from work. Zeke wore a muted look of gratitude as he scanned the expressions and reassuring nods—Father Time in his brutally plaid suit and scowl, X-Man in black fatigues, the brand-new Lucy Flynn, Kofi Asraham, Cash Monroe and the dreadlocked Faustis, dourly frowning with respect.

Turning back, he could see the many paths of what this would mean, at some other distant point, when more links had been connected. That to exist you needed a past to stick with stakes like mileposts mapped in conquest. He knew no promises had been made to any of them, that points like this in the future could be dodged or circumvented, and that each day only brought those odds slowly closer. Outside of Cammi, Booger, and Lotus, not one of these people had even known the person they were here to bury, nor was the day's pay ever considered, to stand here in black, on a freezing hilltop twenty miles outside the city. He knew half of them didn't know each other and, as the afternoon finished, half of them never would. Still, it was one more point claimed, one further acre traversed, and Zeke was here to know it.

$\mathcal{E}$pilogue

SHE WOKE FIRST, THE sun a low disk just breaking the horizon. Seated in his kitchen in the chill morning air, she had her legs pulled up against her chest for added warmth, his stretched T-shirt covering over to the ankles. Having already made coffee, the mug in Cammi's right hand steamed like a winter chimney.

It was going to be a long day, she knew, so she would take a minute more before nudging him awake. Friday's funeral had turned into yesterday's farewell party, and the participants seemed divided. Some, mostly their friends, supported their plan, while others, like Stuart Rigby and Richard Parks, were losing considerably more.

"My two top earners!" Stuart had lamented, theatrically draping a hand across his eyes. "Why, dear Lord, has this foul fate befallen me!"

Richard Parks, minus the hysterics, had later taken Cammi aside. Unlike her somewhat volatile relationship with Stuart, she had always found Richard's steadiness in council and now, with the security of what she knew set to end, tried to savor these last few moments.

"Last night," he said, "Stuart and I were reminiscing. Other than the few months he worked for Billy, and then his time in Suffolk, Zeke's been with us since he was sixteen, and then he met you, brought you in and the two of you fell for each other and had those cute little mohawk haircuts. Do you remember those? God, the two of you looked like a couple of hateful roosters." They shared a laugh until he grew serious again. "We've watched you be together and then apart and then reunite and not once, no matter how ugly it got, did either one of you really quit the other and leave. So I'm not worried in the least. Stuart, well, he still thinks one of you will be coming home in a body bag, but I, well … I happen to think you're right. Once you have to rely on one another, in a strange new city, you might just have a chance."

"I mean, I know how hard this is going to be, but …" She shook her head and returned his smile. "I'm actually looking forward to it."

"So is he."

She knew he must have seen her doubt, because he then said, "Right now, of course, he's preoccupied with this horrible situation. And I know, only because my brother Terry died and I … well, I just know. Burying anyone close is bad enough. But a sibling?" Richard Parks frowned at what this meant. "You only get a set amount of those."

Cammi nodded solemnly as Richard Parks sipped his beer and said, "Zeke is pretty distinct. Once you're through all his bravado and various elements of, well, self-defensive *bullshit,* he is a decidedly conscientious human being."

"I just keep telling myself that if I cannot, like, freak out, and we can align ourselves again before all of that crap of our past creeps back in …" She shrugged, still picturing the vicious odds ahead. "I have to believe, Richie, you know? I mean, what else have we got?"

He put a hand on her shoulder, his plain brown eyes warming as if suddenly dreading this farewell. "Until he puts this nightmare behind him," he said, "your strength is all that matters. As to the depths of that, no one knows it better than Zeke."

Hugging him then, she found that she was thankful. With all that stood in their path yet to come, they had at least, for however long it lasted, with Stuey and Richie and a wide cast of acquaintances, shared these moments in their familiar comfort. Of what would now come next, she knew, no such guarantees existed.

"Zeke?" Sitting on the bed, she pushed gently at his shoulder. "Sweetie, it's almost seven."

He groaned as he rolled over, his nipples hardened beneath the chill. Placing a hand on his stomach, Cammi gently stroked the thin white chest.

"I smell coffee," he said, then cracked open his eyes. She fed him a sip before he collapsed back onto his pillow.

"How're you feeling?" she asked.

"Pretty good." He blinked, rubbing at his sleep-filled eyes. "That was a fun night, huh?"

"About as much fun as one could expect."

"And fucking Stuey …" Zeke yawned and smiled at the same time. "Was he the life of the party or what?"

"Yes," she said. "He certainly was animated."

"And fucked up, man, that little fella put away the brews."

"Towards the end, Richie was just about ready to flip."

Zeke grinned and then caught her glance, holding it in his grip. "We've got a lot to do, Cam."

"I know."

"Jesus …"

"Listen," she said, "we'll get the van, come here for your stuff, go to my place, then I'll close out my bank account and what not and … then I guess we're gone."

"Okay," he said. "This is really happening …"

"I know." She hoped she sounded more confident than she felt. "I'm still worried, Zeke, about that other thing. I mean, how do we know they won't just show up somewhere down the line, looking for money or …" She would not contemplate the alternatives.

"We don't." Resting on the pillow, he rolled her into his gaze. "I'm sorry, babe. I know that ain't shit for an answer, but all I've got is what they told me. Until further notice, Boston is gone forever. And you know what? If that's the cost of getting out from under Josh's fuckshow, so be it. Coming after me is like trying to squeeze blood from a stone. They know that, and they also have Lindy and Boxer on the hook instead." He shrugged. "Fuck everybody, you know?"

"Yes." Still, it was hard to digest the threat. She took his hand and said, "I called Betsy again. She spoke with her roommates and said we can definitely stay at her place. It's way out in Brooklyn, like near Sunset Park, but she says we can bike to the bridge in about twenty minutes."

"And then ...?"

"And then we get jobs and look for a place of our own."

"Just like that?"

"Yes," she said. "Exactly like that. And if we get sick of their fucking faces, I'll call up Mom and maybe get us a hotel room for a night or two."

"Oh yeah?" He grinned lasciviously, snaking a hand beneath her shirt. "Just me and you, in a seedy room in the Bowery?"

"Why," she asked, "must everything be seedy?"

"Because that's what I am," he said, and gently massaged her breast. "Seedy and perverted."

"Dear God," she said in mock horror. "Please give me the strength."

He rose from the sheets and took the mug from her grasp. After a sip, he placed it on the floor, closing in on her neck.

"Coffee and morning breath," she said as he kissed along her throat. "What could be more romantic?"

He laughed, but his tongue stayed active, and she soon found herself grinning inside this pleasure. In that intimacy old friends find by rote, their history came alive again.

They parked the Ryder van outside Cammi's apartment at 110 Parkvale Avenue. Zeke leaned against its flank, waiting as she and her roommates settled up and said good-bye. At three o'clock, they were entirely packed, and Zeke was mindful of this miracle. He had one large army bag stuffed with clothes, his tools, and his music collection; two bikes; and four albums of photos stored in two large boxes. Other than that, the van was jammed near to bursting with her things, flattening its rear wheels. She had two bikes as well, and all four were strapped onto the roof. Her sewing machine and half-torso used for fitting were nestled behind the seats. He remembered the various instances over the years when they had moved or lived together, and the initial rush of solidarity, as if daring the world to stop them. But this time, heading into one of the most competitive places on earth, he took no stock in such illusions. They would either survive and prosper or, more realistically, New York would finish them for good. Either way, Boston, the only place he had ever lived, was firmly squared against him.

Lighting a cigarette, he was still leaning on the van when the maroon

Infiniti sedan slowed to a stop. It was too depressing to think this would be the last time, so Zeke raised a hand in greeting.

"Perfect timing, man."

Lotus nodded and closed the door, a brown bag cradled in his arm. As he approached, Zeke grinned at the black boots scuffing along the pavement. With the leather jacket zipped tight, Lotus's ponytail flagged in the breeze, his face a wind-chilled scowl. Nodding towards the van, he slapped Zeke's hand and said, "Congratulations."

"Tell me about it." Zeke flicked ash from the cigarette. "Never thought we'd do it."

"All set?"

"Supposedly." Zeke shrugged. "She's upstairs leaving money for bills."

He followed Lotus to a stoop, and they took a seat together. Exhaling smoke, Zeke said, "You've got the address and number, right?"

"Yeah." Lotus lit a cigarette of his own. "Big Bad Brooklyn."

"Something like that." Zeke grinned but felt awkward. It was more than the sum of what had happened, he knew, and ended here, with his belongings packed, after fourteen years had passed. Staring into the glow of the cigarette, he finally said, "I talked to him this morning."

"McInnis?"

Zeke nodded, flicking away the butt. "They've got my statement, my new digits and all that."

"He's got no problem with you leaving?"

"Nope. If they need me to testify, I told him I'd be up here in a minute."

"And me?" Lotus did not veil his interest. "He sweat you to death or what?"

"Not really since the last time we spoke." Zeke shrugged. "Without me, you serve him no purpose. And now that I've been cleared ..."

Lotus gazed across the street, smoking in the pause. "I heard the kid took the deal."

"Yep." Zeke stretched out his legs. "You were right. He took the manslaughter and now old Lindy and Boxer—"

"Are probably grabbing ankle as we speak." Lotus grinned, pulling two beers from the brown paper bag. "Thought we might make one last toast to 'em."

"Yeah." Zeke popped the top. "Here's to colostomy bags and a lifetime sucking Gracie's cock."

Lotus laughed appreciatively, and tapped his beer in silence.

"Oh great," Zeke heard her say. Turning his gaze up the staircase to where she stood, her arms were cocked off her hips like wings. She gave both of them a burst of attitude and said, "One last beer with your little playmate and then it's time to leave."

"Yes, dear." He lifted his can, smiled at her warmly, and said, "Here's to the best damn ball and chain a guy could ever ask for."

She gave him the finger and said, "If you're not careful, I'm going to make sure this becomes the biggest mistake of your life." She stuck out her tongue and let the screen door bang closed behind her.

Lotus waited a moment, caught Zeke's eye, and said, "Yeah, you're a lucky guy, all right."

Zeke laughed quietly. "That's what's so sick about this whole thing. I'm actually starting to believe that."

"Here's to it." Lotus raised his beer as their cans collided again. "No one's pulling for you guys more than me, man, you know?" He shrugged. "Seems like you've been earning toward this motherfucker forever."

"We'll see."

The door behind them banged and Zeke heard her footsteps descending. Squeezing in between them for a seat, Cammi draped an arm around each of their necks.

"Zeke," she said, and he could tell that she had been crying, "I can't stay here much longer."

"It's sure not getting any easier," Lotus said, and promptly stood above them. Holding out both hands, he helped them to their feet.

"All right," Zeke said, somewhat disjointedly. "Guess this is it."

Cammi hugged Lotus, her head turned sideways against his chest. "We couldn't have done this without you."

"Be cool, Cam." Lotus disengaged from the embrace, his expression stoic until Zeke came next and clapped him on the back.

"I love you, bro, be careful."

"Yeah, man." Lotus's lips were a twitching seam. "Do the same, man, fuck." He grabbed Zeke by the ears, knocked foreheads with him gently, and said, "No matter what it is, remember, New York's only a couple of hours away."

"We appreciate that."

"I ain't fucking kidding either." Lotus looked aside, as if embarrassed by the intensity of this gesture. "Just call me, okay?"

"You got that." Zeke hugged him one more time and then pulled the keys from his pocket. "Showtime."

Once they were in the van, he quickly started the engine and checked his mirrors, eager to be underway. He saw Cammi waving up at her roommates and Lotus leaning against his car, scowling at the proceedings. Zeke Sandaman gave the horn two blasts and slowly, as if still undecided, turned away from the mirrors for good.

The End
Colorado, September 2001

CPSIA information can be obtained
at www.ICGtesting.com
Printed in the USA
BVHW080737050223
657899BV00019B/196